A SOUL TO KEEP

T0380590

A SOUL TO KEEP

CHRISTOPHER L. HAEFNER

To order additional copies of this book, contact:
Xlibris Corporation
1-888-795-4274
www.Xlibris.com
Orders@Xlibris.com
26395

A Dedication

This book is dedicated to my old friend, or fiend, as you may consider him, James. He really lived, loved, lusted, and lost his life just as the book indicates he did. And, he really did return from the dead!

Book Summary of
A Soul To Keep

Bounded by truth, A Soul To Keep, highlights the diabolical life of James Cuzze as told through the inculcations of Dr. Christopher Haefner. The doctor had always endeavored to help him before it was too late. But then James is killed! The doctor is devastated. As a prominent psychiatrist, he knows that if he could have helped James, he could have helped anybody. Had he succeeded, he could have considered himself a brilliant physician. Now he would never know.

But would he? Ten years after his death, James returns—in ghostly form! Little by little he exacts his purposes into the doctor's life by purporting to his exasperated friend that he has come back only to help him. James has nothing to reconcile with as the doctor does, and he shows him in ways which were like him, wildly wicked. From the first encounter until last, the doctor's life is blasted toward a final enlightenment!

Biography

Christopher Haefner grew up in the city of Lancaster, Pennsylvania.

After completing his college education in 1995, he set about writing novels for both young and adult readers. He is a voracious reader and has learned from the greatest authors of the past 150 years. He is a public speaker and gives lectures to both public and private organizations. He teaches Creative Writing in schools in his spare time.

Currently Chris resides just outside Lancaster, close to the tiny village of Silver Spring. He has a wife Cathy.

A Story Unfolds

The door to Dr. Haefner's office closed. The quiet way in which it did was indicative of the mind-set he proffered to himself each and every day at the conclusion of his work day. Since his very first day as a psychiatric practitioner, he had begun allocating the final hour of his otherwise busy day as a private time, a time in which he could contemplate the day.

Today's last patient was his most complicated. Eddie, thirteen, was suffering from a complex self-destructive disorder in which he would, without provocation, hurl himself through glass-covered apertures such as windows or sliding doors. His face and arms were, over the extent of his illness, always in some stage of recovery from the wounds that bore the result of this unusual sickness. Eddie's mother, embarrassed by her son's condition, always went to great lengths to hide his injuries by coating his healing scars and contusions with skin-colored topical lotions. Before beginning treatment with Dr. Haefner, Eddie's life resembled that of a mental patient's from fifty years ago when someone like him would have been labeled insane and sent to an asylum. No longer. The doctor had taken Eddie on because of the severity of his disorder and had been successful in treating him to the point where he no longer had to be hospitalized or be restrained while sitting in chairs or in his bed at night. By intensifying the method of his therapy and increasing the dosage of the Prozac he was on, the doctor had been able to moderate the boy's illness so that it could be controlled. Now the only remaining precautionary implementation being imposed upon Eddie by the doctor was the stipulation that he wear specially made gloves. Except for sleeping, these had to be worn in between all activities in which he could not have them on. Though the doctor was certain at this point that they were not necessary in the sense that Eddie would need them in case he went berserk, he wanted the boy to be constantly aware of himself, of what he had been doing to himself. Eddie needed to be brought to a state of considerable conscientious consolation.

"I have given new meaning to the phrase 'kid gloves,'" he wrote. "I am helping James." The doctor quickly deleted the erroneous name from the computer file, corrected it, and then turned off his computer. He got up from his comfortable swivel chair and stretched. He strolled behind his desk to one of the open windows which overlooked the now vacant parking lot. The windows, he had opened in advance of Eddie's session as a precaution against inducing any unnecessary temptation to the demonstrative child. The doctor took a comprehensive view of the scant backyard that presided over the larger paved area of what was once a considerable-sized lot of grass, shrubs, and flowers. The doctor lamented that he had to comply with the city's parking regulations and provide for his patient's vehicular facilitations by asphalting so much of what had once been such a visual delight. It had been a splendid appendage to the grand architecture of the Victorian building it had been serving for over a century. From his vantage point the doctor observed the proliferation of spring buds appearing on the two old lilac bushes which abutted the brick wall outside the windows. He knew that, within days, the bushes would be besieged by busy bumble bees buzzing about in search of nectar. He would have to put in the screens very soon if he wanted to continue using the windows. While the doctor stared at the scenic view and his mind reflected, his attention was suddenly diverted.

He detected a movement, a shadow, slipping across the wall directly beside him. He caught it out of the corner of his eye and noticed that it landed on the enclosed newspaper article he had hanging on the wall. When the doctor turned to face it, the shadow had disappeared; and instead of considering it, he began considering the article itself.

He read it for what was probably the thousandth time. It read: "Local man killed the day before his wedding. James Cuzze, thirty, died tragically yesterday as the result of a car crash on a rural road just outside New Orleans, Louisiana. His death occurred when the car he was riding in plunged off a steep embankment, causing his seat belt to strangle him. New Orleans officials listed suffocation as the determining factor in his resultant death. The other occupant in the car, Julie Newcomer, James's fiancée, was unhurt in the accident. At the request of the deceased's family, the body is being returned to Lancaster for burial."

It was a Saturday afternoon, the day after, when the doctor first learned of the tragic event. He had gone to a local park to shoot hoops with his brother, Mark, and their father. His father had immediately related the bad news to him and he recalled the shock of hearing it. "Cuzze is dead."

Having heard that his old friend just died, Christopher was immediately reminded of another startling event that occurred the previous night. It was eleven o'clock and Christopher had just gone to bed. He had just closed his eyes, ready for sleep to overtake him, when unexpectedly the phone began ringing. At first he did not react, but the ringing continued, so begrudgingly he got up to attend to the matter. As he trudged down the steps of his rented home, he lessened his irritability by the consideration that any persistent call this late at night could only be of an important nature. When he reached the downstairs phone, he diligently picked up the receiver and said hello. There was no response, but curiously it appeared as though some connection had been made. There was a static noise coming from the other end which became louder as the moments passed. Chris interjected several hellos into the interference, hoping to induce the unknown caller to respond. There was no response. The second he placed the receiver back down, Chris heard a strange noise coming from the front door. In the darkness, Chris traipsed into the living room with his eyes affixed to the door. It appeared as though some unknown person was there, strangely jiggling the brass doorknob as though they were attempting to enter.

Hoping to catch the unsuspecting person by surprise, Chris slowly crept to the door and cautiously turned back the latch on the door lock. When he was ready, he flicked on the porch light and opened the door simultaneously. His adrenaline was flowing and he was ready and able to pounce on anyone who resisted him. The moment he interceded the porch and was about to apprehend the intruder, he was startled to discover that the porch was empty. Nobody was there and there was nobody on foot fleeing the scene. He had been deceived by someone, somehow, but now they were gone. Whoever had been there had mysteriously vanished into thin air! Other than believing he had been fooled by some prankster, Chris gave the incident no further consideration and traipsed off to bed. It was only when his father related to him the account of James's death that Chris realized the relevance of what happened the night before. Without a mention of the correlative meaning he had concluded about the two events, Christopher went on with his exercise; but in his mind, there was no doubt about it. James, whose life had just ended and whose spirit had yet to realize its determination, had made one final, desperate attempt to seek help. It was James who had tried to make contact with him.

There was a knock on the door. Dr. Haefner's concentration on the regurgitated matter of James's death was broken. "Come in," the doctor responded. The door opened and the pretty face of Annice Colby, his office secretary, appeared. "Doctor, it is after 5:00. Are you all right?"

"Yes, yes. I am fine," he responded in a subdued voice.

Annice noticed his tired appearance and decided otherwise. She went deliberately back to her desk and acted as though she were busy so she could wait him out before leaving. She knew all about Christopher, his moods and his attitudes. She knew him well enough to know that all was not right with him now. They were friends. And once, before, they had been more.

It was the summer of 1976. He was sixteen. She was fifteen. They were both patrons of the old Maple Grove swimming pool. They were both young with their hearts wide open. Through the course of that summer, they became each other's first love. Annice smiled as she thought about Christopher as an adolescent boy. Although people change in the sense that they mature and become more responsible about themselves, they do not ever change the essence of who they are. Christopher was still Christopher. And in that place in her heart where she had loved him once, she loved him still.

A teardrop fell from her eye as she recalled the intensity of her young heart. "We were too young then," she told herself. "Too young to be in love."

"Oh, you're still here," she heard from one side of her desk. Using the tissue she held in her hand, Annice wiped away the wetness from her eyes. Having him so close to her at this moment tortured her heart. If only she could disclose her heart to him now. If only.

He positioned himself beside the door, holding his briefcase. Annice got up reluctantly, grabbed hold of her handbag, and moved toward the door. As she approached him, he noticed a distressed look on her face.

"Annice, you look a little flushed. Are you coming down with something?"

"No," she replied. "I'm fine."

"No, you are not," the doctor said decidedly. He instantly placed his briefcase on the floor beside him and reached his hand up to examine her. He moved his hand from spot to spot on her forehead, feeling for fever. As he did, he could not help but become entirely entranced by her beauty. His touches became strokes of tenderness and affection. He looked at her—soft brown eyes, swirling chestnut hair, and smooth, creamy skin with not a blemish to be seen. He could have lost himself in the moment.

"You don't have a fever," he said affectionately, hoping his affectionate observance of her beauty had not been too obvious. "Are you ready?"

Annice smiled bravely. "I'm ready. I've been waiting for you."

"Yes, yes, I know," Christopher admitted. "I am sorry for detaining you."

"If you're really sorry, you will tell me what is bothering you."

"What makes you think something is bothering me?"

"I know you, Christopher, and I know when something is bothering you."

"You're right. It's that boy, Eddie, my last patient. I'm very concerned about his welfare."

"Is he recovering?"

"He's had only one violent episode during the past five weeks. He's off his nightly restraints. And his mother says that he is much more amicable now."

"Sounds to me you should be feeling relief and not consternation over the matter," Annice said pointedly.

The doctor conceded. "You are persistent, aren't you?"

"I have to be whenever I deal with you," Annice returned. "I know exactly what I have to do to get you to tell me things."

The doctor grinned. "I can not resist your candor but let's walk and talk," he suggested.

Annice's insistence that they react further on the subject was used by the doctor as an excuse to also initiate a subtle form of intimate contact with her. As they proceeded out of the office, he placed his hand on the small of her back to seemingly escort her as a well-intended gentleman might do. As he did so, he felt a warm rush of heat extend to his hand from her body. It made him look. His hand, gently pushing against the lowest point of her back was only inches from being in contact with her exquisite derriere. How easily he could have slipped his hand past the rim of her skirt. How eagerly he desired that should happen.

He felt as though he were playing the fool for the second time in his life. Once they had been lovers—lovers in the sense that they were two teenagers infatuated with each other and caught up in the idea about being in love. Their love though, then, had been confined expressly to passionate kisses and fondling. They had never actually made love.

This thought infuriated Chris as he and Annice stepped out of the James Street building, and appropriately, Chris released his touch on her.

"Tell me before I go," Annice persisted. Chris regarded her intently, her soft brown eyes gazing at him so expectantly. "It's about

Jim," he relented, "my dearly departed James, my friend of old, my friend."

"You mean the James referred to in the article hanging from the wall in your office."

"Yes, him."

"What about him?"

The doctor's mind stared into the past, to a time of its former self. Talking about or even thinking about James was like opening up Pandora's box. But just like Pandora, the doctor was useless to resist. Those times, so filled with the clamor and capacity of the human soul, defined by chaos, bound by indignity and atrocities, and reasoned by possession and possibility, were, for the doctor, his life's blood. The memories, all, were indelibly printed on his mind. Aware that this was neither the time nor place to dwell into something so intricate, the doctor was succinct in his expressing the matter. "I am forty years old. I have been practicing psychiatry for a decade now where I have seen and studied a thousand patients or more. I have also read the case studies of a hundred patients more. But not once, not ever, in all of my erudite study have I come across anyone with a more complicated psyche than James Cuzze."

"Why does it bother you so much to think about him now? After all, he's been dead for a long time."

The doctor, still so captivated by the fond memories of the times he and Annice shared together as a couple, used the conversation as a catalyst to bring up that very fact.

"You know," he began, "you knew him too."

"I did?" she replied dubiously.

"Yes. In fact he was the one who encouraged me to pursue your affection way back when."

"Way back when?" Annice asked awkwardly.

"Don't you remember? The summer of '76? Maple Grove?"

"But we knew each other from Sacred Heart School."

"We knew of each other from Sacred Heart and Catholic High but we didn't really know each other. I'm talking about that summer when we went swimming together. We even kept our towels together every day."

"What did that have to do with Jim?"

The doctor regarded her a moment before complying with an answer. "Up until that time, you were only a pretty face. You were, in regards to James, always the number-one pick in my top-ten list of girls that I liked." Annice looked at him slightly annoyed. Noticing it, Chris responded, "So what if we composed top-ten lists back then? You should be honored. You were always the girl I liked the best. Teenage boys have a right to categorize their potential significant others. It's a way of helping them to understand what specifically they're looking for in another person."

As Christopher continued, Annice began to feel an intense awakening inside herself. She began to feel as she had back when she was that younger girl the doctor was speaking about, about when they were in love. Annice Colby was thirty-nine. She was married but had no children. She had a hard life. She grew up in the city and attended Catholic schools her whole life. Having had no prospect to further her education and no opportunity to hold an appealing job, she married her first serious boyfriend, Leslie, when she was only nineteen. Annice was unhappy.

Leslie Colby was an stubborn man who drank too much. During the past twenty years, he had worked a plethora of jobs until recently he landed a position as a postal clerk. He abused Annice both verbally and physically. Annice, due to the mandates of her strict Catholic upbringing, endured it. Emotionally, she had divorced him long ago, but actually, she could not bring herself to do it for the stigma it would attach to her, and because it was considered a sin.

There had been times early on in her marriage when Annice did relent and confided with members of her family some of the dissatisfactions she was experiencing. But most of it fell on deaf ears as she was told from time to time that she had made her bed and now she must lie in it.

Believing in God the way she did profoundly upset her instead of providing her comfort. How could a God who loved her so deeply have determined such an unhappy life for her? This, Annice could not come to terms with, not understand, and not get out of her mind. She did retaliate. From almost the onset of her marriage, Annice had been secretly taking birth-control pills. She did so furtively by acquiring them from a doctor in adjacent York County. This was her secret joy, that she would never conceive a child with a man as mean as her husband. And now, nearing forty, and her reproductive processes declining, she would soon be alleviated from the bother of having to deceive her husband.

Annice listened as Christopher concluded his articulation about how it was James who was the reason that they had been a couple. She would rather that he focused more on that than the reason behind it. The doctor, who had actualized the purport of conversation for the purpose of bringing up their intimate past, had become lost in the myriad of stimulations and excesses of thought that always accompanied discourses pertaining to the subject of James.

Annice was thinking. So what now. Even if his old friend could be attributed with bringing them together once, how did that help now? For her, for her life, it was too late. Just like James.

"So you see . . ."

"What difference does it make?" Annice interrupted. "He's dead!"

The doctor was oblivious to the reason for her anger and he answered in accordance with her remark. "He's dead, that's true, but I, as you know, deal with the emotional value of things. And in that sense, the evocative sense of what people bring into the world, he is not. There exists in each of us parts, attributes, contributed by others—others who are still with us, contributing; others who are no longer with us, contributing also."

"What do you mean?"

"Take you for example. Anyone who has ever been a part of your life has changed you. To some extent, you are who you are because of the people who have interacted with you throughout your life. It is a process which I call influential continuation. Think about it, Annice. Though you may not be consciously aware of it, some of who you are depended upon the people you have made part of your life."

"Or the people I have not wanted to make part of my life."

"Precisely."

"So how does this continuation thing pertain to James? What did he contribute to me?"

"Me."

They both smiled.

"And to think, Doctor, all of that simply because I stated the fact that your old friend was dead. I think I'm going to have to be a little more careful what I say around you from now on."

"I am sorry to bother you with my extrapolated theories but I must say that I did it with the greatest regard for your insight and intellect. I have always enjoyed discussing esoterics with you."

Annice felt flattered that the doctor regarded her as someone who could stimulate his mind, but because he was obviously not of the mind to stimulate her emotions, she did not pursue the conversation any further. Christopher, too, realized that she was avoiding any interest in his regard to discuss the philosophical aspects of cause and effect. Obviously she was tired and wanted to leave but was too polite to say so, so the doctor offered her an opportunity. He glanced at his watch. "Look at the time."

Annice hesitated. Annice's hesitation confounded the doctor. It contradicted his belief that she was bored and wanted to leave. Christopher didn't know what to say. "Did you forget something?"

"No."

"Then what is it?"

"Nothing."

To give her a chance to speak her mind, the doctor suggested that he walk her to her car. "This street is busy this time of day. I don't want anything to happen to you. I can't afford to lose the best secretary I ever had."

Annice smiled, knowing that she had been the only secretary he had ever had. The doctor took charge, exchanged hands with his briefcase, and grabbed Annice's with the other. For a time, traffic on the two-way street kept them at a standstill.

"This looks like a level-seven Frogger situation," he said jokingly.

As the entourage of cars and trucks clogged both lanes so indiscriminately, Chris continued to hold Annice's hand. Their palms sweated just the way they had when they first held hands as a couple. By the way Chris held on, he tried to convey to her that he had feelings for her, that he loved her. When the moment came, they hurried across the street, still hand in hand. On the other side, their hands released at the exact moment, as if their connection had been part of a theme park ride which had just ended. Annice entered her car and tried starting it. The engine refused to turn over.

"Want me to go inside and call your husband?"

"Him? He would be of no help. I can assure you of that. And besides that, he won't be home until after midnight. He works second shift, and after that he usually hits up the bars."

"You know, you should really become a member of the AAA."

"I know, Christopher. You told me that before. But it takes money to join, money that I just can't spare right now."

"Then how about if I give you a ride home today? Tomorrow, first thing, I will call a tow truck and have your car taken to the nearest garage. Maybe it's something simple and can be fixed in one day. And don't worry about the expense. If it's too much for you to handle, I will pay for it. Consider it a bonus for all of the hard work you do for me."

Annice looked relieved. She got out of her disabled Ford Escort and locked it. Together they waited again to recross the street. As if it were a premeditated act, their hands made contact again and joined as if they were magnet and steel.

Flashbacks

The doctor arrived at his home on Pinnacle Road shortly after 6:00. It was a half-hour commute to and from his practice every day, but he much preferred the seclusion of the sylvan southern woods to the busy city life. To most people who knew him, the extent of privacy he afforded himself on his ten-acre property seemed far too extreme, but he always assured them that he was comfortable living there and content living there alone. The living alone part, of course, was not true, but the doctor was not one to spread his personal problems, like peanut butter and jelly, on public bread.

He longed for love. He wanted to have someone special in his life. He wanted a wife.

During his college years and again as he studied for his doctorate, the doctor had been involved with a considerable number of young attractive women, all of whom he had his fun with but none he had taken seriously enough to try to build a future with. After expending such a large number of eligible bachelorettes, the doctor had gained a somewhat sundry reputation as a cold, callous philanderer. Even his professors had heard of it. Several times they cautioned him against this behavior. "Though you may be very well—intentioned at finding your heart, we must advise you against this reckless abandonment you seem to put each and every one of these poor girls through. Your intended profession requires that you maintain the utmost standards of decency. We do not want to see your career jeopardized by having something as silly and as serious as this ruin your chances."

Christopher took their advice seriously. During his remaining year in medical school, he improved his behavior toward the fairer sex and reduced the frequency of his sexual indulgences.

When it came time for him to begin his four-year stint as a practitioner, he was a changed man. He came highly recommended when chosen by Dr. Brain, a prominent psychiatrist who headed Reading Hospital's Psychiatric Ward, to assist him. The four years he spent there evaluating and caring for actual patients brought out the essence of Dr. Haefner's erudite nature. He became a brilliant psychiatrist and an ineffective "love-her," as he put it. He had been rendered a bachelor, a compensation for years spent in intensive study. He was thirty years old when he began his private practice in his hometown of Lancaster, and hope was still his guide to what he thought would be his eventual, successful finding of someone special. Then came Annice. It was like a dream come true the day she came to assist him in his private practice. She was all he ever wanted in a woman and he cherished every moment of every day they spent together. But she was married, a fact the doctor could never completely come to terms with. Having her with him, he experienced both the agony and the ecstasy that comes with true love. His hope of finding someone special confined itself to his own office from the very first day she came.

He winded his way up the long approach to his house and activated by remote control the automatic opener to his garage when it came into view. It still amused him how, when he had built his home, he had a two-car garage constructed despite his owning and intending to only ever own just one. The idea that it was put there for the eventual purpose of having a spouse who would use it now seemed laughable. Just the same, the doctor only parked his vehicle on the one side, wanting to keep the other in pristine condition should it ever be needed.

After parking the Buick, he closed the garage door then proceeded into the kitchen by an adjoining door. His mail, which he carried with him, he placed down on the oval oak table alongside his briefcase and began perusing it. A considerable amount of it, as usual, was junk. The ones he affirmed as such, he, without even opening them, took one by one and tore in half, tossing the torn sections into a nearby trash can. The bills, he piled neatly and placed back beside his briefcase. One white envelope which was from the Pennsylvania Psychiatric Association or PPA, located in Phoenixville, outside of Philadelphia, the doctor opened. It was a request by the prestigious group, asking the reputable doctor if he would be willing to donate any of his precious time to a cause that the state was now involving itself with: taking an interest to provide in-house psychiatric care of inmates in prisons across Pennsylvania. No psychiatrist could risk becoming disassociated with the PPA, so some contribution would have to be made to the cause—money, perhaps. "I don't do prisons."

Putting the thoughts of what he might do aside, the doctor set about making himself supper. He stepped over to the refrigerator, opened it, then perused its contents for anything that particularly piqued his palate. He picked, from the assorted Tupperware containers, a selection of leftover haddock fillets and half a plate's worth of onion potatoes. He carried them to the counter beside the stove then got out a skillet. After applying butter to the pan, he began frying. For a drink, he returned to the refrigerator and brought out a half-gallon container of milk. He poured about ten ounces of the 2 percent milk into a twelve-ounce glass, then scooped into it twice the recommended amount of Nestlé's Quik to make what he termed a chocolaty chocolate milk. After aptly stirring his concoction into a perfectly blended mixture, he placed it inside the freezer to chill. Then he went back to the stove to cook. When everything was ready he took his hot food and cold drink into his living room where he regularly ate his evening meal. Using his remote control, he switched on the TV news then eased himself down into his comfortable La-Z-Boy recliner. He had just taken his first bite of food when the phone rang. He reached over his plate and picked up the receiver.

"Hello," he said in a mild-mannered voice.

"Hello, Doctor . . . I mean, Christopher. It's me, Annice."

"Annice?"

"Yes. I hope you don't mind me calling you at home."

"Not at all," he assured her. "What can I do for you?"

"I . . . I . . . just wanted you to know how much I appreciate your taking me home today. I . . . I really didn't thank you when you dropped me off. And that was inappropriate of me. I'm sorry."

Something was amiss. The doctor sensed that there was something more to the call than the apology that had just been unnecessarily offered. Could it be that you love me? Could it be that you called just to hear my voice? Could it be that you needed reassurance that when we held hands today we were, in effect, holding each other's heart? These meanderings came into effect in his head but he dared not entreat himself to their possibility. It was an awkward situation for them both. Having regarded her sincere apology, Chris was simply unprepared for what to say next. He didn't want to admonish her for calling him at such an inconvenient time, but he did want to complete his meal before it got cold. "Annice, I am sorry but I am going to have to let you go. I have a hot plate of food in front of me right now and it's not getting any hotter."

"Oh, Christopher, I'm so sorry. I didn't know."

"Don't worry about it. It's no big deal. Look, I'll see you tomorrow. And don't forget I'm picking you up."

They said their goodbyes and hung up their phones. Christopher's heart was pounding at the joy he felt from actually having Annice call him at home. The only other time she had ever called him there was the day, ten years before, when she received notice that he had selected her to work in his office. But he was equally upset by the strangeness of the call itself and how he had handled it. If it were true that Annice had called for reasons other than the apology, he should have tried to find out what they were. By not doing so, he found himself out to be no different than what he had been back when they were teens. Even then, he had found it incredibly hard to open up conversations between them when it involved their feelings. He admonished himself for his apathy toward her. She was obviously in some sort of distress or maybe just lonely, and all he could do was complain about his food getting cold.

"What a fool I am," he pronounced loudly as he commenced with the consumption of his food. He tried to console himself as he ate and watched the television, determined that it would never happen again.

An aura of melancholy enveloped him once the news was over. He collected his dirty dishes and brought them to the kitchen sink and began filling the sink with soapy water. He liked hearing the sound of the splashing water as it spilled into the stainless-steel sink. He liked watching the bubbles and placing his hands in the steamy hot soak. He lingered at the sink for a time, thinking and doing dishes. His mind became interspersed with thoughts about Annice, then went blank.

Most evenings before bed, the doctor would read in his chair, sometimes fall asleep in it, and wake up in the wee hours of the morning, then stumble off to bed. It depended mostly upon the fascination he was having with his latest library acquisition. The doctor was a voracious reader. He had an insatiable appetite for the written word and he would indulge himself as a reader whenever and wherever he could. He had other hobbies too. He collected old American and Canadian coins, fossils, and old brewery memorabilia from the Haefner Brewery, a brewery his family had once owned and operated in Lancaster. Though his interests were quite profound in each of his collections, it was his reading that spurred him on. One of his lifetime goals was to accomplish reading every important book ever written. At age forty, he had already read over one thousand. And as he considered it, he had only nine thousand more to go.

The only book left on the drop-leaf table, the only one left from his latest trip to the Lancaster County Library, was a biography of John Chapman, the man notoriously known as Johnny Appleseed. It was written by a man, a Mr. John Price, back in 1951. He had started reading the book the night before and was now already halfway through it. It was late into the evening when he sat in his recliner and resumed his reading. He read and he read and he read until he read himself to sleep.

It was midnight when he awoke. He checked his book, which was only three chapters from completion. He placed a bookmark at the page and put the book back on the drop-leaf table. He felt his legs and arms were stiff, and so he leaned and stretched until he felt the stiffness go away.

Curiously, he noticed that the stereo system had been turned on. The red indicator light was on. He approached the stereo. When he did, he heard that the system was playing. The sound was so faint that it could only be heard if you were right up against it. He checked the audio control and did find that it was turned just the slightest movement past off. He listened. It was a Pink Floyd song playing. He listened more intently to try to identify it. Then he laughed at himself for not just turning up the volume. It was intense. He brought the music up to full volume—a maneuver he could get away with given the context of his seclusion—and breathed the song into his being. A succession of Pink Floyd's greatest played. It was as it was—music that transcended time. Having perfected the audio controls, the doctor retreated to his recliner and immersed his soul with the sound. Soon his mind relinquished its reality. He found himself capable of reaching back into time, back to where the music took him.

James stood there adjusting the audio controls of the new Fisher stereo as though he were a Renaissance artist perfecting a painting. The reverberant sounds pitched off the black-painted walls of the Third Story. The party was at its peak. James was the master of the ceremony. Pink Floyd's *Dark Side of the Moon* was center stage. Pot smoke from James's hand-carved talc pipe, shaped as an elongated quartz crystal, inundated the now spacious third floor of the Pine Street house. The Third Story, as everybody called it, was as homemade as the pipe which James spent weeks carving.

At sixteen, James controlled the Bollers' home where he had lived since he was six. His aunt Betty and uncle John had effectively given up trying to control James by then. They were afraid of him, of what he might do if they resisted him. So when James took it upon himself to knock out the separating wall between the two rooms in the third floor of their house so he could make one big room, they didn't have much to say. He sledged the walls, painted all the walls and ceilings black, and created the best party place for blocks.

Willie B., one of James's temporary friends, appeared from a dark corner of the party. He had been smoking heavily, the Columbian Red Bud, which was the prized pot of the party. Noticing him and annoyed that he was indulging in more than his share of the precious weed, James called out, "Little Willie, Willie, won't go home. Cause you can't push Willie around. Willie won't go."

"Knock it off, Jim," Jules ordered, "you're ruining my high."

"Here, Jules," James responded, handing him the pipe so he could take another hit. "Put this in your pipe and smoke it."

"Hey, guys, hold off a minute," Christopher cautioned the group. "I hear something. Cuzze, it's your aunt, she's coming up from the first floor. Open a window and turn the music down."

"Forget you!"

"Why are you such a complete idiot? Call down to her before she decides to come up. You're going to be busted."

Angered that his party was being interrupted from inside and out, James lowered the music. He stepped out into the adjoining hall where he heard his aunt Betty calling his name from just outside the closed door at the bottom of the third-floor stairs. Without provocation, he hurled a drinking glass at her the moment she opened the door.

"Get out!" he ordered. "I told you already, you and Mr. Idiot aren't allowed up here any more. And I really mean it!"

Betty had been struck by the thick glass directed toward her head. Blood from her wounds trickled down her face. James motioned as though he was ready to throw something again and Betty fled, crying.

"You fool," Christopher said admonishingly when James reentered the room. "What if Mr. Boller comes up here now? What are you going to do? You can't beat him up."

"I don't have to be able to beat him up," James stated proudly. "If he comes up, I'll kill him. And he knows it."

"I don't believe you," Chris shot back.

"You'd better believe," James said defiantly.

"Is that so?" Chris volleyed back while standing up to fight.

"Hey, don't be so cocky, guys," Jules shouted out.

James relented. He knew the toughness of Chris and he wanted no part of an altercation with him. Of all of the fights James had been in and of the few in which he lost, Chris had been his toughest adversary. Their eyes always spoke of it every time they came close to blows. James's eyes were defiant but yielding while Chris's were victorious and unrelenting. Neither ever forgot the one time their forces had battled.

It had happened only months before and not because of any personal indifference between them. It happened inadvertently. James had, for some time, been sneaking up on the fire escape of the property next to the Haefners. His goal every time he did it was to catch Chris's sister undressing before she went to bed. Previous to the night of the fight, Lisa had mentioned that she was suspicious that someone had been looking in at her, at least once. Chris was going up to bed himself when he heard Lisa shriek from her second-floor bedroom. He ran to her room and flung open the door. She was standing there, naked. As she hurried to cover herself with a nearby pillow, she shouted, "Outside!"

James heard the shriek too and fled down the fire escape, jumping over the side and into the yard once he was closer to the ground. Christopher ran as fast as he could, down the stairs and out the door onto the front porch. It couldn't have been timed any better. The very second James emerged from the tiny alley which ran between the houses, Christopher was there ready to pounce on him. Christopher leaped off the top of the concrete steps and toppled Cuzze to the ground. A horrific fight ensued. They fought like tigers—each fearless of the other. James, who had so much more experience in street fighting, seemed at first to be getting the upper hand. He forced Chris to the ground several times by using underhanded moves—biting and headbutts. But Chris remained steadfast. He knew James's weakness: he threw everything into the first few minutes of a fight and became increasingly tired if the fight lasted beyond that spec of time. He fought defensively, purposely, to outlast his opponent.

A crowd, people from the neighborhood, gathered to watch. By the time Chris was winning, everyone, it seemed, was privy to the spectacle. Everybody was witness as Chris began to prevail. Everyone stood in wait as Chris finished Jim off, holding him by the throat with one hand against the porch railings while delivering blow after blow to his head. James was in tears when it was over. He had been humbled and humiliated in front of so many of the people who feared him. Christopher became, for the rest of his life, the only person James ever feared.

James relented, knowing from their eyes what each of them knew. Deb, James's girlfriend, intervened. She didn't want the party spoiled. She knew that James was boiling mad and she offered herself sexually to him to try to appease him. James resisted. He had found another outlet for his frustration, Willie.

Willie had moved to the corner of one of the two sofas that faced each other in the center of the room. He had been motioned there by Chris who had taken up a place on the opposite couch across a long table which sat between them. On the table were assorted pot-party paraphernalia: papers, roach clips, roaches, two piles of pot—one seeded, one deseeded—and a bong. Willie picked up the bong and moved to fill it up with some of the deseeded Red Bud. James, who was standing close by watching Willie, waited until he had lit the bong and taken one long inhalation. Before he could exhale, Cuzze had forced his hands over his face using one to hold his nose closed and the other to keep him from opening his mouth. Willie struggled for a split second but then acquiesced knowing it was James and realizing that if he offered any resistance Jim would surely harm him given the bad mood he was in. After holding Willie against his will for what was no doubt the longest minute of his life, James released him. Willie had tears in his eyes and he coughed continuously for several minutes as the partyers assessed what had just taken place and why. Nobody said a word but each person came to their own certain conclusions about James and the paradoxical way in which he chose to bolster Willie's high.

"Now you're flying," James said conversely.

"Flying high," Jules interjected.

Willie was black, and to ridicule him further, James insisted that he stand against the far wall. With the wall being black while

Willie was too, he blended into the "blackground," as James called it, so completely that the only parts of him that could be seen were the whites of his eyes, reflecting the dim light offered by the three black lights in the room. James had Willie stand there, stiff and still, while he changed the locations of the black lights until their dim reflections, captured by his eyes, accentuated fully the comical look of Willie. Everybody in the room participated in the amusement, cajoling Willy for looking so silly.

Once James had vented his anger, he allowed Willie to sit back down amongst his companions. The show was over and the attitudes of the partyers shifted to more relevant purposes. James was a master of using people to influence his parties. And Willie was only the latest in a long line of expendables. Willie, like all of the others before him, allowed James to control him, even if it meant humiliating or sometimes hurting him, because of how much he wanted to be a part of the unusual world James had established. James had power. He controlled his aunt and uncle. He controlled the house they lived in. He did anything he wanted; and Willie, like everyone else who experienced this power gone mad, wanted to be part of it.

Willie was not his usual carefree self. He was tense and Chris could sense it. He invited Willie to sit back down with him so he could discuss it. "What's wrong, Willie?"

Willie responded with a wide white-toothed smile. "What are you talking about?"

"I'm talking about you. I know you. And I know you well enough to know that something's bothering you. So why don't you just spill it."

Willie knew Chris too. He knew that he was the type of friend who concerned himself with the well-being of others. And because of the concentrated way in which he dug into other people's problems, he knew he could not hide the truth of what was bothering him for long. "What makes you think there's something wrong?" Willie asked with a fake smile.

For a time Chris did not answer. Then he responded, "We're going to sit here until you decide to tell me."

Willie laughed, but while he laughed, he was determining his surroundings, making sure that if he did confide in Chris their conversation would not be heard. He spoke then with a changed look and a lowered tone in his voice. "It's Cherise. She's been cheating on me."

"How do you know for sure?"

"Oh, I know for positive," Willie explained. "The other day, I got home to my mom's house. Cherise was there. When I got there she was just coming down the stairs. She was surprised to see me. I heard a strange noise coming from upstairs. It wasn't Mom because she was at church. I ran upstairs. It was too late to catch who it was but the bedroom window was wide open and I found a sock which didn't belong to anyone who lived there. She denied it of course. I forced her down on the bed to see if she was interested in doing it with me. She didn't. So I held her down until she admitted that something had happened. I had to use force, I had to. After the longest time, with her struggling to get free, she finally told me. She cried when she told me. She was guilty. And did it in my house too."

"Sounds kind of incriminating, Willie. What do you think you should do?"

"What I want to do is kill her or kill him, maybe."

"That wouldn't be very wise, Willie. You kill him or her and you'll spend the rest of your life behind bars. You would end up in a worse place than either of them. Is that what you want?"

Before Willie could respond, James, who had been eavesdropping on their private conversation, butted in. "What? Your girl's been cheating on you and you're going to let her get away with it? You are a poor excuse for a man, aren't you?" He hastily left Willie's side and went into the wall closet located in a corner of the room. He returned a moment later holding a shotgun. "Here's what I would do to her," he said, pointing the gun straight out in front of him. Next, he pointed the shotgun at Debbie, his girl. "I know this. If you ever fool around on me, I'll put a dozen holes right through your head."

"Hey, Cuzze, put the gun away and don't be crazy," Jules pleaded.

"Forget you, Jules."

"Put the gun down right now!" Chris demanded.

"It's not even loaded," James protested. "You guys are a bunch of sissies."

James returned the gun to the closet but returned to chastise Willie. "You pathetic black boy. Why don't you go home and cry to your mammy?"

"Shut up, Jim. Willie's problems are none of your business anyway."

"They are if he wants to talk about them around me," he declared.

"Don't listen to anything he has to say, Willie," Chris decided.

James mocked Willie. He made up a chant which everyone, except Chris and Willie, began cajoling Willie with, "Willie B., Willie B., Willie B., the Killer B. Willie B., Willie B., Willie B., the Killer B."

The mocking went on incessantly. Willie became upset and nothing Chris said made it any easier for him to take. Chris wanted Willie to leave and even offered to leave with him. They got to him. Willie's agitation turned into anger and not at James and the others as it should have. Willie's face seized as though he were convulsing inside. They had reached the dark side of his soul. He was no longer Willie. James stood behind him as a showman would who was about to display his best act. He held out his hands as if he were presenting a magic act to an audience, and he was. "Look and see. Look and see, everybody, at the changes I have brought about in this peon. I have turned him into something better."

Willie stood up in front of the others, center stage, feeling a fury that he hadn't thought was humanly possible. He could have taken on Cuzze and beaten him, but that was not to be. There were two other individuals who were waiting for him and their punishments had to come first.

Willie left the party. Chris was glad to see him go, and he believed, once Willie got outside, his head would clear and he would go about his business in his usual carefree way.

The story of what happened that night was told the next day. Willie had returned to his mom's house shortly after leaving the party. He was unexpected. His girl, Cherise, was up in bed with another man, probably the same man Willie had accused her of sleeping with before. He heard them and went down into his basement and searched around for a weapon. He found a sledge hammer and a chisel. He crept up both flights of stairs and stood quietly outside the bedroom where Cherise and her lover were heavily involved. Willie waited. When the time was right, when he was sure the other man was on top of her, he burst into the room. The man he took out with one blow to the head. He was knocked unconscious to the floor. Willie then bashed his head several times more with the hammer until he was sure the man was dead. For Cherise, Willie had something better planned. Something worthy of the monster James had created. Something hideous. Using belts, he tied Cherise to the bed. He told her he loved her; then he placed the chisel to her heart and told her goodbye . . .

Striving for Change

It was later that same night that while the doctor was reliving those egregious experiences of his past that Annice was about to experience an egregious situation of her own.

She was upstairs, in her bed, reading. Unexpectedly, she heard the front door suddenly burst open, then, just as quickly, being slammed shut. It was her husband Leslie. He had come home from another night of drinking at the corner bar, earlier than usual. In an act of desperation Annice shut her book, turned off the lamp beside her bed, and plunged her head tightly into her pillow. She listened as Leslie's heavy footsteps ascended to the top of the stairs. She took several deep breaths to try to calm her breathing before he entered the room.

Before stopping off in the bathroom to relieve himself, Leslie opened the bedroom door, poked his head inside, and alerted his wife that he was home and that she needed to remove her bra and panties for him. Annice listened nervously as Leslie tended to his personal needs in the bathroom across the hall. She waited, not knowing what would happen next.

When Leslie returned, he practically stumbled into the room. Annice never flinched. She could tell he was totaled by all the effort he required to take off his clothes. Usually, when her husband was this inebriated he would become hostile toward her at the slightest provocation, but tonight he didn't sound angry. Maybe, she thought, he was so drunk that he would fall asleep the moment he fell into bed.

No such luck came to her though, for when he had successfully removed his clothes, he plopped down onto the bed beside her and began applying sloppy kisses on her forehead, face, and lips. He tore the covers off her, expecting to see her naked body. When he saw that she had disobeyed him and was still wearing her underclothes, he became furious with her. Without wasting a word on her, he tore off her bra and reached down and ripped off her panties.

Annice avoided looking at him so as not to give him the satisfaction of her acknowledgment. Leslie didn't care. He reached down and fondled her breasts then slipped his fingers over the rest of her defeated body. "Oh yeah!" he shouted out. "This is going to be great!"

Annice lay perfectly still as Leslie attended to himself, very selfishly, over her body. She refused to stimulate him the several times he tried to entice her to do so. She refused to show him even the pretense of love.

Leslie continued with her until, finally, they climaxed; or rather, he did.

When Leslie was finished with her, he abruptly moved off of her. He fell down beside her on the bed and instantly fell asleep. Annice lay still until she was sure. Terrible thoughts about her life invaded her mind. Most daunting of all was the "you've made your bed now lie in it" that she often heard her mother say to her when she was a child. She was right. She had made this bed for herself and now she was lying in it, although it wasn't all her fault that things turned out so badly. If she had known of her husband's proclivities for drinking and for using bad language, she never would have married him. For all intents and purposes, she had been deceived, and because of it, the best years of her life had been wasted.

Annice began to cry lonely tears. She cried and cried until the very last tear was spent from her. Then she remained motionless for a time. Her mind was numb. Finally, she realized that she desperately needed to clean up after what happened. She was lying on a huge sweat spot that was now beginning to irritate the skin on the back of her thighs and her backside. Just the thought of her husband being all over her in the way he wanted repulsed her. She sprang up out of bed and flew across the hall into the bathroom.

She quickly filled the sink with warm soapy water and began wiping off her body, top to bottom. As she continued at this, a terrifying thought occurred to her. She had not taken her birth-control pill! Immediately, she flung open the medicine cabinet and sorted through the various pill bottles for the one marked ALLERGIES. This was the bottle she secretly kept her birth-control pills in. She found the bottle and popped the cap, but before she inserted a pill in her mouth, she was struck by the fact that the bathroom door was standing wide open. With one quick pulse of her hand she closed it tight and locked it securely. It would have been hard for her to explain to her drunken husband, if he should wake, why she was so concerned about taking allergy medicine in the middle of the night.

Annice swallowed her pill, taking it down with a glass of tepid drinking water. With the pill safely inside her, she eased up on herself, her fears about her husband. She gazed into the cabinet mirror and began reflecting upon herself. At 39, she did not yet consider age a detriment to her looks. Her dark-brown hair was still lustrous and it was still shaped perfectly down the sides of her head to her shoulders. Her brown eyes still sparkled. And even without make-up on, her lips still possessed a shade of red close to crimson. She had no age spots or blemishes on her face. And most remarkable of all, her body weight was only ten pounds heavier than what it had been when she graduated from high school.

After a prolonged look-see at herself, another set of tears streaked over her cheeks. They proclaimed the assurance she felt at having passed her own scrutiny, assessing that she still retained most of her feminine beauty—the beauty that would be essential for her to have if she ever decided to take up life away from her abusive husband.

In regard of her self, Annice began to dress more provocatively and tended to herself as though each time she went out she was going out on a first date. She would not allow her spirits to slump the way her husband wanted. It was easier for him to manipulate her whenever she was feeling depressed or melancholy.

At work, the doctor noticed her accentuated appearance too and became quite distracted by it. It was hard enough to love her the way he did and have to keep it to himself without watching her work her feminine wiles on him by appearing so desirable. Sooner or later something would give, and it was only three short days into their new office dynamic that their personal natures began to take over.

Dr. Haefner was sitting quietly in his office waiting for his next patient to arrive. He was looking over the contents of a packet on his desk which contained a profile of a thirteen-year-old girl. Her name was Patricia Thome and she was suffering from a severe case of obsessive-compulsive disorder. She had had three hospitalizations during the past year and her case had been referred to him by his old mentor, Dr. Horace Brain, who headed the Reading Hospital's Psychiatric Unit.

Dr. Brain and Dr. Haefner had not seen each other in over ten years since the final day of Dr. Haefner's residence-training period. When Dr. Brain had made recent contact with him regarding Miss Thome, Dr. Haefner thought it to be rather unusual; after all, Dr. Brain was a highly esteemed psychiatrist, and if anything, he was more capable of treating Miss Thome than he was. But Dr. Brain was able to allay some of Dr. Haefner's speculations when he related to him, in further correspondence, that he had once read a paper of his regarding a new standout method of treating people afflicted with severe cases of obsessive-compulsive disorder. It sounded believable even though that particular paper had been written over five years previous to this first-time interest in his methodology.

Entranced in his reading, the doctor was wrested from his intense review by a light tapping on the door. He got up, walked to the door, opened it, and was just about to say hello to the Thomes, when he noticed that it was Annice he was about to speak to.

"I'm sorry, Doctor, but the Thomes just called from their cell phone. They were on their way here and ran into an accident on 222. They won't be able to make their appointment."

"Is it that bad?" the doctor inquired.

"Mrs. Thome told me that apparently a tractor-trailer overturned on the highway. Traffic is backed up for miles and there are no other exits close by. She said they're as stuck as a fly in molasses."

For a moment, the doctor pondered their unfortunate situation and what it meant to him. "We need to get their daughter another appointment as soon as possible."

"I've already discussed that with Mrs. Thome. She is going to call me first thing tomorrow so we can figure something out."

"That's good. So where does that leave us with the rest of our day?"

"That leaves us time to do whatever we want," Annice said. Her reply was a bit strayed from the strictly business tone that usually prevailed between them. The doctor didn't know what to think. He looked at her intently. Was she being suggestive? Was she actually flirting with him?

The doctor had to find out, so he tested her. "Then let's celebrate. Up until this unexpected break, I've had a tedious day. I've had to deal with . . . let's see . . . three nuts, two fruitcakes, and a man who has lost all his marbles."

The two broke into laughter at the doctor's comical comment. Annice feigned reprimanding the doctor by hushing him and telling him it wasn't nice for him to joke about his patients, but it was all done to further their humor.

Once the invocated humor had abated, Annice and the doctor realized they were in a peculiar situation. The intimation was, and they both knew it, that each wanted to spend time together in a personal, rather than a professional, way. Since Annice had been the icebreaker, she took the plunge into what potentially could have been icy-cold water.

"I have a perfect idea. Why don't we just close up early, for the first time in ten years I might add, and go out and get ice cream cones? It's warm enough out for a cold treat."

The doctor couldn't believe what he was hearing. He was experiencing something special between them for the first time since they began working together. He was not going to blow his first opportunity to be together with her. They were still talking through the open door when the doctor gestured for Annice to step back into the outer office. As she did, the doctor took a full appreciative view of her and smiled.

"I'll tell you what. Let's go one better than ice cream. Let's have dinner together."

Annice blinked and looked down. Ice cream, like coffee, seemed harmless and casual. Dinner was more intimate, almost like a date. Her first inclination was to decline, but the stirrings inside her, her instincts toward making herself feel better, offset what she thought was her better judgment. "Where?"

"What are you partial to?"

"I'm partial to food in general," Annice replied humorously.

"Then I know the perfect place," the doctor quipped. "Herkimer's."

"I don't think I know where that is," Annice responded.

"It's my favorite place to eat. I go there often. The owner is a friend of mine. He's a splendid man."

"Where is it?"

"Out on the New Danville Pike just outside the city. I can't believe you've never been there or heard of it before."

"I . . . I never go out."

The doctor caught Annice's hesitation. He knew without having to ask that she was abject to discuss her personal life in the wake of their going out together. He interjected before she felt she had to respond further, "Then it's settled. What do we have to do around here to free ourselves up?"

Like busy beavers, the two office associates flurried through their self-assigned tasks, each of them listening to the other from their respective places and each smiling as they heard the other's stumbling about. The doctor finished ahead of his secretary, and when he did, he poked his head outside his office to inquire of Annice whether she wanted his help. When she declined, he gave her another minute before he poked his head out again and asked, "Ready?"

"Ready. Willing. And able," Annice declared.

A sexual innuendo, the doctor concluded. This is going to be very interesting. He closed his inner office door and walked over to her desk where she was setting the office answering machine. Once it was set, they began a stride toward the door. Just as they cleared Annice's desk, the doctor stumbled. In the process of falling, he tripped Annice, and together they went down, face first, to the floor.

Annice had landed on the carpet with her hands out in front, protecting her as her body thudded against the floor. The doctor landed directly on top of her, straddled over her as though they were in the first stages of intimacy. For several seconds neither of them moved. Neither of them wanted to. They had become inadvertently entangled together in what was a very stimulating position. They both felt the heat from each other's body and it possessed them against what they knew was the right thing to do. For the doctor it was twenty years of lust and love gone mad. The sensations made by the contact between them were sensational to him. He would have given anything to be able to pull down Annice's panties and give himself to her in an undeniable act of love. But fortunately his ethics got the best of him, and hard as it was, he relented.

Dazed and weak, he struggled to get up and he was glad. If anything were to ever happen between them, he would want it to occur in a more elaborate setting, not on the floor in his office. As they apologized to one another and readied themselves to leave, again the doctor began to have flashbacks of the times when he was in college and he had exchanged his sexuality frequently with multiple partners. He recalled vividly the encounters, beautiful women and all. He envisioned their faces as he took them: blonde hair and blue eyes, strained and tired; auburn hair with brown eyes, an excited expression; dark hair with dark eyes, an intense stare. In his mind they were together again. The next moment he was subdued. He found himself face-to-face with several of his professors. They all wore concerned looks on their faces. They were all telling him or rather warning him of the great risks he was taking by involving himself with so many individuals of the fairer sex and how these sexual indulgences could implicate him as being promiscuous. "It could bring detriment to your character and hinder your reputation. It could even lead to scandal. You must take measure against your desires. You must hold yourself up as much in your private life as much as you do publicly. Your success will be determined as much by one as the other."

The couple stood beside the door—Annice picking particles of dirt off her outfit, the doctor adjusting his pants which had become twisted around his waist. Annice watched as he continued to shuffle them and noticed that he had become aroused and what he really was trying to do was hide how he really felt about her at that moment. Too embarrassed to say anything, she clasped her hand in front of her mouth to hide her broadening smile. Seeing that he was getting nowhere with his private concern, the doctor gave up. He extended his hand to her as if to say I'm sorry and moved abruptly toward the door. Annice looked at him appreciatively, took his hand in hers, and held it as if to say everything is all right.

Before departing, the doctor made one look around in an attempt to vindicate himself of the incident. He made an intense scrutiny of the carpeted area around Annice's desk, searching in vain for whatever was the true culprit responsible for making them fall. He shook his head after he determined he had made a futile effort. There was no phone cord, no carpet tuft, no extended computer wire, no loose object lying on the floor, no obstacle whatsoever that could have been in his path as he walked across the floor.

"I wonder what the devil made me trip and fall," he said aloud.

"Probably the devil," Annice replied. "Leave it at that."

Annice knew the doctor and his tenacious personality. He would, if he could, begin adducing possibility upon possibility, contingency upon contingency, in the hope of rendering a verdict in the case of "The Mysterious Fall." In reaction to her assessment, Annice asserted herself by rendering to her partner an unamused look. Preferring to be in her good graces, the doctor gave up his quest and followed her to the door.

They drove together. Just south of the city, they turned south on the New Danville Pike, a picturesque road lined with interspersed woodlots and houses. The left side of the road paralleled the Conestoga River and provided a lovely view. Less than a mile down the pike, the car turned left into Herkimer's parking lot. Annice now recognized where they were though she had never before entered the establishment.

Herkimer's was a quaint out-of-the-way diner which appealed mostly to local people. The owner preferred it to stay that way. He never advertised. Beginning at this time of year, Lancaster County restaurants were inundated by the annual influx of tourists that came to see the Amish. Herkimer's got very few of them. But the business thrived despite its aversion to sightseers. Reliable clientele, of which Dr. Haefner was one, kept the business bustling.

"How do they ever manage to stay in business out here?" Annice asked once they stopped.

"They stay in business much the same as I do," he replied. "Word of mouth. And believe me, there's no better way. It's an old, proven way. I liken it to a handshake when a handshake was the only thing necessary to close a deal. In those days, a person's word was gold. Some of the best business deals ever made in this country were made with a handshake and a smile. Nowadays, everything's transacted with lawyers and contracts—contracts filled with fine print and esoterics. And most of it is caused by one person's lack of trust in another. Most people born today won't ever know the fine feeling of having confidence in others—at least not in the way I'm speaking."

"Do you?"

"Do I what?"

"Do you trust other people?"

"Only those who have earned it. But I am happy to say that in my life I have had the good fortune of knowing quite a few people whom I considered worthy."

"Do you consider me worthy of your trust?"

"Of course I do. You are a good person. I would trust you with my life."

Annice didn't know just how to respond. She still felt anxious and nervous about their being together. Still she felt she needed to reply.

"I . . . I think you are a good person too."

"Good then. How about if, we, two good people, go in for a good meal?"

They both laughed at the remark. The doctor exited the car first and hurried around to the passenger's side to open the door for his companion. Annice was flattered. Never in all her married life had her husband ever opened a door for her. The specialness she started to feel helped her get over the awkwardness she also felt. She thanked him politely. "Thank you, Christopher." Annice liked calling the doctor by his proper name. She could only do it outside the office due to the professional courtesy she had to afford him while they worked. Now, through the course of their time spent together, she could be more personal with him, this idyllic man she cared for so much and wanted to be with.

When the doctor entered Herkimer's, he was chided by Mike, the owner, for having someone special with him.

"Hey, look," he called back to the cook, "the doc has a date."

"Hey, Doc." He turned to the doctor, saying, "I'll have my finest table ready for you and your lady friend in just two shakes of a lamb's tail."

Annice blushed. The couple waited by the checkout counter for the minute it took the restaurateur to prep their table. Being perceived as a couple made them both feel a bit uneasy because they both knew that Annice was a married woman, and they both knew too that their being together had more to it than just two friends going out to eat. Annice felt especially disturbed because she was wearing her wedding ring, and she knew that anyone looking would see it on her finger.

A minute later, the hostess escorted the couple to a cozy table located in an obscure corner of the diner. After they had been seated, they each felt somewhat relieved that their presence was not being so ostentatiously displayed. Their waitress gave them water and menus and told them she'd be back shortly to take their orders.

The doctor knew the menu by heart and he knew exactly what he wanted without looking. Annice perused the selections for a time before the doctor asked her if she was tempted to try anything special. She looked at him.

"I can't seem to make up my mind."

"I have an idea then," the doctor stated. "Why don't you have what I'm having?"

"And what are you having?"

"Hot roast beef sandwiches," he declared. "My favorite. I always get it here. It's lean beef slices laid on homemade bread and covered with, strike that, smothered with rich beef gravy. And the gravy is a feast all its own, made with onion bits and mushrooms. And then, of course, you get your choice of two vegetables too to go with it."

At Christopher's delectable description, Annice folded up her menu and placed it on top of his. She readily replied, "You're one of those people I trust, so I trust that I won't be disappointed with the fare."

"Splendid."

While waiting for their food, Annice asked, "Do you come here often?"

"That depends on what you mean by often. I'd say I come here, on average, twice a week."

"You must really like it here."

"I do. I like the place, the food, and the people."

"The people?"

"Yes. You would be surprised. Sometimes I run into lots of old friends here. Some from Catholic High, some from Sacred Heart."

"Do you ever run into any of your old sweethearts?"

"Yes. You for one," the doctor declared, "but nobody else worth mentioning."

Annice sensed Christopher's disliking the fact that she had brought up the idea of other women, so she abandoned, for the time being, provoking him further on the subject. The doctor had it right, though he really was not particularly annoyed with Annice for bringing it up; in fact, he was flattered. He knew that the only reason she would have for broaching the subject was that she was interested in him herself.

Despite the fact that the owner himself had promised to tend to the matter of their service, their food was delayed in getting to them as they had expected. This delay, unfortunately, gave the doctor too much time to think. His food for thought was the concern he had about how Annice must perceive him in view of the fact that at age forty he was still a bachelor.

How can I possibly explain it to her? he sat there thinking. She must think I'm cuckoo or something. Now that we've entered into this relationship, am I obligated to tell her everything about my past? Must I tell her about all of my sexual exploits even when I was in college? That would really turn her off. Should I tell her the honest truth that I felt I was so superior to every woman I ever met that I convinced myself I could never be happy with any of them? Should I also tell her that the reason I could never fall in love now, now that I've matured, is that since she's come to work with me I think only about her? With at least one of us eligible, it makes it that much easier should something happen to confound her married life. And to think I've been contemplating this for the past ten years.

The doctor took notice that Annice was staring in his direction. Afraid that she might be reading his mind, he quickly let his deliberations about them cease. Just as he was about to begin explaining his quiet contemplations as something other than what they were, Annice stood up and politely excused herself. "I have to go to the ladies' room," she said.

Just after she left the table, their meals arrived. The doctor instructed the waitress to place the appropriate plate at each of their places. "I am having the beef, broccoli, and baked potato," he said. "While . . . ," the doctor thought for a moment how to properly title Annice, "while my date will be having the beef, green beans, and baked potato."

"And here are your drinks, sir."

"That's fine. I'll take the Coke. And the Pepsi goes there," he said while indicating with his finger for her to place it with Annice's food.

By the time the waitress completed her task, Annice still had not returned from the ladies' room. The doctor decided to take advantage of her absence and play a little trick on her. Without her knowledge, he switched their two drinks. He took her Pepsi for himself and gave her his Coke. Annice always drank Pepsi-Cola and she claimed that she detested Coke. The doctor always thought she was speaking nonsense whenever she advocated the one over the other. Most people, he thought, though they may prefer one beverage

over the other, usually liked both. The differences between the two
soft drinks were not so vast as to make some people abhor one. The
doctor believed this wholeheartedly, and to prove it, he intended to
use Annice as his guinea pig.

Minutes later, Annice emerged from the direction of the
restrooms and she promptly seated herself when she saw the delicious
plate of food waiting for her at the table. Unbeknownst to the doctor,
her reasons for the trip to use the facilities had been twofold. Besides
taking care of her bodily functions, she had also extricated her
wedding band from her left hand. Other than after brutal fights with
her husband, she had never removed it, and doing so now liberated
her. Her validation came from her intent to someday leave him.
Having her ring removed made her feel that their being together was
somehow more appropriate. Like most Catholics, Annice didn't like
the feeling of a guilty conscience, and having her wedding ring off
alleviated some measure of her toleration of it. Over the course of
their meal of good food and interesting conversation, Annice boldly
displayed her bare left hand upon the table just in case Christopher
would happen to notice.

When it was time to leave, the two patrons got up. Each had to
stretch their bodies after such an enduring dinner. "We'd better go,"
the doctor insisted. "If we don't, they may not let us return. We have
taken up a valuable amount of time at our table."

"Oh, wait a minute," the doctor stated after they had started to
exit the dining section they had utilized. "I almost forgot the tip."

Feeling somewhat guilty for having extended their dining
experience to what he considered double the appropriate interval of
time, the doctor placed a 30% gratuity back on the table for their
waitress. He then met Annice over at the checkout counter where she
was standing, waiting for him. The hostess intercepted him just as he
approached. "Have a nice time," she asked.

"Yes."

"That will be $15."

"Fine."

Christopher paid the bill. Then, before leaving the counter, he
spied a small serving bowl filled with jelly mints—small white mint

candies with centers of chewy jelly. There were plain mint, lemon, orange, licorice, and cherry. The doctor scooped several times into his left hand. He offered some to Annice and she accepted it by placing her left hand out to receive it. She was delighted. She, too, liked the candy and, any chance now, while it was still pertinent, to show off her ring-free hand.

After they exited the establishment, Annice thanked Christopher for taking her out to eat. She used the thank-you as a way to endear herself to him by softly placing her left hand in his right hand. As they crossed the parking lot, hand in hand, she turned to him, smiled, and said, "She who laughs last, laughs best. I mean, did you really think I wouldn't notice the Pepsi challenge you put me through? The result of which is that you now owe me a Pepsi."

A Psychiatric Past

It was a week later, late Friday morning, that Dr. Haefner was whisking his Buick out of his James Street parking spot and into the city. He spun his car through the city streets and alleys to reach the north end of the city where he picked up the extended road which turned into Route 222.

It was a sparkling day. When the doctor's Buick hit the open highway, he activated the car's cruise control which he set at sixty miles per hour, the speed limit. He also lowered the car's power windows all the way, allowing a continuous rush of warm air to infiltrate the vehicle. The doctor was heading to Reading, a city of similar size to Lancaster, located about thirty miles north and east of it. There, the doctor was to meet with Dr. Brain, his old adviser and mentor from his earliest days as a practicing psychiatrist at Reading Hospital. It was Dr. Brain who had introduced the Thomes to Dr. Haefner's practice prior to their unfortunate highway snafu which had prevented their initial contact.

Now, for a second time, the Thomes were unable to meet with the famed Lancaster physician. Their daughter, Patricia, had taken a turn for the worse and, prior to their rearranged meeting set for today, had been hospitalized again. In a recent telephone communication with his colleague, Dr. Brain had requested that Dr. Haefner please come up and see him and together they could visit Miss Thome at the psychiatric hospital in Westeerville where she had been admitted.

It was exactly 11:45 when the doctor pulled off the Reading highway and onto a connecting road which led into the southeastern extent of the city. At this point, the doctor had to follow the intricately marked directions he had made during his most recent conversation with Dr. Brain during which he had discussed the location of his private office. The notations, Christopher had attached to his dashboard, on standard-sized, Post-it notes. He referred to them in succession and successfully navigated the unfamiliar territory confronting him: Blue Mountain Road to Hills Road to Distant View Road.

He discovered Dr. Brain's office by identifying the building's structural intrigues; a large single-level white-stucco structure made with a capricious dome on top shaped like a human brain. Looking at it, the doctor couldn't help but appreciate its whimsy, and he smiled the entire time he entered and parked his car in the visiting-physician's section of the parking lot. Once he was appropriately facilitated, the doctor raised up his windows, to about a half-inch on both sides, attached himself to his briefcase, and made his way to what looked like the main entrance to the building. Dr. Haefner's stomach grumbled as he pushed on the leading dark-glassed door. Inside he was greeted by a receptionist who informed him that Dr. Brain was indeed expecting him and would he please accept a seat until the doctor could accommodate him. Before seating himself, the doctor perused the counter of the reception area for any treats that offices such as this sometimes leave out as appeasements for any young children that may come as patients or just accompanying their parents. There were none. In his aggravated state, the doctor also perused the lobby area and the adjoining hall for any snack machines, of which there were none.

Having come up empty, he then seated himself on a comfortable large green-and-white-striped sofa. He felt depleted. He began to wonder how many of his own patients would have appreciated it if he had the foresight to provide a little something for them while they waited in his office. It is not an unimportant matter, he contended. He recalled from one of his college classes in philosophy the order of Maslow's hierarchy of human needs, from the essential food and water, all the way up to self-actualization. Food, of course, was the most essential of all. Well, he thought, I'm going to do something about taking better care of my patients' primary needs. After all, who in their right mind would want to sit in my office and listen to me prattle on in my psychobabble about healing them psychologically when they're all the time trying to get past one of their most basic human needs? The doctor set forth the condition he would meet in a self-satisfying thought. Splendid. He congratulated himself for his clever idea. Those jelly mints I like so much at Herkimer's, I'll incorporate them into my plans. I'll buy bags of them and a crystal serving bowl and a silver spoon. That will be nice. I'll have napkins too, and a water dispenser with little Dixie Cups.

As the doctor forged ahead inwardly about the snack-allocation program he intended to implement, his thoughts were abruptly interrupted by the fast approach of a body coming straight for him from across the room. He looked up and met the appreciative eyes of his old friend and colleague, Dr. Brain.

"Dr. Brain, I like your brain," Dr. Haefner stated jovially.

In response, Dr. Brain put his hands to his head and remarked, "I didn't know anything about me having a hole in my head," he laughed.

"I mean the brain atop your building," Dr. Haefner replied.

"Oh that, that was my brainstorm," he continued. "Although you should have seen the look on the face of the architect when I proposed it to him."

It seemed like old times. Dr. Haefner had always appreciated Dr. Brain's humor. It was a great asset especially when one's life was comprised of dealings with seriously sick people.

"You know, I don't usually collaborate with other doctors about my patients but I was especially intrigued by the success of some of your methods. I have read your journals related to treating severe cases of obsessive-compulsive disorder and I wanted to discuss your therapies with you personally. I believe Miss Thome can derive benefit from you. Also, I would like to be involved in the result of what you are able to accomplish with her. I would like to see firsthand what level of enablement you can give her."

"Sort of like giving me an exam, eh?" Dr. Haefner blurted out.

"Oh no, no, my boy. In this case you will be the one teaching me."

"Sounds good then," Dr. Haefner said humorously.

"It was unfortunate that they were unable to see you last week. I read the account of the accident in the paper. Apparently the driver of the tractor-trailer purported that he had seen something or someone crossing the highway up ahead of him. He slammed on his brakes so abruptly that his rig buckled up and fell over sideways onto the road. Traffic heading into Lancaster was backed up for hours. The problem was that there are no exits for miles back from the scene of the incident. Luckily no one was hurt, not even the driver of the truck."

"If he is seeing things, maybe he should be seeing a psychiatrist," Dr. Haefner replied.

"Who can say?" Dr. Brain retorted.

"So what is the status of Miss Thorne currently?"

"She has had a relapse. She was admitted to Reading Hospital three days ago, evaluated, and then transferred to Westeerville State Hospital."

"Where exactly is that from here?"

"Not far. You and I are meeting her and her parents there today around 2:00. First things first though. Are you hungry?"

"Yes."

"Come then. I am taking you to the Pagoda. Do you like Oriental cuisine?"

"I have heard a lot of good things about that place and I do like eating out."

"It is a marvelous place. I'll call ahead and reserve us a table. Sometimes they get awfully busy at lunch. Many of the local business people go there."

Using the phone at the reception desk, Dr. Brain called the Pagoda and arranged to have a table ready for them when they arrived. During his brief interlude on the phone, Dr. Haefner took the time to contemplate his old colleague. Dr. Brain was an older man, older than Dr. Haefner by twenty-three years. Except for his acute abilities as a psychiatrist he was past his prime in everything in life. He was shorter than the average person, stout, and balding. His hair color was a confusing mix of white, gray, and black. Some strands seemed to have all three distinct variations of color, or should it be said, absence of color. The aging process had not been kind to his hair. But despite his deteriorating physical appearance, Dr. Horace Brain had many personal assets of intrinsic distinction. He was an extremely intelligent person who was not self-absorbed. He had no pretensions about himself. He was a very caring individual, an individual who would go out of his way for anybody. He was a very stimulating person to be around. And as for his humor, he always carried it with him in pockets full. If he had not become a prominent psychiatrist, he could have been a cartoon columnist.

The Pagoda was a posh eating establishment set on a high promontory overlooking the entire city of Reading. Due to its prominence, a dominating one hundred feet above the lowland, it could be viewed from anywhere in the city.

When the two doctors arrived, they were situated at a prominent table setting beside a huge glass window which allowed them to view the entire city. It was a spectacular sight.

Within minutes, a lovely young waitress attended them. They gave her their orders then began to converse while their food was being prepared.

"Do you have a penchant for eating Oriental food, Horace?"

"Oh my, yes. Whenever I can actually. And the food here is first-rate too."

"How often do you come here?"

"All the time. How about you? Do you have a proclivity for the food of any specific culture other than your own?"

"I am afraid not. Not that I don't enjoy partaking of ethnic foods should the opportunity present itself. It's just that in and around Lancaster County there are so many delightful places to eat that if I ever got started trying to sample them all I would never finish. The good thing is that because I don't eat much ethnic food, coming here today is a treat and one I intend to make the most of."

Their food came, served by the same lovely waitress they had placed their orders with. Horace's plate, the contents of which

Christopher could not discern, was presented to him, and after making a quick joke about it, the connoisseur began eating heartily of it. Chris's plate was laid down before him, and before partaking of it, he examined its contents with a discriminating eye. He tasted each heaping of rice and noodles, chicken, and sprouts in turn, examining their texture and taste. Once he decided that everything was to his liking, he began devouring his food to appease his grumbling stomach. Both men ate until they were content. Then their attention again turned to the spectacular view outside.

As they were again discussing the cityscape below, their waitress came back to their table to remove their empty plates and offer them dessert. Horace declined, stating that he was as stuffed as a Thanksgiving Day turkey. Dr. Haefner paused while he considered getting a piece of pie or something. Actually, he was smitten by the waitress and her close proximity to him.

She was only inches away from him and it was quite comical, at least from Horace's perspective, to see his associate feinting interest in the dessert menu when all the time his head was turned sideways toward the temptress and his eyes were swooning every time they made contact with her. She was scrumptious. No doubt about it. Horace laughed as he thought how he knew Dr. Haefner would rather have her for dessert than any piece of pie.

Finally, Dr. Haefner yielded to the pressure of having to come up with an answer. "No," he said. "I guess I won't have anything more today."

"Sorry, my dear," Dr. Brain chortled, "not today." Unbeknownst to Dr. Haefner, Dr. Brain winked at the waitress on Dr. Haefner's behalf, indicating to her that he was interested in her. The waitress smiled then excused herself of her duties at the table.

Dr. Brain knew most of the waitresses who worked at the Pagoda. Those he didn't, he didn't because they had not been in the employ of the restaurant very long. This particular woman he knew partially. Her name was Carol. She was thirty-one, single, and had been working the early shift at the Pagoda for about six months. Carol was bright, hard-working, and honest. In Dr. Brain's view, she would make Dr. Haefner very happy if they ever got together.

"I have to thank you, Horace, for a fine dining experience. I'm sure that if I lived up here I would come here often."

"You are not about to get off that easy, my boy."

"What do you mean?"

"You know very well what I mean. That woman over there. The one you couldn't keep your eyes off of. The one you keep turning your head to see. As you know, I'm a very perceptive person. I can plainly see that you're infatuated with her. And, if I'm any judge, I think she sees something in you too."

Dr. Haefner grinned. "OK, Doc, you got the goods on me, but how is it that you're so sure about her?"

"Because I saw what you couldn't see. You were just so obvious. We both knew it. You were not interested in procuring a dessert when she was standing beside you. You were interested in procuring her. You know it. I know it. And she knows it."

"Look, see for yourself," Dr. Brain stated while indicating some proof of his postulation by holding out the dinner bill for his guest to take. "That little annotation on the bottom was written by your female counterpart over there."

Dr. Haefner took the slip and read over it carefully. On it, at the very bottom was a lady's name and number. Written directly under the phone number was the inscription: "Call me." At once the doctor felt conspicuous. He was, for a moment, afraid to look up from the note for fear that he was being observed reading it. Then, finally, he lifted his head and looked for Carol, who was attending to an old couple seated a short distance away. Several times during her interlude with them, she broke her attention from them and glanced over at the doctors' table. Christopher, not knowing what to do, returned a smile.

"Look at you," Dr. Brain began jovially, "one day out on the town and you're already a tomcat on the prowl."

The doctors meandered over to the checkout counter, which they found to be unoccupied by the hostess. Carol, their inspiring waitress, noticed their dilemma and hurried over to respond.

"Hello. Back so soon," she said jokingly.

"We're sorry, but the hostess seems to be misplaced," Dr. Haefner said, attempting something of a silly reply.

"That's OK. I'll take care of you," Carol responded.

"Of that I am sure," Christopher answered with a flair.

Listening to their weak attempts to flirt with one another, Dr. Brain stepped forward to say, "As a supportive bystander, I must intervene and move matters forward, out of the playground so to speak, so we can get going. We have an important appointment to keep and we're not getting any younger. Here, here's thirty dollars. This will pay our bill plus leave you with a nice piece of pie. I'm going. You two have two minutes to sort things out between you."

Horace handed Carol the money then left.

"Dr. Brain, he's your associate?" Carol asked. "So you . . . you're a psychiatrist too?"

"Yes."

"It must be an interesting profession."

"It has its moments."

Just at that moment, Carol was called over to a table behind her. They both became anxious. It was now or never.

"Look," Carol said, initiating the spoken words for their concern. "I have to go now but I would like it if you would call me sometime."

"I will," the doctor said assuredly.

"OK then," Carol replied. "I will talk to you later."

After their brief exchange, Carol returned to her duties. The doctor watched her as she turned and walked away. He admired how her shapely body moved across the dining-room floor as if she were promenading around; a swimsuit model, on stage at a beauty contest. For a moment longer he stared at her, only half-believing he could have her.

Outside, the two doctors collaborated. Before a word was spoken, Dr. Haefner relinquished a smile. Dr. Brain stood, hands on his hips, waiting for a report.

"I guess my only chance of finding out would have been if I were a fly on the wall."

"Doctor, if I may, I really don't believe that my infatuations with Carol were all that obvious. It was as if she already knew about me, as if she were expecting me. Could that be? What I think is that I was the fly, so to speak, the Pagoda a spider web, and Carol the lovely spider."

"My boy, you cut me to the quick. But in my defense I would say that if I ever did say anything in your behalf it was said in the best possible way and with your best interests at heart."

For that, Dr. Haefner had no reply. Without Dr. Haefner sharing any of the aforementioned circumstance to his colleague, they simply entered their vehicle and departed. Once they were off the steep road, Dr. Brain began informing Dr. Haefner about the specifics of their afternoon.

"We're going to Westeerville State Hospital. That is where Miss Thome is. We're meeting her parents there at two—which gives us exactly half an hour to get there."

As they turned onto the south highway, Dr. Haefner gave one last departing look at the magnificent Pagoda and one last departing thought to the marvelous waitress.

A short time later, they arrived at the state hospital. From the turn on the highway, there was a long approach which led directly to the front of the massive brick building. Halfway along the drive, they passed by an old abandoned guardhouse, now padlocked. Dr. Brain took notice of Dr. Haefner's curious stare at it.

"This institution opened some fifty years ago. Things were different then. Society itself was ill-equipped to deal with the mentally disabled. Even doctors were viewed suspiciously—those who treated them. Up until the early 1970s guards were posted all around the building's perimeter. Nobody got in. Nobody got out."

"That sounds deplorable," Dr. Haefner responded.

"If you think that's bad, you should have been around to see what went on inside. There were no therapies such as we have today. There were no effective medicines for treating the poor suffering people. There was no Prozac or Haldol or Cogentin or Valium or the new Lithium. There were no valid medicines available for use."

"What did they use?"

"In some cases the only thing they could: placebos."

"I'm shocked."

"You would have had you been a member of this health club long ago. That was one of the most prominently used therapies: electric-shock therapy."

"Yes, I've read about that practice. I can't believe practitioners condoned it."

"Oh, it was a horrible thing the way sick people were strapped onto a bed, had electrodes strapped onto their heads, and had all that electricity zapped into their brains."

"What happened to all those patients as a result of electroshock?"

"Some got better. Of those, some only because the part of their brain that did work told them they had better fake it rather than go back for more. Others, probably because the parts of their brain that did not work got fried—at least that's my contention."

There was an abeyance of conversation as the doctors absorbed all that had been said. Both, in their minds, went over the suffering endured by early mental-health patients.

"But now we're planted firmly in a modern era of mental-health healing. We're learning more and more each day thanks to this Computer Age we live in.

"But who knows, fifty years from now the psychiatric profession as a whole will probably think that our current methods for treating the mentally ill are abhorrent."

"I say that is to be expected, and in all actuality, that would be a good thing because that would mean that the science used in healing people's minds has improved."

"Right you are, my boy," Dr. Brain agreed.

Dr. Brain parked his Cadillac in a front-row space designated for visiting physicians.

"Privilege precedes us," Dr. Brain contended once they stopped. "And look at that. We are right on time."

The two professional men walked into the building and approached a broad semi-circular admittance counter. After identifying themselves, they were given visiting-physician badges which they were instructed to wear on their shirts. One young intern acknowledged Dr. Brain as the pair made their way down a central hallway toward the elevator. Inside the elevator, Dr. Brain pressed the indicator so they would be transported to the fourth floor. Once they were delivered to Patricia's floor, they proceeded to another station where they received instructions about floor procedures. Then they were off to Patricia's room. Dr. Brain was still cogitating thoughts about their earlier discussion.

"You know, what a horror it would be if some young girl like Miss Thome were to end up in a place like this back some fifty years ago. She would have been mistreated too. Not that I blame the profession. They did the best they could with what they had. Nothing more could ever be expected from anyone. But it still staggers my mind to think of it."

"Those patients were experimented on. They were like prisoners both inside themselves and outside themselves. Psychiatry was incompetent to deal with them. And you know I have been in practice thirty years now, long enough to have seen some of the changes as they were taking place. To this day I am still replete with anger over some of the treatment of patients I personally witnessed when I was coming up in the field."

"Maybe that's something you should deal with professionally, Doctor," Dr. Haefner contended.

"That's something I do deal with professionally, Doctor, every day. It is the reason I care for my patients so personally. It is part of the reason you are here today to help me. I need you to help me help her."

As the doctors continued their walk along the corridor, Dr. Haefner made note of the fact that many of the facility's rooms appeared to be unoccupied.

"You've hit on an inspiring point, Doctor. That fact is a tribute to our profession. Because of science's better understanding of how the brain functions, medicines have improved substantially. Today, many of the patients that would have been here in the yesterdays of our profession no longer have to be. Psychiatry is fast becoming an outpatient service."

Dr. Haefner knew firsthand that what Dr. Brain was saying was true. His own mother was a sufferer of a severe case of obsessive-compulsive disorder. During his childhood and adolescent years, she had been admitted to Embreeville State Hospital several times. There, she underwent the same outmoded treatments they had just discussed, including electroshock therapy. It was Prozac that saved her. She had been one of test patients selected back in the 1980s to use the drug experimentally. Now, twenty years later, she is still depending on it but she is living her life.

Prozac today is dispensed like candy. But, for the memory of Dr. Haefner, it was a life-changing drug. He recalled the plethora of sad memories which had daunted him as he grew up. He recalled the times he watched his mother agonize over her inability to deal with her condition and the incessant way she tried to get her loved ones to understand her—something she didn't understand herself.

Dr. Haefner recalled vividly the experiences of his mother breaking into tears of frustration—the constancy of it. He recalled the inability of his father and other family members, aunts and uncles, to console her. He had a flashback of a particular situation in which he had been in the company of a noted psychiatrist with his mother and father, and how the psychiatrist admitted he had nothing to offer. Until Prozac.

All these thoughts weighed heavily on the doctor's mind. So much so that when they reached Patricia's room, but before entering it, he suddenly blurted out, "You know, Doctor, my mother is a mental-health patient. She was one of the first patients in America to receive Prozac."

"I'm sorry to hear that, Doctor, but I don't recall you ever telling me that when you were a young apprentice at my side."

"I'm sorry. I didn't. I still carry the burden of it. I still feel the pain and stigma of it. It is not something I admit to very often. It is too personal a thing to talk about to most people."

"So your mother is an actual test-case person. I must admit to you that I would be interested to discuss her condition, past and present, with you. She holds valuable insights into the long-term effects of the drug. Tell me, has her prescription changed much over the years? Most people, as you know, build up a certain resistance to it over years of taking it."

"I'm not her doctor so I don't know precisely, but I know that for the first ten years or so the Prozac did wonders for her. Along the way, of course, she had to increase her dosage to get the same effect. Then, some eight years ago, I believe, she started taking another form of the same medicine. It helped get her back to feeling the original relief she felt when she first began taking Prozac."

"Your mother is to be greatly appreciated. She was a brave soul to have undergone the uncertainties of taking what was then an experimental medicine. How is she doing today?"

"Living life."

"It seems that your mother's illness has had a profound effect on your life. Tell me, is she the reason that you became a psychiatrist?"

"You would think so, but no, she's not. Remember, I saw my mother being appreciably helped before I decided to pursue this endeavor. My concerns for her were already being abated when I chose my life's profession. Actually, Doctor, there was another person who I was far more disturbed by, a person I was far more concerned about. He was once one of my best friends, James Cuzze."

Who was this James?

The visit with the Thomes lasted for two hours after which the two doctors decided to review the case privately. To accomplish this, the hospital afforded them the exclusive use of a small conference room located on the same floor. There they deliberated.

"Well, what do you think, Doctor?"

"I was about to ask you the same question."

"I asked you first, Dr. Haefner."

"Well, she is obviously suffering from a severe case of obsessive-compulsive disorder. She seems to have had only limited response to the medications that have been afforded her. Hospitalization will not help her, of that I'm sure. Protecting her will not make her demons go away. I have had similar cases and seen similar results.

"Patricia is an intelligent girl. She has a keen mind, and that will be to our advantage. She also recognizes what is happening to her. But she is making the same mistakes that so many patients who suffer from OCD make. Every day she tries to do battle with her mind. She thinks that to win this thing she has to be able to control the uncontrollable thoughts that plague her. She can not. In order for an OCD patient to win, they must first accept the fact that the thoughts will not go away. What will go away is the way they allow themselves to be controlled by their thoughts. Since their minds will not allow the bad thoughts to leave them, they must learn instead to disregard them. They must learn to not listen to them. They must learn not to react to them."

"Do the medications help at all in your opinion?"

"It varies. Everybody is an individual. Everybody's mind make-up is a little different, so medications work for each person differently. What the medications tend to do is tone down the bombardment of irrational thinking of the individual. This first eases the patients' stress level then actualizes and strengthens their ability to slow down before reacting to their emotions. You see, emotion is the other side of this. It's because of the heavy emotional stresses that accompany the bad thoughts—emotions like fear, guilt, or anger—that the patient has such a hard time coping with the disorder. That is why patients have such a compulsion to cleanse themselves. It is not just the thoughts they are having, it is also the excess of negative emotions they are feeling."

"So what do you do?"

"The first thing I do is to session with them to determine the severity of their disorder. Then I force them to tell me everything they are thinking. Most are reluctant to discuss what they know are completely ludicrous thoughts. But once I assure them that I have already heard them all, they tend to open up. Sometimes I purposely laugh when I hear them telling me things like if they open up a certain closet door they are afraid they will disappear. I laugh because I want to see if they are able to laugh too. If they are, then I know they still have enough control of their cognizant skills to make the therapy work.

"What we do next is to work with each thought and rationalize it. I help the patients to prove to themselves just how ridiculous their fears are. If they insist that something bad will happen to them if they sit in a chair while they are having a bad thought, I make them sit in the chair. If they fear that something they did has harmed someone else because they had a bad thought when they did it, I have them call the person to prove that nothing ever happened. If they think they will die because they ate a certain food, I make them eat it, that is, if it is something they like to eat.

"I call it confrontational therapy. And it can't just be applied in an office-type setting either. It has to work in the real world too.

So, usually on the third or fourth session, I take my patient out into that world where we continue to confront the debacles the disorder throws at us. I usually take them out into traffic or to the Park City Mall where they are inundated by large numbers of cars and people which are great antagonists to their affliction. Then, they are forced to deal with themselves. With me there to help them, they begin to learn how to rationalize instead of ritualize as a reaction to their fears. Then we go back. And in the office I try to get them to laugh at what would have been their reaction to the circumstances that piqued at them while they were out in the world. We do this again and again and again until I feel certain they are gaining control of their reactions."

"What has been your success rate?"

"It doesn't work the same on everybody. But I have had success. And I think in the case of Miss Thome it will help her. It would be to her benefit if we start as soon as possible too. As you know I have already arranged a tentative session with her for next week in Lancaster. I hope she makes it."

There was a brief interlude in which the doctors absorbed their thoughts while listening to the background noise made by the PA system. Both men were in a relaxed pose, enjoying the comforts of their little cubbyhole, when Horace, whose curiosity had already been piqued by his associate's reference to one James Cuzze, decided to call upon Dr. Haefner to explain how it was that an old friend and not his mother, with her detailed medical past, had been the primary reason for his becoming a psychiatrist.

"Who was this James?"

"That's a loaded question, Doctor. If I were to properly enlighten you it would take hours. As it is, with our time being limited, I'll try to tell you as completely and as succinctly as is possible. James was the most complicated person I ever knew. It was perplexing just to be around him. He contradicted even himself.

"He was born in 1959, the same year I was, though I was one week older. Soon after he was five, he was abandoned by his real parents and adopted by his aunt and uncle, Betty and John Boller. I first met him in 1968 when I was eight. We had just moved into the city where my father had bought a home on the one hundred block of Pine Street only one house away from the Bollers.

"The Bollers, James's adoptive parents, were both drunks. Several nights a week and most weekends, they frequented the Moose Lodge, of which they were members, where they drank and drank and drank. James and his younger brother Dave, the Boller's only child, were left on their own during their parents' excessive and often extensive durations at the lodge. Essentially, they spent most of their formative years at each other's throats, riled in conflict.

"For James, who had already started life very dysfunctional, this was confounding. He wanted his life to be right. He wanted parents. He wanted parents to be parents. Inherently, he sensed that this was right. The problem was that he was able to take advantage of the extensive freedom afforded him by his parents' neglect. Because of their blatant indifference, James was able to exercise his unfounded freedom into power. He used his power to influence people. The Bollers, when they weren't in a stage of inebriation or post-inebriation, sometimes made attempts to discipline him. But James saw right past them. He called them drunks to their faces and once even broke into the lodge to confront them and make fools out of them while they were intoxicated. That was when he was ten.

"By the time James was thirteen, he controlled the Bollers' home. You know, even today it still sounds funny to refer to it as the Bollers' home. Everybody, and I mean everybody—friends, neighbors, strangers—all called it Cuzze's place. James turned that house into his own. It was his domain. He was the undisputed dominator of Pine Street then and even after he left home.

"When I turned eighteen and I left home, I lost contact with him. At that point, our lives were going in completely different directions. I was an astute college student living on my own in a small apartment. He was a party person. He had his own place when he could afford it. He smoked pot, drank beer, and sometimes used cocaine. Every time I saw him, he had a different girlfriend. By the time he was thirty, he had fathered three children. To the best of my knowledge, he never got to know any of them.

"James was killed in a car crash one month before he turned thirty-one. It happened outside New Orleans. Supposedly, he was strangled to death by a seat belt. The driver of the car, his fiancée, walked away from the accident unscathed. I believe he was murdered. James was probably showing his fiancée the first signs of his abusive nature; you see, they had only met three weeks prior to his leaving to Louisiana. Cuzze's problem was that down there he was out of his element. He had no place to run, no place to hide. So, when things got bad between them, she was able to have him subdued by her friends. He was probably choked to death with a seat belt. But not in a car as the coroner's report indicated. It was done by somebody. Then his dead body was placed in the car and the car was run off the road way out in the boonies where no one could witness it.

"I had planned to help him before it was too late. Being associated with him was very distracting, so I couldn't afford too much interaction with him while I was in college. I had only just started my private practice when he met his unfortunate demise. I had intended to call him in for a personal visit once he got back from New Orleans. You know, it was strange. It was as if James had known his fate. He called me about a week before the wedding and asked me to come down and be best man at the ceremony. He told me that of all the people he had ever known, I was the only one he considered a friend. He told me he loved me. Can you believe that? In all of our life together I had never heard him say that, not to me, not to his parents, not even to any of the many ladies in his life."

"Tell me, did he have any real brothers or sisters?"

"Yes. He had a sister, Paula, who had also been adopted out. I only ever saw her once. He also had a brother, Ron, who visited him from time to time. Every time Ron came to see James, they ended up in a fight. James always won. He also had a sister, Deb. There were many instances when they interacted with each other."

"You make it sound as if that was significant."

"Do you want to hear an example?"

"Why not."

"It's a sordid story but here goes. One summer day when James and I were fifteen, James had the notion to go over to his real parents' house on Pearl Street which was only about six blocks from Pine Street. James had been asking about visiting with his real family and had been told no. His real parents did not want to see him. He was forbidden from ever going over. So, of course, James went. I went with him. I did it to support his cause: the right to see his real family.

"Prior to the day we went, James had been making inquiries of other members of his extended family and was able to find out when his real mom and dad would be working or out of the house. When we arrived at the house, James just walked in as if he had lived there all his life. I can remember it as if it were yesterday."

The doctor told the tale. He unfolded the story in such a complete manner that he and his listener felt as though it were a live experience.

"Who's there? Who's down there?" Debbie called out from the upstairs hall.

"It's me," James replied in a loud voice.

"Who? Ron?"

"No, it's not your wimpy brother. It's me, James."

"Jimmy! What in the world are you doing here?"

"I came here to see you."

Deb was still wet from the shower she had just taken and she had a towel wrapped around her body. She was standing at the top of the stairs, conversing with her brother who had moved from the living room to the dining room to the staircase. James stared at his sister, at her vulnerability.

"I like what I see," he commented openly to her.

That was all it took for Deb to realize what James intended to do. Though she didn't live with him, she knew enough about him to know that anything James wants, James gets. She tried to act nonchalant about it by just casually turning and walking away. James retaliated by charging up the steps after her. Before Deb had made her escape complete by closing and locking her bedroom door, James burst into her room and tackled her to the bed.

The towel she was wearing came loose where she had it folded together at the top of her chest. She gripped it tightly in advance of

James's attempts to remove it. For the first minute, James remained quiet, being quite content just to feel the power of his strong body over her. She was his. He had conquered her. After that long minute, James lifted up his head and looked intently into his sister's eyes and spoke, "And to the victor goes the spoils."

Deb struggled to free herself. James had fun with it by allowing her to almost get free several times before smothering her with his upper body and locking up her legs in his. He wanted her to expend most of her energy so she wouldn't do anything rash once he was vulnerably inside her.

Finally Deb gave up. She knew it was futile to try to escape and that it would only infuriate her brother into possibly hurting her. She was unaware that James had a companion waiting for him in the living room so she never called for help. Chris didn't know to what extent James's interactions were with his sister. In desperation, Deb pleaded with James.

"Jimmy, please don't. I'm your sister."

James put his hands on her neck and started to strangle her. "This is it," he began. "I'm having you whether you like it or not. If you say one word about it to anyone, one single word, I'll come back. I'll come back, have you again, and then kill you. Right now I want you to make love to me as though I were one of your boyfriends. If you mess up and act like you're not enjoying it, I'll punch you in the head until your dead!"

Acting as though he were her lover, James began caressing his sister's body. He unwrapped her towel, laying it down around her sides. He gazed upon her lustfully. He stripped out of his clothes while warning her not to move a muscle. Then he straddled her. Deb did everything James commanded from start to finish. When it was over, James left.

"I heard it. I heard it all. I believe he did it to entertain me as much as himself."

"Did you think to intervene at all for his sister's sake?"

"The reason I did not intervene was for his sister's sake. If I had she would have been the one who got hurt. And besides, in a weird sort of way, I actually believe she liked it."

"What?"

"Yes. You see that was James's appeal. He had a way of breaking people down to their basest level. He knew that at the core of everyone there lurked their self-interests. He exploited that in people. He used the basic three—sex, drugs, and money—to get to people. In this case he knew how much his sister liked sex. He knew that once he forced her past the stigma of their being brother and sister she would acquiesce to him. He was right. Remember she was no angel either. So once they were actually involved in the act and she had passed the moral boundary, she let herself go. I heard her shrieking, 'take me, take me,' to him when they were climaxing."

"Was that an isolated incident?"

"No, that was only the beginning. Several times after that, they got together to have intercourse. As I'm sure James kept reminding her that once her Pandora's box was opened, what difference did it make anyway."

"Whatever happened to James's sister?"

"I know that at age seventeen she got pregnant. It wasn't James's. She left home and went to live with her boyfriend. Eventually, they got married, but soon after, divorced. Then for a while she lived by herself and raised her son. Two or three times she and her ex-husband got back together before, finally, they gave up on each other. Then, sometime later, I know she had an intimate relationship with another woman who lived with her. I know that because I remember being over at her apartment once with James and he was riding her about it. To date, I have not seen her in ten years. I do not have a clue where she is. Too bad too for she would make for an interesting patient. I do know she suffers from acute depression because even way back then she was on some kind of medication."

There was a break in the conversation as each man contemplated James's abhorrent behavior toward his sister when they were younger. Then, Dr. Brain inquired, "What was he like with his girlfriends?"

"At every age, members of the opposite sex were fascinated with him. He was relatively tall, dark-haired, and good-looking. He was always so self-assured, too, that his peers were commonly interested in finding out about him.

"Most of the decent girls would lose interest in him after the first couple of days. He was obnoxious and rude to them, in part, but that was what James did on purpose so he could weed out the weak. He understood himself very well. He knew that only the strong could survive around him. Pity to those who fell in love with him.

"There was one young lady who turned out to be a real fighter. She tried everything to make a go of their relationship. Her name was Deb too. She and James met at Luckee's Bar. Luckee's was a place where you could get served underage if you were cool about it. I went there myself a few times, although I did not consume any beer or alcohol. James introduced me to Deb there. It was an unusual bar in that there was a back room where patrons openly smoked pot and made out. Once I remember watching a couple having sex in a booth. The place went into an uproar as, on a dare, the couple took off their clothes and did it for everyone to see. The loud chants and applause that followed even brought back the owner who advised everybody to keep it down. He saw the naked couple too, but he didn't care. Later, as Luckee's became even more decadent, the police began raiding the place periodically, and eventually Luckee sold it. Soon after that, the place shut down for good.

"But anyway, about Deb, like I said, she was a person who possessed an amazing amount of resolve. She wasn't easily overcome by James's audacious character or outlandish behavior. At his request, she even abandoned her apartment and moved into his parents' house on Pine Street with him. Betty and John, of course, had no say in the matter.

"Actually James went to great lengths to accommodate Deb in his house without having his parents be involved. He took control of the third floor of the house and converted it into a private living space exclusively for them. It became known as the Third Story. How he did it is a story in itself. One day, about a week before Deb was to move in, James made use of a ten-pound sledge hammer he found lying in the basement. He took out the partitioning wall between the two rooms which comprised the upper floor of the house. Now the entire third floor was one large space. From that moment on, the Third Story became the premiere party place on Pine Street.

"To accentuate his achievement further, James went so far as to paint the entire third floor black, everything—walls, ceilings, floors. He got black lights and reflective posters and arranged them around the room. In the center of everything, he built a bar which had a built-in refrigerator. He kept beer, liquors, and stashes of marijuana on hand for the plethora of get-togethers which occurred there on an almost-daily basis. He filled the room with an eclectic mix of assorted seating apparatus—arm chairs, wooden chairs, recliners, swivel rockers, a sofa, stools, an old love seat—you name it.

"Except for when they cooked, showered, or went to the bathroom, Deb and James lived up there. At any given time, day or night, there could be visitors there. Often, people spent the night. The Bollers were helpless too to do anything about it. Strangers came and went from their house all the time, and besides acting gruff about it, there was little they could do. James had effectively warned them that if they resisted they would die in their sleep.

"At first, Deb went along with everything James had devised for them. Although I am sure she held some sympathy for James's poor parents, she enjoyed the way he prevailed on everyone. The life style was one of excess without boundaries. She contributed to it freely. For a while she and James got along. They smoked pot, drank beer, and had sex. But soon, as with all of James's acquaintances, he became bored with her. They began to fight with each other, sometimes over nonsensical things which only proved that their complicity was overwhelming. Day after day the hostilities grew, until finally James decided that Deb needed to be subdued. To keep her in line, he needed to hurt her in a way that she would be forever intimidated by him.

"I was there that night. I was a witness to it. And like all the times before, there was little I could do to prevent it and little I could do to stop it once it started. It was late at night. There were five of us still there: James, Deb, me, Pete, and Steve. Everyone was stoned. All at once, James, who had been acting nice toward Deb the entire evening, took her by the hand and settled down on top of a bearskin rug, which was in the center of the room, with her. He began kissing her more and more passionately as everyone in the room looked on.

Soon the kissing turned into foreplay. He was sliding his hand down her pants and up under her blouse. At first, she insisted that they quit there and continue elsewhere, but James refused. He was forceful with her. She was so out of it that she didn't put up much of a fight.

"It was unbelievable. Soon they were completely naked. He was feeling and fondling her and she was holding onto him. The onlookers in the room were astonished at the blatant display of public sex. Finally, once James knew Deb was past the point of no return he turned toward us and asked for volunteers. He said that earlier Deb had agreed to engage in a fantasy-sex scenario. She would have us all perform sex on her one after the other. At first no one believed him but he insisted that it was true.

"The stage was set. James knew that if the wild sex party played out as he had planned, he would have forever humiliated her. He knew that from that moment forward she would forever be without any moral ground to stand on to ward off any other sordid acts that were to follow. There was nothing she could do.

"As for the ogling eyes of the onlookers, no further persuasion was necessary. Though they were somewhat stunned by the proposition and reluctant to come right out and agree to it, they did each consider it. Each of them, delighted by the unexpected offer, moved forward upon the spectacle before them to see for themselves if Deb, herself, had anything to say for or against it.

"Deb, of course, had nothing to say nor had she contrived with James to partake in the unusual sex act. For her part though, she had already been stimulated past the point of no return. She was already under the heavy influence of alcohol, pot, and sexual foreplay. In her defense it must be stated that what woman under these strenuous circumstances would be able to defend herself? And it might be added, she was getting something too. After all, despite there being a certain sordidness to this act, it was a sexual fantasy which some women actually think about. Here was a real chance to experience it with three or four good-looking men.

"To go on, Deb lay there, vulnerable, on the bearskin rug. She was only marginally aware of what was going on around her. James sat beside her continually stroking her body, keeping her aroused. I recall there was some commotion about the order in which we were about to take her. I was truly fascinated by it all. I felt like I was watching a scene from a porno movie being filmed—a movie I had no intention of being part of. As the squabbling continued, it was James that took charge and established the order of business amongst us. He looked at me and said, 'Best friends first.'

"Now that the actual moment to 'perform or die trying'—as James so eloquently put it—arrived, I had to make up my mind too, so I simply deferred saying, 'Thanks but no thanks.' That was hard for I was enticed to the extreme myself, sitting there looking intently upon Deb's voluptuous body. What actually saved me was my modesty. I couldn't, for the life of me, undress and do it in the company of others. But as for the others, modesty seemed in short supply that day. Once I relinquished my fortunate position, they took over. They were like unfed animals—a lion, a tiger, a hyena—all ready to pounce on the first fresh meat in days.

"I sensed the embarrassment that would follow such an event, so before anything further happened, I left. I expect James got what he wanted out of it too because it wasn't long after that that Deb left him for good."

"Your life back then must have been one exhilarating experience after another. It's a wonder you got through it."

"You have no idea, Doctor. Just think, those two stories I just told you, they were just two exiguous accounts of what life was like with James."

"And you purport that he, James, was the reason you became a psychiatrist."

"Yes," Dr. Haefner returned adamantly.

"You wanted to help him but back then you couldn't. You knew that past that disturbed character of his was a boy in pain, a boy in a lot of pain."

"I did what I could for him back then. He leaned on me when he looked to do things right. I was a shining example for him to see about how to act, about how to behave, about how to treat people. It ended up being about half-and-half as far as he and I went. Though he got away with doing countless things wrong I was able to stop him half of the time. If I had tried to stop him more than that, he would have terminated our relationship, and then he would have hurt far more people in his lifetime. So basically I did all I could, all things considered."

"What you say makes sense but I can't help but think that in thinking back you consider your efforts ineffective. Why else would you dwell on the past like you do? I can tell by the way you tell your stories about way back when that you have already spent an immeasurable amount of time weighing out the importance of what you did for him against what you weren't able to do for him. Am I right?"

Everything Black and Blue

The drive back to Lancaster was uneventful. This meant that the doctor had a chance to unwind his mind from the stresses of the day. As he approached the northern edge of the city from the straight-shot of Route 222 that connected Reading to Lancaster, the doctor noted the time on the digital car clock. It was 5:30, and already past the time when Annice would be gone for the day. So instead of returning directly to the James Street office, he decided to make a run to the grocery store to purchase several bags of the jelly mints he had promised himself he would buy for his patients who waited for their appointments.

Entering the city off the highway exit, the doctor swerved his vehicle into the merging traffic lane that led to the Lancaster Shopping Center, the location of a Giant Food Store. The doctor quickly parked his car and went inside. Despite the busy appearance of the store, the doctor knew he was lucky to have gotten there when he did, before the droves of usual Friday-night shoppers arrived.

Once inside, the doctor located the candy aisle and began perusing the different confections for the mints he intended to buy. He found the mints on the bottom shelf midway down the aisle. They were being sold only in small one-pound packages, so in order to purchase an adequate supply the doctor had to appropriate ten bags. With his hands full, he carried the bags of mints up to the register, where he had to stand waiting for five minutes before he could pay for them. While transacting the purchase of the mints, the doctor inquired of the cashier if she knew whether or not the mint candies came in larger packaging. When she stated that she had only recently become an employee of the store and she wasn't sure, the doctor relented from acquiring an answer.

By the time he exited the Giant, the parking lot was burgeoning with cars. Traffic on the streets was heavy and it took the doctor an exceptional effort to cut across the two-lane road which he had to take to get back to his office. When he arrived at the office, he pulled up into the back parking lot and stopped. Holding his grocery bag full of candy mints, he walked around to the building front and went inside. Once inside, he walked down the short corridor and one-handedly opened the office door. The moment he stepped inside, the phone began ringing. He quickly flicked on the lights then thudded the grocery bag down on the secretary's desk so he could answer it.

"Hello, this is Dr. Haefner's office," he said amiably.

"Hello, Christopher, it's me, Annice."

"Annice?" he answered quizzically.

"Yes," she replied in a mused tone. "I was just calling to leave myself a reminder on the answering machine about something I have to do on Monday."

As she spoke with her sweet melodic voice, the doctor was reminded of the fact that he would not be seeing her until next week. It happened the same every week, the weak feeling he would get in his stomach just knowing that Saturday and Sunday would pass before they would be together again. The misery he felt now was no different from the misery he felt then, back when they had attended high school together. Every Friday afternoon at the end of the school day, he would intentionally pass by her locker just for the chance of their saying hello; and even if they did and his heart felt a momentary reprieve, it would soon return to its emptiness. His whole life he had been intimidated by her beauty.

"Should I hang up and just let you leave your message?" he answered succinctly.

"Should you?" Annice replied curtly.

The doctor realized from Annice's terse reply that he had responded improperly. He could feel the tension rising between them. He knew that Annice did not like being put off for anything. Above all, she did not like being short-changed in a conversation. He should have at least talked to her for a few minutes, perhaps tell her a little about his day. Now it was too late. If he did not remedy the situation immediately he knew there would be awkward feelings between them for days to come starting on Monday. Angry at himself for hurting Annice's feelings, the doctor was also angry at Annice for being the way she was, so sensitive about improprieties connected to their relationship. In a surge of self-righteousness, he defied his inner weaknesses and blurted out, "If you really want to talk, why don't we get together right now?"

Annice didn't know what to say. Her whole life she had been accustomed to Christopher's shyness around her. Now, now he was blatantly asking her out. Now, after she was married twenty years, now after there was virtually no hope of their ever getting together. Annice was dumbfounded. She hesitated before replying to consider the moral implications, if any, of their getting together.

Knowing that she needed to respond, Annice finally asked, "What should we get together for?"

"I think I was asserting that we get together to have dinner," the doctor responded even though he had just made it up.

They had had meals together before, lunches mostly, when they had become caught up in circumstances beyond their control. In those circumstances, Annice had never felt compunction about it. But this seemed different. She knew that deep inside her were feelings about them. Would she be acting on them simply by complying to Chris's request to have her have dinner with him? Would she? She searched for a way to resolve the bittersweet conflict she felt growing inside her. In her silence, the doctor continually tried to convince her to go. Since he had already taken the initiative, he wanted to see it through. Then, it dawned on her, a way to look at it without her having to feel guilty. The phone call, the phone call itself had been inadvertent. The fact that they first happened to speak to each other happened only by chance, not by choice; therefore, there had been no initial intention for their getting together.

"You know what, I think I can make it," Annice said determinedly.

"Great! How about thirty minutes then? You can come over to the office. I'll wait right here."

During the intervening half-hour, the doctor acted out the part of a high-school boy who had just received word that the cheerleader he liked would go out with him. He was delirious with joy. Despite his best efforts, he couldn't seem to calm himself. The best thing he could do was keep busy, so to that end, he took his bag of mints and emptied out a place in a storage cabinet for them, all but one. That bag he opened up and treated himself to a few of his favorite candies. The remainder, he kept in the bag, rubber-banded it, and set it down on a table in the waiting room until he found a dish to put them in. Keeping on course, he next went into his office and began making notes about his newest patient, Miss Thorne. Once he had accomplished writing his notes, he went to the bathroom to arrange his attire and comb his hair. When he felt he was in one piece, the doctor stood before the mirror to admire himself a little. Then he noticed something protruding from the corner of his shirt pocket. He removed the slip of paper and saw what it was—the Pagoda receipt with the annotated phone number scribbled on it. The doctor thought about the waitress—was it, Carol, Carolyn or who? He recalled her face, her body, her smile. "No," he finally said, stopping himself, "Annice is better." He crumpled up the phone number and tossed it into a nearby wastepaper basket.

After conversing with Christopher on the phone, Annice readied herself for their intended get-together by taking a quick shower then re-dressing in a more elegant dress, one of the dresses she would wear to church. Next, she sat at her dresser mirror and applied a liberal coating of cinnamon-flavored lipstick to her lips. Then she began dabbing her earlobes, wrists, and neck with just the right enticement of Chanel No. 5 perfume. When she had herself just right, she picked up her pocketbook, flung it over her shoulder, and headed out of the bedroom. On her way downstairs, she was startled by a loud voice shouting from her porch. She raced over to the door and opened it.

"Leslie! What are you doing home!" she declared.

"Shut up!" he shouted and ordered her back inside the door. "This isn't your business!"

Leslie Colby was a despised man. He, at one time or another, had had problems with everyone who lived on his block of College Avenue. "Everyone" also included the various neighborhood pets that he had occasion to encounter. In this case, his unexpected return home had caught his next-door neighbor, Mrs. Gantner, off guard. Aware of the comings and goings of the mean Mr. Colby, she had leashed her pet dog Krimpet on her front porch, expecting to leave him there until a little later when she would bring him in for his evening meal. Krimpet, who had been teased and tormented by Leslie on countless occasions, became extremely agitated at seeing him now. The hound dog, feeling vulnerable because he was tied to a porch rail, tugged and tugged at the leash until the simple knot came undone. Krimpet responded to Leslie's appearance by making a stand at the porch rails which separated the two semi-detached properties. He stuck his snout in between two rails and expected the worst to happen. It did. When Leslie saw the dog, he pretended not to notice him and walked very nonchalantly up the porch steps and toward the house. He had actually walked past the dog's position when he made an abrupt turn and, in a split second, sent a flying kick which hit Krimpet squarely on the nose and in the process knocked out both porch rails which protected him. The dog fell back and began sneezing blood out of his nose onto the porch. Leslie, proud of what he had done, perched one leg up on the top of the railing and laughed.

After ordering his wife back inside, Leslie was confronted by both Mr. and Mrs. Gantner about what he had done. Because they already disliked each other so much, the confrontation started off as a brutal shouting match.

"What the hell did you do to my dog!" Mr. Gantner shouted.

"Keep your dog off my porch!" Leslie retaliated.

"Our dog wasn't even on your porch," Mrs. Gantner contended.

"Look what you did! You kicked out the porch rails! And the porch rails aren't on your property. They are on the property line!"

"I had the dog tied up on the porch. What did you do? Unleash him so you could kick him? You're an evil man, Mr. Colby."

"I don't care what you believe. Your dog had his snout through the rail and through the rail constitutes my side, and once he's on my side he's mine!"

"There's no talking to you, Mr. Colby. You know what I'm going to do? I'm going to call the police. Let's let them decide if you have the right to do as you please to a poor innocent dog just because he has his nose in your air space."

"Go ahead, call the cops. I don't care."

"And that language of yours. Do you know who I feel sorry for? Do you know who I feel sorry for the most? Your poor wife. I can't imagine what it's like to have to put up with you all the time. I can't believe you even have a wife, Mr. Colby," Mrs. Gantner concluded.

"Forget the both of you," Leslie said, ending his conversation.

At that moment, a far-off police siren was heard. The Gantners took Krimpet inside and attended to his injury. They, by hearing the siren's sound, felt self-satisfied that if they did call the police, the police would surely take their side and arrest their mean neighbor. Leslie stood on the porch for a short time thinking of what to say should the police actually come. Once he had established an estimable lie, he went inside.

Annice had retreated to a chair in the living room where she listened with fright to the altercation on the porch. She feared her husband and anything he might do to her whenever he was this mad. Then she was struck by a terrifying thought. She was all dressed up and ready to go out to eat with Christopher, another man!

Leslie entered the house and slammed the door behind him. He noticed his wife sitting quietly in the chair and gave her a cold stare. "Next time, I'm going to kill that dog. I'm telling you plain and simple I'm going to kill him."

Annice remained silent. Leslie paced around the two front windows nervously, watching for the police. Several minutes passed. He became surer of himself and soon professed, "You see they're afraid of me too. They aren't going to call the cops." He stared directly at his wife when he said, "And do you know why? Because they know that I would have to kill them too. I'll kill anyone I have to."

Then Leslie moved closer to Annice. "Hey, wait a minute! What the hell are you doing all dressed up!"

"Nothing," Annice answered simply.

"Nothing! You'd better tell me the truth, girl!"

Before Annice could respond further, Leslie slapped her on the face. Annice winced and started to cry. Leslie slapped her again, harder. Annice covered her face entirely.

"Tell me! Tell me!" Leslie demanded.

Annice was in pain and crying but she attempted to answer him.

"I . . . I just got home before you did. I . . . I am still dressed from this morning."

"You're a liar," Leslie shouted. "You weren't wearing that dress when you went to work today."

"Yes, I was," Annice pleaded.

There was a moment of silence then Annice boldly asked, "Since when do you ever pay attention to anything I'm wearing?"

"Is that so?" Leslie contended. "Well, I'm paying attention to you now," he said, then placed his hand on one of her breasts and began fondling her. Annice was repulsed by his callous touch but didn't dare show it. She knew if she reacted adversely, at all, Leslie would become infuriated and she would become his punching bag. She had no choice but to endure his advances. Leslie continued with her as she sat sadly in the chair, waiting for him to take her right then and there as she suspected he would, until the phone rang. Annice thought that the interruption might be her reprieve. If he got tied up in a phone conversation, maybe with his work, she might be able to sneak upstairs and lock herself in the bathroom. But the phone continued to ring and Leslie refused to answer it.

"Aren't you going to answer the phone?" Annice intervened.

"No, and neither are you," Leslie responded.

"Why not?" Annice persisted.

"Because right now I'm answering one of nature's calls," Leslie returned in a wry voice.

Dr. Haefner finally put down the phone. Apparently Annice, for whatever reason, was not going to answer. Forty-five minutes had elapsed since he had last spoken to her and they had arranged to meet.

It was obvious that something had happened and she wasn't coming. The strange thing was that she hadn't bothered to call him to explain why. That was the part that upset the doctor the most. Could it be that she didn't take the invitation seriously, he wondered? Could it be that she just decided no? The doctor pondered the possibilities.

After an entire hour had elapsed, the doctor departed. There was nothing left to do except go and eat by himself as he always did. He locked up the building and headed to Herkimer's. His mood had gone from ebullient to sullen in the short span of an hour and now he would have to put up with feeling sorry for himself for the remainder of the weekend.

Once he situated himself in Herkimer's, he began to feel slightly better but he knew that was only because he had just ordered his favorite meal—two hot roast beef sandwiches with mushroom-and-onion gravy. When the food was served to him, he ate it forlornly. Several times he looked up while he ate, as though he were almost anticipating Annice to arrive to join him. But she never did and the doctor felt foolish for ever allowing himself to think so illogically. The special night that he had, on a whim, contrived for them had collapsed, collapsed like a sandcastle being washed away by the tide. And should it resurface, in any form, it would wait three days to do so.

While finishing up his dessert, a piece of Boston cream pie, the doctor took note of the activities in the restaurant around him. In particular, he noticed several of the pretty waitresses as they whisked by him on their way to the kitchen or back to a table they were serving to. He wondered about them, their lives, their loves. He wondered if any of their love lives were as complicated as his. Here he was, age forty, in love with a married woman and desiring to love no one else. He thought about Carol, the waitress from the Pagoda. She, no doubt, was interested in him but there were things about their situation that would hinder their relationship. If they got together, their relationship would be a long-distance relationship and the doctor was not too keen about the difficulties that would arise from that—long-distance phone calls and only being able to see each other on weekends, sometimes not even then. If they got together, would they be happy with each other, he being erudite; she being, most likely, much less so than he. And the thing that concerned him the most was that if they got together would he be able to stop himself from being carried to the altar by what he knew would be an extremely satisfying sexual relationship.

The doctor went home. He tried to encourage himself with a good book but he found himself too distracted by his thoughts to entertain his mind with anything else. He sat in his recliner half-reading, half-listening for the phone to ring suddenly. Several times he picked up the phone, wanting to dial, wanting to assuage his fears. He tried to think up reasons, other than the truth, to explain his call, especially if Annice's husband should answer. He stayed up late. He never called.

If the doctor had known what was happening to Annice during the interludes when he almost picked up the phone to call her, not only would he have called her, he would also have left his intimidations behind him and gone to her: After fondling his wife in the chair, Leslie again began accusing her of some intended infidelity. He became incensed when he tried to question her further and got only the same reply. To teach her a lesson, he spent hours asking her about who it was that she intended to see. He did it to torture her. He knew that each time her response would be the same—that she had only just arrived home and she hadn't intended to see anyone. Each time she replied that way, he slapped her in the face. Each time he slapped her, he slapped her harder and harder.

Finally Annice couldn't take it any more. For her the grilling was over. Her face had been slapped red and blood was spilling out from her nose. Leslie commented jokingly that she and Krimpet both got what they deserved and now both bore the same red badge of courage.

In one desperate attempt to escape, Annice leapt out of the chair and made a dash across the room and started up the stairs. She had just cleared the top step when suddenly she felt herself being taken to the floor by a tremendous push from her husband. As she lay crying on the floor he stood over her and removed all of his clothing, then hers. He warned her to remain obedient as he took her in the face-down position she was in. Several times he punched her on her side and on her arms just to prove to her he was serious about hurting her if she provoked him.

Annice cried herself to sleep. When she awoke the next morning, she was still wearing the tattered dress that Leslie had torn down the middle of her back to have her sexually. Leslie was gone. She struggled to get out of bed. She got up, removed the dress and discarded it. Next, she stood in front of the full-length mirror attached to one of the closets and examined her body. The space in front of the mirror was splashed in sunlight, which allowed her a clear view of herself.

Dried blood was stuck to a small area around her nose and upper lip. There were several black-and-blue marks on one of her arms and one really large one on the right side of her hip. Annice was appalled. Instantly she flung open the closet door and made a frantic search for her Polaroid OneStep camera. She found it inside one of her carrying cases. When she opened it, she was ecstatic to discover that it still had film. She quickly closed the closet and set to work taking pictures of her bruises.

Once she had completed her task, she showered and dressed. She would take the already-developed pictures and hide them out of the house. She took one look at herself after she had dressed and noted, deridingly, that she had dressed herself in a black skirt and a pale-blue shirt—black and blue, just like me, she thought.

Leslie, she knew, was at work since he worked every-other Saturday and had been home last week. It was late, already past 1:00 in the afternoon. Apparently, Leslie, who had already gone before Annice awoke and didn't actually start work until one o'clock, must have felt apprehensive about seeing her after what he had done and made sure he wasn't around when she got up. Annice was just as glad.

Once she was on the porch, she looked up and down the street just to be sure. When she turned to lock the door, she was approached by her next-door neighbor, Mrs. Gantner.

"Good morning, Annice," she spoke softly.

"Good morning . . . or rather afternoon, Mrs. Gantner."

"Oh yes, you're right, dear. I've been so busy I lost track of time."

Once the pleasantries were over, there was an awkward pause in their conversation. Each knew that the other's thoughts were tilted toward the incident of yesterday. Mrs. Gantner spoke of it first.

"I'm so sorry about what happened yesterday. I want you to know I don't blame you one bit. It's that husband of yours. He's just so cruel to our Krimpet. And that language of his . . . Why, he's just . . . He's . . ."

Mrs. Gantner's eyes were tearing. She hated having to say mean things to Annice whom she liked very much. Annice was moved by her tears and stepped over to where she was standing beside the porch rail that Leslie had smashed when he kicked Krimpet. Without saying a word to her, she reached out her arms and they embraced.

On her walk to the James Street building, Annice had a chance to clear her head. She thought about Christopher. She reflected on how her detainment had left him waiting and wondering about her. What should she tell him?

She arrived at the office and went inside. She noticed the bag of jelly mints sitting on the table and instantly recalled how much Christopher liked them. She sat down at her desk, removed the photos from her handbag, and hid them among some unused folders in one of her drawers. Annice began to think about what it would have been like last evening had she been able to have dinner with Chris. When he asked her out to eat, it was so unexpected. It wasn't like before when they both found the time to be together. That was like a doctor and his secretary being together—at least she assumed it was from his perspective. Only she, so she assumed, had assumed more. But Annice had a woman's heart and a woman's intuition and her intuition was telling her that now there was something more. Last evening when he spoke to her she sensed it. Last evening, if it had endured, would have proved it.

Annice felt tense about what to do. If she let things go, she would go home, do nothing, and wait for Leslie. In desperation she picked up the phone and debated calling Chris. She dialed. The phone rang. Before Chris could pick up, Annice got nervous and hung up. She dialed again and again hung up before someone answered. Annice felt anxious. She was reluctant to call a third time. She had ruined it without realizing it. If she called now he would put two and two together and know it was her who had been calling. Despondent, she got up from her chair, grabbed her handbag, and started for the door. As she was about to leave the phone started ringing. She paused for a moment but decided to answer.

"Hello," she said in an amiable voice.

"Hello, Annice, is that you?"

Dark Clouds

On Monday, Dr. Haefner's practice was busier than usual. He and Annice were so busy dealing with patients that they scarcely had time to converse with one another. The phone connection they had had over the weekend had done much to soothe each other's concerns about what had occurred. Annice had been forthcoming and told Christopher about the incident on the porch but she declined to tell him anything about her husband's brutality toward her. That, she adamantly told herself, would be told someday, face-to-face.

Several times during the very-brief intervals between patients, the doctor would come all the way out of his office and head for the candy dish to grab a handful of jelly mints for himself. His patients were amused, watching their doctor oblige himself so purposefully. Annice too, at one point, commented to him as he whisked back to his office. "You had better be careful with those jelly mints or you will become addicted." The doctor smiled. "I'll accept your advice," he countered, "that is, if you will agree to give me another shot at taking you out for dinner again."

Annice remained silent. She wanted to afford him the opportunity, especially since their previous opportunity had gone awry. She wanted to just because she wanted to but there was a dark cloud over her head and the predicament she was in regarding her husband and his suspicious attitude toward anything she did prevented her from taking even the slightest risk.

At three o'clock in the afternoon, the doctor was waiting out another interlude before seeing a new patient. The patient was a twelve-year-old boy who had a propensity for torturing defenseless animals. He had just been released from the psychiatric unit at the Lancaster City Hospital after a ten-day stay. His latest stint had been using a butcher's knife to cut off the tail of a stray cat. For the offense, he was arrested and sentenced to confinement in the hospital for evaluation and treatment. The boy had prior arrests for the same type of misconduct, which the doctor was reading over when suddenly he heard Annice announce over the intercom that Joshua had arrived for his appointment.

When Joshua and his mother entered his office, the doctor noticed that the boy had a handful of jelly mints clenched in his fist and a mouthful which he was chewing. The doctor shook both their hands and situated them in the two plush chairs that sat opposite his desk.

"Sit down. Sit down," he directed them both.

The interview lasted an hour, after which the doctor handed the mother her son's next-week's appointment and dispensed him some sample medicine along with a prescription.

When they had gone, the doctor contemplated the boy's condition. He began making notes on his computer file. Cutting off cat's tails is not a normal occupation for a twelve-year-old boy. Josh doesn't do it to amuse himself, nor does he do it to watch the animal suffer. He does it rather as a type of therapy for himself. Josh suffers from an accentuated fear of injury or dismemberment. He is irrationally afraid of losing a limb or becoming permanently disabled. What he's trying to accomplish by severing the tails of cats and squirrels and other animals is to see how the animal actually deals with it. He watches as the animal tries to overcome their sudden tragedy and finds a way to cope with it. He sees that they do manage to survive and they do manage to continue with their lives despite their circumstance. This helps Josh. It helps him to realize that he could manage too if something like losing an arm or a leg should happen to him. He's extremely afraid and he manages his fear in this unusual way. He's so afraid. He's so afraid. So much like James. So much like James.

The doctor's mind slipped away from the immediacy of Josh's problem. He thought about James, about the aspect of fear. The memories inculcated him—memories about James and how he carried out what could have been a similar reaction to a similar fear. The doctor tendered this new insight in application of James's behavior toward the two dogs his adoptive parents owned.

One of the incredible aspects of James was his cruelty toward his own pets. Snoopy was a young brown-and-black-spotted hound dog. Taffy was a snappy, fat, older mutt. Both dogs had been living with the Bollers prior to James's adoption. At first, James seemed to enjoy having the dogs around, especially Snoopy who was energetic and liked to frolic. Later, when James began to experience his detachment from his real parents who wanted nothing to do with him, and the associated disrespect for his adoptive parents who also wanted nothing to do with him, he began to inflict deliberate harm on the dogs. Sometimes he would kick them as he walked past. Sometimes he would tie them up for hours in the kitchen or down in the cellar just to hear them plead to be freed. About the age of thirteen, James was introduced to marijuana by his sister Deb, and he began smoking it whenever he got hold of some. Under the influence of smoking pot, James's behavior toward the animals worsened. Now, when he tied them up he would blow pot smoke in their faces, forcing them to get high. Then, sometimes, he would hurt them just to watch them experience pain while being potently high on THC. One thing in particular he did was to stand above the dog, usually Taffy, and drop his pocket knife, blade first, into the dog's back. If it stuck, the dog would yelp fiercely and James would laugh.

The doctor wanted to get his thoughts down on paper, so he began to print on the computer the words he had just summarized in his mind; then he continued.

Several times I intervened on the dogs' behalf and James stopped whatever it was he was doing to inflict pain and suffering on them. Usually, then, James excluded me from seeing it. His half brother, Dave, would sometimes tell me the stories of what he saw James do.

Back then, I always believed that James did it to get back at the Bollers for slighting him the way they did, which they did due to their increasing fear of him. Now, I am beginning to wonder if that was entirely true. James, who in essence grew up without ever being loved, was so afraid of what would happen to him as a result of that, that he intentionally inflicted harm on all those around him so he could see, so he could learn from them, just how to deal with an unjust world.

James, like Josh, was terribly, terribly afraid, terribly afraid of the uncertainties of life and how to deal with them. Fortunately for Josh, caring people—his parents, the authorities, and I—have intervened, and he will be helped with his condition. James condition worsened. One day, Snoopy, in a desperate attempt to flee from James who was chasing her through the house with a baseball bat, jumped right through a glass window. She was bleeding so profusely that the veterinarian actually came over to Pine Street to administer the care necessary to keep the dog alive long enough to have surgery. Snoopy's wounds required a whopping 150 stitches. She had to have glass removed from several of her internal organs before she was sewn back up. Snoopy was never the same after that. She had a nervous breakdown and the Bollers eventually had her put to sleep.

Taffy had a similar fate. Being despondent over Snoopy's sudden disappearance from the house, she took to hiding all day. Often, she would wedge herself behind the stove and hope that James would not be in a mood where he would want to torture her for kicks. James hated her for being obstinate. Once, James went to great lengths to pull Taffy out from behind the stove and Taffy, in retaliation, bit him in the hand. James went crazy. The first thing he did was immobilize Taffy by getting her stoned. Then, when Taffy was incapacitated, James dragged her to the top of the cellar steps and slammed the open door on her body. Taffy cringed in pain. Next, he booted her with his steel-toed shoes until she fell helplessly down the flight of wooden steps.

Taffy lay still. Blood trickled out from her mouth. James descended the stairs and approached Taffy cautiously, fearing that she might snap at him if he got too close. Taffy began panting and gasping for breath. James touched her once on her side and the dog winced at him with tears in her eyes. She was in excruciating pain and James began to think about how his parents might react if they witnessed such a sight. As far as he was concerned, Taffy was as good as dead, so to put her out of her misery he decided to crush the remaining life out of her and do both her and him a favor. He went to John's workbench and unbolted a huge forty-pound vise from its mounting. He lifted it up over his head and carried it over to where Taffy was lying in agony. Without hesitation, he readied and steadied himself for the execution that was about to take place. He hurled the heavy vise down onto Taffy's head, crushing her skull the instant she was hit. Taffy was dead.

The worst James got out of it was a quick trip to the emergency room to have seven stitches sewn into his hand from the bite Taffy gave him, and a tetanus shot. The Bollers were afraid to reprimand him or report the incident to the proper authorities. They buried their dog in the backyard. James wore his injured arm in a sling for a week and gladly recanted the tale, from his vantage point, to anyone interested in hearing it.

I remember with vivid clarity an event which followed several days later in which James was confronted by a dog-loving neighbor, Pete, about what he had done to both his dogs. I didn't see exactly how it all began but I did witness the event once it had reached its crescendo when the confrontation had escalated into a backyard brawl in the Bollers' yard. By this time, there was a large group of neighbors gathering in their adjacent yards listening to the argument between James and Pete.

"You worthless little piece of dirt! You killed both of your dogs and now you go around telling everybody your story about it. Look at you, you're even happy about it. How would you like it if I did to you what you did to those innocent dogs?"

"Why don't you just learn to mind your own business?"

"Because I'm making it my business! That will show you!"

"Don't!" shouted Chris.

"Beat the hell out of him!" several onlookers shouted at once.

"Don't!" shouted Chris again. "It won't prove anything. He will have God to answer to for what he did."

Just then John Boller came out. He surveyed what was occurring and recognized the volatility of everyone. He stood on the top of his back-porch steps and shouted for everyone to leave his property at once.

"I want all of you to leave my yard at once. Jim, I want you to get the hell in the house."

Some of the people started to leave. Others, more certain that something yet would transpire, retained their positions around the incident by hopping the fences and standing in a neighbor's yard to watch. Then Mr. Boller directed his attention to Pete.

"What are you getting so personally involved for? As far as I'm concerned the incident is over and there is nothing you or I can do about it. What Jim did was a hell of a thing, I know, but it's done."

"You wouldn't care if he killed a person, let alone a dog, would you?"

"Oh, I care all right. What I care more about is my own life. That's the part you don't understand. With Jim in the house, I have to care about whether or not I'm going to wake the next morning or not."

"That's it!" Pete declared. "You're afraid of him."

"No wonder he's so messed up in the head," another onlooker shouted. "His own father's afraid of him."

"You would be too," Mr. Boller said pointedly, "if you had to live under the same roof as him. I'm afraid. He's already told me he'll stick a knife in my throat in the middle of the night if I ever give him reason to."

Mr. Boller's confession infuriated Pete further. He was only inches away from James and with all his heart he wanted to pound him one. His right fist was clenched in readiness should he be provoked any further. Chris intervened.

"All right the both of you. Pete, you're a lot bigger than Jim. What is it going to prove to beat him up? It isn't going to bring the dog back. Is it?"

"Yeah, smart guy," James got up the nerve to reply.

At that moment Pete lunged at James. James, anticipating Pete's maneuver, backed out of the way just as the burly man advanced toward him. Pete fell to the ground. James fled. He wanted no part of Pete's fury. Pete got up, stumbled in his haste to start the chase, got up again, then was met by the strong arm of John Boller before he could pursue James who had fled into the house and was now watching the backyard from the back kitchen window.

"If you want to go after him you'll do it when I'm not around and not on my property. If you won't accept that, then let's have at it right now."

"Get the hell off me!" Pete declared.

"Now look at who is chicken now!" James shouted out the window.

Pete raised his fist at Jim. He wanted no part of Mr. Boller and he was careful not to have eye contact with him as he shouted back.

"You're day is coming, Jimmy! Guaranteed, I'm going to beat you up!"

Pete now realized it wasn't the time or the place to try anything further with Jim. The altercation was over. He began to move swiftly up through the yard in order to leave. James, who was still stationed at the back kitchen window, added one last insult against his aggressor by opening the screen and spitting at him as he rounded the corner of the house. Pete heard it, stopped dead in his tracks for a split second, then resumed his hasty departure.

The doctor's reminiscence was suddenly voided by Annice's voice over the office intercom reminding him that his final patient had arrived.

"Send her in," he replied while massaging his forehead with his fingers as he usually did every time he thought with such intensity.

The young woman who entered the office and seated herself in front of him suffered from a mild case of depression. Cases like hers were not ones Dr. Haefner ordinarily undertook but he had made an exception for her because she was a friend of a friend and he was a person who was inclined to do favors for people he knew and liked.

Judging from the looks of her, he suspected that her condition had more to do with nutrition, or rather, the lack of it. She was in her twenties, tall and very slender. Whenever she came to see him he always asked her questions about her diet. She was an attractive woman with long strawberry-blonde hair, and she attended Franklin and Marshall College, his alma mater. He didn't quite remember but he believed she was an international-studies student.

She was so delightful a person to be around that the doctor couldn't help but flirt with her whenever he sensed that the mood was right for it. She reminded him of the so, so many young Franklin and Marshall women he used to socialize with when he attended the prestigious college.

"Too bad," he always reminded himself every time she got up to leave, "if I were only five years younger or she were only five years older."

Dr. Haefner followed her to the office door and said goodbye to her as she left. His eyes followed her out the main door as he always gave her a good last look. But then, just as quickly, she was forgotten. All the doctor had to ever do was take one riveting glance at his loveliest of all ladies and his heart was back in place.

The doctor returned to his desk and relaxed in his swivel chair. He noticed his mail again and decided to open some of it. He sorted it and discovered the letter he wanted to open most. It was a letter from Dr. Brain. He opened it.

"Dr. Haefner, I hope all is well with you. I am greatly pleased that you have agreed to help Miss Thome. I remain hopeful that your initiatives with her will work well. Please keep me apprised of her progress as I am very interested in how your therapy can be applied to such a severe case as hers. By the way, I was wondering whether or not you have decided on your other initiative, our lovely Carol from the Pagoda. Maybe we should, or rather you should, go back for a second course. What do you think? Well, as you know I'm a busy man and I have to leave you with just those thoughts. Please write back ASAP. PS. I hope you are making progress with your personal appeasements regarding that James friend you knew."

Dr. Haefner put down the letter. He smiled, thinking about Carol, the waitress. After just enjoying the lovely presence of his last patient, he was tempted to take Dr. Brain up on his offer to visit Carol. He could sure use some of what she could give him. But the doctor only paid a trifling amount of effort toward that concern. Dr.

Brain's last comment had affected him more. His mind-set was still connected to James. Dr. Brain had once mentioned that he believed Dr. Haefner's strife over his friend's life and death could somehow be associated with Dr. Haefner's inability to reconcile with himself both the grief and guilt he felt over James's sins of the past. Could this be true? Dr. Haefner decided to put it to the test.

"I was only fifteen when Taffy and Snoopy died. I was a child. I was like any fifteen-year-old today. I have to remind myself of that because I think much older. I regret what happened. Of course I feel grief over it but the difference is that I feel more grief for James than the dogs he killed. He is a higher order of living thing so of course he must be regarded first and foremost. That is the part of it that most people leave out whenever they throw stones at James for what he did.

"Do I feel guilty? To some extent, maybe. But I was not an accomplice to a killer. Was I my brother's keeper? Certainly in regard to all I did for him. My interventions prevented him from committing a thousand more sins. That is the integral part in my reprieve.

"I have rendered the verdict unto myself and I find myself not guilty. My responsibilities to James included telling him right from wrong, included intervening when I thought any real harm could come to others. These I did. But as it applies to his dogs, I did what I could to prevent him from doing what he did. The times I saw him drop the knife into Taffy, it was unexpected as were most things in relation to James. I know I laughed as the others did, at first. So, I am guilty of finding humor in a situation that was no laughing matter. So what? Should I be punished for having a sense of humor even though it was a morbid spectacle? I laughed at it and other things like it more because of the outrageousness of it rather than the actuality of it. And I'm not saying that in retrospect."

The doctor was still lost in his attempt to exonerate himself from the involvement he had in regard to what James did to his dogs, when he heard a light tapping on the door.

"Come in," he announced.

Annice entered and informed him that it was late and she was ready to leave for the day unless the doctor needed her. The doctor glanced at the wall clock. It was exactly 5:15.

"No," he answered. "As a matter of fact, I'm leaving too. I didn't realize how late it was."

Once everything was put in order—the answering machine activated, the intruder alarm set, and the lights turned out—the couple proceeded out the building. The doctor escorted Annice to her Escort then headed back across the street to where his Buick was parked. As he was about to enter his car, it occurred to him that he had forgotten something. Earlier he had tried to remember to take home some stamps.

"This happens every time I neglect writing myself a note," he said in an admonishing voice to himself as he locked up his car again and walked back toward the building.

Once inside, he moved hastily to Annice's desk and began rummaging through the drawers in search of the elusive roll of postage stamps which were never to be found in the same place twice. He found them in the third-drawer down on the right-hand side in the back corner among various other miscellaneous items. He counted out what he considered an adequate amount, fifteen, tore the perforation, pocketed them, and tossed the roll back into the drawer. Before closing the drawer he counted out the allocation against his needs. While doing so, he happened to take notice of what appeared to be the corner edge of a photograph sticking out of a large, opened envelope. He debated the should-I-or-shouldn't-I dilemma just long enough for his curiosity to get the best of him. Besides, he contended, Annice knows that at times I go into her desk. If she didn't want me to see any of her pictures she would not have brought them to work, or if she did she would have taken them home with her.

Once the doctor had contented himself with his reasoning, he lifted out the large envelope to examine its contents. He seated himself in Annice's chair and opened the flap so that the pictures inside would spill out onto the desk.

"Oh my dear God in heaven!" he declared when he saw the top prints on the pile. The doctor was in a state of total disbelief. There was Annice, in partial stages of undress, standing in her bedroom, taking pictures of her body. The doctor rapidly shuffled through each and every picture to see if they were all like the first. In several of the photos she was completely naked, but the doctor soon understood that it was not the naked aspect of her that she was trying to portray. In each of the photos the real aspect could be determined. On each picture there was some section of her body which displayed a telltale mark that she had been beaten.

Near her hip was a black-and-blue mark about the size of a man's fist. On her arms, just below her shoulders, were several more, smaller in size. It was painfully obvious. Annice was attempting to profile a case of abuse against her husband.

The pictures, one in each hand, fell from his fingers. The doctor collapsed in the chair by the sheer enormity of the revelation. In front of his eyes was one of the most consternating matters he had ever encountered. Simultaneously he was viewing the very thing he wanted to see most and the very thing he wanted to see least. He was infuriated at seeing Annice's body being treated like a punching bag. But at the same time and for the first time, he saw the true beauty of her body. She was a spectacular woman in every sense of the word. He couldn't help himself and he picked up one of the most revealing photos and looked at it admiringly. This was his woman with her curved hips, soft supple breasts, smooth flat tummy, and sensuously shaped legs, all of her, all for him, He could do nothing to stop himself from being aroused at the sight of her.

Then he began to ponder, very seriously, what he should do about the whole thing. Should he tell her the truth, that he, inadvertently, had come across the pictures while perusing for postage stamps and, letting his curiosity get the better of him, looked at them? How would she feel knowing that I had seen naked photos of her? How would she feel knowing that I know that her husband has beaten her? This is a very private matter and it must be handled delicately. She is my rose and I will not allow her to be trampled. I will bide my time until I can think of a suitable approach to the situation.

A Cry from the Past

On the way home the doctor stopped off at Herkimer's for another of his favorite hot roast beef sandwich meals. While he was enjoying his food, he continuously made an effort to come up with a suitable solution for assisting Annice's cause. He was determined to help her.

Once he completed his meal he got up, paid his bill, and scooped up a handful of the jelly mints he liked so much. Standing at the cashier counter he recollected, fondly, the memory of not so long ago, when he and Annice had shared a table of their own here. Now, because of their more-recent episode in which she had been unable to attend their intended get-together, it seemed almost as if the previous encounter never happened. That experience he likened to having been stranded on a deserted island, alone and lonely.

Then it struck him. What if Annice's inability to join him that day had something to do with her husband finding out and possibly forcibly preventing her from going, possibly hitting and hurting her. The doctor suddenly felt queasy considering that he could have inadvertently been responsible for Annice being harmed.

He drove home. Turning into his driveway, he stopped the car and retrieved his mail. At the top of the drive he activated the automatic garage door then parked. After closing the garage, he entered the kitchen holding his briefcase in one hand, his mail in the other. He took from his shirt pocket the last few mints and popped them into his mouth after setting down his briefcase on the oval oak table that was the centerpiece of the spacious kitchen. He looked through the stack of mail and discovered nothing of particular importance. Disregarding the mail, he went to the refrigerator and poured himself a drink of lemonade for his parched throat. He drank one full glass while standing with the refrigerator door open—something he would have never been allowed to do as a child without his mother or father yelling at him to close it—filled his glass again, and then carried it through the living room and into the study. It had been several days since he last looked at his collections—something he always enjoyed doing. Christopher was a collector and had been since boyhood. He collected coins, fossils, minerals, old books, and old Haefner Brewery memorabilia from the brewery began by his great-great-grandfather in 1885. The Haefner Brewery operated for sixty-five years until 1949. It had been a prosperous Lancaster business until it met its demise due to the myopic business practice of its last owner in not attempting to market the beer outside the locality of Lancaster County.

It irked Christopher that, having been born in 1959, he had missed out completely on the opportunity to have had something to do with the family business. He had been born with a keen mind and he knew that if he had an opportunity with the brewery before it went out of business, he would have not only saved it but also made it prosper as it did in its early years.

While taking sips of his lemonade, he eyeballed the entire collection of brewery items which included thirty old bottles, some from each period of the brewery's history; one old quarter-keg, dating from the 1890s; two ashtrays made of pewter; and two ruby-red shot glasses from 1935, depicting the fiftieth anniversary of the brewery. The quarter-barrel though was the prize of the collection. It was constructed of three-quarter-inch teak wood and had an impressed insignia reading Lancaster's Haefner Brewery Lancaster, Pa. The collection was looking a bit dusty, and the doctor made a mental note to make a written note to allocate some time, soon, to dust everything.

Once his glass was empty, he returned it to the kitchen where he rinsed it and set it aside on the counter with other accumulated dishes. Next, he went into the living room and seated himself comfortably in his La-Z-Boy recliner. His contemplations again turned to the complexity of Annice's situation. He was determined to advocate for her in some effective way, regardless of the consequences that would inevitably come about as a result of any outside interference.

What should he say? What should he do? As a person who dealt exclusively with matters of the mind he felt entirely inadequate to deal with Annice's personal problems. What would be the best approach to broach the subject with her? Should he go straight for the jugular and simply tell her everything he knew, or would that make her angry or defensive?

He wasn't quite sure how she would respond to any approach. He knew her but he didn't know her heart and this situation certainly was bound in her emotional state of being. One thing the doctor figured would be in his favor would be to wait for one week or more before taking any specific action. This would allow her more time to initiate her concerns personally to him. It also would lessen the likelihood that she would suspect him of viewing her private photos.

Professionally, the doctor had very little dealings with the matters of spousal abuse, though there had been a few cases in the past where a patient's loved one, overwhelmed by their partner's affliction, had become either verbally or physically abusive toward them. But those were isolated incidents and they were not deliberate acts of violence but rather a crying out from all the accumulated secondary suffering that affiliated persons deal with.

Then, unexpectedly, the doctor thought of something, or rather someone, who might be able to help.

"Detweiler! Dr. Detweiler!"

Dr. Jean Detweiler was a noted child psychologist who was on staff at the city hospital. Before working for the hospital, she had worked for the Child Protective Services locally, dealing with adolescents who had been ordered out of their homes by the court and into protective custody. She was the ideal person to at least assist in the doctor's endeavor to help Annice. She and the doctor had interacted several times in the past as together they worked to stabilize young patients as they acclimated themselves in their newly arranged living conditions.

Finding a notepad and pencil in a drawer in the kitchen, the doctor made a quick note about calling Dr. Jean and finding the time to dust off his brewery bottles.

Feeling mildly better for having at least initiated some course of action for Annice, the doctor settled himself in for the evening by hopping into his recliner and clicking on the television by remote control and surfing through the channels for something entertaining to watch. When he got to the local PBS affiliate, Channel 33, he paused to see what was being broadcast. The doctor was a member of PBS and contributed both time and money to the Harrisburg station. On occasion, he would set aside a Saturday afternoon during a pledge campaign and drive up to Harrisburg to participate. There, he would answer phones and fill out new-member cards. Sometimes he would be induced to go on-air and express his personal feelings to the Channel 33 viewers about being a member.

Tonight the public television station was broadcasting a special program series dedicated to correlating biblical tales with historical fact. Tonight's episode followed a team of biblical scholars as they searched for evidence to prove that there had once existed the Great Flood. The team had assembled at the base of Mount Ararat in eastern Turkey. Mount Ararat, they believed, was the final resting place of Noah's Ark.

The program was a delight to the doctor, just the ticket to unburden his mind from all of its associated stresses. Though his interest in the program never waned in the least, the doctor eventually drifted off into a soothing light sleep. Once his conscious mind was blocked, the doctor's subconscious mind took over. It was still in a panic. He wanted to take Annice away from the brutality that was being perpetrated upon her by her husband, the beast. And he wanted . . . wanted . . . wanted . . . her.

Then, as if to guide him, his dream state laid before him the events of a similar circumstance in which he had participated in the rescue of a young lady from a beast even worse than Mr. Colby. He went back in time to a place of familiar faces.

"Chris! You are the only person I can count on. Please help me. I can't stay in that house any longer. He will kill me if I do. The other day he put a knife to my throat. He told me that my stereo and everything else that's mine now belongs to him. He told me that because I belong to him, everything else does too."

"Deb, what are you talking about?"

"Christopher, listen to me! I had to lie on the floor for hours or he would have killed me. He told me, 'If you make the slightest move, witch, this blade I'm holding will cut right through you.' So, you see, I stayed right there. Later, he took the knife and cut off all my clothes and raped me for hours. But I was strong. I endured it, knowing that every bad thing he did to me would be the last. So, now I'm asking you to help me. Help me, please. Help me get away from him."

I did. The following Saturday I had arranged for a small moving truck to be used to transport Deb's belongings back to her parents' house in York. Included in her belongings would be the prized Fisher stereo system which James now considered his. I had notified Deb's mother as to her daughter's plight and she seemed understanding. Hearing Deb's story from someone other than her gave credence to what most people would have considered a fairy tale.

To make the plan work, James and the Bollers would have to be taken out of the way for the duration of the move. The Bollers were no problem. They were both barflies, and every Saturday they left their Pine Street home in the late afternoon to spend that late afternoon, evening, and night drinking. Their favorite watering hole was the Moose, a private club for people who enjoyed drinking to the point of bliss.

James, on the other hand, was a problem. He was no fool. No last-minute ruse would coax him away from his female property especially since, of late, they were having extreme difficulties. Unwisely, Deb had already threatened James that she intended to leave him. To get rid of Jim I would have to rely on the help of two other friends: Art and Jules.

Recently, Art and Jules had introduced skateboarding into the neighborhood. A new skateboarding park had been built at the Price Elementary School about one mile away. Art and Jules went there all the time and had become expert skaters. They also had extra boards and pads which they offered to anyone who was interested in joining them. James was intrigued by the pastime and if he was bored at the time he was asked to go, he might. But because the stakes were so high, James would have to be enticed further. The entertainment was just the thing, but along with it, I decided to provide James with something irresistible: pot.

When Saturday arrived, everything went according to plan. The Bollers departed even earlier than expected. The moving truck had been appropriated and was parked on the next block. Dave, the driver, was waiting inside his house for the signal to bring the truck down. James was waiting too for Art and Jules and the small bag of pot they had promised him they would bring if he went with them to the skateboarding park. I had been in contact with Deb several times during the week and reminded her how important it was for her not to act too conspicuous about the whole thing or James would catch on and the whole thing would be over. Though I had been invited to go along too, I insisted that I couldn't because my father wanted me to clean up the cellar. Actually my parents and three of my younger siblings were off visiting friends, and I sat nervously on the couch in my living room waiting for the phone call that would initiate everything.

"Art and I are ready," Jules stated. "How is everything there?"

"Just fine," I replied. "The Bollers are gone and James is up in the Third Story waiting for you two. I just left him and Deb only twenty minutes ago. How long will it take you two to get here?"

"We will be there in less than ten minutes. We're up at my house on James Street and we're going to ride down to your house on our skateboards."

"Do you have the pot?"

"Right here," he replied and indicated so by rustling the baggie it was in so I could hear it over the phone.

"Now remember, when you get here go right up to his place. Don't stop off here or he might get suspicious. And don't take too much time getting ready to go. Don't let him talk you into smoking any up there."

"But what if . . ."

"Stop what-iffing and get going. Goodbye."

A short while later, I witnessed Jules and Art skateboarding down Pine Street. Jules was coming down one side of the street; Art, the other. I peeked out my front window and watched as they converged on the pavement outside my house. I listened as they began arguing with each other as to who got there first.

"I won!" Art said smiling.

"I won!" Jules shouted back.

"I got here first," Art stated.

"Yeah, but I was beating you the whole way down until my board hit that broken concrete. That's what got me," Jules complained.

"Hey, that's too bad. That's the way the cookie crumbles," Art said with a grin.

"You just wait until we get to the park," Jules challenged him.

Up in the Third Story, James had been anxiously awaiting his two pot-toting companions. Though he had been periodically glancing out the front window he had not seen his two buddies when they came down the street. He was playing the stereo loudly and was also fully involved in a nasty argument with Deb.

"Stop your complaining," James roared out like a lion. "We can go to the Laundromat tomorrow. And if you don't shut your mouth it will be the tomorrow after tomorrow."

"But you promised," Deb insisted. "The bear rug has beer and food stains all over it."

"Keep it up and I'll add blood stains to it too," James declared intensely.

Just at that moment, Jules and Art bounded up the third-floor stairs. Deb's eyes lit up when she saw them, knowing she was only hours away from freedom.

"Where is it!" James demanded when he encountered his friends.

"How about a hello?" Jules insisted.

"How about a goodbye if you came up here empty-handed?" James replied.

"Right here," replied Art, who followed up his acknowledgment with a smile and compliantly digging into his pants' pocket and retrieving the half-ounce of pot he had promised.

"Open it!" James shouted.

Jules opened the bag and together he and James took a lingering whiff of the aromatic substance. Just a breath of the THC seemed to placate James. His disposition mellowed and he even spoke nicely to Deb and asked her if she wanted to go along with them. She refused, saying that she had just gotten a headache and was feeling poorly. James responded by stating, "More for us then, guys."

"Hey, Jim, why don't we get started?" Jules suggested.

"Hey, Jules, why don't you shut up and fire up a joint?"

"Wait a minute," Art intervened. "I know you, Jim. If I fire one up we'll end up smoking the whole bag up here. That wasn't the deal. You said you'd go skateboarding with us. Look, I even brought you a board."

"Where!" James demanded.

"Relax," Jules intervened, "it's down on the porch."

"It's like we agreed, Jim," Art added jovially, "if you say nope then you don't get the dope."

"You know what?" Jules decided, "We're leaving. You're either coming or you're staying."

Jules and Art glanced at each other and pushed their way past James out of the room and started down the steps leading to the second floor. Deb was standing beside the rug, staring down at it as though it were the only thing of importance on her mind.

"I'll let you clean the rug tomorrow," he said impatiently, knowing he was down to his last minute. Deb didn't speak. The last words Deb ever heard from James were, "If you are not here when I get back, you will be sorry."

James bounded down both flights of stairs to catch up with his companions. They were on the porch—Jules balancing himself on his skateboard as he tried to go backward; Art sitting on the porch railing, fidgeting with his skateboard's wheel. When the pair became a trio they started out. I witnessed their departure from the walkway between our house and the apartment building next door. When they were out of sight, I quickly reentered my home and called Dave who was ready with the truck. Deb was downstairs in the Bollers' living room waiting for me, when I knocked on the door. She was expecting me.

"Ready!" I cried when I encountered her.

She was a sight. I likened her elation to a spirit who had just left a body, free at last. She spoke at a rapid-fire pace about what had to be done and how little time there seemed to accomplish it.

"The truck will be here any minute. I just spoke to Dave. Hurry up and put two kitchen chairs out in front of the house so nobody else takes up the parking space. I'll go up and begin disconnecting your stereo. What time did you say your mom will be here?"

Within an hour, all of Deb's belongings were packed inside the rental truck. Dave had been given directions by Deb's mother on how to get to her house in York and he left without delay. Before departing herself with her daughter, Deb's mother asked if she could go into my house and make a phone call. While she was in the process of doing that, the unthinkable happened. Deb, who had been nervously pacing on the front porch, alerted me to it. I immediately stepped out from the house, looked up the street, and sure enough there was the figure of a person on a skateboard making his way toward us. I couldn't make out the identity of the person until he reached the intersection of Pine Street and Orange Street, at which point there were now two more skateboarding figures heading down Pine Street behind Jules.

"Hurry up and get inside," I ordered. "And don't worry, I'll make sure you get out OK."

I purposely lingered on the porch. Because of the lead Jules had on the others, there was time to make contact with him before James and Art arrived. I cast myself out over the steps like a flag waving in the wind, allowing Jules to take notice of me. Once I was sure he had spotted me, I exited the porch and stood at the entrance to the walkway and waved my hand for him to see. When he arrived, he was out of breath.

"What happened? Why are you back already?"

"It was Cuzze's fault. He started harassing some kid in the park and the kid's dad came out and started a fight with Jim. We couldn't stay because if the cops came they would have smelled us and we had already smoked about half of the amount in the bag. We would have all been arrested."

"Well, the situation here is this: we already got everything of Deb's out of the house. Dave already left with it. He's taking it to Deb's mom's house. She and her mom are still here. They're inside. What you have to do is get James up to the Third Story and keep him there until Deb can leave. Deb's mom's car is right over there, but now that James is back, I'm going to have her move it. After what James is going to see, I don't want Deb trying to leave right in front of his nose. Here they come. You had better leave."

I entered the house and gave Deb's mom the instruction to go at once and move her car to a less obvious position one block farther up the other way on Pine Street. Ten minutes from now Deb would leave with me out the back of the house and we would take the back way to meet up with her mom.

The three of us listened by the front window of my living room to the three of them who were congregated around the Bollers' porch. It was easy to see just how high they were by their loud obnoxious behavior. James was attempting to jump over the porch steps, side to side, with his skateboard. Each time, he failed and fell onto the hard concrete laughing. Finally, Jules convinced the others to go up to the Third Story. It was a relief.

"OK, Mom," Deb said, "time for you to make your move."

"OK, sweetie," she replied and softly touched her daughter's face.

Just after Deb's mother got in her car and drove away, we heard the violent volcanic eruption of Mount James once he discovered how he had been deceived. We could have closed the window and still been able to hear the exploding expletives. Deb began shaking.

"Don't worry, Deb. James doesn't know you're here."

"Why don't we leave right now?"

"No! Until he settles down a bit, we'll stay right here. Right now he's in such a fury he could come down out of the house. Imagine if he saw you. Imagine what he would do. He's so angry I couldn't stop him."

Deb was still shaking. To comfort her, I reached out for her. She responded by falling into my arms as though I was a magnet and she was steel. She pressed her body into mine and I held her tight. Soon we became voracious with each other. We, who had coveted each other for months, were now together as one body. It happened without a word spoken between us. I took her up to my room where we quickly undressed. We hopped up on the bed like a pair of rabbits. We never felt better. Deb and I had always, secretly, desired each other but it took a now-or-never situation to bring it out in us. It was glorious!

When it was over, we dressed. We exited the house out the back and together made our way through the back alleys and back out to Pine Street, one block up. Deb's mom thanked me for all I did and drove off up the alley that Deb and I had just come out of.

James created his own dramatic ending to the story. It befitted him. For the first time in his life someone had gotten one over him. He was humiliated. In response to that, he raged about his home like a tornado. He destroyed everything in his path: chairs, tables, mirrors, windows, doors, a typewriter, knickknacks, a broom, the television set . . . The loud, raucous noise attracted the attention of everybody in the Pine Street neighborhood. A crowd gathered outside his home. Soon, James became aware of the outsiders and he fell into a rage about them.

To express how he felt about their intrusion, James kicked open the door to the closet on the stairs which was located on a landing two steps up the first flight of stairs. The closet was always kept locked by Mr. Boller who kept two 12-gauge shotguns in it. James retrieved one of the guns, never checking to see if it was loaded, and, armed, went onto the porch to confront the crowd. Upon seeing the shotgun, one of the neighbors slipped back inside his home and called the police.

Minutes later the police arrived, one by one, until five cruisers had converged on Pine Street. Coordinating their efforts, they blocked off the street to all oncoming traffic. Next, they dispersed the crowd which I was now part of. James retreated inside his home while the police began questioning witnesses. After a few minutes, two of the officers walked up to James's door and knocked. James made contact with them but informed them that he would not venture out onto the porch and instead they could communicate to him through the closed door. Because of his seemingly sensible suggestion, they agreed. At one point, the two officers left the porch to converse with a detective who had just arrived at the scene. Taking advantage of this reprieve, James stuck his head out of the door. He noticed me standing on my porch and he called over to me.

I intervened on James's behalf and convinced the officers that he had not actually threatened anybody. Acting as liaison, I was able to convince James to go with the officers to make a statement down at the police station. He came out, apprehensively, and was handcuffed and taken into custody. His arrest lasted less than one hour and he appeared back on Pine Street, boasting to everyone of his notoriety. "It took ten cops to keep me from wiping out the whole block. And if that whore ever shows her face around here again, I'll kill her too!"

Help is on the Way

Annice was a smart, savvy woman, and to actually be able to help her without being too obvious about it would require a certain amount of savvy on the doctor's part—something easier said than done, he knew. So as not to arouse any undue curiosity in her, the doctor held his efforts in abeyance for several weeks before enacting anything.

To prepare personal time together, the doctor began adjusting the schedule, eliminating a patient or two per week so he could spend that time with her. Because the variance was so slight, Annice did not detect that the doctor had done something intentional.

When the intended time came about, the doctor strolled casually out of his office and expressed how jubilant he was at having some free time on his hands.

"For the first time in months I have a little extra time to do with as I please," he said, validating his presence with her.

"Oho," Annice responded, "remember what your mother told you about having too much free time on your hands?"

"What's that?"

"Something about their being the devil's workshop," she replied humorously.

"That's just plain silly," the doctor responded wryly.

The time was right. Annice was in a good mood and might be receptive to his subtle inquiries about her personal life as long as he continued to seem as though he had no real purpose for questioning her about anything. To add to his concealed intent, the doctor purposefully walked away from her desk and into the waiting room where he could indulge himself with a handful of jelly mints. He would wait, seemingly uninterested in anything particular, except eating candy, until Annice decided to strike up a conversation with him. That way, anything that resulted from it would be because of her.

Finally it happened. While the doctor sat and plopped mint after mint into his mouth, Annice finally spoke up.

"My, you really do enjoy those mints, don't you?"

"I can't help it," the doctor quipped. "I've liked them ever since I was a small boy. You know, it's funny. Something like these candies I probably would have forgotten about long ago if I had not found them again down at Herkimer's. And now that I have, I can't let go."

Just the mention of Herkimer's brought a guilty conscience to Annice. It also raised a cloud of suspicion over her that Christopher still had hurt feelings about their recent unrealized rendezvous that was supposed to have taken place there. Added to that was the still-unfulfilled promise she had made to him that they would go out again to make up for it. Though several weeks had elapsed, she had failed to actualize it. It had to be settled.

"About that," she began, giving no consideration to whether or not Christopher had actually intended the meaning she had applied to the mentioning of the restaurant. "I really would like to go back there with you. How about this Friday?"

The doctor was dumbfounded. Their interlude was only minutes old and already it had strayed way off course. The course of their conversation had been meant to enhance the level of their relational discourse as a precursor to his asking her personal questions about her marriage. But now it was too late. The doctor was so gripped by the knowledge that he and she would be . . . His thoughts stopped there. He liked that unfinished sentence. He and she would be. He kept repeating it in his mind until finally he realized that Annice was waiting for a response.

"Fantastic!" he blurted out without caution.

"Then Friday it is," Annice bounced back. "We'll call it Fantastic Friday!"

The doctor was so proudly possessed with the realization that they would be sharing an intimate dinner together that all thoughts about being the supportive friend in her time of crisis left him, all but one. He made a mental note that there would be ample time to do that, and that no matter what, he would not renege on his purpose to help her.

Other than to regard his obligation to her, the doctor himself was helpless to help her. For the moment, he had been cast out of his erudite self. He was the embodiment of a high-school boy who had just scored a date with the head cheerleader. He was incapable of serious thought. Since he could not capitalize on what had transpired between them already, the doctor decided to abrogate their interactive discourse by politely excusing himself from her presence and returning to his office.

Once he had retreated to his private office, the doctor paced the floor to and fro. His emotional state was torn like a piece of paper cut in two. He had not achieved his initiative, yet he was overjoyed about how the situation turned out.

"Tomorrow!" he shouted out finally. "Tomorrow, I shall begin my endeavor!"

The doctor spent the remainder of the day buried in his work. He read over patient files and made numerous annotations about how they were doing. He also tape-recorded several ideas he had thought of for several patients regarding their individualized therapies. This taping of his thoughts, as the doctor always did, was a valuable tool for him in that it allowed him to hear himself think. By allowing himself to hear himself think, the doctor could prevent the occasional occurrence when, while attempting to put his thoughts down on paper as quickly as they came, he would sometimes lose what he had thought of somewhere in the stream of thought.

Once he had pertained to his personal perspectives he leaned back in his chair, yawned, and stretched his arms out wide. He was about to leave the office when it struck him that there was something more he could do for Annice right away. The note he had made to remind him to call Dr. Detweiler was still in his briefcase. He had forgotten to take it out and place it somewhere prominent, but nonetheless he had remembered on his own about calling her.

He wanted to implement it. He wanted Annice to go down to the city hospital on some ruse and meet with her personally. He retrieved her personal office number from his phone list and dialed.

"Lancaster City Hospital, may I help you?"

"Yes, please. I thought I had her personal number . . . could you please connect me with Dr. Detweiler."

"One moment please. Who's calling?"

"Tell her it is Dr. Haefner."

"Hold please."

"Hello, Dr. Haefner."

"Hello, yes, it's me. Dr. Detweiler I need your help."

The remainder of the week, Dr. Haefner's office was busier than expected. The times the doctor had allocated for them to share privately had invariably dried up due to patients showing up late for appointments and appointments extending beyond their allotted times. Casual conversation between Chris and Annice had been reduced to an occasional sentence or two between patients. Once, though, midweek, the doctor approached Annice just to confirm that Friday was still on.

It spurred a lot of thinking on Annice's part when he reminded her that she would be with him. Her feelings were intensifying. She spent most of her solitary time contemplating both men in her life.

It bothered her most of all that for the past several weeks her husband, Leslie, had been unusually nice to her. It was almost as if he had some uncanny sense that she was actually contemplating leaving and divorcing him. She began to wonder if, faced with the choice, he could redeem himself, could actually begin again to appreciate her as he once did so, so many years ago. She also wondered whether or not her husband's anger toward her had anything to do with her holding out on him in regard to not bearing him any children. Wouldn't he, or any man for that matter, have the right to be mad about that?

Having children is one of the inevitabilities of marriage, especially in the context of a Catholic union where birth control is forbidden unless pregnancy could result in irreparable harm to the mother.

So, so many years had passed. She recalled how, during the first years of their marriage, it was he who hadn't wanted any children and she had. She recalled their strict adherence to the rhythm method and how often they had to abstain from having sex because of the possibility that she might conceive.

Leslie, though, didn't want children for selfish reasons. Aside from his job, he spent much of his time with his drinking buddies, and he didn't want anything, much less a child, to take him away from that. She recalled vividly how he would slander her in front of them every time they gathered at their house socially. As the years passed, his abuse got uglier. Sometimes he would hit her in their presence just to prove to them that he had the upper hand in their relationship.

It brought her to her senses. Leslie was a brute, and no amount of interjecting could alter that fact. His behavior toward her was atrocious, and despite any tendency she still may have had to defend him because he was still her husband, she could no longer overlook his overall unhusbandlike treatment of her any more.

Friday of that week, the office started off quite busily, but by early afternoon it had slacked quite a bit. The uncharacteristic dullness had been deliberately arranged. Unbeknownst to Annice, the doctor had canceled two patients' appointments so that he could open up part of the day to have Annice sent to city hospital on an intended errand for him. Her mission was to see Dr. Detweiler and retrieve a case-file folder for him. The doctor explained to her that it was imperative he have it ASAP.

It was not quite one o'clock when he strolled out of his office with his latest patient and subtly suggested that now would be as good a time as any to go since his next patient wouldn't be coming until 2:30. "That will give you ample time to get there, meet with her, and retrieve that file I so desperately need."

Annice didn't mind. The doctor very seldom asked her for favors, and when he did, she knew there was an importance attached to it. Taking up her delegated task, she compliantly put away a few papers lying on her desk, grabbed her handbag, and departed. Dr. Haefner, enthralled that part one of his plan was taking shape, treated himself to a handful of jelly mints and plopped himself down on the waiting-room sofa to relax and enjoy his respite.

Traffic was sparse and Annice arrived in the city hospital's parking lot in less than ten minutes. She immediately went inside and visited the central information desk, where she was told to go up to the sixth floor and inquire about Dr. Detweiler. Annice responded by taking the elevator up six flights, then visiting the sixth-floor desk. A huge brass plaque fastened to the front of the desk indicated that this part of the sixth floor was the children's psychiatric unit, and Annice knew she was in the right place to find Dr. Detweiler. She introduced herself to the staff member standing behind the counter and apprised her of her intent to see Dr. Detweiler. After checking a schedule, the attendant informed her that the doctor was busy making rounds but would be informed of her arrival.

Several minutes later, a dark-haired woman wearing whites appeared at the desk. Annice was sitting patiently in a small cane-back chair. The woman in white came right up to her as if they were friends.

"Hello, Annice Colby? Dr. Haefner's secretary?"

"Hello," Annice replied in an introductory voice. "I'm she."

"I'm Dr. Jeanne Detweiler. I'm head of the children's psychiatric unit here."

"I'm glad to meet you," Annice said amicably and extended her hand toward the doctor.

"I'm glad to meet you too. Would you come with me please? I promise not to keep you too long. I'm in a bit of a hurry. I've got to complete my rounds lickety-split before my patients are called for their afternoon medications. I only have two more patients I have to check in with, then I'll get those papers for you. Ordinarily I wouldn't take a visitor along with me on my rounds, but seeing that you're in the profession, I guess it would be all right. It's a discretionary thing."

Annice could see what she believed was an infusion of stress underlying the doctor's seemingly calm countenance. She deemed for herself that her presence in front of the hospital children would be innocuous so she decided to comply.

"Are you sure I won't be interfering with your work?" she asked out of politeness rather than necessity.

"Only if you decide to interfere," the doctor shot back with a dose of intense humor.

They walked and talked. After moving down the main hall behind the front desk, they turned a corridor and continued down the side hall until they reached nearly the end. At a door marked 610 they stopped. Dr. Detweiler tapped lightly on it and listened for a response. She tapped again, louder, and this time a faint voice was heard offering whoever it was to come in. They entered.

"Timmy, how are you?"

Propped up by a plethora of pillows was a small boy, maybe nine or ten, sitting on an inclined bed in the center of an extraordinarily white room. Everything was white, from the walls to the bed linen to the storage cabinets.

Timmy's head was entirely shaven. He had a pale complexion, sunken eyes, and was frail, almost skeletal.

"Hello, Dr. Jeanne," Timmy stated in a stoical voice.

"Hello, Timmy," Dr. Jeanne returned enthusiastically.

"Who are you?" Timmy asked, directing his stare toward Annice.

Annice looked furtively at Dr. Jeanne for approval before she commented to the boy. Dr. Jeanne smiled assuringly at her.

"My . . . my . . . name is Annice, Annice . . ." She was about to divulge her last name but the word "Colby" got stuck in her throat as she was more and more attempting to disassociate herself from her marital bond.

"That's a pretty name," Timmy responded sincerely.

"So, Timmy, how are you doing today?"

"OK, I guess. I just wish the TVs around here got more of the cable channels. Do you even realize what shows I'm missing? I can't even get *Nick at Nite*! And another thing, when can I get something decent to wear besides this split-open gown? This thing is the poorest excuse for clothing I've ever seen! Do you really think it's a good idea to have me exposing myself to everybody!"

Dr. Jeanne patiently listened to Timmy's complaints. She wanted him to assert himself as he was just doing. Part of his therapy was to only introduce improvements to his living condition once he had demanded a change, once he had determined for himself that he wasn't going to take it any more! That's why the room was white, bland. That's why the food he was eating started off with meager rations and no variety. That's why the television had been programmed to get only three stations. That's why he only had a white gown to wear. That's why he had few visitors.

Timmy had almost lost his life due to his inability to cope with difficult living conditions and now, to assure him that he had it in him to deal with depravity in a more successful manner, he had to learn how to be strong. Everything, from the bottom up, he had to fight for—from attention, to colored bed sheets, to better clothing, to an increase in television-channel capability, to a greater selection of food.

Despite his efforts to assert himself, Timmy broke down and began to whimper. Because his retaliation was weak, Dr. Jeanne decided not to grant any of his requests. She declined from divulging any of this pertinent relevance to her guest for reasons she would not understand.

Out in the hall, Annice raised a concern about Timmy.

"What happened to him?"

"Timmy came from a broken home. His mother and father were boyfriend and girlfriend and didn't ever live together. The mother raised him. They lived in town in an old, dirty apartment. Apparently his mother was drug addicted—cocaine and marijuana—at least that was what evidence was found in the home when it was investigated. One day, his mother just up and left. She abandoned him. He lived alone in the apartment with no food, no money, no resources of any kind. Neighbors became suspicious when they started seeing the boy out in the street without his mother. Several times he was caught stealing candy from one of the local mom-and-pop groceries. They felt sorry for the boy and did nothing. That apparent act of kindness actually prolonged his suffering. Timmy survived mainly because he had access to tap water from the kitchen sink. If it hadn't been for that he'd have died. What finally happened to bring the situation out was that Timmy collapsed in a neighbor's yard. He had been attempting to eat leaves from some of the plants in their garden and they called the police."

Tears streaked down Annice's face as she painfully listened to the details of Timmy's hardship. At the point of Dr. Jeanne's telling her about the neighbor's intervention she abruptly asked, "What about his mother?"

"Who knows? According to Timmy, she disappeared about two weeks before he was finally found in the neighbor's backyard."

"That's a horrific story."

"Yes, but one that has a happy ending. Timmy's alive and doing well. He survived his abuse—he survived his abuse but not on his own merit, and that is how we're dealing with it with him. Timmy must learn how not to accept abuse from others any more. He must learn how to fight for himself and fend for himself in this world. People that are caught in an abusive situation must take action for themselves. They must realize that they can go on to happier lives. No one has to accept any situation that is a hardship to them. No one."

Annice felt singed by Dr. Jeanne's words. It was as though she was being spoken to directly. She began to feel uneasy, and the uneasiness she felt piqued her. She wanted to tell Dr. Jeanne something of the pain she felt as an abused woman. One further remark from her and she would have but her determination was interrupted by Dr. Jeanne's insistence that they move on.

"Come on, Annice, one more patient before I get you those reports."

The two women continued on down the same corridor two doors until they reached door 614. Again Dr. Jeanne tapped lightly on the door which was slightly ajar. Inside was a young teenage girl. She was slender, attractive and had dangling strands of dirty-blonde hair covering her face.

"Hello, Cheryl," Dr. Jeanne said gracefully.

"Hello," Cheryl replied. "Who's that with you?"

"This is my friend Annice."

"Hello, Cheryl."

"Hello."

Cheryl's room was dimly lit due to the fact that she had all of the window curtains drawn up tight. Without comment or compromise, Dr. Jeanne went to each window and opened each curtain fully. Then she addressed her patient again.

"How are you doing today?"

"Why should today be any different from any other day?" Cheryl retorted.

"Every day is a precious gift. Every day our life begins again. Every day is a new opportunity for us, an opportunity for us to do anything we want."

"That may be true for you or for her, maybe, but I don't feel anything like what you're talking about."

"Nonsense," Dr. Jeanne said tersely. "Look at you, you're young, bright, and beautiful. You can make your life anything you want it to be."

Cheryl sulked.

"This afternoon I'm ordering you out of here. First, you have a medical appointment with the gynecologist. After that, I have someone who is going to take you down to Millersville University. You are going to be reviewed for admittance in the fall. Your days of lounging around here are over."

Cheryl was obviously disturbed that anything of the magnitude spoken to her by Dr. Jeanne was being expected of her.

"Dr. Jeanne, why do you put on such an act? Why do you act like you really care about me when all you're really doing is putting in time?"

There was a short stiff abeyance in the conversation as each party considered what to say.

Finally, Cheryl spoke, "I mean, after all, after I'm gone you will probably never think of me again. You'll never come to see me no matter where I go or what I do. So why pretend? Why pretend like you really care?"

Dr. Jeanne remained reflective for a moment. She wanted a listening space to grow between them so that her reply would have more emphasis.

"You're probably right, Cheryl. I may not ever come to see you once you leave here. But that's not what I want. What I want is for you to make your life better and go on with it. I want you to develop yourself as well as you possibly can so that you can be happy. Then, I want you to come back. I want you to come back here, back here to me, and show me that you've made it. I want you to show me how happy and successful you've become. Then, I want you to tell me it was all because of me and how I encouraged you. That, my dear, will be my reward."

Dr. Jeanne moved forward and placed her arm around Cheryl and hugged her. Cheryl responded and returned Dr. Jeanne's embrace.

"You really handled that situation well," Annice commented once they were outside the room.

"Cheryl is a hard case. She is only seventeen. Her mother died of cancer two years ago. Because of that, Cheryl effectively took her mother's place in the home. She's an only child. She did everything on her own—the cooking, cleaning, all the shopping—all while still attending high school. Things went too far. Cheryl's role-playing enticed her father to want a complete wife in Cheryl. His affections toward her turned intimate. Eventually, Cheryl found herself in bed with her father every night, performing her wifely duty. Unfortunately they never took precautions. Cheryl got pregnant. She's expecting."

"Oh my God!"

"What's worse is that she blames herself entirely. She wants to have her father's baby. She insists that it's not the baby's fault what happened, and that the baby can still be loved regardless of the unusual circumstances of how it got here."

"What about adoption? Wouldn't that be a better option?"

"No!" Dr. Jeanne replied adamantly. "Adoption, abortion, they're both out of the question. The problem now is only how Cheryl can cope with it. Secretly, she is in agony about things though she refuses to admit it. She wakes up every day hoping it was all some kind of nightmare. The nurses say she cries every morning, sometimes for hours.

"Unlike most people, Cheryl is not assertive. She internalizes everything. Though she puts on a calm demeanor, inside she is out of control. It's my mission to motivate her to get beyond her problem and get back to herself as a person. If she can grasp onto who she was, who she really is, she can advance herself out of the mental quagmire that has her in its grasp."

The women walked and talked all the way back to Dr. Jeanne's office. Once they entered the office, Annice noticed the time and reported that she must leave at once.

"It's almost 2:30 and Dr. Haefner, I'm sure, is expecting me back by now. He had a one-hour lull but his next patient is probably walking through the front door this very minute."

"Don't worry, Annice. I'm sure he will be very understanding. Dr. Haefner's a kind man."

The doctor went to her desk and pulled out a folder. She opened it up then took a separate piece of paper, wrote a sentence on it, then placed it in the file, which she sealed with a clasp. She handed the sealed folder to Annice and thanked her for coming.

Once Annice had departed, Dr. Jeanne got on the phone and called Dr. Haefner's office.

"Look," she said after exchanging greetings. "I didn't have the time to write down my evaluation of her so I decided to call you before she got back to you."

"What do you think?"

"It's difficult to come to any conclusions after only one encounter with a person, but in Annice's case I believe that given time and opportunity she will be willing to let go of her fear, her reluctance to divulge her abuse. She just needs the right person to respond to. I took her with me when I visited some patients—all who suffered from abuse and neglect. She reacted emotionally. I could see how deeply it affected her. The best thing for her right now is to have someone to be her guide, someone to encourage her. She needs you, Doctor, to be there for her."

When Annice returned, Dr. Haefner was already busy with a patient and had a patient waiting. Annice busied herself at her desk until the current session ended, then she walked briskly into his office, and handed him the folder she had retrieved from Dr. Jeanne.

She appeared anxious and her face was flushed as though she had recently been crying. The doctor pretended not to notice and thanked her for her good deed.

During the duration of the workday, the doctor made no special mention of Annice's encounter with Dr. Jeanne. It had been, he was sure, an emotional experience for her, and he wanted her to have ample time to apply her experience to herself. He would talk about it with her only if she initiated a conversation.

Though Annice felt emotionally flustered, she was not about to back out on the evening together she had planned with Christopher. She wanted their evening out to be a success from beginning to end, and to ensure that it would start out right, she insisted that they leave directly from the office instead of her going home first to freshen up like she had tried to do the last time. So instead, she used the facility in their office to brush her hair, wash her face, and apply fractional amounts of perfume and makeup to herself. She wanted their evening out to be a replica of the one several weeks before.

Once they arrived and were seated at Herkimer's, the doctor ordered his usual Friday special—two hot roast beef sandwiches smothered in gravy, and a pile of soft-cooked baby carrots. Annice ordered the same except for the carrots. Instead, she ordered steamed broccoli. And as always, he ordered a Coca-Cola and she a Pepsi-Cola.

"You know, Coca-Cola is the original cola, not Pepsi. Coke started back in the 1880s. Pepsi came later."

The doctor enjoyed regaling Coke in front of Annice who liked Pepsi better.

"Pepsi has a sweeter taste which I think is second to none," she insisted.

The doctor tapped off the thin paper covering from his straw and inserted it into his drinking glass. He swirled it around to hear the ice cubes rattle and see the carbonated bubbles rise to the top of the mixture. He picked up the glass and held it out in front of him as though it were a holy object, and then had communion with it by slowly bringing it to his lips and taking tiny sips from it.

"I predict that eventually, by spending time with me, you'll start being a Coke drinker too. You'll have to. It's the only drink, other than milk and orange juice, that I keep around the house. I must have four or five cases of it in the garage at any one time. Once you start drinking it on a regular basis you won't want to switch back."

"Oh, I won't, won't I?" Annice returned. "And just when do you intend to begin inviting me down to your secluded little homestead?"

The doctor hadn't realized what he had said. It had slipped out unintentionally. He quickly adjusted his thinking to come up with a true response.

"How about tomorrow?" he replied while gulping down more of his soda in an effort to conceal his nervousness.

The doctor, by asking Annice to his home, had inadvertently taken their intentions about being in a real relationship to a new level. It was now about staging a setting in which they could privately pursue their intimate feelings for one another. If Annice said yes, even in fun, it would mean that she too wanted more out of their relationship. If she adamantly refused, then it would certainly be over between them.

"What is tomorrow?"

"Tomorrow," he stated, "I'm having a little get-together down at my place. Two couples and myself. We're going to throw barbeque chicken on the grill, maybe some steaks. My brother Mark just retired from the military. He spent twenty years in the Marines. He's bringing his third wife, Michelle, along. They live in Oceanside, California. Also, one of my old friends, Dave Cool, and his girlfriend Kelly are coming. Both couples are lots of fun to be around. You'll like it if you come."

The doctor was grateful that he had a legitimate reason for asking her to his place. Even if she rejected his invitation, it was still valid and the event he had invited her to had no suggestive sexual association—they would not be alone.

"Wow! It all sounds great," Annice replied. "But just how do you propose I get away from you-know-who?"

"I'm afraid I'll have to leave that up to you. Only you know the best way to manipulate your situation. I only know that I'll be waiting there for you regardless."

Annice was flattered at being invited to Christopher's home. Although she had never actually been there before, she did know where it was. Once, a year or so before, she and her little sister Amy had been on their way to Maryland and Annice suggested they take a picturesque shortcut through the hills of Pequea, and along their way she deliberately had her sister drive past the stretch of Pinnacle Road where the doctor's house was located. Even then, on that particular occasion she fantasized about seeing him, about being with him, about what it would be like to live with him in that wonderful secluded house.

Once they had eaten, they exited the diner and began strolling through the parking lot. There was a small path on the backside of the building which led to the Conestoga River. They took the path, hand in hand, uncaring as to the implications of doing so, and traversed the river bank. They watched as a pair of wild ducks floated in unison along the opposite shore.

"They're probably a mated pair," the doctor suggested.

"They're beautiful," Annice observed.

"And they're probably looking for an ideal nesting site," the doctor marveled. "Look at how they're investigating all those thickets of thistle."

"Nature is beautiful. Isn't it?"

"It is. And we're part of it too," the doctor let go, smiling, as his eyes fell upon her. "As long as I'm with you."

Party Interrupted

Had it really happened? The doctor thought to pinch himself when he awoke in his bed the following morning. He felt as excited as ever whenever he thought about the experience he had shared with Annice. He envisioned it over and over again in his mind—their words, their visual exchanges, the love he was sure existed in each of their hearts.

As he sat up in bed, he surveyed what was around him—the two sun-struck windows casting radiant light in patterns of geometrical symmetry across the room, one window's light shadowing a potted African violet's image on the wall; the other's, shining directly on the wall beside it. He scanned other contents in the room—a maple dresser, a lounge chair, an overfilled bookcase, all of it, all of it seemingly different somehow.

The doctor's eyes turned to the African violet, still covered in a splash of white light. He regarded the purple flowers intensely. Purple was and always had been his favorite color, though it was not a color he wanted to be used in large quantities about him. The color purple looks best when it is used sparingly, like as decoration on a towel or a tie.

"I hope Annice likes the color purple," the doctor stated aloud from his bed.

A short while later the doctor arose. He wore only his Fruit of the Loom underwear, and he stood before the dressing mirror and pondered whether or not to get fully dressed. Instead he put on his favorite blue robe and slipped on a pair of moccasins.

The air was crisp and cool when the doctor exited his home to retrieve the morning paper at the end of his drive. Songbirds, abundant at this time of year, scattered themselves among the treetop branches and sang for him as he flopped along the stony drive toward Pinnacle Road. Possessed by the sparkling day that was before him and the extraordinary happiness he felt in his heart, the doctor too joined in the bird song. At first he tried to repeat the various chirps and tweets he heard, then he began to just whistle, and soon the whistling turned into song. He began whistling the tune of an old '70s song. His whistling soon broke into song, "I've got this feeling . . . I've got this feeling . . . . I've got this feeling . . . ." Because he couldn't remember all the lyrics, the doctor soon returned to whistling. As he made his way closer and closer to the end of the drive, he tried harder and harder to remember the name of the '70s group that had the hit. It eluded him. Then he remembered with a smile that his old friend Dave Cool would be paying him a visit later today and Dave would, without a doubt, remember.

He retrieved his paper and returned to the house, stopping once to be fascinated by a family of gray squirrels as they chased each other in the upper branches of a huge oak. Back in the house, he prepared himself a hefty breakfast of country-style potato and eggs, orange juice, and a tall glass of cold chocolate milk. As he sat down at his breakfast table to eat, he had with him a sharp pencil and a notepad of clean white paper. In between bites, he began writing down a list of grocery items, essentials he needed to purchase for the party.

"Let's see," he began summarizing out loud. "napkins, paper plates, plastic knives, forks, and spoons. I have the steaks and chicken. I believe I have enough charcoal briquettes, though I'd better check their condition. They have been sitting around for—since last summer. I do have the Coca-Cola but I'd better put a few carriers in the fridge. Oh, and yes, I have to buy ice."

By the time breakfast was over, he was sure the list was complete. Later, he would make a trip to Pequea, the closest little town, where he could purchase his supplies. He began pondering the party, the intricate details; in particular his date, Annice. Would she come? Would she come or would she disappoint him once more? Panic pervaded his spirit over whether or not she would come. He needed assurance. He spirited over to the phone and dialed her number which he knew by heart. He was exceedingly anxious as her number rang and he suddenly felt thwarted by the complex issue of what would he say if her husband answered. Could he just ask for her? What would happen to her if he wasn't given the opportunity to identify himself and explain himself before a jealous Leslie Colby hung up? The thought struck him with terror.

Annice was roused out of bed by the ringing of the phone, but by the time she got out of bed and picked up, the caller had broken the connection. She was very sleepy and debated going back to bed for more much-needed sleep. Leslie had come home very late last night, past 2:00 in the morning, drunk and angry. While out at the corner bar, he had expended a great deal of time and money trying to hustle, and unsuccessfully so, an attractive young woman, blonde, with a slender figure. In the end she had managed to take advantage of him for all his wallet was worth and then carelessly tossed him aside like a used Kleenex. To sustain his generosity, she had flirted with him the entire time, shamelessly, while they drank, and she even had offered him the time of his life before finally making a hasty departure by deceptively claiming she needed to use the ladies' room, then making for the door instead. All Leslie was left with was an empty wallet and a seething anger.

He came home frustrated and furious. When he entered the house, he deliberately smashed a vase of artificial flowers Annice had set on a small table. He then trudged upstairs to take out his sexual frustration on his wife. Though she was asleep, he woke her and ordered her to assume a sexually receptive position so he could have her. Annice obeyed. In her husband's condition, she knew he would beat her if she resisted. Annice braced herself for Leslie's assault. Just as he began having his way with her, he got very sick. He was so drunk he could neither stop vomiting nor stop violating his wife. Being relieved made him feel better and he continued until he had jostled all of the excess, energy and alcohol, out.

The moment it was over, he was so relieved and so exhausted, he pulled away from Annice, rolled over her to the wrong side of the bed, and fell to the floor. To Annice, the act had been so wicked she remained in bed, stricken. For the longest time, she lay there, sick to her stomach, shrouded in fear. She was afraid. Then, finally, she took hold. It was the odor covering her body that forced her out of her self-induced trance and into the bathroom to shower. She instinctively locked the bathroom door then rummaged through the medicine cabinet for her secret stash of birth-control pills. Though she had already taken her dose for the twenty-four-hour period she was in, she insisted on taking more. It was her overreaction to her husband's abhorrent behavior toward her that she would never, not ever, conceive him a child.

She began to feel better once the stink of sweat and dirt were cleansed off of her body. After drying off, she slipped quietly into the bedroom again and sat down on a corner of the bed. She debated dressing and spending the duration of the night downstairs but decided against it. She knew that if her husband awoke and found her missing, he would only become angry again and in retribution she would be beaten and raped once more. So, cautiously, she slid back into bed, without making a sound. She lay awake through the remainder of the night, waiting for the moment when her husband woke up. If he asked, she would tell him nothing of what he had done.

Though he never received a last-minute assurance that Annice would be coming, the doctor carried on with his party plans with an alacrity similar to when he had done so in his college days. In the early afternoon, he made the short drive into Pequea to purchase all of the essential items he had on his list. He even bought a few extra snacks, potato chips and pretzels, to make things more complete.

His old friend, Dave Cool, and his live-in partner, Kelly, arrived first. Their arrival was well-marked by the loud thunderous roar of Dave's 1970 Dodge Challenger. It was Dave's original high-performance car, a car he had purchased all the way back in 1976 when he first was privileged to drive.

Standing in the driveway opening, the doctor regarded the sound of the super 340 engine and the memories it brought back to him. He examined Dave, sitting in the car, revving up the engine just the way he used to do when he was twenty years younger. The doctor smiled as he juxtaposed the Dave of now with the Dave of yesteryears. Except for a little less hair, a little more paunch, Dave was the same. Dave was Dave. His prodigious appetite for fast cars and pretty girls never left him.

Once Dave turned off the engine, he lowered his driver's-side window which had only been cracked open. Both men smiled. Kelly unbuckled her seat belt and sat patiently in the car for Dave to initiate their next move. The doctor and Dave shook hands through the open window.

Dave got out of the car.

"Long time no see."

"Not long enough," the doctor returned facetiously. "I was thinking that after twenty-four years you might have at least grown up, at least a little."

"I don't ever plan on growing up," Dave responded. "Life is too much of an adventure and I'm having too much fun as an adventurer."

"Good answer," the doctor replied earnestly.

"Oh, by the way, I brought some of that adventure with me."

With that, Dave turned and walked toward the rear of the Challenger, opened the trunk, and retrieved from it a case of cold beer.

"We stopped off in Conestoga on the way and picked up a case of what used to be your favorite, Stroh's. It's still cold but we better put it on ice if you want to keep it cold. Where can we put it?"

They made room in the auxiliary refrigerator, taking out several carriers of Coke and filling in the space with single bottles of beer. With that done, Chris, Dave, and Kelly made their way into the house, where they situated themselves in the spacious living room so they could converse.

Dave made himself at home by stopping off at the entertainment system and perusing through the collection of old albums his old friend possessed. He was amazed at the size and condition of the collection.

"I can't believe you still have all these," Dave said admiringly.

Though Dave and Chris still considered each other close friends, they seldom saw each other. Usually they would run into each other in Lancaster, in a store or on the street, but because their friendship had been so intense when they were in their later teens they would never consider their relationship less than what it had been.

Dave poured through the LPs, his eyes reveling in each and every one: Foreigner, Bob Seger, Aerosmith, Led Zeppelin, Eagles . . . he stopped there.

"That's it! Hotel California. I haven't heard that for . . . for a decade or more!"

Dave enthusiastically extricated the vinyl disc out of the cardboard cover and examined it in full.

"This," he stated, "is music worth listening to."

He placed the album on the holder expertly and turned on the system. The record dropped and the crackling that always preceded an album's beginning sounded through the speakers.

"Not too loud, Dave," Chris cautioned.

"Why, you afraid the squirrels will complain?" Dave chortled.

"No, it's not that. I don't have a neighbor within a mile of here. It's just that I have other company arriving. If you play that thing too loud I won't be able to hear him when he arrives."

"Oh, that's right, Mark and Michelle are coming. Well, boohoo for them."

"And besides that, Dave, how are we going to be able to talk if the music's playing too loud?"

"You're not supposed to talk when you're listening to this type of music," Dave responded. "The music is supposed to do all the talking."

Dave moderated the volume so that conversation could be heard along with the music. Chris instinctively looked out the front bay window to see if his brother was there. Dave situated himself on the floor in front of Kelly who was seated on the sofa. He begged her to rub his head and neck while he listened to the song. The song played and both Dave and Kelly became absorbed in it. They never heard or saw when Chris left the room to go greet his brother and his wife.

Mark pulled up beside Dave's Challenger in his Firebird. When the cars were nose to nose, Mark began revving up his engine as though a race was about to begin. Seconds later, Dave was out of the house, standing beside his car and staring at Mark, grinning. Mark motioned Dave to get into his car and enticed him to do so by revving up his engine again. Dave got into the Challenger and began revving his engine alongside Mark. The two looked at each other from their driver positions and made smiling gestures toward each other as if they should proceed in a race, but what the race was really about was to allow the rivals a chance to hear the distinctive power of each car's motor. Finally, the situation broke into hilarity, causing the rivals to cease their antical behavior. Simultaneously they turned off their engines. Dave and Mark exited their vehicles.

"Should we call it a tie?" Mark proposed.

"Not on your life," Dave responded.

"OK, OK, you two," Chris intervened. "Shake hands and call it even just for today. There's no place to race around here anyway."

For a short while outside, Mark and Dave exchanged details about their cars. Kelly emerged from the house and introduced herself to Michelle. Once the conversation about whose car could outperform the other subsided, the standing invitation for everyone to rejoin inside was accepted. Dave apprised the new guests of the awesome albums that awaited them inside. Once everyone was situated in the living room, Dave went to work immediately and entertained his listeners with a Bob Seger album, *Night Moves*. After the album played out and before another was selected to play, there was an interlude of catch-up conversation between the acquaintances.

"So, Dave, how is your business doing?" asked Mark.

"I'm so busy right now I shouldn't even be here today. I have projects lined up straight through the season and I'm even booking work for next year already. And that doesn't even count the less-lucrative jobs that I keep turning down."

"Sounds enterprising. Do you think you'll be able to retire soon?"

"It's not my goal to retire, not in the sense of quitting the business. The ultimate goal of any business person is to get into a position in which the business can be run from behind a desk. Right now I have two dependable masons and one really dependable apprentice working for me. If I can double that in the next few years, I can surely ease myself into that comfortable chair behind that elusive desk I speak of."

"Wow!"

"How about you?"

"I'm already retired, just last year. I spent twenty years in the military."

"The Marines, right?"

"Yes. I retired as an E-7. I have a pension of $950.00 a month for life. We live out in Oceanside, California but we're not sure that that's where we're going to stay. Michelle has family there. So that's where we're staying for now."

"What are you going to do now?"

"He's not doing anything." Michelle interjected. The only thing he does is go down to the beach every day and watch the sea lions or watch other women in their skimpy bathing suits."

"That's not true," Mark replied in earnest.

"And when he's not doing that, he's sitting around the house getting on my nerves."

"Don't listen to her. She's just jealous because she has to work and I don't." Mark gave Michelle a hard look as if to say, let me finish what I have to say. "Anyway, what I really want to do, that is if things work out right, is to start up a gym. I had a great time lifting weights all those years in the service. Everywhere I went they had facilities. Now I want to take that training and apply it on my own. I just have to find the right place, the right location, and the right building to convert. I'm only thirty-nine. I could run a gym for thirty years if I wanted to."

"Sounds intriguing," Kelly said, joining the discussion. "Where all were you stationed when you were in the . . . what branch of the service did you say you were in?"

"I was a Marine, a lifer," Mark replied. He began counting the years, the places he had been. "I first went to Parris Island, South Carolina. That's where basic training is held for lots of Marines.

Next, I was stationed in Oceanside, California, where we are now. After two years there, I was sent to Okinawa, Japan, for eighteen months. After that, it was back to Parris Island for another three years. From there I was sent to Hawaii for two years. That was the best place I stayed in, in my entire military career. Then I went to Cuba for a little over a year. From there I went to join the forces in the Gulf War. I spent eight months supplying divisions out of an exchange in Kuwait. Then, after going back to Cuba for a few months, it was off to Somalia in East Africa to take food and supplies to the starving people there. Then I came back again to Oceanside. That's when I met Michelle. We stayed there for another five years before I was finally sent to Quantico, Virginia, where I spent the last two years at the base outside Washington. That's where I officially retired from. Then we moved back to California so she could be near her family. We still haven't decided if we're going to stay or go."

Getting back to the main matter of the discourse, Mark's brother asked, "Mark, what do you think is the feasibility of opening up a civilian gym so close to a military base that adequately provides those needs for all the attending personnel? Isn't Oceanside just an auxiliary zone to the military installation? Is there enough of a civilian population there to justify opening up a business of that concern?"

Mark laughed in reaction to his brother's rendition. Not having been around his older brother, Mark wasn't used to hearing his high-profiled use of the English language. This turned the conversation.

"You don't have to answer that," Dave interrupted. "Anything you don't understand you don't have to answer."

"Didn't we used to have a name for him?" Mark asked.

"We had a name for him for all the little perks he had," Dave stated. "Let's see, we called him 'professor' because of his word power, and yes, we called him 'poverty' because he used to pick up pennies from the street."

"And when he was little my mom called him 'Pip' because he was her little Pipper," Mark pointed out.

"Did you really, I mean, pick up pennies from the street?" Kelly inquired, looking at Chris curiously.

"He picked up change wherever he found it—streets, stores, other people's cars, on the floor in someone's home, everywhere," Dave answered for him.

"How much did it ever amount to?" Kelly inquired further.

Proudly, Chris got up out of his recliner and walked quietly out of the room. Minutes later he returned holding a large glass jar. He placed the heavy container on the coffee table in front of his guests. The jar was entirely full of various coins and even a few bills. Chris unscrewed the tin lid so the money could be viewed more easily.

"Every penny, nickel, dime, quarter, and half dollar I ever found is inside this jar, including several one-dollar bills and a five-dollar bill. I've saved everything ever since—let's see . . ." He examined the exterior of the jar which still had the old label on it, displaying the brand of pickles which were originally sold in it. On a clear part of the paper label was an old date written in pen. "It says, October 14, 1975."

"That means for twenty-five years you have been saving every bit of money you ever found," Kelly stated profoundly.

"Did you ever count it?" Michelle asked.

"Yes," Chris explained. "Once a jar is full I count it and write down the amount on the outside of the glass. This one is the original jar. There are three now. Two are full. This one contains—let's see— eighty-seven dollars and thirty cents to be exact."

"That's just remarkable that you endeavored to do that," Kelly stated.

"Persistence usually pays off," Chris returned matter-of-factly.

Then as the doctor capped the jar and returned it to its safe place on the upper shelf in his clothes closet, Mark and Dave broke out into an uncontrollable laugh.

"I can't believe it. I just can't believe it," Mark and Dave both said agreeably.

Once the laughter ceased, Dave offered to go to the garage and bring back beer. The afternoon progressed with the group listening to selected music, predominately from the '70s, and engaging in casual conversation related to their lives past and present. Finally, it was the doctor who concluded that it was time to get things cooking by which he meant to actually begin with the preparations to eat.

Everybody extended helping hands and soon the charcoal grill was set a-fire and pieces of chicken and steaks were placed on it to cook. In addition to the meats, baked potatoes were set in the oven and green beans were standing ready to be heated up once everything was within five minutes of completion.

The meal was to be eaten on the outside patio which was located to the front of the house, adjoining the large stone driveway opening. All of the place settings were arranged by Kelly and Michelle. Dave attended the fire and the doctor concerned himself with the stove. An hour later, all the food was ready to eat and the participants joined around the serving table just outside the patio where all the food was placed. Everyone in turn filled their plates then situated themselves around the dining table inside the enclosed patio.

While everyone's appetite was being appeased, the newly formed group found many topics of conversation to engage in and they became quite talkative. The doctor purposefully left himself out of much of the conversation. He felt awkward about being the only single person in the group and he was growing increasingly concerned about whether Annice was going to show. Often, he stared over at the parking space that still remained for her Escort if she bothered to come. Then, it suddenly occurred to him that Annice could very easily pass by his driveway entirely and never know it. The directions he had given her spoke of distances and did not really connect the road to any available landmarks, except for his mailbox. Disturbed by this, the doctor strained to quickly think of some sort of way in which he could denote the entrance to his property so that it was easily found.

He left the group. Inside the garage, he appropriated a three-inch-wide roll of yellow tape, left behind by the surveyors who, years before, staked out the boundaries of his acreage. While he held onto the tape, a humorous idea dawned on him. He would tie a yellow ribbon round an old oak tree. He was, of course, remembering the old Tony Orlando song from his early teen years. Inwardly he chuckled at the possibility—the possibility that by applying the yellow ribbon in the same way that Tony Orlando did and for almost the same reason, Annice would see it for its other purpose.

Once he had accomplished his secret task, he returned to the others. In the garage, he was met by Dave who was bringing out a few empty beer bottles and exchanging them for full ones.

"You got a nice place here, professor, but why did you build a two-car garage when it's only you?"

Dave, of course, was kidding but the doctor didn't feel like explaining, for fear of sounding like a whiner, about the hope of someday finding someone who could occupy that ostentatious spot next to his. In replacement of that, he came up with a comical comment.

"You know, Dave, I've always wondered, why is a garage called a garage? Why isn't it called a 'carage'? Wouldn't that make more sense, after all isn't it a car that's being parked there?"

"Oh, you have the driest sense of humor," Dave blurted out. "Take one of these and splash down that overused brain of yours."

To quell his growing anxiety, the doctor immersed himself in the society of his friends as they gathered in steeped conversation about when they were young and joined each other in slugging bottles of beer. It was to his complete surprise when, forty-five minutes later, a blue Ford Escort came bounding up the stone driveway.

"She's here!"

"Expecting someone?" Dave said in a pitched voice responding to his friend's excitement.

"I can't believe it!"

Annice parked her car in the select spot. She exited her car, latched and locked the driver's door, then turned toward the outdoor porch where the others were assembled. She made an impressive appearance when she approached them. She wore dark sunglasses and had on a purple plaid dress which draped her to her knees. The dress was unrecognizable to the doctor and he wholly wondered if she had just recently brought it and worn it especially for him.

"Christopher, how are you?" she spoke softly.

"I'm . . . I'm . . . aghast," he answered meekly.

"What a terrible thing to say," she said reproachfully.

"Forgive me," he countered. "It was getting so late that I really didn't expect that you were going to make it."

"Make it? How could I miss it with that special little marker you left for me along the road?"

"What marker?" Mark interjected.

The doctor turned to Annice and replied, "That was just for you and me. I confided in no one else."

Ignoring everyone's interest in what they were talking about, the doctor began making formal introductions all around. "Annice, this is Dave Cool. We've been friends for twenty-five years. And this is Kelly, Dave's sexy girlfriend. This is Mark and Michelle, my brother and his wife. They've been married for eight years now."

Once Annice had shaken hands with each of Chris's friends, she sat down with them in the enclosed porch. Michelle, acting ahead of the doctor, readied a plate of hot food for her. Annice, after seating herself in one of the wrought-iron armchairs, took exception to the fact that these old-time friends of Christopher's would know something about the James he always spoke of, the James he always thought about.

"Did any of you know this James person Christopher always talks about from when he was young?"

Immediately, Dave, Mark, and the doctor exchanged glances.

"You mean the Cuz," Dave responded.

"The Cuz," Mark reiterated."

"That's the one," Annice returned.

"What do you know about him?" Dave asked.

"Only that he was a diabolical person. He was abandoned by his parents at a very young age and adopted by his aunt and uncle. I know that he died in a car crash ten years ago down in New Orleans. Other than that, not a whole lot."

"Then you know only the beginning and ending. You don't know about all the good stuff that comes in the middle," Dave stated.

"Yeah, Cuzze was sort of like an Oreo cookie," Mark analogized. "His life was stuffed in the middle with unbelievable stories."

"You mean double-stuffed," Dave interjected.

All this while, the doctor said nothing, hoping the discussion would die by attrition. Instead, he picked up a paper plate and served himself a second portion of barbequed chicken and beans. He sat down next to Annice to join her while she ate.

"I ate only small portions before you came," he said, "hoping that you and I could eat together."

"That was thoughtful," Annice stated cheerfully. "And by the way, I do appreciate what you did with the tree down at the end of the drive. Your place isn't the easiest to find. It's like you're hiding out from the world in these woods."

"Maybe I am," the doctor announced, laughing.

"What are you laughing about?" Annice asked.

"The yellow ribbon," he answered wryly. "You noticed it but did you notice it?"

"What do you mean, Chris?"

"I'll show you what I mean. Wait here. I'll be right back."

The doctor took one lasting bite of chicken, got up, and raced into the house. Moments later, two of the front bay windows could be heard opening and soon after a song could be heard playing on the stereo. It was the old "Tie a Yellow Ribbon Round the Ole Oak Tree," by Tony Orlando and Dawn from the 1970s.

When the doctor returned, Annice was smiling. She understood.

The evening progressed and dusk fell, sooner in the heavily wooded hills surrounding the social gathering than elsewhere beyond. It was only an hour after darkness that hints were being dropped by everyone that it would soon be time to go. Before his guests departed, the doctor made certain that the women rather than the men were the ones driving home. To make certain of this, he even escorted each couple to their vehicles when they left, and watched. Kelly and Michelle were far less inebriated than their significant others and were better able to drive without the chance of their getting into an accident. Alcohol-related deaths were among the life tragedies that had hit home recently in the doctor's family. Tony Haefner, a cousin, had been killed, along with his fiancée, in a fiery car crash, in adjacent York County, just days before Christmas, three years ago. The driver of the vehicle that caused the crash was drunk. Ever since, the doctor has been adamant about things like buckling up, obeying posted speed limits, and driving defensively.

"Are you leaving too?" the doctor asked Annice in a mild voice after the Challenger and the Firebird were gone.

"Are you asking me to?" Annice countered in a whimsical voice.
"No, certainly not. Your answer to that is out there, tied up around that tree. That yellow ribbon is for you. But the real question is, would you have tied a yellow ribbon for me?"

They were alone. It was late. A nervous tension hung between them like a mist. It was emotions and sexual desire and strife brought on by the desire to do what is right. Together, as they cleaned up, they purposefully tested each other's resolve by asking and answering questions that could be taken to mean more than what was apparent. Neither one wanted to be bold. In the end, it was the doctor who determined that it was neither the time nor the place for them to have what he so desperately wanted: intimate relations. To appease any misgivings she might have regarding his adamant suggestion that she should get going before it got too late, the doctor approached her, enclosed his arms around her, and held her tightly. She knew by the way he held her that his feelings for her were intense.

"I'd like you to stay," he put to her delicately, "but I just don't want to see you get into trouble, if you know what I mean."

Annice, entranced by Chris's hold, threw caution to the wind, turned her face to his, and kissed him on the lips. It was a kiss that told him exactly where her heart was at that moment, a kiss that professed where her heart would be whenever he wanted it.

They walked quietly to the car together, his hand around her waist. When they arrived at the car, they looked at each other expectantly, their eyes then their lips met once more.

On the way back into the house, the doctor wondered if by doing the right thing he had done the right thing. If he had made love to her, they would have crossed a threshold together, a threshold from which there would be no going back. By letting her go now, she would be given the chance to reconsider what had happened and possibly back away before it was too late. But it was too late.

The doctor locked up the house and slipped into bed. How he wished that Annice were there beside him. What a perfect partner she would be. He slipped off to sleep with his head acting out scenarios between them.

It was late into the night when the doctor was jarred from his sleep by the blaring noise of the stereo. Startled, the doctor jolted out of bed and into the living room to investigate. Upon entering the living room and fully expecting to find that one of his guests had returned unannounced and was playing a trick on him, the doctor was shocked to discover, once the lights had been turned on, the room empty of all possible suspects. The stereo, however, was playing at full blast. Immediately, he shut it off, but curious, he turned it back on to listen to the tune playing. The stereo was tuned in to a classic-rock station high up on the frequency modulation, a station the doctor hadn't listened to before. The song still playing was "Lonesome Loser" by the Little River Band. The doctor listened intently to the music, still attempting to ascertain the mystery of how the music came to play. He checked both the front door and the kitchen door which led into the garage, jiggling their locks to see if either had been opened. Both were secure. Uncertain that there was anything more he could do, he turned off the music, then the light, and turned to go back to bed. Maybe the stereo had been on the entire time and just now, for some unknown reason, turned itself up. What else could have done it?

The doctor was a footstep away from entering his room when he heard the unmistakable sound of a person laughing coming from the living room. He whirled around and raced back to find out. This time, when he threw on the light he would be met by one of his companions, Dave, Mark, or somebody.

"All right you!" he shouted. "All right! You've gone too far! What right do you have entering my home in the middle . . ."

The doctor ceased shouting. He heard the laughter again. He stood in silence as the sound of it seemed to echo across the room. The laughter came loud but died with each successive sound. Attempting to ascertain the identity of the mystery person, the doctor went hurriedly into each adjoining room and flooded them with light. Next, he took his house keys and unlocked first the garage then the front door, looking for the interloper. No one was to be found. On a hunch, he raced back into the garage and opened his car to see if someone was hiding in it. The car was empty. The only other possibility was that whoever it was, was outside and maybe now escaping. He raced back into his bedroom, found his flashlight, and carried it outside where he began projecting its beam of light into the nearby woods and down the stony lane. He found no trace that anyone had been around.

As he walked slowly back up the lane, he wondered if it had been his imagination that had gotten the best of him. But no. The laughter was real and he had had only four or five beers by his best estimate the entire night, and the effect of what he'd had had almost completely worn off. He reentered the house not knowing what to think. When he walked into the living room, he froze. The flashlight fell from his hand as if he had just been shot. There, sitting in his favorite La-Z-Boy recliner was an apparition—an apparition of what appeared to be . . . It was unmistakable. The phantom occupying his comfortable chair was James!

Together we Can . . .

Dr. Haefner was an exceptionally rational man, just as any eminent psychiatrist would be expected to be. As such, he was averse to believing in anything like specters or ghosts. But seeing is believing, and the doctor had a great difficulty before him in that he did believe that he had seen the apparition of his long-lost friend.

During the days that immediately followed the strange event, he meditated and mediated with himself on the certainties of the situation and as well the uncertainties.

He recalled the catastrophic event of James's death a decade ago. He remembered how, as James's life was ending, his fleeting spirit had desperately tried to make contact with him. He thought about the phone that night which rang and rang as though it were frantically trying to speak out. He thought about how he picked up the receiver, and even though no one spoke, he knew that someone was there. Then the front door sounded as if somebody was jiggling the knob, as if trying to get in. How much like tonight that night was.

Over and over he weighed out the possibilities in his mind; the events of the past and present. It was perplexing to believe that James could have possibly come back. It was one thing to believe that someone's life force could have one last chance to cling to life like the doctor was sure James's had done so many years ago, but it was entirely different to believe that someone whose spirit had been gone for so long a period of time could suddenly, and for no apparent reason, appear. The questions came without answers. Why would he come back now instead of more immediately after his death? Why would he appear here to me? Why not to people who were closer to him like his half brother Dave, or some of his pot-head friends? Why not to his other real brother or sisters? Why not to his aunt Betty or uncle John? Why would he come back at all?

All during his appointments on the days that followed, the doctor found that he was perpetually distracted by his thoughts on the matter. He was doubly distracted by the new sort of relationship that had been established between him and Annice. He wanted to confide in her what he had seen but he couldn't. He didn't want their blossoming romance ruined by including in their daily discourses and flirtations a diet of unexplained nuance concerning the sighting of James's ghost. He needed someone to talk to, someone he could open up to.

By midweek, the doctor was so perplexed by the enigma of seeing James's ghost that he had Annice place a call for him to Dr. Brain at the Reading Hospital. He continually went through the motions with his patients, attempting to heal their sufferings and misery but it was only a patching of plaster that he applied to their wounded minds, for in his mind he was plagued by, haunted by, the startling revelation of James.

At the end of the day, Dr. Brain's return call finally came. Annice notified him on the intercom and put the doctor's call through.

"Hello, Dr. Brain?"

"Hello. Dr. Haefner, how are you?"

"I'm fine, just fine. Look I need to talk to you, or better yet, I need to see you about something. Do you have any free time available soon?"

"Free time!" the doctor spoke out loudly and with a laugh. "No, you'll have to pay me like everyone else."

"You know, Doctor," the doctor replied jovially, "in this particular instance, maybe I should."

"Is it as serious as all that, my boy?" Dr. Brain returned affably.

"More so than I can say," Dr. Haefner replied.

"How about cluing me in on just what this is all about?"

"No, not on the phone. You'll have a hard time believing what I have to say in person."

Dr. Haefner deliberately held in abeyance the facts of the matter, knowing that the enticement he had delivered up to his celebrated mentor would be cause enough to ensure a face-to-face meeting. Dr. Haefner waited patiently as Dr. Brain fumbled through his schedule.

"How about . . . no, no, that won't do. Let's see . . . I've got . . . no, that won't do either. Wait a minute . . . no, no, yes. I've got it! How about this Friday? I have a conference at the hospital—just a monthly agenda meeting. I could blow it off and send one of my interns as my proxy."

"Are you sure, Doctor? I don't want to be responsible for keeping you from your . . ."

It was settled.

Dr. Haefner made a note of the proposed meeting and notified Annice about it too. After annotating the information on her computer, she aptly informed the doctor that his next patient had arrived.

This was the patient he was waiting to see, the one who could probably take his mind off James. It was Miss Thome, Patricia, and she was accompanied by her mother. As they entered the office together, Mrs. Thome handed the doctor Patricia's release file which contained all of the latest and most pertinent information regarding her daughter's most recent hospitalization. The doctor, after being handed the file folder, cordially greeted first Mrs. Thome then Patricia. He was delighted when, after shaking Miss Thome's hand, he witnessed her taking out a fistful of tissues from the Kleenex box he had on the edge of his desk. Immediately she proceeded to wipe her hands in a rhythmic motion, a characteristic of her disease.

"No!" the doctor shouted. "Please remove the tissues from your hand, Miss Thome."

"What on earth!" Mrs. Thome remonstrated. "For goodness sakes, Doctor, she's only wiping dirt off her hand," she pleaded.

The doctor gave them each a cold hard stare. His eyes told them that he believed otherwise and that he had the collateral to back up his belief.

"Your daughter, Mrs. Thome," he said, addressing Patricia's mother, "is attempting, not to clean her hand as her actions might dictate, but rather, as I believe it, cleanse her mind of some thought or fear she may have had when she shook my hand. And now, in a ritualistic fashion, she is listening to her emotionally overloaded mind as it tells her what she must do to compensate. Isn't that right, Patricia? Without waiting for any response he continued. And how do I know that this is so? Simple. If Patricia truly had intended to remove some dust or dirt from her hands as you purport, why wouldn't she have reached for the box of tissues prior to shaking my hand? If clean hands were the issue, wouldn't she have desired to clean them before she would have dirtied mine? Wouldn't she?"

The doctor allowed his visitors a brief interlude to situate themselves in the chairs he had facing his desk and for the mother and daughter to render upon each other a look of suspicion and a look of guilt.

"Now we begin," the doctor said plainly. "Mrs. Thome, Miss Thome, listen carefully to what I am about to tell you. The therapy I have proposed in Patricia's case is a radical one I admit; in fact, I invented it. It is called confrontational therapy.

"In it, I call upon the afflicted person—in this case you, Patricia—to confront your obsessive-compulsive behavior head-on. What we will do is put our patient in direct contact with everyday, ordinary, circumstances. Through it, I will observe every action and reaction exemplified by Patricia. Whenever I see her stressing in response to her illness, especially, enacting rituals, I will stop her and make her realize that there is no consequence for not having abided by her petty tortures. She will see, one instance at a time, that even though we may not be able to beat back the intense emotive side of this illness, we can control how we react to it. And that is how we begin to defeat the demon.

"This therapy is of no use here, in the safety and confines of this inner sanctum. To be really effective it must be aptly applied outside, in the real world. I want Patricia's mind to be inculcated with stimulus, the kind of stimulus that affects her each and every day."

The Thomes looked solemnly at each other, not knowing what to expect. Dr. Haefner got up and announced that they were leaving at once.

"We are leaving at once and I know the perfect place to take Patricia."

"Where?" asked Mrs. Thome with a puzzled voice.

"The Park City Shopping Mall," the doctor returned.

The trio promptly departed. Using the doctor's car, they whisked through the few blocks to the Harrisburg Pike and traveled the three extra miles until they reached the huge shopping center.

Once they entered the mall, they spent the next twenty-five minutes going from shop to shop, perusing things of interest. The doctor made certain that the three of them stayed together in a tight group so he could observe Patricia closely. Several times he caught her. Once she attempted to continuously wipe off her hands on an article of clothing. The doctor immediately grabbed her hand and stopped her. Patricia was noticeably upset, but the doctor forced her past the immediacy of her imagined need. By forcing her out so she couldn't complete her self-inflicted punishment, he showed her just how unnecessary it was for her to oblige her fear.

A short while later, the doctor decided to treat himself and the others to a soft pretzel and a Coke. He seated Mrs. Thome at a table at the center court, and he and Patricia purchased the pretzels and drinks.

On their way from the food stand to the table, the doctor asked, "Well, Miss Thome, did you enjoy your little shopping spree today?"

"Shopping spree?" she asked with a bewildered look on her face. "I didn't buy anything today."

"Oh, but you did, my young friend. You went on a spree to free your mind, to free your mind of its tightening grip on your reactive behavior. And you accomplished much in the way of it. I expect it to have a hold on you. I expect you to take from here what you have learned and expound on it. I expect you to do for yourself what I have shown you to do. You, only you, have the power to free yourself. I have only shown you how. Exercise your power. Let your will be free, be stronger than your demon. Together we will fight this thing. Together we will win."

Once they returned to the James Street office, it was just time for the Thomes to leave. The doctor escorted them from his car, parked out front, to theirs, parked out back. Mrs. Thome pointed out the cranberry-colored Cadillac parked nearest the building, and as they approached it, she expeditiously removed a small electronic device from her handbag and pointed it at the car for the doors to automatically unlock. When they arrived at the vehicle, Mrs. Thome ordered her daughter into the front passenger's seat and asked for her cooperation and patience while she had a brief word with the doctor.

"What do you think, Doctor?"

"What do I think? I think your daughter suffers from a severe case of obsessive-compulsive disorder. I also think there's hope for her. Believe it or not, but there is a one-in-three chance she could have a complete recovery. Sometimes the body can heal itself. Her brain, at any time, could begin connecting its impulses again and she would be cured. And if not, she will surely learn from me how to cope with the behavioral part of it. Certainly she will get better."

"Will she?" Mrs. Thome asked.

"She will," the doctor said with certainty. "You will have to help her though until she is better able to help herself. Make sure she keeps taking her medication. Stop her whenever she starts acting out behaviors like we discussed. Encourage her in the hope of succeeding. If you help her, if I help her, she will succeed, all the way to a better life. She has the potential to complete her education, hold a job, get married, and even have children, if she desires. Help me help her, Mrs. Thome. Help me help her."

Mrs. Thome was in a highly emotional state. Tears were welling up in her eyes. Due to her sensitive condition, she felt compelled to broach the subject of the doctor's seemingly harsh demeanor with her daughter.

"One more thing, Doctor, I don't suppose doctors are very personable people but you seem to be very hard on Patricia. Are you always so hard on your patients?"

"I am intentionally hard on your daughter, Mrs. Thome, and everyone else too. While Patricia is under my care, it is important for her to see me as someone who can help her. She must regard me as someone with absolute authority. It is only through that kind of authority that I can assert my ideas on her. The only way she will implement my ideas is if she respects what I have to tell her.

"Patricia is a lovely girl and I like her already, but if I become too amiable with her, if I become her friend, she will not regard what I say in the same way she would under the strict authoritative relations that exist between a doctor and his patient. Believe me, everything I'm doing, I'm doing with Patricia's best interest at heart."

"I . . . I . . . believe you," Mrs. Thome said reluctantly. "I just want my little girl to get better."

"She will. I assure you of that," the doctor said assuredly.

Responding to the pain he knew she was feeling, the doctor placed his hands on her shoulders to touch her. Mrs. Thome responded by wrapping her arms around him and allowing herself to cry. To ease the awkward moment, the doctor remarked jokingly. "Well, now that I no longer have you under my spell, what shall I do?"

The doctor waved goodbye to the Thomes as they exited the back lot. He began a slow approach around the building and entered through the front. Once inside, he took a good hard look at Annice, busy at her desk. He moved toward her and commented when he noticed she was working on a backlog of insurance paperwork. He deliberately picked up one of the forms, and pretending interest, began perusing it intently.

"I'm glad I don't have your job," he announced while placing the form back on its pile.

"I see you're all done for the day. How nice for you."

"Actually I have one last patient," the doctor stated firmly. "And I'm seeing her this very moment."

Annice really was his final patient of the day just as the doctor had intended. Under the ruse of being uncertain as to how much time he would have needed for the Thomes, he had allocated the remainder of the afternoon for them even though he had really intended to split the time between them and Annice. He had forty-five minutes left to give her. He thought it wise to act facetiously by telling her that she was his last patient; that way, she would probably not wise up to it.

"Where are the Thomes?" she asked politely.

"They left as soon as we got back," he replied. "Mrs. Thome insisted."

"How is the young girl?"

"She had a good first lesson today. I'm expecting she will improve a great deal in the time to come."

Having Annice open up a conversation about Patricia was opportunistic for the doctor. It gave him the opening he needed to discuss how people overcome their problems in general. Time was running out. Still hovering in front of her desk, he quickly commented, "You know, Patricia is a very determined young lady."

Before Annice could comment the doctor continued.

"The result of her success will come about largely because of her own ability to be obstinate toward failure. Most times in life we determine our happiness. The problems we face become our successes or failures by the decisions we make in response to them. No problem is insurmountable. We have only to decide for ourselves what course of action we are going to take in regards to it. It's all about philosophy.

"It's especially true when it comes to dealing with afflictions of the mind. We have choices about how we live outside ourselves as well as inside ourselves. In our minds. The two are not unalike. Let's say you have a job you don't like . . ."

Annice interrupted him by smiling up at him as if to indicate that the task before her was one that he was speaking about.

"I would offer to help you but I don't really know what to do," the doctor admitted.

"Anyway," he began again. "If somebody doesn't like what they're doing in life, they have the power to change it. Some things, of course, are harder to control than others but it is still possible to change them."

Intentionally, the doctor held his next thought in abeyance so it would have its own impact on her.

"If you are in a bad relationship, end it!" he snapped.

Annice felt the sting of his words in her heart. She deferred to him a look that told him she did not wish to discuss her own personal problems. It did not matter, though, for the doctor had said what he wanted to say albeit in the guise of speaking in general terms. Satisfied that he had rankled her, he continued.

"The best example I can give is how we fight a bad habit. Some are very hard to control like cigarette smoking, spitting, or cursing. Each of these requires our utmost perseverance to control and conquer. The key to it all, however, is confrontation. If we confront ourselves with the unhappy truth about what is wrong in our lives and we keep that confrontation constant, we are better able to assert ourselves toward bettering ourselves."

At this point, Annice had several papers completed which required the doctor's signature.

"Sign these please," she said as she held up the appropriate forms.

The doctor complied, taking out his Cross pen from his shirt pocket and applying his signature on the necessary places Annice indicated. The doctor could tell from her nonchalant attitude that she was not hit as hard as he thought from his mentioning her spousal problem.

"She's not going to get off that easy," he said to himself. He decided to escalate matters.

"By the way, I never did ask you what you thought about Dr. Jeanne."

Annice stopped her typing and looked directly at him.

"I really liked her. I think she is a wonderful person and she is so personable with her patients. The work she's doing must have a profound impact on their lives. She is what I would call a real-life lifesaver."

"I think she's a step above that," the doctor replied earnestly. "I would go as far as to call her a life-savior!"

Annice smiled.

"You know, she too, advocates a person's self-reliance. Most of the children she deals with have even come to her attention through their own ability to survive. And even though our lives are not as compromised as those she deals with, I think the philosophy being stated is one that is valuable to us all. Wouldn't you agree?"

Annice did not respond, but somehow the doctor felt as though she had taken it to heart. Rather than arouse in her a disdain for his suggestive line of questioning, the doctor deferred to another matter.

"By the way, Dr. Brain is coming here on Friday. Here, I have his number," he said, handing her an old business card. "The new number is the one written in blue ink. Could you please call him sometime later today or tomorrow and give him directions? He's never been to my office before. He will be coming from Reading."

The directions Annice had called in for the doctor suited him perfectly, in fact, they were so expeditious that the doctor managed to arrive early even though he had departed late. He arrived at the office at precisely 1:50, ten minutes ahead of the scheduled two o'clock.

"You are the model of efficiency, my dear," Dr. Brain stated cordially, once he had made Annice's acquaintance. "I could certainly use someone like you at my office—someone with brains as well as beauty."

Dr. Haefner, whose last patient had departed and whose door had been left ajar, heard Horace's adulation of Annice and came bounding out of his office.

"She'll never leave me," he rebuffed his old mentor. "She's mine for life."

"Hello, good doctor!" Dr. Brain shouted, elated at seeing his old friend.

"Hello, Horace," Dr. Haefner returned with enthusiasm.

Dr. Haefner showed his colleague into his private office then paused to confer with Annice.

"Annice, if any calls come in please take a message. Unless it is an emergency please do not disturb us. Dr. Brain and I are collaborating on a matter of personal importance to me."

"Certainly," Annice responded, smiling.

Before joining his friend, Dr. Haefner whisked into the little break room adjoining the main office area and collected two cans of cold Coke from the refrigerator and a fresh bag of the jelly mints he enjoyed so much. When he entered his own office, he found his colleague busy scrutinizing the personal effects displayed around his room.

"You remind me of a police dog, sniffing about, searching for even the tiniest particle of evidence. Tell me, good doctor, or better yet, enthrall me with your acumen."

"Relax, my old friend. I have engaged myself in a mental exercise concerning you. On the way down here I began a formulation in my mind, a formulation about you, about who you are in relation to who you were back all those years when I knew you so well. I just wanted to see if what I hypothesized about who you had become was true."

"Wouldn't that be somewhat easier to do based on having spent time in my company rather than having tried to piece together a synopsis of who I am based on what personal belongings I stash in my office."

"I'll be the first to admit that the evidence is exiguous and I can't come to an explanatory conclusion about who you are—who you have become—but one thing is certain. The items that you have carefully selected to be your companions while here in this office speak only the truth about you; whereas you, with your bright shining mind, could easily cover up some truth about yourself. A lot can be detected of a person by what they surround themselves with."

"That's very interesting, Doctor. Tell me, what do you see about me in all of this?"

"You are, essentially, as I knew you all those years ago. You haven't really changed except that you may have accentuated your interests in the things that were most important to you. Like most people, you surround yourself with your identity. Let me expound on that. You are a precise and accurate person. I can tell by the order in which you keep things. You are learned. The books that you keep on your shelves are testimony to that. Most are esoteric and would not be given the opportunity to rest on a shelf space that could be given over to much more interesting reading. Your knowledge extends beyond the eruditions of your profession, for your volumes cover all of the sciences and philosophies that humankind has attested to."

Dr. Brain paused for a moment to open his can of Coke and quench his parched throat. Dr. Haefner did too.

"One other thing of note, Doctor. You are extremely interested in your past. Take for instance this old newspaper article you have framed and hung on your wall. It faces you every day as though it holds some special meaning."

Horace stood before it and began reading the article in a voice that could only be slightly heard by Dr. Haefner. Dr. Haefner allowed his friend the time he required to read the article before he began to explain anything about it. But before he could, Dr. Brain suddenly turned toward him and announced, "This is James! This is the James from your childhood! The James you have not reconciled with in your mind!

"He has a high hold on you. You keep his memory alive and with you every day. Why else would you keep this article displayed so ostentatiously on your office wall, facing your desk, instead of in some old scrapbook tucked away in a seldom-used closet? I remember the conversation we had about him when you visited me recently. So is this what's troubling you, my boy?

"You admonish yourself for not having prevented all of the tragedies that befell him during his lifetime. Possibly, you believe you could have even prevented his death. You knew him even better than any real patient you ever had, and still, still you could not find a way to help him. And you hold this against yourself. What do you hope to do, bring him back to life?"

"You get an A for your evaluation of me, Doctor. I am intrigued beyond repair about my former friend; his life, his death. But understand why; he baffled me more than any other soul I ever knew on this earth. If I could ever understand him, I could decipher the mystery of anybody."

"How can you ever hope to understand someone who's dead? You know, it takes a great deal of interactivity to get to know someone well enough to evaluate them and help them. And that kind of interaction is best achieved with someone you can have conversations with—you know, like someone who's alive."

"I disagree, Doctor. What about case files? We study those; in detail, I might add. Don't we adduce things from those—those whom we have never personally known?"

"But you're forgetting, the information compiled in those studies was actually derived from someone who actually knew those people. So the information, albeit indirect, is as accurate as the day it was first put to paper. References are a good source of knowledge."

"James is more than a reference to me. I was an integral part of his life for ten years. My mind is full of instances, scenes, scenarios, depictions, interactions, involving him and me, and I am fully aware of them as though they happened days instead of years ago. I have my memories, Doctor, and they are sharp and clear as a blue sky."

"Are you so sure that blue sky isn't just a little clouded? How can you remember exact details, exact words, and therefore have an exact depiction of the context, of the meaning of your interpretations? Remember, you weren't a psychiatrist back then, and although you undoubtedly took a great deal of mental notes about your unusual friend, you did not, I assume, write down any thoughts or feelings you had about him at the time. Did you?"

Dr. Haefner didn't answer. It wasn't because the answer was no but more because the intellectual path he had taken them on was not the one he wanted to go on. He had thought that maybe there was some possible way to lead into the real discussion he wanted to have, but there wasn't. So he just blurted it out.

"James is not dead, Doctor!"

Horace was startled by the bold statement but he held himself in abeyance for several moments, purposely waiting for his esteemed colleague to follow up with an esoteric explanation of his hard-hitting statement.

Neither man moved. Dr. Haefner leaned farther forward on his desk and repeated his words. His eyes were blazing and Dr. Brain thought he looked like a man possessed. He was afraid that any moment the good doctor might jump across the desk or possibly jump up to the ceiling light and swing from it. Then he might, in a fit of insanity, throw himself through the window and fall to the concrete walkway below, hitting his head hard. "Oh, the blood, the gore," the doctor lamented.

Nothing happened in the seconds that followed. Both men were thinking of something to say.

"What do you mean James is not dead, Doctor?"

"I saw him!"

"You saw him. You mean he didn't really die?"

"No. I don't mean he didn't die. I went to his funeral. I saw his dead body."

"Then explain what you mean."

"I can't, except to say that James, his body, his spirit, his spiritual body exists."

"That can't be."

"It is!"

Dr. Brain was becoming increasingly concerned for his friend. Was he being consumed by guilt? How extraordinary that someone could become so intensely depressed over the death of someone other than a loved one. James was not his brother. It's true that friendships kindled in childhood can be of a profound nature but not to the point of this.

"I know what you're thinking, Doctor," Dr. Haefner said, smiling, "but I am not obsessed with the death of James. James did die. He was a dead man but I saw him, nonetheless. It was just days ago. I was awakened from my sleep when I heard music playing from my stereo. I went to the living room. After turning off the music, I checked the house to see if someone had gained entry. After establishing that there had been no entry, I was readying myself to go back to sleep when suddenly, to my disbelief, I saw James, or rather an apparition of him, sitting comfortably, leaning back, knees crossed, in my favorite recliner. The image soon faded and he was gone. I . . . I . . . . thought he was trying to make contact with me.

"Before that night, I admit I kept him on my mind but that was only because of the clinical value he held for me as a psychiatrist. It's also true that I do strongly regret the fact that I was unable to establish a lifeline to him during our childhood and adolescence. But that in no way has made me go mad over it.

"Doctor, you would have had to know him yourself to understand what fascination I hold for him."

"Seems to me that he's the one who holds a fascination for you," Dr. Brain replied facetiously.

"True."

"Doctor, I think I may have something of an explanation for the way you feel about your old friend. James, it seems, was an overwhelming person. You, at a very young age got caught up, or rather, entangled in, his extraordinary life. Its complexities were too complicated for you understand, try as you did. You have tried ever since to unravel this mysterious person whom you knew too well. But don't forget that when you were actually part of his life you, *you*, were only a young boy yourself. Thinking back, do you really believe you possessed the knowledge and the skill to successfully help someone so obviously in need of special help? Do you really hold yourself in such high esteem?"

"You are right, you know, about that aspect of me. I have considered that myself. But still, Doctor, if you only knew him, as he was, I believe he would have a hold on you too. If I were to diagnose him today, I would have to make up a new term to classify him. I would call him an ephemeral man or someone who suffers from ephemerality. James was an actor, and on the broad stage of the world on which he played, he played a different character every day. He was literally a different person every day of his life. It didn't matter if any two days were exactly the same in what he did or who he was with, he was not. And his characters were extreme. They—"

"I'm sorry to interrupt, Doctor, but don't you see you're doing it to yourself right now?"

"Doing what?"

"Don't you see? You can't get past the confusion that you carry over him. It's because you perceived him from your perspective when you were too young to really understand him. I believe you when you tell me he was the greatest challenge to your intellectual mind; that's why, because you weren't able to establish yourself over him when you were young—you were young too. Your mind wasn't ready to cope with the calamities you faced with him. That's why you can't let go. He's the mystery that can't be solved."

"So you don't believe I saw him?"

"I don't know. You could have conjured him up yourself."

"And if I didn't?"

"If you didn't, what? I have no experience dealing with ghosts myself. You will just have to deal with it yourself, but call me if you do encounter him again; better yet, compile some evidence that you are being contacted from the great beyond after all. If you claim you can see him, capture him on film. Then I'll believe you."

Dr. Haefner didn't know if Dr. Brain was being a little patronizing with him, so he changed the context of the conversation. He asked Dr. Brain, hypothetically, "If James actually did appear to me as I portend, why would he come now, after all the years he's been gone?"

Dr. Brain indulged him.

"Time is a component of life. It holds merit only for the living. It places boundaries upon us, upon all living things. We are born, we live, and then we die. But what could the dead be bound by?"

"They are bound by existence."

"Yes, only by existence. Not time. So then, if they do continue to exist they could not be bound by something that is defined by the cycle of substance called living matter. They would simply be and they could do anything with it they wanted."

"But that still doesn't explain why he would only come back now."

"The 'now' you speak of is only relevant to you."

"Then why at all?"

"That's the question. Why at all?"

Silence fell between them as they each pondered the question in their minds. Finally, Dr. Brain spoke up. "Well, I guess you'll have to ask him that if and when you see him again. Try to make verbal contact. See what happens."

It was getting late.

"Well, Dr. Haefner, we will have to resume this interesting conversation another time. I'm famished. I don't suppose you could direct me to some good eating establishment, could you?"

"Better than that, I'll accompany you," Dr. Haefner replied. "Just allow me a few minutes to get my things put away."

Knowing that they were going out to partake of the pleasure of some scrumptious local fare, the mood became lighter. Once Dr. Haefner was ready, Dr. Brain commented, "Now, it will be just the two of us for dinner, right? No spooks, specters, or ghosts, right?"

"The dearly departed have no itinerary to follow. They are bound by nothing except existence. And if they already exist, then they are not even bound by that, remember, Doctor?"

Dr. Brain laughed. He then turned the conversation over to a more delicate matter. They were on their way out of the office when Dr. Brain said directly, "Why on earth did you ever turn down the opportunity with that delightful woman who waitresses at the Pagoda? Carol?"

What Dr. Haefner wanted to say was that his heart belonged to someone else and that she was sitting right here in the very room where they stood. Instead, he made the popular excuse that he did not want to be involved in a long-distance relationship, a complaint many people make when they are in a situation similar to his.

Annice, making ready to leave herself, heard their abbreviated conversation and inferred from it that Dr. Haefner was slightly involved with another woman. She was infuriated.

As the doctors left, she acknowledged their departure with a handshake from Dr. Brain and a soft touch on the shoulder from her doctor. While they were walking the hall, she further heard something about sampling of fruit and a response of, "Why should I eat grapes when I can have wine."

Take a chance on Me

Alone at home, Annice sat on the edge of her bed. She thought about the office incident, about what the doctors were saying. Her intuition told her that there was reason to believe another woman was vying for Christopher.

She got up and stood before the closet mirror. "So, Christopher's got an admirer," she proposed. "She's probably twenty-five, dirty-blonde, dirty mind . . ." She stopped herself.

Annice began to undress. When she was naked she viewed herself fully. She began scrutinizing her body, her attributes. For a woman of forty she thought herself still extremely attractive. Her proportions were nearly perfect. Her breasts were supple, her legs slender, her stomach as flat as when she was twenty, mostly due to the fact that she had never conceived a child. The perception of herself in her exposure was that she was still a very desirable woman possessing all of the superficial qualities that would make any man glad he was a man.

But despite all of the reassurances, Annice felt insecure. Despite having access to her beloved forty hours a week, it wasn't the same as having one hour's access to him in his free time. Her rival, if there was one, had the advantage. She plopped down at the foot of the bed and began asking herself questions. Was Christopher really the type of man who would succumb to the wiles of a woman half his age? If she were only younger. If she were only free. She took a hard disapproving look at the wedding ring on her finger, stuck there as if it were a part of her appendage. "If only I were single," she lamented.

Her reconciliation came about due to the recognition that with age came experience, maturity, and depth, all qualities she knew Christopher relished in any relationship. "That well I do know him," she considered.

Then Annice came to the hard fact of her husband, a word she seldom if ever used anymore; a word which choked her whenever she inadvertently evoked it. This battle will have to be fought on two fronts, she thought, one in vying for a divorce, another in keeping the doctor's attention on the possibility of "us."

Abrogating her relationship with her hus . . . with *him*, would be difficult, to say the least. Making herself available to Christopher would be fraught with even more danger. If she made herself so desirable to the doctor, he would want her and it wouldn't be right for her to refuse him after she had enticed him, and that, she knew, would lead to having an affair—adultery!

It was hard for Annice to contemplate what she would be getting herself into. Her strict Catholic upbringing forbade her from even considering a divorce. And add to that, adultery! The thought brought a queasy upset to her stomach. The crosses she would and might have to bear as a consequence for the changes she wanted for her life would be excruciating. And even worse was the fact that she would have to do it alone. There was absolutely no one in her circle of family and friends whom she could count on to help her. Christopher would but his help depended upon at what point she involved him, at least in her divorce. She would have to guard against involving him too early. He too had been brought up a strict Catholic and it might be reprehensible for him if he found himself cheating with someone else's wife and then taking her for his bride. If he felt the least responsible for that then someday it might come back to haunt their relationship.

"No!" Annice said adamantly. "I will do this alone!"

Then another possibility played itself out in her mind. What if she went through a divorce only to find out that Christopher had no intentions for her? What if the flirtations she occasionally received from him now were only due to the fact that she was actually protected, at least morally, from anything more. Maybe he felt safe in that assumption. Annice pondered that thought for a while but finally concluded that it was still better for her to be free of her abusive husband.

She reminded herself of some of the recent abuses she had received at his hands: the punches, the rapes, being spit on. No, despite any implications she would find her freedom.

She paused. Visualizations of her wedding day danced through her head. How happy they were. The contradictions of then and now made her cry. She cried and cried and soon scrunched herself up on her bed and fell asleep.

The day was growing late when she finally emerged from the crumple she had been in on her bed. The sun was setting and inside her room it was difficult to differentiate the darkness from the many shades of furniture around her. She slowly propped herself up from the ball she was in and immediately began ironing out sore, stiff muscles in her legs. As she started to get up, a thigh muscle in one of her legs began to cramp and she collapsed on the floor beside the bed.

Just then she heard the unmistakable sound of the downstairs phone ringing.

"That's odd," she thought. "Why would the phone be ringing down there and not up here?"

She struggled, with her pained leg in tow, to investigate the peculiarity. Making it to the night table, she leaned over and picked up the receiver. For some reason the phone ringer had been turned off. The instant she clicked it on it rang.

"Hello," she automatically said.

"Hello, Annice," a reticent voice answered.

"Christopher!" Annice declared.

"Yes, it's me," he responded. "I'm sorry to call you so unexpectedly but I . . . but I . . . I sensed that you were a little upset at the way Dr. Brain and I left the office today—you know, so abruptly. It was rude. I didn't want either of us spending our weekend being mad at each other when a simple apology could spare us our feelings."

Although Dr. Haefner was being sincere in apologizing for the hasty departure he and his colleague made in her presence, the doctor's real intent in calling was to find out whether Annice had been privy to the personal remarks Dr. Brain had made in regards to the Pagoda waitress while they were leaving.

"It was sweet of you to call but your leaving the way you did didn't bother me at all. I knew you were probably just trying to get your friend back on the road before rush hour, or something similar to that."

"Yes. Yes, that's it," the doctor pronounced.

The doctor made his apology again, and as Annice listened, she caught sight of the fact that she was stark naked, lying stretched out across the bed while speaking to the one man she wanted most. It was exceedingly amusing for her to listen to him go on and on about how sorry he was for offending her while she was picturing them being together at that very moment. She tried but couldn't help herself from erupting into laughter as the peculiar scenario played on.

The doctor discontinued his prattling at once and actually had to hold the receiver away from his ear due to Annice's loud, spontaneous laughter. He waited until she was silent.

"That's the first time I have ever been laughed at while attempting to reconcile differences with someone," he said humorously.

"I'm so sorry," Annice responded.

Though the situation seemed very humorous to her, Annice was also very aroused. It was an opportunity to go beyond flirting, which in her opinion was something they very much needed. She gathered up the courage as she prepared to disclose to him what had made her laugh.

"I wasn't laughing at you, Chris. It's just that you caught me at an awkward time. You see, I'm lying here on the bed." She paused.

"Yes, you are lying there on the bed," the doctor repeated.

"I'm lying here on the bed . . . entirely naked."

Annice was glad she had said it but felt embarrassed. To help her ease her conscience, she began explaining the whys and wherefores of her case.

"You see, after I came home I had gone upstairs to undress and change outfits. I managed to get half the job done when suddenly I felt so tired I decided I would take a little nap on the bed. Suffice to say that little nap turned into a three-hour sleep. Just when I awoke, the phone rang and it was you, with me still in my birthday suit."

"Talk about timing," the doctor responded forwardly. "I'm certain your birthday suit is your most becoming outfit of all."

The doctor felt a tinge of alarm after his comment but his mind went immediately to work assuaging his apprehensions with the assurance that Annice had actually been the one who initiated the awkward conversation between them.

"Thank you," Annice said of the compliment.

A prolonged silence began to grow as neither knew how to proceed. The doctor finally took the next bold move.

"You know, Annice, in a way I'm glad you're not mad about anything but in a way I'm not."

"What do you mean?" she said in a rebuking voice.

"What I mean is that, well, if matters were not settled between us I would have asked you to have dinner with me tomorrow so we could work on the rectification of this circumstance."

Annice, thinking he was probably being sincere but also detecting a hint of the insincerity she so desperately wanted, thought hard and fast how to capture some time together with him.

"How about breakfast?" she blurted out at once.

"Breakfast? For real? Are you allow . . . I mean, are you able?"

"I can have breakfast with you if I want," she said sternly. "Can you meet me at the Holiday Inn on Route 501?"

"Isn't that a Chinese restaurant?"

"Yes, the, Eastern Garden, but they also serve a regular breakfast, lunch, and dinner. Sometimes I like to go there for Sunday lunch with my sister Amy. The place is always so lively with all the tourists. Have you ever been there?"

"No, but I've heard that the food is exquisite."

"Then tomorrow it is," Annice said firmly.

"What time would you like me to meet you there?"

"Let's eat around 7:00. I get hungry early."

"Seven sounds fine. I'll set my alarm for 6:00."

The breakfast was arranged, though each of them knew that it was more than a breakfast that had been arranged. A flurry of thoughts and feelings induced them privately as they each began to grasp what had just taken place between them. Annice, anxious for tomorrow, wanted to end their conversation so she could begin her personal preparations.

"Oh, and by the way, thank you. Thank you for being concerned enough about my feelings to call me. That was so sweet of you."

Chris wanted to say more but relented except to say, "I do care for you."

The doctor clapped his hands with joy after the call. He tried to remain calm about the unbelievable success he had with her but he couldn't. He paced nervously back and forth between the kitchen, the living room, and the hall, like a tiger in a cage. He felt enormously proud of his overachievement. At one point, he paused in the living room and stared over at his favorite recliner and recalled the appearance of the apparition of James.

James was the master stud, the stud who never dudded with women. Initially, he was the coolest of all the cool with every woman he ever met, at least until they had a chance to find out who he really was.

James, as it actually happened, was the one responsible for letting Annice know how much Chris cared for her. He had taken it upon himself, without Chris's knowledge, to call her up one evening and confess Chris's true feelings to her. The doctor remembered. But it also made him remember how suspicious he was back then that James had called Annice at other times, and who knows what he may have said to her. His relationship with Annice had been so up and down that it could have been attributed to James's antics. "He could have been responsible."

Infuriated and surging with elation, the doctor stared directly at the chair and shouted.

"How about that, Cuz! How about that! I've got her now and there's nothing you can do to screw things up for me! Nothing!"

The doctor stood in perfect silence. His right fist was clenched and waiting should James decide to appear. He didn't know what good it would do to take a swing at a ghost, but it felt important just to let him know he was ready. Minutes ticked off the clock. The doctor's adrenaline subsided. The emotion which had overtaken him eased and now cautioned him. He had tempted fate—something he rarely did.

Pride comes before a fall, volleyed back and forth between his mind and his lips.

"I need to be extra cautious. There's so much I don't know yet. If James has found a way back into the realm of the living, he may possess the capacity to interfere with those he has made contact with. I can't take any chances. It's scary enough just thinking about him being around in any capacity."

The doctor wanted to forget James for the moment. He needed to keep his attention on tomorrow and what it could bring. In that regard, he exited the living room and trotted down the hall to reach his bedroom. He entered. The first thing he did was set the alarm clock for early the next morning. Next, he opened the walk-in closet, stepped inside, and yanked on the chain to turn on the light. He immediately began perusing the contents of the spacious alcove for the proper attire to wear for his intended rendezvous.

While still fully engrossed in the detail of selecting his next-day's wardrobe, he alertly heard the faint sound of a far-off phone. Reacting, he retreated from the closet's confines and proceeded in haste toward the inveigling rings. Halfway to the kitchen he stopped short. In that instant he realized that the phone extension beside his bed was not ringing too. Evidently it had been turned off and forgotten about. He paused as though he should return to it but just as quickly he pressed on to deal to the more immediate concern of just answering the phone.

During the last part of the interrupted dash, he anticipated it would be Annice calling again. He thought so. Excitedly he picked up the phone, cleared his throat, then elicited an expectant, "Hello."

The hello that followed indicated that it did indeed belong to a member of the opposite sex, but much to his chagrin, it was not Annice. Dejected, he responded with a subdued inquiry as to who he was speaking to. At first, the unfamiliar voice faded into the background and now he heard two distinct voices conversing for their own sake. After a few moments the confusion passed and an abrupt-sounding voice spoke up.

"Chris, it's me, Mark."

"So, what do you want?"

"So, what do I want? What kind of a question is that to ask? I'm your brother like it or not. Do I need to have a special reason to call you?"

The doctor heard the humor in his brother's pretended annoyance and decided to advance it further.

"Little brother, you know that I'm always of a serious mind and as such I fully expect others are too whenever they wish to engage me in conversation. Time is a precious commodity and should not be wasted by trivialities."

"Oh, just shut up," Mark replied tartly, not taking the bait. "Anyway, the reason I called, or should I say, the ridiculous reason I called was to harass you about your new girlfriend."

"Well, she is a girl and she is a friend."

"Knock it off, smarty. You love her. You've always loved her. So tell me. Did you?"

"Did I what?"

"You know what."

"No, actually I do not."

"Yes, actually you do."

"If by that you are referring to the physical aspect of our intimacy, choose your words in reference to the question. Did I hug and kiss her? Did I ask her to spend the night? Did she? Did we take our relationship to the next level? Are we now a couple?

Mark was bursting out with laughter.

"You said it, brother. All of the above."

The doctor broke into laughter now too.

"You know me. I never kiss and tell."

"Come on. You can tell me."

"Yes, obviously I could but I won't."

"OK, smarty, your not telling me tells me everything. I'm glad for you, brother. Now, maybe you'll be more personable with people and maybe socialize more. Like the other day. Say, by the way, when are you going to host another party? You could bring Annice, snicker, snicker."

"Maybe soon. I would have to arrange for it first then set a tentative date. We'll see."

"Hold the phone. Hey, Michelle, get me a dictionary. Christopher's using his high-Q again. How do you spell tentative?"

The doctor and his brother always ended their conversations in a jovial mood. He hung up the phone and was about to resume his task when unexpectedly the phone rang. Believing it was his good-natured brother again, he picked up and answered in a mundane voice a solemn, "Hello."

This time the doctor recognized the voice at the other end. It was Dave Cool. The doctor, still influenced by the jovial mood created by the previous conversation he had had with Mark, produced a remark conducive to what he considered a Dave attitude.

"Hey, Cool, how's it going?"

"Hey, Haef, it's definitely going. I just called to catch a rap. Just the other day a weird thing occurred. Kelly and I were out at Park City, and guess who we ran into? John and Betty Boller. Can you believe it? The last time I saw them was at James's funeral, at the viewing. When I first looked at them I didn't even know who they were. They recognized me. I stopped and talked to them for a while. They asked about you too. I reminded them what you did for a living. Mr. Boller commented that it was too bad that you came into your profession a little too late to help Jim. When was the last time you saw either of them?"

"Same as you before the other day. 1990."

There was a pause in the conversation, indicating that neither one wanted to continue the pertaining dialogue. Dave quickly remedied the awkwardness by referring their discussion to another matter.

"Hey, Haef, Kelly and I are arranging to rent a condo down at the shore in late July. We are getting the place for two weeks. Why don't you come down one of the weekends?"

"Where?"

"Ocean City, Maryland."

"That's where I like to go when I go to the shore."

"Hey, there are a lot of hot babes down there," Dave said enticingly.

"I know. I know. But it's one thing to admire the scenery and entirely another to become part of it—if you know what I mean. Most of the women down there are much younger than me. I wouldn't stand a chance."

"Oh, come on. Don't be a wimp. Besides there's a simple solution to your problem: BYOB, bring your own babe!" Dave elicited with a shout.

Before the doctor could respond, he heard Kelly's voice in the background calling Dave, asking him if he was ready to leave. Dave answered her tersely to wait a minute then turned back to Chris and insisted for him to come. After that he made a quick goodbye.

The doctor contemplated the idea of bringing Annice to the shore. It sounded good but he was dubious she could make it. It's hard enough for us to see each other for just an hour outside the office. How would it be possible for her to sneak away for a few days?

Returning to his room, he had already abandoned the idea and went back to his task of preparing to see her in the morning. No sooner had he reentered his closet when the phone rang for the third time. He began a mad dash to the kitchen again, when he suddenly stopped short of the threshold to his room. Even though the ringer was off on his bed phone he could still use it. How silly that he didn't use it the first time the phone rang. Just because he hadn't heard that phone ring he never thought to pick it up. This time he did.

This time he was received by another familiar voice at the other end. It was Dr. Jeanne Detweiler.

"Dr. Haefner," she said in an appreciative voice. "I'm so, so glad I got hold of you. I've been calling for a while and I was beginning to feel like I was trying to be the twenty-ninth caller or something."

"Dr. Jeanne, it's always nice to hear your voice. I'm sorry about your trying to reach me but I'm happy to say that you've finally hit the jackpot."

"Doctor, I must apologize for calling you at your private residence but I felt it best considering the sensitivity of the discussion."

"Don't worry. It's no imposition."

"It's about Annice Colby. I wanted to talk to you about her."

"Tell me everything."

"When she visited me the other day I sensed a great deal about her. I purposefully took her with me when I went on my afternoon rounds. I wanted her to see the result of harm done to other people at the hands of abusers. I also wanted her to see their recovery and I wanted her to know just how important they were to their recovery. She was very concerned about their condition and care and I could see she had taken it to heart. We talked. We talked about the individual causes of all of my patients' conditions and then we talked in general about abuse and how important it was for anyone being abused to seek help. I didn't come on too strong though but it went against every fiber in my being. I believe it's best to just come out with it. But at least Annice now understands me for being related to this type of thing and she knows that I'm someone she could come to if things really got bad."

"Bravo, Doctor. You did a great job. I think what you need to do now is just stay in touch with her. Send her a 'thinking of you' card or invite her out for lunch some day. I'll accommodate her. Annice is precious to me and she needs our help."

With a smile on her face that the doctor could see through the phone, Dr. Jeanne inquired, "Dr. Haefner, do I detect a more than professional interest in you for her?"

The doctor, in his embodiment of love for Annice, had inadvertently spilled the beans to Dr. Jeanne about how he felt about her.

"It may be fate, Doctor. I loved her when I was growing up. I love her now. But I have never done anything to attest my love to her. My conduct for her has always been above reproach."

Dr. Jeanne ignored the doctor's defenses. She was charmed by the intrigue of the scenario that existed between them.

"Your love for her is intrinsic, Doctor. You have been living the life of someone with a lead role in a soap opera."

"Yes, except nobody's selling any soap," the doctor responded facetiously.

"If you love her then you are the answer," Dr. Jeanne pointed out.

"Yes, I know. At least I know I could be if she lets me. To tell you the truth, I don't know very much about her personal life despite the fact that she works with me. She's very reticent about divulging facts involving her relationship with her husband."

"Then become more than a boss to her. Relate to her. This may be a chance of a lifetime for you."

"You're absolutely right. As a matter of fact, I'm meeting her tomorrow morning for breakfast. We had a little misunderstanding at work and we're going to work it out with a little coffee."

"I'm not so sure you're not in for a little coffee, tea, or me," Dr. Jeanne responded.

"Wouldn't that be lovely," the doctor responded.

"Well, good luck to the both of you."

"We'll be needing it."

Breakfast and Bed

Saturday. Alerted by his internal clock, the doctor was awake just a minute before the alarm went off. After resetting the alarm to its usual time, he hastened out of bed and headed into the bathroom to shower and shave. Next, he proceeded to dress in the selected casuals he had appropriated for himself the night before.

On him, once he was dressed, was a pair of loose-fitting beige pants, a cream-colored buttoned shirt, and a flared yellow tie. He looked at himself carefully in the bathroom mirror and admired the unassuming way which he had attired himself. While he was still reflecting on his good looks, he happened to notice a pimple on his face, and immediately took out a small bottle of dermatological soap so he could scrub himself clean. The doctor, though forty years of age, was still prone to breaking out with acne once in a while.

After the cleansing, the doctor stepped into his bedroom to consult with himself on which cologne to wear. On the top of his maple dresser, he had a vast collection of various colognes, all of which he had received as Christmas gifts over the past years. It seemed that cologne and new ties were the choice gifts given to psychiatrists by their family and friends. His tie collection, because there were so many, were now kept in an opened box in a corner of the walk-in.

The colognes that were his favorites he arranged in a row at the front of the dresser where he opened their tops and afforded each one a sincere sniff. It occurred to him as he went down the line that he did not know which fragrance Annice might be partial to. In all the years since she had worked with him at his practice, she had never once commented on his choice of cologne. This thought bothered him until he convinced himself that it didn't matter, and that it was understandable in that it's not something a married secretary would say to her boss. But that didn't mean she didn't think to compliment him.

After careful consideration, he chose his personal favorite, English Leather. He dabbed suitable amounts on his neck and under his chin and even a little on the inside of his collar and cuffs for a more long-lasting effect. The last thing the doctor did was fasten his wristwatch on his left wrist. He glanced at the time. If he intended to arrive at the Holiday Inn on time he had to leave promptly. The location of his home on Pinnacle Road, situated in the rolling southern hills of Lancaster County, was a thirty-minute drive to the city. He hoped, as he entered his car and drove away, that the early Saturday-morning traffic would be light. It would be even better, he speculated as he drove along under the spreading branches of tall trees that lined the old two-lane road, if I actually arrived early. In situations like these, women liked to think that the men were the aggressors and therefore be first to initiate every act.

A short time later the doctor was pulling into the parking lot of the Holiday Inn. The Eastern Garden restaurant was adjacent to the main lobby of the inn and connected to it on the inside by huge glass partitions, which when opened, opened up to a long wooden footbridge, surrounded by artificial tropical plants, and suspended over a real pond into which patrons threw coins.

The doctor was elated at being punctual and he hopped out of his car with the zest of a college-age boy out on a first date. When he raised his head toward the restaurant-motel lobby, he unexpectedly came face-to-face with Annice who appeared to have been waiting for him for some time. She looked upset.

When they met, the doctor was stunned by her appearance. Annice looked better than she had ever looked before despite all of the nice outfits she had worn while in the office. The difference being that these clothes, adorning her head to toe, were for his eyes only.

She was wearing a white silk blouse with a single pink rose stitched above the right breast. She also had on a pleated purple skirt which came to just above her knees. To match the outfit, she wore light-purple socks which jutted out only three inches above the crest of her white shoes, a style unfamiliar to her admirer.

"Is this really you?" the doctor asked in an astonished voice.

"I'll take that as a compliment," Annice expressed with anxiety.

"I adore the way you look," the doctor continued in a flattering display of words and wonder.

"Thank you," Annice replied. "We had better go inside now. I don't want us to lose our table."

"Our table?" the doctor responded in a dumbfounded tone.

"Yes, I'll explain once we're seated."

The doctor followed Annice inside the restaurant, across the wooden bridge, past the artificial plants, and over to a secluded corner of the restaurant where their table was waiting.

In a polite manner, the doctor pulled out a chair for her.

"I've been here for some time already," she explained. "It was the only way. Sometimes I come here with my sister Amy. Today I invited her here for coffee and coffeecake. They make absolutely scrumptious coffeecake here. I needed to spend a little time with Amy, purposefully, so I would have an alibi as to where I was and who I was with this morning should I need one. My husband makes me tell him the who, what, where, when, and why of everything I do. This way, most of what I might have to tell him would be the truth, and the truth is so much easier to tell."

The doctor situated himself closer to Annice by moving his chair toward her. He did not want anything she was saying to be heard by the strangers around them. He did not want to delve into the particulars of her contrived contingency plan but he did admit, at least to himself, that her precaution was ingenious. Rather than escalate that matter, he wanted to concentrate solely on her.

"Have you already eaten then?"

"Only one cup of coffee and a serving of coffeecake."

"I'm starving. I'm counting on what you told me about this place to ease my empty stomach."

Just at that moment, a waitress arrived and asked if they were ready to order. Annice was glad to see that she had moved far enough away from the table she had shared with her sister and that this was a new waitress waiting on them. Annice asked for a few more minutes.

"I'll be back," the waitress responded.

"OK, Christopher. Open up your menu. I think you will be pleasantly surprised to find various breakfast items you would enjoy."

The doctor perused the menu and gave several approving nods as he read it. Annice already knew what she was ordering and just waited. When the doctor was finished, he placed his menu beside him on the table.

"I know what I'm having," he spurted out.

"I know what I'm having," Annice countered.

When the waitress returned they each ordered. Annice ordered a stack of light, fluffy pancakes, syrup, butter, and a cup of coffee. The doctor ordered country-style potato and eggs, toast, and a cup of hot cocoa.

"Now you know one of my weaknesses," the doctor grumbled playfully.

"What's that?" Annice asked.

"My fondness for anything chocolate to drink. I can't go a day without drinking something chocolate. You name it, I drink it: Nestlé's Quik, Hershey's syrup, Ovaltine, Bosco. Those are my milk mixtures. In water there's Carnation, Swiss Miss, Borden. I like them all."

"That's strange," Annice declared. "Then explain why I don't see you drinking anything chocolate at the office?"

"That's quite simple. If I did, if I drank any more than I already did, at home or on the road, then, then, I would have to consider myself addicted. And doctors are always keen about crossing that boundary line, my dear."

"So you drink it exclusively at home and in restaurants, I see."

"You see, too much of anything is no good. Excess is wasteful.

"Too much of anything," Annice smiled saying.

The doctor, anticipating her reference, replied with a wry smile, "Well," he admitted, "there are exceptions."

Once the selections were served the couple sat and ate quietly. The expectations they had of each other were greatly surpassed and it made their meal taste all the better. All through his potatoes and eggs and with every bite of toast, the doctor kept telling himself how incredible Annice was. Annice, who had been a bundle of nerves prior to Christopher's arrival, was now confident that she could do the unthinkable and make a move on the man she wanted.

Once the main portion of their meal was over, the couple sat contentedly and engaged in ordinary conversation about each other. Then, without warning, Annice announced, "You know, I am not happily married."

Her sudden burst of confidence in him took the doctor by surprise. He did not know how to respond. Instead he folded his hands and waited for more. Annice checked his reaction then continued past the silent interlude.

"I mean simply this. I'm not in love with my husband any more; in fact, I don't even like him. He's a brute."

The doctor leaned forward and uncrossed his arms.

"But you've been with him for such a long time. Are you sure that you're not just temporarily upset with him or something?"

"Are you kidding? Christopher, trust me on this. The only feelings I have left for him are contempt and loathing," she answered sarcastically.

Annice's voice was carrying beyond the realm of their privacy. Other patrons, nearest them, began ogling the couple. Annice noticed and stopped talking.

"Maybe this isn't the best place to hold this kind of conversation," the doctor stated politely. He consoled her by reaching across the table and grasping her hand which was holding the coffee cup.

"Yes, you're right," Annice concurred. "Let's go someplace else."

"How about back to the office?" the doctor suggested innocently. "We could have a nice private discussion there with no one to interrupt us."

"No, not there," Annice countered. "For me the office is not conducive to a personal discussion of this nature. There, I would feel like one of your patients, and this isn't about that. I don't want you feeling like you're helping me professionally."

The doctor had a burgeoning urge to suggest that they go back to his place but he reluctantly decided against it. Now that he had made it all this way he didn't want to push.

"How about if we just leave here and take a nice walk on the grounds?"

"OK," Annice replied.

After getting their check, the couple got up from the table and went to see the hostess. There the doctor paid for their breakfasts. Departing the restaurant, they walked down a wide hall with openings on both sides, one was for the bar; the other, a game room. Halfway down the hall, Annice reached over and grasped Christopher's hand. Exiting the building, they came across a quaint garden rise that abutted the back wall. They strolled through a flagstone walking path which led from one end of the garden to the other.

Beyond the garden there was a central courtyard enclosed on three sides by three two-story sections of buildings which comprised the inn's room complex. In the interior of the central courtyard was a large swimming pool, complete with a diving area and a single low diving board. When they entered the courtyard, they noticed an employee busy cleaning the pool with a long vacuum-cleaning hose.

"This looks like a nice place," the doctor commented as they strolled down a pavement alongside a section of ground-floor rooms. "I still favor going to a nice Holiday Inn rather than spending my money at one of those bed and breakfasts that seem to be all the rage these days."

"You don't like bed and breakfasts?" Annice asked with a cute smile on her face.

"No, not especially," the doctor returned in a matter-of-fact way.

"Well then, how about breakfast and bed?" she returned wryly.

For a brief moment the doctor did not consider the comment anything other than ordinary. Then it occurred to him what she had said. They had just reached the intersection where the one long side-section adjoined the backside-section of the building complex.

Without saying a word, the doctor led them to an alcove at the end of the longer section of building. Fitted into the alcove were a soda machine and an ice machine. Both machines were busy humming, keeping their contents cold on the warm spring day. They stopped. Trembling, the doctor placed his hands, first on Annice's shoulders, then down along her sides, and then steadied them courageously on her hips. His heart was pounding out through his chest.

"No more kidding between you and me. Do you want to make love to me?"

Annice leaned into him making full contact. She looked at him intensely.

"I want you."

This would be easier than he thought. All of the earlier inhibitions concerning the unfaithfulness and selfishness on both their parts diminished in the heat of passion. Neither could refuse the other.

Eager to begin, the doctor contemplated what to do. "The best thing," he suggested to himself, "would be to take her home to my place. There we would have the privacy we need to complete our need." Before he could divulge his plan, Annice boldly whispered to him, "Why don't we get a room?"

"Here?" he questioned back at her. "Won't that look kind of obvious, us having breakfast here then ordering up a room?"

"No one will know," Annice said assuredly. "The motel and the restaurant operate independently of each other. No one from the motel has even seen us today."

"There might be a problem. This is the beginning of the busy season. There might not be any rooms available. And unless there was a vacancy from last night, a room that might be available wouldn't be available until after the morning, after the room has been adequately serviced."

Annice's adrenaline was pumping. She was too worked up sexually to be thwarted by a process of procedure.

"I have an answer," she claimed. Making sure there were no peering eyes pointing in their direction, she said, "Let's find a room that's already been serviced. By checking, we'll be able to tell if someone has checked out or not, or if the room isn't occupied, we'll be able to tell that too. Like you said, if we do find an empty room it's unlikely the motel would allow anybody in until later. Most check-in times are between 11:00 and 2:00. That gives us a couple of hours at least."

"A couple of hours to couple," the doctor returned spontaneously. "Your plan just might work."

"Come on, let's hurry. Let's go around to the back building, up on the second level. It's the most obscure area. Let's try our luck there."

It was a risk, but for the sake of sex, it was a risk both were willing to take. As they climbed the steps to the second level, the doctor was already hard at work trying to think up excuses to tell the maid, the manager, or some irate tenant, about their inadvertently entering the wrong room.

Annice led the way. As she moved cautiously up the concrete steps, the doctor looked over the shape of the breathtaking body that would soon be revealed to him.

Around the back of the building, halfway down, there was a maid's cart, unattended for the moment. It was full of cleaning supplies and assorted tissue boxes, hand soaps, and toilet paper. The couple stopped short of the room being pertained to by the maid and maintained the pretense of a married pair interested only in taking in the view of the little meadow which served as the backdrop of the inn. Out of the corners of their eyes, they watched patiently as the young girl moved freely back and forth from the stationary cart to the room.

After an uncertain amount of time, Annice and the doctor finally ventured toward the room. Passing by slowly, Annice peered inside and ascertained from her view that the room was no longer occupied.

"There's nothing left behind in there. This one's ours," she quipped.

Leaving the room behind, the couple proceeded down the remaining extent of the second-level walkway and turned back into the courtyard area again.

"Wait a minute," the doctor stated suddenly. "I just thought of something. She'll lock the door after she's done. How will we ever get in?"

"Good point," Annice said retrospectively. "I neglected to think of that."

Both their minds went blank. Neither had anticipated the fact that vacant rooms would be locked. They walked and talked their way around the entire upper, inner level before Annice, determined to find a solution to their unexpected predicament, thought of a possibility. She stopped and turned to her accomplice.

"Wait! I have an idea! I remember the room number. It's 223. I'll just simply go up to the front desk and ask for a key. I won't explain anything else. I won't give them anything to contemplate. I'll pretend I'm in a god-awful hurry and ask for a spare key to our room. If they ask me for identification I'll just root through my pocketbook, supposedly looking for my ID, then, in the act of finding that, I'll pretend to find my key and leave. Either way no one would be the wiser."

"Sounds like a plan. Do you want me to go with you?"

"No! Most definitely not! It's better if only one of us tries. That way they can't fall back on you if they decide to question me."

Annice went on and the doctor waited anxious and nervous as to whether she would succeed. He watched as she turned into the same stairwell they had come up; then he followed her as she proceeded back into the main building.

Several minutes elapsed and the doctor began to worry. Against her wishes he was just about to descend the stairs and see what had happened when suddenly she appeared exiting through the garden rise, visible from his vantage point. When she spotted him, she extended her right arm high in the air. Dangling from her fingers was a key.

The doctor met her while standing at the top of the landing.

"You are something!" he remarked admiringly.

"Follow me!" she proclaimed victoriously as they marched off to the back of the building again.

When they arrived, the maid's cart was gone, moved farther away. The attendant was working in a hurried pace, and during her brief interludes at her cart, she appeared inattentive to the mysterious couple loitering around room 223. After the maid had made several quick trips to replenish supplies, Annice decided it was time for them to make a move.

"It's now or never," she said boldly.

She inserted the key into the door slot and turned it. The door opened.

"Quick! Get in!" she insisted.

Once they were both safe and secure inside the room, Annice turned and relocked the door.

"This is just for precaution."

"What happened at the front desk?" the doctor inquired with a curious stare.

"Everything happened better than expected," Annice announced. "To my advantage there was a long line. The wait would have been tedious so I took my chances and butted in line, acting as if my life depended on having an immediate resolution to my conflict. Twice, the clerk attempted to question me further but I was abrupt with him and insisted that he please hurry."

"You're absolutely wonderful," the doctor proceeded to say, though he was feeling a bit overwhelmed by the events taking place.

"You're wonderful too," Annice shot back. Then she turned to him provocatively and kissed him on the lips.

No further words were necessary. Their actions now were dictated by a process of attraction between a man and a woman which has been played out countless times before, a process which culminates in the completion of sexual desire.

The kissing itself could have gone on for hours more had the two lovers had the time. But their purpose was exact. Though their inclination was to take their time, they had to complete their love-making within a certain time constraint.

Acting hurriedly, Annice excused herself and fled to the bathroom. The doctor, meanwhile, undressed and situated himself on one side of the freshly made queen-sized bed. When Annice returned, she was wearing an alluring pair of purple panties and a matching bra. These she wanted her lover to have the pleasure of

removing himself. The foreplay continued. Lying beside him on the
bed, Annice gazed at his body, firm and muscular. Christopher gazed
at Annice. She was as amazing, as beautiful, as a woman could be.
They were ready for each other. They had been ready for all of their
lives but only cheated from it by the circumstances of their youth.
Now they were here, in a place so unexpected, but ready to make up
for the mistakes of the past. All of their hopes had now come to be.
All of their dreams were now coming true. It was a fantasy.

No one could ever imagine what the effects of a twenty-five-year
wait can do to a person's heart. It hardly ever happens. Emotions were
carried to the extreme. They were not shy. They were not awkward
with each other. They had rehearsed this event thousands of times
in their minds and now they were able to play at parts they knew
so well. What they had believed for so long was now becoming a
reality—they were made for each other! They had been, since the
first! Tears fell from their eyes as their hearts finally met. Nothing like
it had ever happened before!

A Step in Time

The couple parted, though each would have easily preferred to stay together. In retrospect, though, the doctor was glad that their departures were urged on by Annice's insistence. Usually it is the man who leaves the trysting place first, but this way the doctor knew he would be spared the accompanying awkward excuses which sometimes had to come up in situations like this.

Before they actually left, the doctor had them each drive their vehicles to a seldom-used end of the back lot. There they stood outside their cars and talked for a few minutes until Annice insisted their time was up. After opening up her door for her, the doctor reached over and pulled her close. They kissed, softly, then passionately, as though they were putting on a fireworks display and the end came only after a grand finale.

No goodbyes were spoken. Words were not necessary.

Now that it was over, the doctor had no regrets. No second thoughts pervaded his conscience. Being with Annice, the splendor of it, told him that. It didn't matter now that they had not been together from the first. It didn't matter.

Because he was already in the city, the doctor decided to check up on things over at the office. There he could find solace, a place to interact with himself about the new and unusual circumstance. He drove his Buick into the back parking lot which he seldom used and parked it in a spot nearest the building. After entering through the front, he locked each door behind him.

The morning escapade had been tiring, and the doctor, depleted of his energies, tendered himself a handful of jelly mints and poured himself a cupful of Cherry Coke from a bottle in the break room. There he remained, eating his mints and drinking his Coke. When his respite was over, he sauntered over to Annice's desk, sat down on the edge of it, and contemplated their new beginning.

"Everything will be different now."

While dallying around the desk, it occurred to the doctor that he was now, officially, a part of Annice's life, personally. Their recent intimacy provided it. Now, his helping her with any personal problem would be welcomed and expected, would it not? He thought of the revealing photos hidden in the desk and he wanted to retrieve them.

He went into the drawer where Annice had stashed them previously and began searching for the familiar envelope. Now he could view them with a new purpose. He felt he no longer had to guard himself against their discovery. Their twofold depictions had a stronger personal meaning to him now.

The revelation of her personal beauty was now flesh to him. He had tasted the forbidden fruit. He could look upon her now and know he had tasted the cup of her wine. It was no longer an illusion. The passion they had shared was like a blossoming rosebud, now freed to grow and bloom into love.

The revelation of her tragic abuse, her tainted flesh, was as to him. It required retribution.

Despite a frantic search, the photos could not be found. The doctor furthered the search by investigating the remaining drawers in the desk, but the packet was gone. After what he considered a thorough search, the doctor sat back in her chair and pondered the situation. Had she intentionally moved them? Why? They would be safe anywhere in the office. And as far as she was concerned, he did not know they even existed. The doctor's frustration grew as he rifled through the plethora of forms, files, and folders for a second time. The one daunting theme that ran through his mind was that the photos were evidence, evidence that may one day be needed for the purpose of extricating Annice from her marriage. It's hard to claim abuse without evidence. If there was any hope that they would be together, together as man and wife, they would need to be able to prove Annice's allegations that she was being abused.

After the second search, the doctor, dejected, slumped down into Annice's chair for an interlude of quiet reflection. Thoughts ran through his mind. "Obviously she's taken them. But where? If she took them home that could be terrible. There's always the chance that he would find them. And then what? He'd destroy them and we would lose our best evidence. And not only that. If he found them, he would most likely brutally beat her for having taken them. I'll tell you what. If he ever so much as lays a hand on her again, I will go over there and see to him personally. I will beat the . . ."

The doctor's solemn vow was surreptitiously interrupted by a faint disturbance coming, he thought, from his private office. He looked over at the door which had remained locked the entire time he had been in the office. He regarded the sounds as he sat motionless in the chair. It was hard to ascertain what, exactly, it was.

"Maybe it was just a squirrel who managed to get to one of the window ledges and was having a hard time getting back down," he wondered.

The noise continued. To offset his curiosity, he got up and crept slowly, quietly, toward the door. Just as he had known, the knob wouldn't open when he tried it. Cautiously he slipped out his keys from his pants' front pocket and inserted the proper one into the slot. The door was unlocked. Courageously he turned the knob. The door opened.

The doctor was aghast when he looked inside. Straight ahead, standing only a few feet away, was the same apparition he had seen at his home. It was the apparition of a man. It was the apparition of James.

The ghost appeared to turn to him and smile then it disappeared. Nothing can prepare a person when they actually encounter a ghost. There's no experience like it. A ghost is not a being. A ghost is not a thing. It is more a 'thieng', a combination of the two.

"If this turns out to be true, I'll advocate that a new word be added to our English language," the doctor thought loudly. The doctor moved over to the area where the 'thieng' had appeared. He faced the wall where the ghost had been looking. Then it was clear—the position, the amused look. James was reading the article. He was musing at the write-up about his death. "That proves it! That proves it was James! No other ghost would be so interested in reading an old newspaper article. James is back!"

A chill ran up the doctor's spine, a chill that grabbed hold of him, refusing to let go. It was as though the ghost were holding him in place. To diffuse his fears, the doctor began shouting out past his fear, "James! James! Where the hell are you!"

The room remained unchanged. The doctor was beyond his fear and began moving about, shouting out challenges to James to appear. "Why don't you come out chicken!"

Then the doctor's mind regarded another aspect of James's arrival among the living again.

"What kind of power must it take for someone who's dead to actually come back to life, even in the manner of a ghost?" It was a great disappointment to the doctor that James did not appear upon command. "I wonder what controls his comings and goings.

"Others must try. Very few make it. Very few. Consider the vastness of the number of people who have populated the earth and weigh that against the number of believable sightings. It must require some special force or power to transcend the realms. The great Harry Houdini proclaimed to all the world that he would do it. And he did not. Despite all his conceit, all his tricks, all his illusions, he failed. Today he is dust! But James! Consider him. He was no Houdini. He was a failed human being, but in death he refused to face oblivion."

There was a profound silence as the doctor rendered himself to the task of identifying the great mystery.

"James was a nobody. He was nobody. Yet he found a way. He has cheated death."

What to do. The doctor, without taking his eyes off the spot where James had stood, slipped quietly behind his desk and surrendered himself to his chair. He folded his arms as he lounged backward to begin thinking. He was no paranormal expert but he was willing to become one if these unexplained sightings of James continued.

"What should I try to accomplish with this? The first thing should be to establish the fact that I made contact. But the evidence is all in my head. I need proof, proof that I really saw him, proof that it really is James."

Then he had it. He reached into one of the lower drawers of his desk and retrieved the Lancaster phone directory. He immediately went to the yellow pages where he began perusing through the S section.

"Security, security, security," he sounded out as he scrutinized the security and surveillance sections.

The proof the doctor wanted was to be had. Just as Annice had done, he would validate his ghost sighting by taking advantage of technology. If he could see his ghost, then couldn't a camera as well? He called Eye on You, a local security company in business since 1985. Fifteen years in business was proof they were established. During the discourse that followed, the doctor requested a state-of-the-art surveillance system which included twelve-hour interval audio and video tapes on a closed-circuit monitor. The monitor could even be kept at his private residence where he would be able to watch and listen in on what goes on in his office, where the system would be placed.

The Eye on You assistant promised the doctor that within one week the new system would be installed.

"The sensitivities of these new systems are truly remarkable," he told the doctor. "The video has such clarity you can even detect pimples on somebody's face, even from a distance of ten feet. The audio is so heightened you could hear a moth fluttering around the room."

"Good then," the doctor responded.

He thumped the thick book back into its drawer.

"It's too bad I just couldn't call the Ghostbusters," he announced to himself amusingly.

The doctor was on a roll. He suddenly thought of another action to further his plans. He took out the phone directory again and this time began perusing last names and numbers and scribbling those which supported his cause. After paging through the white pages, he had handy a list of people, friends, and family, of those who knew James. When the list was complete, with the exception of one, it included: John and Betty Boller, James's adoptive parents; Deb, his sister; and one of James's closest friends after the abrogated friendship between James and the doctor, Jules. The one person the doctor couldn't find the whereabouts of was Dave Boller, James's half brother. But the doctor was certain that by contacting the others he would acquire it.

Judging from the day, Saturday, and the time of day, almost noon, the doctor realized that it would be hit or miss in his attempts to make contact with any of the individuals. His goal would be to see, without coming right out and asking, if anybody had any of the same experiences he had and had James appearing to them.

The Bollers still lived there on North Pine Street. When the doctor began dialing the number, he was amazed to realize that he still remembered it. It was still the same.

When contact was made, a person on the other end answered in a gruff voice, "Who's there?"

It was awkward starting out. For a moment the doctor was at a loss for words, taken back by the brash demeanor of Mr. Boller. He had forgotten.

"Hello, Mr. Boller. Hello. It's me. Christopher Haefner. You know? Jim's old friend. Do you remember me?"

"Yes, I remember you. You're Pip? Right?"

"Yes," the doctor replied jovially in response to hearing his old nickname. "I hope my call did not interrupt anything important you were doing."

"No."

"I'm sorry to have called you out of the blue like this but I needed to talk to you. As you may or may not know, I'm a psychiatrist and I'm compiling data to do an extensive profile on phenomenal cases. One of those cases is about James. Although James was never one of my patients actually, I would still like to use information about him as a reference. James was, as you know, an unusual person and he had a personality that no one could understand."

"So what's your point, Pip?"

The doctor refused to allow Mr. Boller's attitude to inveigle him into saying harsh words. Instead, he carried on as though he were speaking to a learned colleague.

"What I need is some valuable background information about Jim. Professional papers should always be accurate and I'd like this one to be as accurate as possible."

"James is dead. Why bother writing anything about him now?"

"Though James is dead, I'm still trying to figure out who he was. If I can piece together why he was the way he was, I can use it to try to help others like him. And the more information I have about him, the more I can piece together, sort of like a puzzle. The more pieces you have to put together, the more you can see of the picture."

"OK, Pip. What do you want?"

"OK then," the doctor returned in a firm voice. This is what I'd like . . ."

After reciting the list and before allowing Mr. Boller to comply, the doctor went on to say, "James was the most complex individual I ever encountered. But through his complexities, I learned enough to pique my curiosity to the point of becoming a psychiatrist. It was through knowing James that I became enticed enough to enter into this prestigious profession. The unfortunate part of all this was that I only earned my PhD just before his death; otherwise, I would have used the privilege of my profession to help him. So, now I would like to use him to help others."

The doctor's concern for James hit Mr. Boller hard. In the ten years since his death, he and his wife had hardly held a conversation about him. To them, James's death was a fitting end to a life of destructiveness and the bitter frustration that enveloped all those that were part of his life. They loved him because they considered him their son. They hated him for the person he turned out to be. They hated themselves, for what parent can not help but feel partly responsible for who their child becomes? A measure of things gone wrong came over John and he wanted only to get things over with.

"Tell me what you want to know once more and I'll help you," he relented.

The question-and-answer period went on for a few minutes, with the doctor acting the part of an interviewer superbly. When the session was about over, the doctor finally asked the one question that mattered most, "When was the last time you had contact with him?"

The phone went quiet. The doctor grew anxious, wondering whether he had hit pay dirt. Had he? Had the ghost visited his adoptive parents? But all too soon the discouraging reply resonated through the phone.

"I'm sorry, Pip. I really can't remember. Maybe it was a couple of weeks before his death."

The doctor believed him.

Next on the calling list was Jules. Jules was an old friend of James's who came around frequently to smoke pot and drink beer. At one point between 1980 and 1990, Jules had moved to south Florida to work on a road-and-bridges project connecting the Florida Keys. He returned sometime before James's death and the two had reestablished their relationship. Jules now worked as a tow-motor operator for a building-supply company. This information he had heard, inadvertently through conversations with his brother. The doctor, himself, had not seen Jules since the time of James's funeral. The call would be awkward, but nothing compared to talking to John Boller.

As the call to Jules was in progress, the doctor clunked himself in the head lightly with the receiver end of the phone. He had totally forgotten to ask Mr. Boller about the whereabouts of Dave Boller, his son, and James's half brother. "Stupid, stupid, stupid me," he repeated to himself. Unless he could get the number off one of his other callers, he would have to go through the ordeal of calling back.

"What's up," was the jocular expression the doctor heard when the phone was picked up.

"Is that you, Jules?"

"Yes it's me," Jules replied. "Who's calling?"

"It's me, Christopher Haefner. Remember me?"

"Remember," said Jules, sounding bewildered. "I see you all the time. Every time I visit my parents. Well, not every time. You have your office right across the street from their house, on James Street, right?"

"Yes, that's me. I didn't know you knew. How come you never came over and said hello?"

"Because I don't need a shrink. I'm happy with my life the way it is," he laughed.

Before the doctor had a chance to delve into the delicate matter of whether or not Jules had had contact with a ghost, he heard the voice of another man calling out to Jules. They were apparently in the same room and the conversation could be heard in its entirety. Apparently, Jules, and his brother, Jeff, had been playing poker. It seemed that one of them was winning big, the other, losing big. The stakes were high! Like so many times before, it was about money! The doctor, listening to all of this, decided not to inquire of Jules the information he originally wanted. Instead he asked about Dave.

"Jules, I called because I wanted to know if you knew how I could get in touch with Dave Boller."

"Oh, that's easy. Dave's in jail.

"What!"

"That's right. It happened about a year ago. Dave and some other guy were caught stealing parts off a car in a junkyard after dark. Dave got sentenced because it was his second or third offense."

"I can hardly believe it, to think, mild-mannered Dave Boller. I can't ever remember him getting into trouble with the law while he was growing up."

"Believe it."

"Where can I contact him? Lancaster County Prison?"

"That's right."

At that point, Jules's brother was growing increasingly impatient at spending the duration of the phone conversation doing nothing. He pleaded to Jules to come back. Jules, anxious too, told his old friend he had to go.

"Look, I'd talk longer if I could but I have somebody waiting for me here. I have to go."

The doctor felt deeply troubled at hearing that Dave was spending time in jail; Dave, who he had always been so proud of while growing up in the midst of a maelstrom; Dave, who had never become corrupted by his older half brother; Dave, who was a rock.

The doctor debated the status of the situation as he intended it. He had spoken to the Bollers—zilch. He had yet to speak to Jim's sister Deb. He had gotten information off of Jules about Dave. Nothing about James had been revealed in any of the contacts. And what about Dave? Much as he disliked the idea of getting involved with someone in prison, the doctor knew he had to. He knew he had to do more than a phone call too. Knowing Dave and feeling sorry for him, the doctor could never forgive himself if he quick-called then let it go at that. It would probably be a godsend for Dave too—spending all those hours, day after day, locked up like that.

The doctor paused for a time to think about Dave's personal life.

"He doesn't have a wife or children. And who knows how often the Bollers go to see him. Gosh, it's a good thing I did forget to ask John about him. That would have made things even more difficult."

Thinking more about the impending call, the doctor regarded the fact that he was, indeed, a healer. This brought him to a higher realm.

"How can I refuse an old pal like Dave, especially in the circumstance he's in? I will do it," he said determinedly.

Next on the calling list was James's older sister, Deb. This was the sister James had sexual relations with when they were younger. While in his late teens, the doctor had been with James and his sister only rarely, a time or two over at her First Street apartment, and a time or two when she dropped by Pine Street. Most often on those occasions, the doctor's encounter with Deb lasted only a brief period of time. Often, James and his sister spoke privately. It was entirely possible that whenever they did get together they got together sexually. Their sordid sexual relationship probably lasted far beyond the specific encounter witnessed by the doctor when they were young. It could have endured up until James left for Louisiana to marry his fiancée. Probably.

In his mind, the doctor knew all to well how James would have been able to seduce his sister and keep her in a state of perpetual seduction. He acted out the key scenario mentally.

"What difference does it make now anyhow? We've already done it."

"I know, Jim, but it doesn't seem right. I feel funny about it."

"You don't feel funny while I'm doing you. Then you keep saying, 'take me, take me.'"

"Shut up, Jim. I don't want any of the neighbors to hear you."

"The only way to shut me up is to take care of me."

"Jimmy, no!"

"You're a liar! You don't care about me! The first time we did it you told me you would always be there for me! You said always! Always means right here, right now!"

Deb started to cry. The first time she had relations with her brother she did so because of the sadness she felt for him. Her parents had given him up, and because she was part of that, in the sense that her life remained intact, she felt guilty. To make up for it, she had allowed James to have sex with her, to give him some pleasure in his disadvantaged life.

"All right, Jim," she finally conceded. "But you're not going to like doing it. I'm not feeling good."

"I don't care," Jim said without objection. "I have you just where I want you."

The scenario played out in the doctor's mind and whether it was fact or fiction didn't really matter. James had been clever enough to strike at his sister's vulnerability and use it to his advantage.

Still undecided whether to call Deb, the interlude continued. The doctor stared at the open space in front of him where only minutes before the apparition had appeared. He stared ahead as though he were applying his mind to try to conjure up James himself. His determination grew the longer he applied himself to the task. Finally he relented. James could not be forced into being.

Reluctantly he picked up the phone and dialed Deb's number.

"Who's this?" came the rude reply from some woman cracking gum.

"Deb?"

"Yeah?"

"Deb. This is Dr. Christopher Haefner. You probably know me as Pip. I knew you through your brother James."

"Yeah, I know you," she now said more clearly. "You and Jim used to be friends. I saw you at the funeral. That was one of the worst days in my life. I couldn't stay. I couldn't stand seeing Jim's body lying there, breathless. I was just too freaked out by the whole thing."

There was an unexpected abeyance in the conversation as the doctor sensed that Deb was becoming upset. He waited for her to calm herself.

"He was killed by someone and you know it, Pip! How could he be strangled to death by a seat belt while rolling over a fifteen-foot embankment? And she, she walks away without a scratch! Tell me, Pip!"

"I agree with you. The circumstances surrounding James's death are suspicious. I, too, questioned it when it happened. I actually called James's fiancée and talked to her about the incident. And I have to say I didn't really believe much of what she told me. The problem was that the accident occurred so far away. Nobody here could get involved in the investigation or what there was of one."

"I believe that the authorities there didn't take Jim's death seriously. He wasn't from around there. There wasn't anybody down there advocating for the truth on Jim's behalf. And it would have been too expensive from this end to do anything about it. In the end, I think the Bollers just realized that James was dead and there was nothing anybody could do about it."

"The motive, I believe, as far as the Louisiana authorities were concerned or should I say unconcerned, probably came from checking Jim's background. They realized they had one dead male, thirty years old, no wife, no children found, and whatever family he had had not represented themselves with a show of force. They assumed, correctly, that there would be no contention to their discovery. Also, in doing some fact-finding about James, they probably came across his criminal record. He had that incident in Florida and numerous altercations with the Lancaster police. To them, then, James just wasn't worth any special consideration. They closed his case just as quickly as the law allowed."

Deb was somewhat satiated by the doctor's considerable interest in James's unfortunate death. He believed as she believed that there was more to the story.

"Hey, I'm sorry, Pip, I never asked why you called."

The doctor was sorry he had called, not for his sake but for hers. She was obviously very upset at having to recall the events of her brother's death. It was one of the worst days of her life and he had brought it back. If she had encountered him or even thought she had, the doctor was certain she would have told him. He tried to think of another excuse for having called.

"I called to ask you if you had any photographs of Jim. I was appalled to realize, only recently, that I had no memorabilia of when we were young. All I have are memories."

The doctor's excuse worked like a charm. Deb was overjoyed that one of Jim's oldest and closest friends had felt so remiss at not having something tangible to remember him by.

"Why of course I can find something for you," Deb said in a brightening tone of voice. "You come over to see me sometime and we'll do it."

"I will," the doctor promised.

"Three strikes," the doctor declared after the phone conversation with Deb was terminated. "That leaves only one. Dave Boller, I need you to be my ace in the hole."

The prison call would be the worst, for Dave, for him; but because of the lackluster response so far, the doctor felt like finding out once and for all if anybody had made contact with James.

The call had to be made. When the doctor got through, he found himself speaking to a prison official who informed him, upon inquiry, that Dave Boller was currently being incarcerated at the facility. After a short abeyance, another official got on the line and again asked the doctor to state his name, occupation, and purpose for calling. After giving the second official the relevant information, the doctor was again put on hold. This time when the line was reconnected, a harsh, uncaring voice answered.

"Hello," Dave called out abruptly.

"Hello. Dave Boller?"

"I hope so," he returned sarcastically.

"Dave, it's me, Dr. Haefner, Pip."

"Pip? What the hell are you doing calling me? How the hell did you find out I was here?

Dave's terse questions made the doctor feel uncomfortable but he pressed on with the situation. He told Dave how recently he had been reconnecting with friends from the past and that the account of Dave's tragic circumstance inadvertently came up in a conversation. Telling Dave the truth but not the whole truth, helped very little to appease the tension he felt, for he knew he had called for a selfish reason, inappropriate considering Dave's suffering. To alleviate his guilt, the doctor assured himself that he would, despite his uneasiness, visit Dave personally.

It never came up. The doctor never mentioned James to Dave. The two men enjoyed their conversation so much that the doctor didn't want to spoil it. And besides, he told himself, he had already promised Dave that he would visit him tomorrow.

After the call, the doctor thought about Dave. He noticed how easily Dave's crusty exterior crumbled once they began opening up to one another.

"I like Dave just like I liked him before. It's a funny thing about friendships. Friendships must be kindled. But if one had been kindled for such a long time so long ago, it can be stoked into flame again. Time, no matter how long, can not put it out. And the same can be said of love."

Blonde and Beautiful

All that evening the doctor was in agony. Spurred on by his rejuvenated feelings about friendship and love, the doctor had slipped by Annice's home on his way home. Much to his utter disbelief, he had caught a glimpse of her and her husband standing together on their front porch. They were holding each other affectionately while talking.

He pondered it over and over in his mind. What did it mean? Seeing them together made it seem as if the events of the early morning had never taken place, as though it were a dream. Could it be that Annice was just using him, seducing him, seeking pleasure?

The doctor pounded his fist down on the kitchen table. "No, no, no," he repeatedly told himself. "Annice would not, could not, ever enter into an illicit affair. In the entire span of her discontented marriage, she had remained faithful, even to that brute of a husband. There was proof in that. Her infidelity with me had not been entered into lightly. We, who had been together for years had only now succumbed to our love." These rationalizations helped the doctor overcome his anxieties and fears. Several times he picked up the phone and dialed her number only to have Leslie pick up. The doctor spoke not a word, not wanting to infuriate him and leave Annice suspect. After the third attempt the doctor gave up. Apparently Annice was forbidden from answering.

That night the doctor was restless in his bed. He tossed and turned and was awakened from bad dreams, dreams which always centered on her. She was at risk. She was in peril. She needed rescuing.

The next morning his mind was jittery. It was like his brain had been put in a freezer overnight then placed back into his head. He could not keep coherent thoughts. Annice was on his mind and in his heart. Love had taken over.

Despite his high state of anxiety, the doctor kept to the routine he needed to keep himself and his day settled. He prepared a breakfast of scrambled eggs, toast, and hot chocolate, and ate while sedately reading the Sunday news. He remained tense, however, desperately hoping that at any moment the phone would ring and Annice would be there telling him how much she loved him and wanted to be with him.

The call never came. At 1:30 in the early afternoon, the doctor turned out of his stone driveway en route to the Lancaster County Prison. He would meet his obligation despite his troubled heart.

Approximately thirty minutes later, the doctor arrived at the prison. He guessed at what was the appropriate entrance by the proximity of other cars and parked in accordance to them; he had never been to the prison before. After getting out and locking his car, he walked briskly to the building's center and entered through a set of huge doors.

Immediately upon entering, the doctor encountered a county sheriff who was manning a metal detector.

"Step right this way, please. Place any metal objects in this basket and pass through the sensor."

After passing through, the doctor reached another checkpoint. At this station, another sheriff awaited.

"I'll need your identification and you need to state the purpose of your visit."

The words spoken by the sheriff were spoken in a way that offended the doctor, spoken to represent authority. To rebuke the obnoxious man the doctor whisked out his identification card, displaying his photo and credentials. The diminutive man winced at the doctor and motioned for him to proceed.

The doctor proceeded down a central hall and was met by a prison guard at a station. Here he told the guard who he expected to see and the guard asked him to wait while he placed a call back to the main cellblock. Several minutes elapsed before an escorted prisoner was brought to the station.

"Prisoner 15799, reporting for visitation," the attending guard attested to the counter guard.

The counter guard had the doctor sign in as a visitor assigned to prisoner 15799 on the day's date, and reminded them of the specified hours for their association.

When they met, the doctor was confronted by Dave's ghastly appearance. Like most of the Pine Street pals, he hadn't seen Dave for years. And like most of them Dave had taken a wrong turn on the road of life. And it showed. From their first moments together, the doctor could see that Dave had had a rough time of it. He was of average height and had a ruddy complexion. He looked several days unshaven, judging by the stubby appearance of his facial hair. The hair on his head was thin, straggly, and balding. It almost matched the color of his skin, pale, bland, orange-red. The oversized orange jumpsuit he had on hid his obviously obese body. When they first met and smiled, the doctor saw that Dave was also neglecting the care of his teeth. Both front teeth were the color of smoky quartz, probably dead, and if they were not, would be before Dave was.

"Good to see you, Pip," Dave addressed his old friend.

"Good to see you," the doctor returned amiably.

The guard at the desk was staring at the two men, indicating subtly that they were interfering with his work area, and should promptly move on. Dave noticed and knew and suggested to the doctor that they should get the hell out of there. He gave his guest several options of places inside the four walls, where they could go to talk. Of the available places, the doctor picked the cafeteria. Once there, they seated themselves at a long uncovered table and sat across from each other.

"So, what brings a special person like you down to a dump like this to take a few licks on an old sucker like me?"

The doctor was feeling a bit apprehensive. Dave's personal condition made him feel sorry for him. Now that he was here, it seemed rather callous to just say what he had to say but he felt he had no other choice. It would be worse to beat around the bush and talk of other irrelevant issues and then charge back with the astounding news of Jim's ghost followed up by inquiring if Dave had also had an encounter with him.

Dave could see that something important was troubling the doctor. The doctor, by taking too much time with his thoughts, had made himself vulnerable to Dave's suspicions.

"Come on, Pip, out with it. I can tell you got something on your mind."

The doctor remained quiet for a moment, squirmed in his chair, and looked around them, making sure they were located far enough away from any would-be listeners. Then he looked across the table at Dave.

"Dave, I'll get right to the point. I came here to see you but I also came to talk about James."

"You came to see me so you could talk about Jim?" Dave said in an abject, bewildered voice.

"Hold on, Dave. Before you get mad, hear me out. I was making inquiries about your brother . . ."

"You mean half brother." Dave interrupted.

"Yes, half brother," the doctor corrected himself. "Anyway, I was making inquiries about your half brother when I stumbled across that fact that you were being detained here. When I found that out, my mission here became twofold. I wanted to get in touch with you to see how you were doing, and I also wanted to speak to you regarding James."

"Well, what is it? What do you want to speak to me about that jerk?"

"Dave, you're not going to believe what I'm about to tell you but here goes. James is back. Twice in the past two weeks I have been visited by his ghost. Twice, mind you. If it had only been that one incident I may not have believed it myself, but two times, two times I'm a believer."

There was a sustained silence that fell between the two seated men as each came to an understanding of what had been said. Finally Dave raised his head high toward the ceiling and declared poignantly, "Oh my God in high heaven! God help us! God help us all!"

"Do you believe me?" the doctor asked in a dubious voice.

"With Jim, anything is possible," Dave declared.

"Believe me, Dave, I'm not making this up. I don't want James around either, especially as a ghost. He was scary enough in real life. But just the same, he's returned and I'm trying to find out why."

"What do you want me to do about it?"

"Have you seen him? Have you noticed any sign of his presence? Has anybody else contacted you with a story like the one I'm telling you?"

"No for everything."

"I'm sorry that I had to tell you, Dave. I know you are understandably upset at having me come here and relate this to you but it was the only way I could find out if anyone else has made contact with him. I know he's probably the last person, living or dead, you ever want to see again."

"I'll add to that," Dave interjected. "He would probably kill me if he ever had the chance."

"What do you mean?"

"I mean at the viewing. I spit on him. I spit on him as he lay dead in his casket."

"Seriously?"

"Seriously. When no one else was looking, I slipped up there and spit a big wet glob of mucus and saliva on his dreaded dead face. And I enjoyed it too."

"I guess we all had our reasons to hate him."

"He deserved it. He was the most evil person I ever knew in my life. He was the son of the devil. He hurt people. He hurt every person he ever knew. I'll hate him until the day I die."

There was a brief pause in the discussion while Dave calmed his nerves. The doctor gave him ample time to do so.

"You know what, that girl he was going to marry, she did to him what I would have done a long time before if I had help. He was murdered. You know that. She arranged for his murder. Down there when things went bad for him he had nowhere to run, nowhere to hide. He was alone, vulnerable. And they got him. Saved us the time. Sure as you and I were born, they got him. They strangled him then put his dead body into that car and drove him into the bayou. There they staged the so-called accident."

Dave hesitated again before completing his thoughts.

"You know, Pip, the way I look at it, he was lucky he lasted until age thirty."

The doctor and Dave continued their conversation for some time, with their conversation peaking every time James was mentioned. The doctor was sensitive to Dave's plight and refused to discuss with him the intrusive details of his incarceration. When they were ready to part company, Dave made some closing remarks.

"Pip, this may sound kind of weird, but you know, it was probably a good thing for me that Jim was killed when he was. If not, I might have killed him myself. Then, you would be in here visiting me for life. But I promise, if I'm ever spooked at night by my half brother's ghost, you will be the first person I'll call. And by the way, I'll need your number."

In compliance, the doctor handed Dave one of his professional cards. He also promised Dave he would stay in touch regardless of the outcome with James.

While returning home, the doctor felt satisfied that things between him and Dave had gone well. He felt confident that Dave would call him should something unusual happen, and he felt confident that he had displayed a genuine concern for Dave as a person. It had been a lot dealing with Dave and the doctor was glad when he reached the solace of his southern woods.

Forgetting about Dave, the doctor's thoughts turned to Annice. And as soon as his thoughts returned to her, his feelings for her intensified. Evening was approaching. It had been far beyond a day and a half since their tryst. It seemed so long ago, yesterday. He checked his message machine which he seldom, if ever, used. Often, during the course of any year he unplugged it, thinking that he really didn't want to be bothered. He got enough junk messages through the mail that he didn't want the same thing happening through his phone. But since yesterday he had reconnected it and it was now in use again. But Annice had not called.

He thought about her. The what-ifs began to bother him. What if her husband suspected she had been unfaithful? What if he beat her and beat her until she confessed? What if she was unable to call because she had been beaten to the bone, broken and bloody?

These poignant questions plagued him and plagued him throughout the course of the evening. He fought them off, each and every one, as though he were flinging his limbs against an onslaught of wasps. But each thought stung him, again and again and again.

It was midnight when he reluctantly traipsed off to bed. His thoughts went with him though they had been rendered harmless now by extreme tiredness.

Monday morning, the doctor awoke, refreshed and renewed. His exceedingly tired state had put him into a deep, deep sleep through the night, and as a result his body and spirit had had a chance to replenish themselves. The resurgence he felt carried over into all things, including his once-dashed hopes about Annice. He felt incentive enough to go-all-out again to foster his new relationship with her.

He was so interested in doing something special to show her how he felt, that on the way to the office he stopped off at a local florist and purchased a bouquet of pink rosebuds for her. Along with the flowers, he purchased a crystal vase so that she could keep them on her desk. And, the doctor promised, I will do my best to make sure that vase keeps filling up with flowers in the future. He smiled as he continued on his way, glad that he had taken the initiative to please her. "Every woman loves getting flowers," he said decidedly.

The doctor was bursting with joy and exhilaration when he pulled up into one of his prized parking spaces in the front of his building. He all but dashed from his car with his briefcase in one hand and the delicate rosebuds in the other. He was earlier than usual and he wanted to have the flowers neatly arranged on Annice's desk long before she arrived. He decided against writing an accompanying note, attesting to the fact that the flowers, budding and beautiful, said it all.

He took the roses into the other room and arranged them in the crystal vase and then took the vase to the sink to fill it with cool water. Having accomplished that, he sat the vase on a corner of her desk and then walked briskly back into his back office to await her arrival. He kept his door wide open so he could easily hear the sound of the main door opening, signaling her presence.

Time passed. Three times he peeped out into the adjoining room, nervous for her.

"She will just love me for this," he declared.

More time elapsed. The doctor began staring at the large circular clock on the wall—8:01, 8:02, 8:03, 8:04, 8:05. More time passed. He began to get edgy. Where was she?

Once she was ten minutes late, he ventured over to her desk and began perusing her open desk planner just to see if she had intended to be a little late for some reason. Perhaps she has told him already and he had forgotten. But the planner revealed nothing unusual about the start to her day. He did notice, though, his patient schedule for the day and realized that his first arrival would come at 8:30. Five minutes later, he anxiously picked up the phone and dialed her number. It was a tense moment. What would he find out?

On the fifth ring, the phone was picked up. It was Annice.

"Hello," she whispered in a soft, delicate voice.

"Annice, is that you?"

"Oh, I'm so sorry, Christopher. You obviously did not get my message, did you?"

"What message?" the doctor asked with a tinge of annoyance in his voice.

"On the answering machine, silly," Annice put in firmly.

"Oh my goodness. I never even thought to check it," the doctor fretted.

Annice smiled for a moment, imagining the competent doctor as some lost little boy, helpless in things that pertained to her expertise. The doctor glanced at the recorder and noticed the tiny pulsing red light. Ignoring the device, he asked her instead, "Annice, how are you? Are you all right? Do you need me to come and pick you up?"

"No," she replied in an uncomplaining voice. "I have a severe headache today and I'm feeling a bit feverish too. I hope I'm not coming down with something serious. Oh, and by the way, I've already called the temporary service so they can provide you with a fill-in secretary for the day."

"But I need you," the doctor protested.

"Oh, that's so sweet. But if I come today I may get worse. Then I may be out for more than a day. And I could make someone else sick, including you."

"You're right."

"The service said that because our call was last-minute they wouldn't be able to get someone over until about 9:00. Think you can make it until then?"

"I guess I'll have to," the doctor conceded.

"Don't worry, Christopher. The agency usually sends competent people out on assignments. Maybe you'll get that elderly woman they sent six months ago when I was laid up with the flu for a week. You said she was great."

"Yes, she was a godsend, I remember. I hope you're right and I hope you get well soon," he said considerately. "If you need me for anything don't hesitate to call."

"Oh, I will," Annice promised.

The call was over. The doctor was confused by the changed circumstance. He looked down at the pink roses and became instantly angered that they would no longer be able to serve their intended purpose. He stomped his foot down on the carpeted floor. The softened impact did little to quell his frustration. As a result, he raised his left arm in a position that he could swoop it down on the vase of roses, but his inclination ceased when he heard the light footsteps of someone passing through the hall.

It was 8:18 and already Mrs. Steinbaecher, his first patient, had arrived.

"Hello, Doctor," she said in a haughty German accent.

"Good morning to you," the doctor replied amicably. "And how are you?"

"Miserable, just plain miserable, Doctor," she complained as they walked into his office.

Annice felt miserable too. Added to her distress was the pressure she now felt for lying to Chris about being sick. For two days now since they had been together she had been in a state of misery and confusion. Outwardly, she appeared melancholy, but on the inside she was in the middle of a tempest. All of the aspects of her life were coming together at once. A maelstrom of emotions surged inside her as the seriousness of what she had done impacted her.

Above all was the fact that she had committed serious sin. According to her Catholic life, she had committed adultery. Despite the issues that had led her to it, she had taken a bite from the forbidden fruit, she had taken naked pleasure in the arms of another man against the vows of her marriage, against God. She felt like Eve in the Garden of Eden. She needed to hide, take refuge from God, from Christopher, from everybody.

But there was nowhere to run, nowhere to hide, nowhere to seek refuge. She was the culprit and there is nowhere to hide from yourself. What had she done?

Throughout the ordeal she prayed openly to God. "Dear God, what is your will for me? I have loved you and obligated myself to you ever since I was young. I have guided my life with you beside me, giving your love my every consideration. Is this to be? Am I to spend my life loving you and in return have my life in ruins? I feel as if you have abandoned me, as if long ago you let go of my hand and left me desolate, desolate and alone.

"Please, God, don't force me to live my life in a loveless marriage. I need love. I have so much love to give. But no longer can I give my love to him. I have accused you of abandoning me, but if you have not, then you know, you know. I have sinned but my sin came from my heart, from a heart that needs healing. I have sinned but my sin came because I loved.

"His sins—humiliation, abuse, rape—all come from hate. He despises me and hates me, and in return, I have grown to hate him. And hate is all that is left despite the acts we sometimes display for one another. Please, God, show me what to do. Please, God, strengthen me and guide me through this. Make me feel your loving presence like I did when I was a child in your arms. With you I cannot fail."

Annice sank to her knees at the bottom of the bed. Her prayers turned to tears and she wept bitterly.

The doctor concluded his session with Mrs. Steinbaecher and escorted her out of his office, her arm, as always, tucked in his. Due to her age and fragility, the doctor never minded. They were met in the waiting room by Mr. Steinbaecher who always dropped off his wife for her appointment, left, and then returned once she was done. The doctor really liked the old couple, and always took the time to talk to them before they left. Doing so, the doctor was surprised when he took note of someone else's presence behind him. His assistant had already arrived and was attempting to acclimate herself to her ephemeral duties. When the Steinbaechers had gone, he turned to greet her.

All during the interlude before she had arrived, the doctor had envisioned her as someone experienced in age as well as ability, someone who had possibly recently lost a job and needed work, or possibly someone who was returning to the work force after a stay at home. She would be forty, wear glasses, be somewhat stout or somewhat thin, and have intricate gray hairs woven into her head.

When the doctor turned to have a look-see at her, the woman was still turned and bent over an opened file-cabinet drawer. She appeared to be examining the overall contents of it as she went from one folder to another, reading titles and moving on. The doctor approached her. She heard his approach and turned herself toward him.

The doctor couldn't believe his eyes. She was beautiful. She was young. His mind worked like a computer, ascertaining all the discernable facts about her. The input was maddening. She had shoulder-length blonde hair which fell about the sides of her face in perfect symmetry. She possessed sparkling baby-blue eyes which pierced him to the core every time she cast them at him. She was slender, and had, as far as he could determine, perfect proportions. Her breasts, as far as he could determine, were ample-sized either for

the pleasures of a man or the needs of a baby. Her legs, below her
skirt, were slender and toned as if she indulged in some activity that
served to keep them fit. The doctor was so captivated by the sight of
her as compared to what he had expected, he couldn't take his eyes
off of her.

Finally, the young lady spoke.

"Hello. Dr. Haefner, I presume?"

"Hello."

"My name is Linda. Linda Brant. I was sent here today by the
temp service to fill in for you. I was told your secretary is out sick."

"Yes, that's true."

"I hope you don't mind if I did a little snooping. I realized that
you were in session and rather than waste time, I thought I would try
to familiarize myself with your office, you know, like where things go.
I see you have a Compaq computer system with Microsoft software:
Windows. I can use any system that's been developed so I won't have
any trouble filing or retrieving data."

"Splendid," the doctor managed to put out while he still
marveled at her splendor and beauty.

"So, what's on the agenda for today?" Linda inquired in a lively
voice.

Instinctively, the doctor grabbed Linda's hand and escorted her
directly to Annice's desk. Together they pulled up the data on the
day's schedule. Linda, who had already familiarized herself with the
printer, printed out a schedule of it. The doctor was pleased that she
could so easily acclimate herself to the office's business.

"The main thing I need you for today is to pertain to the patients'
comings and goings, and take phone messages. If anyone calls with
an emergency situation, use the intercom there to get me even if I'm
in session. Be polite to everyone. Sometimes some patients of mine
have a tendency to speak or act out. Their behaviors are a part of their
illness. Don't concern yourself with insurance forms right now, unless
one of the companies call and really need something. And, if there's
anything you're not sure about, don't hesitate to ask."

The doctor perused the schedule with all of the day's information
on it.

"Today's no big deal," he surmised. "You should be all right. By the way, what is your experience with this type of work?"

"Well, to begin with, I'm twenty-seven so I obviously don't have as much experience as what you were probably expecting. I'm three years out of grad school where I earned a degree in business math. I've spent the last three years working in the college's administration office."

"What college?" the doctor interjected.

"F&M."

"F&M. That's wonderful. That's my alma mater too."

"Really?"

"Yes. I went all the way through BS, MS, and Ph.D."

"I'm impressed. Are you from around here?"

"Yes, I'm a local."

Both the doctor and his interim secretary felt an instant rapport with each other. Already they found that they had many things in common. Both felt that it was an important beginning. One thing, though, the doctor was relieved that Linda had not inquired as to when he had graduated from college. It would have implied his age which he now knew was thirteen years advanced from hers.

The doctor left Linda to her tasks. Before entering his office to prepare for his next patient, he turned to look at her. How lovely she looked sitting there. Her mere presence brightened the office atmosphere as much as day versus night. She reminded him of his early college days and the many young women he had been with during that time. How he wished she had been among them. Linda topped them all. She would have been the one. She would have been the one worth making a commitment to, the commitment he could never make to anyone.

All through the day, the doctor visited his new secretary. Halfway through the morning, she inquired about the pink roses which remained at her desk.

"These roses are absolutely beautiful. Their fragrance makes me feel like I'm outside sitting in a garden. I just love them. Who are they for?"

The doctor, enamored by Linda's compliment, responded without thinking.

"They are for you," he said softly, and turned and walked away.

Fervent Sex!

Annice called off the following days. And on a day-to-day basis she, in turn, called the temporary service to let them know she was not going to make it back to work. She called the doctor too, apologizing each day for her unexpected absence. Not since she had gotten the flu the previous winter had she missed so many consecutive days from the office. She felt bad.

Annice was taking her private contemplations about ending her unfortunate marriage very seriously. It consumed her night and day. During her brief conversations with the doctor, she assured him that each day she was feeling better, which in her mind meant she was becoming increasingly sure about her personal situation. Neither of them mentioned their intimate relations, though it was foremost on their minds. On the third day, Annice insisted that due to her steady improvement, she expected to return by Friday. So as not to let all of their personal feelings go unmentioned, they did express what they considered appropriate emotions, concern and sympathy, freely toward each other, though these exchanges did tend to be exaggerated.

"I really do miss you, Annice," the doctor would say at the conclusion of each one of their conversations.

"I really miss you too," Annice would say in return.

On Thursday, Annice spoke to the doctor and reiterated that she would be returning the next day as expected. Aside from her personal problems she was beginning to feel a little insecure about leaving her position in the hands of another capable woman. She became aware that at no time had the doctor mentioned anything, good or bad, about her replacement. She imagined that she had left the doctor in quite a state of consternation, about her, about them.

Annice was right. The doctor didn't know what to think, and for a thinking person like the doctor, that meant trouble. When he wasn't around Linda, he wondered about Annice all the time. He wondered why she was avoiding him, avoiding any sincere discussion about the fact that they had been intimate. Had her husband anything to do with her avoidance? Had she confessed what had happened to him?

In conjunction with his confusion about Annice, the doctor was finding it harder and harder to suppress his attraction for Linda. She was, after all, available.

The doctor knew, too, that Linda was no innocent bystander in all this. She had made certain that the agency would continue to send her in Annice's stead as long as the doctor needed her. The agency willingly obliged. At the start of her second day, they had placed a routine call to the doctor and inquired as to his satisfaction with her. The doctor gave her high praises.

"She's intelligent and diligent in her work. Why, if I didn't have a secretary I'd hire her on the spot!"

Linda's lovely looks and lively personality did much to soothe the sore ego the doctor was feeling. Just standing beside her, he felt like a new man.

Linda knew too, as a woman does, when a man desires a woman. She felt the doctor's abbreviated stares, try as he might to conceal them. She felt, too, a special tenderness in his voice whenever he spoke to her. She thought the doctor was awesome in mind and body. He was a man in the prime of his life. Though age wasn't really an issue, she perceived him to be about ten years older than she was. He had a strong handsome face with piercing blue eyes. His hair was the color of a walnut, rich and full, with not the slightest recession on its covering. He stood about 5' 9", and was muscular throughout his body. This, Linda left mostly to her imagination.

Besides his apparent physical appeal, Linda was mostly attracted to the doctor for who he was. She had only spent the interludes of their working days together but it was enough for her to gather some useful insight into who he really was. He was the most intelligent person, male or female, she had ever met. He was insightful, modest, and pleasant to be around. He was a deep thinker, a problem solver. Best of all, she liked how he valued her opinions too. Whenever he was solving a problem, which he often did aloud, he would come to her and bounce things off her and ask her opinion.

It was on the afternoon of their fourth day working together that, the doctor and Linda, as fate would have it, had their first real chance to get to know one another. This was the day when Eye on You, the surveillance-systems company, had arranged to come to the office and complete their work. In regard to what the doctor was doing, he explained to Linda that in the cases of certain patients a more thorough evaluation could be obtained if their sessions were recorded on videotape. That way, when it came time to make assessments about their therapies, a review of what they said and how they said it could help the process of determining the process of results. It's hard to remember everything that happens during therapy. With the audio and visual aids, it would be easier. He could make decisions accurately.

"Wow! That's so interesting."

"Yes."

The Eye on You technician cell-phoned Dr. Haefner's office just prior to their scheduled arrival. A short time later, a foreman and two workers entered the James Street building carrying the equipment and installation gear. The doctor met them and directed them into his office where he told them the story about having his interviews with patients recorded for future use. Then, he explained his intention to leave for a time to allow them full use of the office while they did their work.

"If it's OK with you fellows, we'll just leave here for a while so you can do your work. When do you expect the work to be finished?"

"Probably about an hour. It's hard to say," the foreman said as he stepped forward from the others.

"OK then," the doctor replied as he turned into the outer office. "Linda, we have to leave for a while. Are you ready?"

"Ready, willing, and able," she replied with a chuckle.

They departed. Outside they stood at the front of the building, one waiting for the other, to suggest where they should go.

"Do you have any personal errands that need your time or attention?"

"Nothing that I could do in the space of time I have."

"I'm sorry," the doctor conceded. "I'm afraid I didn't give this part of the plan much consideration.

"I know, then," Linda said beaming. "Let's go to my place."

"Your place?" the doctor said incredulously.

"Yes, why not?" Linda said adamantly. "I live really close. I have an apartment on Lancaster Avenue. It's only three blocks from here and we can walk."

The doctor, not knowing what else to do, nodded his approval.

They were off. The doctor and his temporary assistant began a diligent walk to Linda's apartment. Lancaster Avenue connected to James Street only one block from the office building and Linda's 515 address was less than two blocks farther.

Linda's building was a three-story brick row house which now accommodated three apartments. Linda's was on the second floor. It consisted of a large kitchen, living room, a bedroom complete with balcony, a spare room, and a full bath.

As they entered, Linda stopped to collect her mail.

"Wow! You've got your mail already," the doctor commented. "My office is so close to here and I don't get my business mail until late afternoon. I can't believe it."

"Believe it," she stated succinctly as she ascended the central stairs.

At the top of the steps, Linda fumbled in her pocket for her door key then inserted it, turned it, and went inside. The doctor followed. The front door opened into a spacious living room and the doctor commented on how neat and clean everything appeared.

"You're like me," he said, attesting to the fact of his being such a neat person too.

"I'm a bit quirky," Linda admitted. "I've always been fastidious. My mother made me that way. I always felt like I was in competition with her about doing things right and taking care of the house. But that," she confessed ruefully, "is something that should be discussed in therapy."

The doctor laughed but didn't respond, uncertain whether she was serious or just being facetious. Linda looked around at the room, then at the doctor.

"Well, would you like the grand tour?" she asked pleasantly.

"Sure, why not," the doctor responded aptly.

"Then follow me."

They proceeded out of the living room and into the hall where they were intercepted by a white cat who came bounding out from the kitchen. The racing feline jumped into Linda's arms. Linda clasped the cat tightly to her and began petting her affectionately. Then, noticing the doctor, the cat hissed and clawed.

"Tabby! Stop it!" Linda shouted.

"Amazing," the doctor purported. "I've never seen someone's cat run and jump on them like that before."

"We're best buddies. Aren't we, Tabby?" Linda told the cat in a style of voice that started her feline friend purring for further attention.

The trio of friends continued through the hall then stopped in the kitchen where Linda noticed that her precious pet's food dish was all but empty. After putting Tabby down, she bent down, retrieved the food dish, and refilled it from a box of dry food which was on top of the refrigerator. Anxious, Tabby was waiting impatiently in front of the tile square where her food dish was always placed.

"There you go, precious," Linda said in a soothing voice as she used first one free hand then the other to stroke the cat's back. Tabby was all a-purr as she began steadily crunching and crunching on her tasty tidbits. After spending a bit of time petting Tabby, Linda turned up to the doctor to ask if he wanted anything.

"Would you like me to get you something too?"

"No, not right now," he replied.

"Then come with me," Linda continued. "The tour continues."

They exited out of the kitchen and turned down an adjoining hall where Linda led him into a brightly lit room. It was Linda's bedroom.

"Well, except for the bathroom across the hall, this is the last stop. This is my glorious bedroom—where all the good stuff happens." She gave the doctor a furtive glance and noticed he was smiling and his face was flushed. Her flirtatious remark had landed on him just as she had hoped. Outwardly he appeared stolid and he was too flustered to comment, but on the inside she could tell he was tinged with expectation. Linda was excited too but she hesitated to go further until the doctor was ready to make a move.

Linda's alluring remark provoked the doctor to take action but he remained reticent, for the moment at least. He required another assurance, another provocation, to act. One flirtation, he thought, could just be teasing. Two, though, he considered a flagrant attempt at seduction. If he could just get one more, then, then he could have her.

To dispel the quiet that was growing between them, Linda suggested that they move out onto the balcony so she could show the doctor the splendid view. She motioned him out. She moved out to the outer rails and summoned him to join her. From her upper floor, a detectable breeze was blowing, which farther below wouldn't have been felt at all. It added to the quaint setting which they began admiring below. The balcony too, was arranged very comfortably, and the doctor found it much to his liking. It was outfitted with a five-piece white wicker set: a love seat, two armchairs, a glass-top center table, and one glass-top end table. Flower pots were suspended from the ceiling, each one brimming with red-shaded blooms—geraniums. In another pot, which sat on the end table, was an African violet. Its blunt purple flower enclosed behind a protective see-through covering. It caught the doctor's attention.

"You have an African violet, I see," he said.

"Yes. I do," she replied.

"They are very hard to keep. They require the utmost of time and attention. Actually, they do best in a greenhouse where they have constant heat and humidity, sort of like what you did there with your plant."

Conversing about African violets put the doctor at ease from all the tension he was feeling.

"You know, two years ago, a friend of mine, an old college buddy, put together an idea to open a public greenhouse. He did it. He built one on an adjacent lot beside his home. He allows amateur plant and flower enthusiasts to rent space inside it year-round. They can grow exotic plants like orchids, African violets, and other rare and delicate flora, then periodically take them home to show off or take them to shows to try to win contests and prize money. But the real winner in all of it is my friend. He makes a mint off of it."

"What a brilliant idea he had," Linda stated. "I might be interested too. Would you take me to see it sometime?"

"Sure," the doctor said, unequivocally. "I'll have to arrange it first though."

The doctor shifted over to a corner of the balcony and leaned against the wooden railing.

"You have a nice view from up here," the doctor spouted out in a tense voice.

It was. The contiguous yards below were vividly alive with splashes of various colors from a plethora of flowering plants, each yard individualized according to its owner's liking. There were trees of all sorts, prodigious gardens, and groupings of shrubbery strewn about as though they themselves were visitors admiring the view they were part of. There was one tree in a neighboring yard which captured the doctor's attention. It was a flowering tree smaller than any of the other backyarders. It looked as though it belonged in the tropics with its long curved branches, its bark looking like it had been painted on, and spiky pastel-pink flowers.

"That's a mimosa tree," he pointed out.

Linda, who had moved up beside him, listened attentively.

"It looks tropical, like it doesn't belong here, but it does. This tree is indigenous to this area. Long ago when this area was semitropical, mimosas thrived here. Then, as the continent drifted north and the climate became temperate, area trees that thrived in the warmth began to retreat south. But this tree adapted to the change in temperature. It resisted the cold and now as a result we, here, have a once-tropical tree growing in our own backyards."

As Linda listened, she slid in front of the doctor to see and hear him better. Their bodies touched. He placed his hand on top of her shoulder while pointing to the tree with his other. Enticed by the awesome warmth of her body, he allowed his hand to trace down her back and rest at her waist. In response, Linda shifted her body until she was standing directly in front of him. She wiggled her posterior into position against him so they could slightly feel each other. It was beyond belief! Linda could feel the doctor's body hard against her. In her light dress and sheer panties, it felt almost as though it was pressing against her flesh. To show the doctor she was receptive, she shifted herself even more toward him to show him she wanted more. The doctor did too.

It had all happened so fast but each of them knew where it was leading. There being no point in acting otherwise, the doctor decidedly placed both hands around Linda's waist. Their bodies were of one form, sculptured together as though they were both formed from the same slab of stone. For a time they remained mingled, enjoying the feeling of oneness, of completeness. Finally the doctor began kissing Linda. He kissed the side of her forehead, her earlobe, her soft cheek, and neck. Linda completed the advance by turning around and kissing the doctor squarely on the mouth. They kissed and kissed, their mouths opening and closing as rapidly as a revolving door at a business during the lunch hour.

The overactive couple grew bolder with each other. Linda passed her hands over the doctor's body, titillating him. The doctor boldly placed his hands around Linda's back and ran them smoothly across her various bulges. Next he lifted up her dress and did the same against her front. They both knew they were at the point of no return and it would be too indiscreet to advance any further while they were on public display. Linda overtly suggested they move off the balcony and into the bedroom.

Once inside, Linda proceeded to lock both the balcony door and the door to her room.

"I don't want Tabby running in here and pouncing on us while we're doing it. Sometimes she does that while I'm sleeping and I get scratches."

Before the doctor had a chance to undress, Linda directed him to close several of the curtains.

"It's too bright in here," she explained. "I don't want it to seem like we're outside in the middle of the day."

At her request, the doctor darkened the room. Two of the curtains, he closed completely. One he left partly opened to allow a hint of soft light to enhance the atmosphere.

First-time lovers want to see each other just as the doctor wanted to see every visible part of Linda's voluptuous body. He wanted to see every crack on her lips, every lock of her hair, everything that she had to offer as a woman.

Linda proceeded faster than the doctor. Before he had his shirt removed, she already had her dress, panty hose, socks, and shoes off. The doctor stopped when she got to her bra and panties and watched intently. He then hurried out of his trappings and they were naked.

He stood beside his untidy pile of clothes on the floor and stared at Linda. He could see that she was everything he imagined her to be. He knew that if anything happened, anything to stop their sexual encounter, he would be sleepless thinking about her, about what he might have had. He would never tire thinking about her.

Linda too was equally impressed by her would-be partner. She indulged herself to satisfaction just looking at him. He stood before her like the statue of a Greek god. He had a solid upper body with well-defined muscles outlining his chest, arms, and shoulders. He had strong legs which were proportional to his waist and upper body. Giving that its due, Linda next focused on the doctor's eyes, to see what he was thinking. They told her that he, like she, was just as eager to participate in what was expected to happen. It was becoming one of those strangest of times in one's life when things turned out even better than imagined—imagine that! Anticipation was at its peak. Linda was ready. The doctor was too.

When their prolonged, mutual, staring contest ended, the couple flung together to act as one. Time had no meaning as the partners gave themselves selflessly to one another. Several times they worked each other to climax, until finally each of them fell, weak and exhausted, on the bed.

They held each other for the longest time without a word being spoken, until they had wound down enough to notice that the sheets they were lying on were a bit damp. Both lovers had engaged themselves fully in the exercise and were now covered in a layer of sweat. As a remedy to their discomfort, Linda suggested they take a shower together.

While waiting to rinse the rich lathery shampoo from each other's heads, the couple exchanged warm tender kisses.

"This is something that would have been good as a precursor to having sex," the doctor suggested.

"Oh, you mean like this," Linda responded and playfully began applying tender touches and kisses to the doctor's face and lips, arms and hands, legs and feet. Her initiative would have gone further—but it couldn't.

Later, once they were clean and clothed, the doctor noticed just how long an interval of time had passed since they left the office.

Their extended stay at Linda's apartment had lasted several hours and by now the surveillance-systems workers were probably gone. The doctor felt remorseful, knowing that he had intended to settle with them before they departed. Together they dashed out of the Lancaster Avenue apartment and walked briskly toward James Street. As they hurried along, they talked little, each uncertain as to how to act toward the other after what they had just experienced together.

When they arrived at the office, they were relieved to find everything in order. The outer door had been securely locked and there was a note left on the doctor's desk informing him as to the extent of work that was done. Along with that, there was some literature listing the details of how to activate and operate the surveillance system. The doctor perused the brochures briefly then noted the time. It was fifteen minutes from quitting time and he stepped out of his office to inform Linda.

Linda, who had been on the phone, put down the receiver and began playing the phone-recording tape which she just realized had received messages while they were away. The tiny red indicator light was blinking a series of two flashes. The distinct beeps that ordinarily accompany the flashes were silent since Linda had purposefully turned off the volume before they left. She hadn't wanted the constant beeping of any messages annoying the installation crew while they worked.

The second she began playing the tape, the doctor was beside her. Both calls were of extreme interest to the doctor. The first call was from Annice stating emphatically that she would be returning to work the next day. Upon hearing that news, Linda became noticeably upset. The doctor, paying close attention to her reaction, was just about to console her when the second message began playing. The doctor was dumbfounded by who it was and what he said.

The voice was out of breath, succinct, frightened.

"Doc, it's me! Dave! It happened! It happened last night!"

That was it. The message was over but the meaning was clear. Linda noticed the doctor's sudden alarm and grasped his arm.

"What's wrong?"

"It's a very personal matter. But I know what it is and how to deal with it. It's nothing you have to worry your pretty little head about."

The doctor's condescending remark hurt Linda's feelings. She pulled away.

The situation, as it was, was most bewildering. More and more strange events, as never before, were compounding the doctor's life—Annice, Linda, and James's afterlife. The doctor had no choice but to deal with things, one thing at a time. He looked first to reassure Linda.

"Look, Linda, there's a story behind that call. It was from Dave Boller, an old friend. He's involved in a very complicated, potentially dangerous situation right now and I'm trying to help him. It would be useless to try to explain any of it to you unless I explained everything, and quite frankly I don't have either the time or inclination to do so. As for you, you just heard for yourself that Annice expects to be back tomorrow. There's nothing I can do about that. It is her job. As far as we're concerned, I had the best experience of my life with you today. And I don't think I want it to end today. Regardless of whether you work here or not, we can still see each other, that is, if that's what you want."

The doctor lifted her up out of the chair and continued to speak to her softly. As he did, he could see she was sad. The look on her face was like that of a small child being told by her mother that it was time to leave some favorite place. "What happened today between us was half your fault," the doctor reminded her. "So it's half up to you what happens next. I would like to continue seeing you. What do you want to do?"

Linda, still looking forlorn, reached over to her desk—her desk, she contemplated, how she wished that were true—and picked up a piece of paper. She wrote down her home phone number, folded it, and then slipped it into the doctor's shirt pocket.

"Here's my number if you ever want to call me," she said sadly.

She picked up her pocketbook and the doctor escorted her to the door. Before exiting, the doctor stopped her and whirled her back to him. He softly touched the side of her face with his hand then he reached down and kissed her where he had his hand. As a parting gesture, the doctor had her wait at the door for a minute while he gathered up the bunched rosebuds for her.

"For your eyes only," he said when he handed them to her.

Once Linda departed, the doctor's attention turned immediately to Dave Boller. He played the message again, listening intently to the serious inflections in Dave's voice. He was serious about what he said. The doctor went into his office and retrieved a piece of paper which issued the visiting hours for the prison. Verifying what he remembered, he knew that daily visiting hours were from 6:00 to 9:00. To go, he would have to kill an hour or so, either in the office or somewhere in the city.

While deciding what to do, the doctor read over the literature that came with the new office equipment. The system was all set up and ready to go. All he had to do was turn it on.

While contemplating what to do, the doctor turned on the test button to the mechanism. This would provide one-minute's worth of viewing on the tape, allowing the viewer to see if everything was right. As the tape began recording, the doctor became lost in thought about everything that was happening in his life. Only a short while ago he had been alone and lonely. Now it was though he was a different person living a different life. He had spent the afternoon delighting in the company of an attractive young woman. And prior to that, he had had the most intense sex imaginable with the woman he loved most in all the world. It was perplexing. Why did both have to come at the same time? Why? Now he would have to pick and choose from between them; Annice whom he loved and Linda whom he desired.

A short time into his deliberations, his stomach began to complain that it was hungry. To offset his discomfort, he grabbed some jelly mints from the candy dish in the waiting room and ate some as he closed up. The time he needed to kill, he would kill at Herkimer's.

Dead Man's Curve

At Herkimer's, the doctor treated himself to his favorite meal—two hot roast beef sandwiches, a sizeable portion of potatoes, and carrots. It was just the sort of replenishment needed by a man of forty who had just expended himself upon the wiles of a young woman thirteen years his junior.

After the enjoyment of his meal, the doctor hastened to leave the eatery and get to the prison. Again, as he strode across the paved parking lot, the doctor felt that queer peculiar feeling, a feeling that he was somewhere he didn't belong. He went aptly up the front concrete steps and made his way into the building where he was again subject to the same harsh scrutiny as before, before being permitted to see Dave.

As Dave had instructed, the doctor requested a private meeting, a privilege permitted for personal reasons; in this case, a doctor seeing his patient. The doctor, after showing his professional identification, was granted permission to visit with Dave in his cell.

With his credentials established, the doctor was duly escorted past the usual visitation areas and into a wide well-lit corridor. The corridor was a split hall in which the prisoners from one side were not permitted to walk or otherwise occupy the boundary of the other. The doctor noticed that every cell they passed was empty and mentioned it to his escort.

"Tonight is not a typical night for the inmates," she began, "every once in a while, if the prison as a whole has been getting along, the warden sets aside a special night when the whole population is allowed extended recreation. Most of the inmates participate too. They can play cards, watch movies, shoot basketball, anything they like really, as long as it's something already offered for recreational purposes."

Not feeling very interactive, the doctor only nodded. When they reached Dave's cell, the guard had Dave identify who the doctor was and corroborate that he wanted to see him for personal reasons, and in private. To all of these inquiries, Dave responded adamantly, "Yes."

The guard then informed them that special privileges such as they were receiving were allowable for only a specified period of time; in this case, one hour.

"It's discretionary," she told them.

Both Dave and the doctor made no comment back to the guard. The guard then abruptly left.

"Boy, she's a real stuck-up witch," Dave stated earnestly once she was gone. "She thinks she's a big shot. She likes to go around all day telling people what they can and can't do. I hate her."

"So what are we supposed to do," the doctor inquired, "stand here and talk to each other through the bars?"

"Give her a minute," Dave replied. "These bars are locked electronically. She will open them, but it will depend on whether or not she liked you as to how long you'll have to wait."

Just then, the locking mechanism across the opening automatically disengaged and the doorway was accessible. The doctor entered. He greeted Dave with a firm handshake and a smile. He then looked around the confines of the cell for a place to sit. Dave, realizing that no provision for him had been made, apologized for the inconvenience.

"That's all right," the doctor replied. "If you can tolerate the inconvenience of being here day after day, I can sure tolerate the inconvenience of being here for an hour with or without having a place to sit.

"Look, I got your message," the doctor continued. "I'm sorry I didn't respond right away but I was out for the afternoon. What happened?"

"I don't know exactly," Dave replied. "It happened last night. I was asleep in my bunk when all of a sudden I felt this strange sensation that I wasn't alone. I awoke. I felt a cold chill run up my spine. I sat up and tried to stay alert. At first I thought someone was trying to play a trick on me and maybe had been standing outside the cell. I thought maybe it was that smarty that brought you here. It was dark. The only light at night comes from the hall and those lights are dimmed so that you can't really see anything in here. The cell lights are automatically shut off after 11:00. They do that to conserve electricity. Ha! Ha!

"What happened next happened without tricks. As I sat in my bunk, I focused my vision on a figure that appeared across the room. It was hard to see, I admit, but the figure took shape. It brought with it its own sense of visualization, as if it were being constructed by particles of light. That's the best I can describe it. I have a tiny flashlight that I keep. It's something that I've managed to keep hidden ever since I was put here. Anyway, I reached for it and I shone the light over, in the direction of the . . . ghost . . . or whatever you want to call it. And I saw it. It was him! It was Jim!"

"I believe you, Dave," the doctor countered. "That was pretty much how it happened to me. And now it makes more sense, now that James encountered you, because why would he enter our realm just to see one of us?"

Throughout the doctor's reply, Dave was in a trance. He had continued to talk.

"It was James, James coming to haunt me. He was standing right there with his back leaning against the wall, one foot propped up behind him. He was staring straight at me as though I were the ghost, as though I were the something that didn't belong. I didn't move. I didn't say anything. He just kept looking. I don't know how long the whole thing lasted, but near the end of it I noticed an expression on the demon's face. It was a smirk. He smirked, then he smiled, and the changes on his face appeared to take place in slow motion. It was like motion captured in phases, like what you see when you see a strobe light.

"And I know exactly what he was doing. He was getting his jollies at seeing me in jail. And you know why. His whole life he avoided doing time despite the fact that he broke probably every law imaginable. I . . . I do just one little thing wrong and I'm in while that . . ."

Sensing Dave's anger, the doctor broke in and asked, "What happened next?"

"I became infuriated. I picked up anything that was within my reach and threw it at him. I told him to go back to hell where he belongs. But I guess even Satan himself didn't want him. He's probably afraid Jim will take over hell."

"Is that when he left?"

"Not exactly. After I threw everything I could, I got up myself. I wanted to go over and slug him. That's when he disappeared."

"Did he reappear?"

"No."

"Dave, I think you should know that I've made recent contact with your mom and dad. I also contacted Deb, Jim's sister, and Jules. You remember him. I didn't tell them anything like what I've told you. I called them up under the ruse that I was compiling information about Jim's formative years for a profile I was writing about him. My real curiosity was in finding out whether any of them had an encounter similar to the one you had. I figured that if I had seen him, then probably somebody else did too. By just mentioning James, I was sure I had opened up an avenue for them to talk about it. But, I'm sorry to say, nobody else has seen him."

Dave came out of his concentrated stare. His anger over the recollection subsided and now he wanted to indulge his interest in the peculiar event. He felt an intense bond with the doctor, knowing that the two of them were sharing a secret that no one else in the whole world knew about.

"So tell me, Doc, what's going on here? Why has he come back?"

"I don't really know myself, Dave. At this point I can only speculate. Knowing James, knowing his personality, it could be he did it just to prove that he could. James didn't need a reason for doing anything. When he was alive, his only purpose was to live for the moment. He was a seeker of all of life's experiences. In death, maybe he became a seeker too. And what is there to seek in death? In death, the ultimate thing to seek would be life again.

"James has found a way back. He's probably doing it just to fascinate us, you and me."

"How come he doesn't do anything or say anything when he's here?"

"I've begun to think about that. It could be that transcending death is an exceedingly difficult thing to do. If it were easy, there would be ghosts everywhere. I know that all sounds silly but it's probably true. James is one of the few who have made it. And maybe it's true too that he needs to get better at it. For instance, when you had contact with him, you said he appeared to smirk. His face changed. Whereas when I first encountered him, he didn't move at all. He's practicing and he's getting better. Next time we see him he would be predictably more advanced. James, sorry to say, is finding his way back into the world, slowly but surely."

"That doesn't sound too good for me being locked up here inside this birdcage day in and day out. He won't have any trouble finding me, that's for sure."

"You couldn't hide from him even if you wanted to, Dave. You can't hide from a ghost."

"Then, I guess, we're at his mercy."

"Not entirely. James is a specter, a ghost, nothing more. Even if he manages to maximize his abilities at things like making more visible contact or making contact more frequently, he'll never be like a living, breathing person. I believe we must be wary of him but not give him powers he doesn't possess."

"Then what influence will he have over us?"

"None I believe. But if he does manage to communicate with us, our only defense will be to find out what his limitations are and what his weaknesses are."

"How will we go about that?"

"If he does have the power to alter events, we need to find out why. If we can speak to him, we must ask him questions, questions like why he is here and how had he managed to get here. The more we know about him, the better off we will be. Another way we can study him is to capture his image on videotape. I have installed a surveillance camera in my office where I saw him. If he comes back, I will record his appearance."

Dave felt disturbed by the doctor's nonchalant attitude and responded, "Aren't you afraid?"

"Not afraid. I'm apprehensive though. I, too, turn out the lights at night and wonder whether while I'm sleeping James would appear."

"And do god-knows-what to you."

"I don't think so, Dave. In life, aside from a few scuffles, James never tried to harm, seriously, either you or me, and because of that, I don't believe he'd do so now. And believe me, he had plenty of opportunities. I have a belief based on this. Once a person's dead, they can not alter who they are. They are the sum of their life's experiences. The extent of who you were remains. All of the person you once were in life is the sum of all you can be. James's recurrent life will be dictated by this premise. So feel safe."

"You think so?"

"Think about it from another perspective, Dave. While James was living, his whole life was about self-indulgence. His motivation for doing anything centered around how he could best gain from any situation. What could he gain from harming us?"

"I'm not convinced you're right, Doc. In life Jimmy thrived on hurting people for self-pleasure. He may not have seriously injured me before but he did hurt me lots of times. And suppose you're right and he can't alter life events now. Won't that just make him mad? When he finds out that he's made it back but he can't do the things he liked best, what do you think he'll do? Remember, that's how he got his jollies."

"I don't know, Dave. If you're right, God help us. I guess we'll just have to wait and see how this thing plays out. If James comes again, try to initiate contact with him. Let him know you are not afraid of him even if you are. Stand up to him. Take control. And most importantly, call me. Tell me if you notice any further changes in his abilities."

Time was up. When the doctor was getting up to leave, he handed Dave one of his professional cards.

"My number is on there, my personal number. Call me day or night if anything happens."

"Will do," Dave replied compliantly. "But remember phone calls around here are limited to specified times."

"Don't worry about that. I will notify the proper authorities here that you are a patient of mine and that it is imperative that you have access to me whenever you need me."

"What if they ask me what's wrong with me?"

"Then tell them you have been diagnosed with an anxiety disorder. I'll send them a correspondence to that effect."

Assured that they were in this together, Dave's disposition improved. The doctor's did too. It was a great relief to have someone whom he could share this bizarre situation with.

"This has been quite a day, quite a day indeed," the doctor gasped once he had reached the prison parking lot.

He left the city, exhausted body and soul. He cut through the south-side city streets hurriedly until he reached the light where the New Danville Pike beckoned him. This was the point where the influence of Lancaster City abruptly ended and the exemplified countryside of Lancaster County began. Each day as he passed through this special place, he became a different person.

The ten miles from here to home were filled with natural enchantment. Countless fields and farms abutted the highway. Country roads leading off of the Pike meandered lazily into acres of corn, wheat, soybean, and tobacco. From higher hills, farm buildings and barns dotted the landscape. Stands of trees stood firm between farms and fields, leaving refuge for indigenous wildlife: pheasants, bunnies, squirrels, skunks, and opossum. Everywhere small streams trickled over rich thick topsoil, and on every fifty acres pop-up ponds of varying depths and sizes appeared.

Farther along, the farms became more scant as the open landscape yielded to the higher hills and woodlands which spread out from and followed the mighty Susquehanna River. Each day the doctor would drink fully of the pleasure and delight of seeing, hearing, and smelling the wonderful countryside setting.

Today, more than most days, he needed its sedentary comfort. Today, due to the later hour, the doctor would be treated to scenes from his ride that ordinarily he did not encounter. His journey would be marked by the coming of night—thousands of dairy cows making their way along lazy paths back to the refuge of their huge barns, countless blackbirds settling into trees to wait out the darkness soon to fall, myriads of fruit bats swarming in from the distant dark caves which dotted the Susquehanna River hills.

To take in this ephemeral display, the doctor automatically lowered his car's front windows so he would be splashed with the cool sweet air.

He drove along, carefree, unburdened. The stretch of highway he was on was a curved stretch of road, made so by the influence of the close-by meander of the Conestoga River. One bend in the road, known locally as Dead Man's Curve, was coming up. The curve was notorious for one-car crashes, usually involving young reckless drivers who attempt to take the turn too fast. The doctor checked his speed, fifty, which was fifteen-miles-per-hour over the recommended speed limit. To compensate for the excess, he removed his foot from the accelerator and reduced his velocity gradually—fifty, forty-five, forty. As an added precaution, he turned on his high beams and double-checked the roadway in front of him and behind. He observed that there was no traffic in either direction just as he proceeded into the curve.

He was rounding the first part of the curve, smoothly, cautiously, when suddenly the doctor slammed on his brakes. The Buick immediately locked up on a thick peel of black rubber which brought the car to a screeching halt. The doctor was shaken. While braking, the car had careened to a point beyond the double yellow line. After shaking off the intense upset he felt, the doctor threw the car into gear, backed up to the center of his lane, then guided the car past the point of circumstance, past the curve itself. So as to avert any potential accident from occurring, he pulled the car over onto the shoulder of the road, to a select spot wide enough to avoid being hit by any on-coming cars. As a further inducement to safety, he left the car in Park with its lights on and emergency flashers blinking. Before getting out, he leaned over to the glove compartment and retrieved his new flashlight and checked it to make sure it was operational. Getting out, he began walking, cautiously, back to where he had halted his car, back to where he had risked his life, back to where he had seen the specter.

With his heart pounding and adrenaline coursing through his veins, the doctor made a frantic search of the vicinity. While remaining safely on one side of the road then the other, the doctor played his steady shaft of light over the darkening road and into the jumble of woods and weeds that outlined it.

Just as he expected there was nothing to see, nothing to recover. The mysterious figure he swore he had seen had vanished without a trace. He played out the illusion again in his mind. He had seen, without a doubt, the shadow of a person crossing the highway directly in front of him as he rounded the curve. If it had been an actual person, there undoubtedly would have been a collision, a death! The only way things could have ended up as they did, without any fatalities, was for the fact that the figure in the road was not of this earth. It was a specter, a ghost. It was James!

Certain that his apparition had disappeared for good, the doctor decided to return to his vehicle, fearful that something terrible could yet occur, due to his car's precarious position alongside the dangerous stretch of road. He gave one last fleeting look at the tire marks—two jagged black fish hooks jaunted across the center of the pale-gray asphalt—to make sure it had really happened, then remarked, "I wonder what Dave would think of these two beauties. Not exactly up to par with what a high-performance engine could put out, but nonetheless . . ." He nodded approval.

In a hurry to leave, the doctor jogged the remainder of the distance back to his car and departed. He drove off, apprehensively examining every square inch of road before him. Around each bend he expected the unexpected. James could pop up anywhere. The ride home seemed to take forever. To the doctor it seemed as if he were on the ultimate Halloween ride ever. The thrill of knowing or not knowing if or when James's ghost would appear had the doctor in a state of exhilaration he had never known before. All the way home he could feel the pulse beat in his body so profoundly, he thought his heart had increased in size immensely.

When he eventually arrived home, he pulled anxiously into his stony drive and proceeded without stopping to retrieve his mail. The sky overhead had already darkened enough to activate the sensor lights surrounding his house and garage. He encroached into the area flooded by brightness and activated the automatic garage door, which opened upon demand. As a precaution, he activated the door-closing without leaving his vehicle.

Though it was early by his standard for going to bed, the doctor felt extremely tired and opted not to stay up. After locking up, he proceeded to his room and quickly undressed and slipped into bed.

As he lay in the stillness of the night, he contemplated all that the day had brought him. His thoughts involuntarily carried him to and fro, from Dave's debacle to his own with Linda. Each one carried with it a plethora of possibilities. Had Dave really seen James? Would James come again? Would James try to harm him? Was Linda's coming into his life at just the right time, fate? Was there to be a future between them? The doctor's mind was like a frying pan full of scrambled eggs, tossing these and other related thoughts over and over and over, hoping to get them done.

And then there was the question of Annice. What would happen between them was the hardest thing of all to predict. Made hardest because the doctor knew her best, knew her morals, her sentiments, her ideals. Annice, he knew, must be in the most dire straits, morally, ethically. It had taken her twenty years to finally, finally decide to renounce her wedding vows. For twenty long years she had tolerated being a partner in a bad marriage. That's how long she struggled with her inner self, her faith. So when she opened herself up to having extramarital relations, she had done so in accordance with having first spent countless hours rectifying it between herself and God. Because of this, this exhausting rectification, Annice's decision would have to be true.

And finally there was the doctor, the last part of the equation. Here's where he was. He had spent almost his entire life fending for James, when they were young, when they were older. And now here he is, again. How should he perceive him? He tried not to. He had spent most of his life loving Annice, near to her when they were teens, from afar after she had left him, and nearer again once she had come to work for him. Somehow, someway, these two are connected. He didn't know if it was true but somehow he believed it.

These relevant matters mattered less and less as the night progressed and the doctor's mind finally gave up trying to bring them to conclusion, and fell into unconscious sleep. There would be no resolutions this night.

Tasteless Tactics

Morning came. The doctor awoke refreshed and in surprisingly high spirits. The jumbled mood that had daunted him the previous night was gone and had been replaced by an elated single-mindedness about seeing Annice again.

It had been since just after they made love that he had been with her and his heart found its place just knowing they would be together. The torturous days of in-between time had been forgotten. Linda would be forgotten. This he vowed as he drove steadily toward the city.

"It will be like old times. Now that we are lovers we can pick up right where we left off so, so many years ago. We will love each other as lovers do."

His heart rejoiced when he pulled into a parking space in front of the James Street building and saw Annice's blue Ford already parked in a spot across the street. He hurried into the building, his heart pounding like a school boy's on a first date.

When he entered the building, he stopped for a moment to catch his breath. When he entered the office, their eyes met. It was an awkward moment as each of them tried to tell each other things with their eyes. The doctor's expression was easy to read. He was overjoyed at seeing her. His face was flushed and told of excitement and desire. Annice's expression was unclear at best. Her face was pale and the smile she wore was not above suspicion. Giving her the benefit of the doubt, the doctor attributed her melancholy look to her lacking health and he rushed over beside her to ascertain the state of her condition.

He approached her, put down his briefcase on the floor beside her, and placed his hand on her forehead.

"Annice, are you feeling all right? You look so pale and tired. Are you certain you are ready to come back?"

"I'm fine," she replied in a subdued voice.

"Is there something I should know?" the doctor asked in a deliberate tone.

"No."

The doctor's question had meant more than asking about her physical condition. He had given her the opportunity to talk about anything. Her refusal shocked him. Her attitude toward him was as if nothing of any consequence had happened recently in her life. She seemed complacent toward him, about life, about anything. It was as though their lives had never touched. In her defense, the doctor speculated that maybe, for her, this was neither the time nor place for them to begin delving into their personal matters. He shrugged off her rather noncompliant attitude, but was still annoyed by it. As he made his retreat, he remarked, "If you need me you know where I am."

To make his annoyance known, he walked off, briefcase in hand, and huffed as he entered his own office. Once inside, he came face-to-face with his newly added decor, the detector. The previous day he had activated both recorders to record for a period of twelve hours, which was their maximum surveillance time. This period, which began yesterday at five o'clock in the afternoon, had just ended at five o'clock this morning. The doctor was curious whether they contained anything worthwhile to his cause.

One of the remarkable features of this latest, greatest technology was that neither tape had to be reviewed in its entirety to pick out any variances which were recorded. Both had a built-in sensing system which could search the tape and lock into any anomaly picked up during the tape's recording. How it worked was that the tapes would become coded whenever a variation of sound or a fluctuation of light occurred during the tape's play time. Upon rewinding the tapes, the codes would be imprinted electronically, and when replayed, could be set to go right from one to another and played from those points of variance.

The doctor diligently went about rewinding both tapes. As he did, he contemplated his chances of finding anything James-related on them. He doubted it. Because of his encounter with the specter on Dead Man's Curve the previous evening, he didn't think it possible to have the extra luck of capturing his old nemesis on film. But he was particularly curious to see just how effective the expensive extrasensory equipment was.

First he examined the audio tape. He set the audio player to search for anomalies and began playing the tape. For the entire twelve hours which had been recorded, there turned up only one coded segment, a span of about three minutes in the middle of the tape in which the doctor heard what he believed to be the sound of a backyard tree branch tapping against the window.

"The wind on the window," he stated to himself.

Next he played the videotape through to search for recorded variances but was disappointed to find out that there were none. Despite this, he played a long segment anyway just to see how clearly the camera's depictions were. While the camera was on, it threw a soft-white light into the camera's view, barely enough light to see by but sufficient for the system's intended purpose.

He looked intently into the tiny viewer at the familiar setting, hoping against hope he would find something, anything. His success was not that he found anything but rather now he knew he could.

He was still perusing the tape when Annice paged him on the intercom and announced his first patient of the day. It was Mrs. Gerdy. Mrs. Gerdy was an elderly woman who had been a patient of the doctor's for almost two years. She was seventy, gray-haired, and as thin as a cord of rope. She was amazingly spry for her age and in good health. Mentally there was nothing wrong with her except for the fact that there was nothing wrong. Mrs. Gerdy had met the doctor unexpectedly once while she was out walking and the doctor helped her to cross the street. She was so taken by his kindness that she insisted, shortly thereafter, to call—call, meaning make an appointment to see him in his office.

During their initial visit, Mrs. Gerdy informed the doctor that her only son, Paul, was a physician too and was currently practicing in Chicago—Chicago, the doctor believed, just so he could get away from her, in a nice sort of way.

Once, during the interim of her care, Paul called the doctor to find out why his mother was seeing a psychiatrist. The doctor told Paul that initially he had evaluated his mother and found nothing wrong with her but that she insisted on seeing him. The doctor suggested too, that maybe she did so to fill the void in her life caused by not seeing her own son. She did not get to experience on a day-to-day basis, having her own son, an esteemed professional physician, and obviously her pride and joy, close.

About the matter of money, the doctor assured Paul that except for her initial appointment he had never again charged his mother for time spent in his office. The once-a-month office visit the doctor considered a contribution to society, as he put it to Paul. Paul then insisted that the doctor be paid something for his time, and to appease Paul, the doctor suggested that Paul make an annual contribution to some mental-health organization, to which Paul agreed. The doctor also suggested that for the time being, Paul's mother should still be allowed to continue with her unnecessary visits, because they were uplifting to her and that she might become distraught if he tried to forbid her from it.

After seeing Mrs. Gerdy, the doctor saw four more patients for forty-five minutes each. During their comings and goings, the doctor had hardly a chance to see or speak to Annice. But once the morning appointments were over, he made another attempt to talk to her.

During the course of the long morning, the doctor had contemplated how Annice had shirked their relational matters when he had wanted to open up to her earlier. He was determined not to let that happen now. He was going to forcefully let her know just how she had let him down and hurt his feelings. He walked determinedly out of his office, battle ready—his thoughts and opinions his ammunition—when he came upon her.

All at once his armor melted, his stash of collected phrases lost. The battle was over before it began and his disposition changed. He was at her mercy. Annice was hunched over on her desk, her hands to her face, attempting to hold back tears which streamed down her red cheeks. The doctor was stunned by the about-face she had done. Earlier she had seemed so reserved. Besieged by pity, the doctor rushed to her and knelt at her side. He leaned his head against hers and began whispering her name, "Annice, Annice, Annice."

After several repetitions, she reluctantly responded and looked up at him with her glistening eyes as more tears erupted from her breaking heart. On impulse, the doctor reached over on her desk and grabbed at the Kleenex box. He began wiping her tears and she appreciably reached over and clasped his free hand as he did so. After an appreciable duration, the doctor finally asked, "Why are you crying?"

Annice remained silent a moment longer.

"Tell me! Tell me!" he demanded. "For your own good, tell me."

He wanted to shake her, shake her and make her tell him everything. He clenched his fists tightly, holding his anger in check— holding back with every fiber of his being, to his sagacity. Annice could not see his demonstration of restraint but she must have felt it, for at the moment when he was about to vent his anger, she finally burst into a crying jag.

"It's no use. It's no use pretending any more. I hate him! I hate him!" she cried in a jittery voice.

"Hate who?" the doctor asked in a tactful reply though he knew fully well who she was speaking about.

"He's the most horrible person in the whole world and I mean it!"

"Who? You're husband?"

"Yes."

"What did he do?"

The doctor's voice was hard and demanding and Annice knew he wanted to hear the truth, whatever it was. Annice looked into his eyes which seemed to be piercing into her soul. She wanted to be truthful with him. He loved her.

She wiped her tear-stricken face one final time, then used the Kleenex to blow her nose.

"I'm ready now," she announced in a resolved voice. "Last Saturday when we were together, he, Leslie, suspected that something was out of line. When I got home he was there. He asked me where I had been and I told him. I told him I was having coffee with Amy at the Holiday Inn."

"But that's what you told me you were going to tell him," the doctor interjected.

"Yes, I know," Annice replied.

"Didn't he believe you?"

"He called her. He asked her what time we were together and what time we left. Amy told the truth. She didn't know any better. So then he wanted to know why I got home so late after Amy. I told him I stayed because I ran into an old friend. Of course he didn't believe me."

"So what happened?"

"Well, we argued for a while and he just got madder and madder. Then he forced me up to the bedroom. He told me to undress and as I did he began slapping me around. When my clothes were off he threw me onto the bed and ordered me to lay still. If I moved he would punch me harder than he ever has before. He made me lie there for him, just for his amusement. I felt like I was being tortured. And I was. He knew. He knew. At that point I was more terrified of him than I'd ever been. He beat me mercilessly."

At that point the doctor almost didn't want Annice to go further. His eyes began searching Annice's body over for the telltale signs of Leslie's abuse. But much to his chagrin, he could see no indications, apparent, that she had been violated. Her face appeared whole, except for the crimson flush on her cheeks from crying as intensely as she had been. Her arms and legs, as far as he could see on them, appeared without the slightest mark or bruise.

"Where did he hurt you?"

"Where do you think!" Annice shouted back, angered at the insinuation.

Instead of provoking Annice further the doctor remained silent. If she wanted to reveal the information she would. He waited for her to continue.

During the brief interval as the doctor bided his time, Annice was becoming increasingly upset. She wanted to be under no restraint. She wanted him to know, to know everything of the awful truth. She wanted him to know the extent to which she had been humiliated and hurt.

"Down there! He forced me to lie still while he punched me in many places. He beat me over and over and over again. He beat me black and blue. When it was over, I was in so much pain I wanted to die!. He left me crying and hurt. The last thing he did was threaten me that if I ever told anyone or if I went to see a doctor he would kill me. He then left the house and got drunk. When he came back he wanted to have sex. I told him he hurt me so much that it was impossible. But he took me anyway, and laughed while he did it. I stayed in bed for days healing. That's why I couldn't come to work. He wouldn't let me leave the house until he thought I was healed enough that I wouldn't want to go to a doctor. I think he still feels threatened that I might go see a doctor."

"I think you should."

"I don't know if I should," Annice said doubtfully. "That might make matters worse. What if I did and the doctor reported the incident to the police. What then? He might go berserk."

"He's already doing that now. If I were you, I would be the one calling the police. Your husband doesn't have the right to hurt you."

For a moment they both kept silent. Each was thinking about what to do. The doctor's heart was beating fast. Though he was angered at the fact that Annice had been harmed, he also felt a surge of elation at the prospect that inevitably she would be free. It was all happening so, so fast.

"What's the matter with you anyway!" the doctor demanded. "Why do you stay there? How can I protect . . ."

Annice leaned over to him and circled her arms around his neck.

"Hold me," she said.

Both stood up and their embrace was enduring. Each felt the other's heart beating as if it were their own. They were as one. Eventually, they loosened their grip on each other and Annice began speaking softly into the doctor's ear.

"I promise you, Christopher, I'm leaving him. Just not today. Not right now. It's a very involved process and it will take time to prepare for it properly. I have to get together some money and find a place to live. In the meantime, it's better that I go along pretending that everything is all right. Trust me now. Trust what I'm going to do."

Annice had pledged that she was going to find her freedom but the doctor was bewildered by one aspect of her planned escape. She had not asked him for his help, not financially, not strategically, not even emotionally. He felt bothered by her lack of demonstrative need.

Not another word was said about the subject as the doctor and Annice scurried off together to have a quick meal before any afternoon patients arrived. Together they retrieved their packed lunches from the refrigerator. The doctor had a homemade sub fixed with lettuce, onions, ham, and several different types of bolognas. With it he had a container of homemade lemonade. Annice had a chicken salad, crackers, and a can of Pepsi-Cola. Their luncheon conversation was sporadic and limited to issues that were relevant to mainly their work. Suppressed deep within their minds were the thoughts that related to each other. But it would have been futile to discuss them now for there wasn't the time.

The doctor, especially, went ahead in his thoughts to exacting the implications of everything that had happened. Annice was in a fragile state and the doctor knew he couldn't provoke her into taking action she wasn't ready to take. Soon, Annice would be abrogated from her marriage, and when she did take that first step toward her freedom, he would be there to help her.

As they continued their meal, the doctor decided that he would help Annice do something that would invariably help with her escape. He waited until they were done before he proposed it.

"Annice, I'm very concerned for your physical being after what you have been through. I have a close friend who is a gynecology specialist. She has an office very close to here and I'm recommending that you see her as soon as possible. I can call her to see if she has an opening, today, if possible. I can have her promise to keep the matter strictly confidential. The only result for having gone will be having the peace of mind that everything, at least everything down there, as you so eloquently put it, is OK, OK?"

The doctor looked squarely into Annice's eyes and he sensed that there was a conflict growing inside her. He knew he had to act quickly to get her to react to his proposition. Fear, once it finds its place inside someone, festers and grows until it has grown over everything. Thinking that she was thinking of a way out of it, the doctor then sought out another contingency and squashed it.

"Further more, I'll pay for it. You won't have to submit anything to insurance and have the worry of phone calls, of forms arriving in the mail. Anything, anything at all that needs to come to you can be sent directly to this office, and in my name if you like."

"OK," Annice said meekly.

Before she could change her mind, the doctor left. He raced to the phone inside his office, and on the way, shut the door. Using the yellow pages, he found the number and placed the call. Before he knew it, he had arranged for a 2:30 appointment for Annice, his cause aided by a last-minute cancellation.

The swift execution of his plan to have Annice cared for, served to inspire him, and as a result, he added to that essential call with two others. The first he placed to Dr. Jeanne at the city hospital, where he contacted her and apprised her of Annice's latest difficulties.

"She will have further incontrovertible evidence of his abuse," he stated in closing.

The second call he placed to Dr. Brain. Dr. Brain was not immediately available for conversation according to his secretary, so the doctor left an at-length message about his concerns.

"Despite any uncertainty, I can assure you that my old pal, James, is back among us. Call me and I'll fill you in on the details of my latest encounter and an encounter someone else had with him."

To ensure that contact would be made without delay, the doctor concluded his message by giving Dr. Brain his personal telephone number and requesting that Dr. Brain call him, even at home.

The doctor saw two more patients before 2:20 rolled around. At precisely that time, he exited his office to remind Annice that she should be leaving. When he joined her in the outer office, she already had her handbag in hand and was conversing with the doctor's next patient, something about her having to be temporarily absent from the office but that she would return promptly. She caught sight of the doctor's insistent stare and hurried herself out of the building. The doctor escorted her out and to her car.

"You remember where I told you it was?"

"Yes. The 1100 block of Columbia Avenue. It's on the right-hand side about midway down the block."

"Exactly."

The doctor gave her a quick kiss for luck then watched as she sped off. He turned then strode back into his building, a feeling of pride elevating every footstep on the way. He had done a good job of helping her.

The doctor's next patient was a young Catholic woman, twenty-five, and pregnant with her third child. She had come to the doctor only recently, assigned to him through a counseling service at Catholic Charities.

Cathy was suffering from an acute case of anxiety disorder brought on by the stressful demands of her extremely busy life; specifically, dealing with the concerns of two young children, with a third on the way. Both of her children were toddlers, ages three and one. The baby, expected in three months, would make for three children all under three.

Even before the conception of her expected child, Cathy had discussed with her husband, on numerous occasions, her reluctance to have any more children. Her husband, an adamant Catholic, argued, as Church Law dictates, that every act of sexual intercourse between a husband and wife should be open to the possibility of conception. Cathy disagreed. She argued that for practical purposes, such as being capable of providing properly for their children, they should limit the size of their family in accordance with their abilities, abilities meaning their available amount of time and money.

As a result of their discord, they had visited their parish priest to seek his counsel. His advice was in accordance with the Church.

Cathy had protested her views sternly and during the final visit stormed out of the rectory.

The doctor, a Catholic too, knew fully well the Catholic Church's position on marriage and conception. He sympathized with Cathy. At the initial meeting, both Cathy and Chris were present. The doctor did his best to try to explain to Chris that God had not intended for every woman to procreate in great numbers.

"Not everybody's the same. Some women enjoy having a lot of children, others do not. In Cathy's case she has already given you two beautiful children, a girl and a boy, with a girl on the way. You should be grateful for that. Your wife can't handle any more right now. For her sake you should consider using contraceptives after your next child is born. For Cathy's sake."

But the doctor's advice had fallen on deaf ears. Cathy's husband had said he would not allow her to use any form of birth control. So, knowing that she had found an ally in the doctor, Cathy continued her visits. The reassurance helped her. But today was Cathy's lucky day, for the doctor was inspired. He had now decided to help her in a way she didn't expect.

"Cathy, I'm going to do you a favor, a really big favor. I understand the predicament you are in with your husband and I've decided to offer you help in that direction. Besides the pills I have prescribed for you, I'm also offering you the opportunity, at my ethical expense, to go on birth control. I have decided, after much internal debate and soul searching, that you deserve to have control over whether or not you conceive any more children. I have the power to prescribe birth-control pills for you.

"It is my considered opinion that your mental health is at stake here and it is my responsibility to help you. Therefore, beginning in ten weeks I want you to come here and I will dispense a one-month prescription. After that, you will receive a prescription every month, meaning that you will come here to get them. I will, of course consult a physician. I know a general practitioner. He's a very good friend of mine. I am certain he will help.

"I think that your problem lies not in being able to handle being a mother but it's your worry that you are unable to control having more and more and more children. If you have any more than the three you will soon have, you will be overwhelmed by them and may not be able to function at all. I . . . we can't let that happen. You owe it to yourself and your children to be able to be the best mother you can be."

Cathy's eyes were lit up the entire time the doctor was speaking to her. She was elated that the doctor, who hadn't known her for very long, was helping her in such a personal way. She was touched.

"Oh, Doctor, how can I ever thank you," she said solemnly.

Then the entirety of the doctor's plan began rushing to her. Her nightmare would be over. Cathy became ecstatic. She clapped her hands together in congratulations of what benefit this would be to her.

"Oh, Doctor! You are a lifesaver! I will be forever grateful for what you are doing for me."

"Remember, though, this is being done in the strictest confidence. It's just between you and me. Don't tell anyone."

"There, two lives saved," The doctor said aloud from his desk once Cathy had departed.

Once Cathy had departed, the doctor checked the agenda to see who his next patient was. To his surprise he found out that there was only an open schedule. The final patient had called and canceled earlier in the day, made known by a small annotation alongside the patient's name. The doctor was now unexpectedly free. He had time now to think to himself.

He stepped into the reception room and scooped up a handful of jelly mints to eat. He felt like being idle and didn't want to take up any patient analysis as he might have done. He plopped down on a waiting-room chair content doing nothing. The doctor idled away a few minutes, when suddenly the outer door to the office burst open. Startled, the doctor turned. It was Linda!

She looked a wreck with her hair all tangled, her face agitated, and her eyes glazed over. The doctor got up and went to her. While looking directly at her, he could see that her eyes were covered with red striations as though she hadn't slept for days. But soon the doctor's eyes were off Linda's facial appearance and on to the rest of her. She was wearing a very provocative ensemble of clothes—a see-through white blouse under which she was braless, a short black pleated skirt, and cuffed black socks which were folded up from a pair of black heels. She looked every part the prostitute and the doctor knew he was in trouble. She had come purposefully and with a scheme to seduce him.

"There you are," she announced the moment she laid eyes upon him. "Thought you could hide away from me in this tiny, little office."

With her keen sexual senses, Linda noticed the doctor noticing her. Like a predator to prey, she was upon him. She engaged their bodies in full contact, pressing hers to his so tightly that the doctor could feel the warmth of her entirely. He was captured and could not escape.

They began kissing. Then the doctor noticed it. The odor was faint but nonetheless present in her hair and as a residue on her clothing. It was marijuana. Clearly this spontaneous course of action was due to Linda's enhanced state of mind. There was no doubt that she had just recently smoked a potent amount of pot, and now under its influence, she was being spurred into this awkwardly bold display of emotion.

The doctor was mad that she had barged into his office, but his resolve to remain mad melted within minutes under the heat of her passion. What could he do? She would obviously never leave if he ordered her to, not without a fight. He observed the clock. Annice would be back soon. In Linda's condition she would probably become hostile if he refused her advances. The only thing to do was to indulge her and do it quickly before Annice returned. It was a scary plan with resounding implications but the doctor knew he had to do it.

The doctor took Linda forcefully by the hand and proceeded with her back into his office. He locked the door. When he turned around, Linda had already removed her button-down blouse and she stood before him flaunting herself. He went over to fondle her. "No," he cried out once he relinquished his tremulous hold on the shoulders of his former lover. The doctor knew his weakness well.

One thing would lead to another and another and another. Hastily he retreated. By the time he ended up behind his desk Linda was already lunging for him. Anticipating her approach he swooped her up and together they fell backward into the swivel chair. Linda was exhausted and collapsed in the doctor's lap. When the event was over, Linda appeared to be coming down off her high. She seemed reticent and tactfully apologized to the doctor for having offended him at his place of business this way.

"Why in God's name did you feel you had to come down here in the middle of the day when you know I'm working? You were just lucky my secretary was out and my last patient canceled."

"I'm so sorry," Linda contended. "I'm as bewildered about it as you are."

"How can that be?"

"It all happened so fast. It was so strange how it came over me. I was leaving my apartment when I bumped into this strange guy. He looked so weird too. He was wearing blue jeans, a denim jacket, and had his hair all slicked back too. He looked like someone from the past. He had no qualms about approaching me either. He called out my name and pretended he knew me. We sat down together on the steps trying to figure out if he did. I wasn't afraid of him. He seemed weird but personable. And there were people around in my neighborhood. So we sat down and talked. It was clear though that he didn't really know me. So I thought he wanted to hit on me but he didn't do that either. I didn't know what to think. Then, suddenly, he removed his jacket. Underneath he had on a plain white tee shirt, and rolled up on his left-arm's sleeve was a Marlboro cigarette pack. He unrolled his undershirt and took out the pack. Of course I thought he was just going to light up a smoke, which he did, but it was a different kind of smoke. I couldn't believe he was lighting up a joint right there in broad daylight. He seemed so unconcerned about it, like no matter what, he wouldn't get into any trouble if he were caught.

"So, we sat there. We smoked pot right there on the steps in front of my apartment building, right there for every eye to see. And it was even weirder. As we smoked, he began talking about you. I mean like he really, really knew you. He told me things—things that I don't know are true, things that didn't really make sense—about you, about you when you were young."

Linda appeared to be exhausted. She was coming down off her high. If she stayed any longer, the doctor feared she would fall asleep right there in the office. And time was running out. Annice would definitely be back soon. He helped her back up and hurried her out of the office. He helped her down the steps in the front of the building then directed her to go straight back to her apartment.

"I'll call you in a few minutes to make sure you got home safely," he called out to her once she began walking down the block.

Of Sex and Sin

Back in the office the doctor noticed there was a saliva stain on the cushion of his chair. He proceeded to clean it by wiping it with a handful of wet Kleenex. Once he had effectively cleaned the stain, he relaxed in one of the chairs opposite his desk. This business of jostling two women around is far more than I can handle," he thought.

It was James! was the next thought out of his head. James has made it back in full. And he's playing me for a fool. He's trying to manipulate my sex life with Linda, and who knows, maybe my love life with Annice.

"Now, not only is he back, he's back doing the same crazy things he did when he was really here. He's even come back as far as smoking pot and manipulating women. I wonder where he got the stash of marijuana though. He probably had some secret supply hidden away from way back when. That joint he and Linda smoked was probably some vintage reefer from the '70s, maybe Columbian Red Bud, Rainbow, or Gold. Or could have been something even more potent like Hawaiian or Thai stick. James always did smoke the top pot.

"Now the question is why did he want to influence her to get to me? If he was trying so desperately to get to me before why, why would he further his communicative powers on Linda instead of coming directly to me. He knows I'm here. And he knows that I know he's here. Maybe he thinks I needed a good one.

"That would be James, though, always thinking he was the best at it. And always believing everyone else was just pathetic at getting women. Jimmy always was a stud. I remember how frustrating it was when we were together as adolescents. James was always so good at finding available girls while I always played in his shadow. His anything-goes attitude always piqued a girl's curiosity. They certainly did pay attention to him. But I had a greater respect for myself. I was not about to give myself up so easily to anyone. I wanted love to be the issue between me and any special someone, not sex. But I have to admit, looking back, I was jealous of James and his way with women.

"But by comparison, I did better. James was a showman but the show didn't last long. I was a sure thing. If I loved somebody and somebody loved me, it was worthwhile. Girls were always infatuated with James. But infatuation never lasts, even when it's good. Girls, especially girls in their teens, are more easily attracted, or should I say distracted, by guys like James; but most of the time they end up hating them. He had a lot of love-hate relationships. He was both a Don Juan and a Henry VIII all at once."

"But how to get to the point of all this, how does this conjecture relate to me specifically? What could possibly be his doing? Why would he come all the way back from the dead just to involve himself with me and my relationships? Why?"

While the good doctor was considering why James, in the form of a specter, would contrive to aid the doctor's faulty sex life, Annice slipped into the office and quietly resumed her duties. On her desk there were piles of insurance forms to be filled out. These had been held in abeyance since her absence because neither the doctor nor Linda had the pertinent information about the patients they pertained to. She readied herself to begin work on them, but then relented, deciding she should inform the doctor that she had returned.

Promptly she switched on the intercom and waited for the doctor to respond. Upon realizing she was back, the doctor immediately called for her to come into his office for a private conversation.

"Is everything OK?"

"Yes," she replied in a mild tone as if she were somewhat embarrassed.

"Is that all?" he asked in a pleading voice. "Please tell me more."

Annice, who was looking toward the floor, lifted up her head and met his eyes with hers. Though she and the doctor had already been intimate, they had not had much practice at being intimate in their discussions about each other. She could tell, though, by his stare, that he was totally interested in what she was about to say. She gulped. She felt like she was getting naked in front of him for the first time.

"I can still make babies," she began openly. "There is no permanent damage to me, reproductively. It's just going to be a long time in healing. I did explain that my husband was drunk and took me forcefully. But I didn't press the issue. I could tell they were not amused, and more than a little suspicious. I won't be able to do it for a while."

After speaking, she gazed at him intently, hoping to interpret by his countenance whether his concern was mild or maddening. Was he truly in love with her or had his feelings faded? It was a poignant moment as she waited out his response.

For the doctor it was nothing short of an opportunity. Her openness made it possible for him to talk to her about the whole measure of this predicament they were in and he wasted no time expressing it.

"I'm both relieved and elated that you are going to be well again. But, be that as it may, I think it's time we discussed what's really important here. What about us?"

Annice had been unprepared for any conversation regarding their personal relationship. An anguish started to grow inside her over it. She had gotten up the gumption to discuss, intimately, the details of her personal injury but she never thought their discussion would turn into everything else. She felt distressed. The doctor's three simple words had opened up a Pandora's box of emotions she had been repressing for times only when she felt strong enough to deal with them. They began to surface in her mind. All the time she was struggling to repress them, she heard the doctor's soothing voice asking over and over, "Are you unhappy about us?"

Finally Annice had control enough of her emotions to respond. She would have to address the issues firsthand for they would not leave her.

"No!" she fired back at his persistent question. "I am not unhappy about us."

"Then what?"

Annice was on the verge of tears and the doctor beckoned her out of her chair to comfort her. They met and their bodies locked together. Like long-lost lovers they clung to each other, their bodies intertwined as if one depended on the other for life. Finally Annice spoke.

"It's . . . it's all so complicated, Christopher. I'm a married woman. Twenty years ago I committed myself in a marriage blessed by the Church. And now . . . now I've committed adultery. I've committed a mortal sin. I feel sorrow and anger and guilt about it. These feelings are now knotted around my brain like a ball of twine that seems to keep growing tighter."

Annice paused to reflect on her thoughts for a moment.

"I love you, Christopher. I really do. I just don't know whether it's fair for me to put you through all this. You have become entangled in my sin. I blame myself for what happened. What I did with you, I did willingly."

"Yes, that's right," the doctor interjected. "But I think your perspective is flawed. You're taking this way too personally. Remember, you are not the only person involved in this situation. There's me and your husband. Nothing happened that couldn't have happened unless all three of us had been responsible for it. Let me clarify that. Nothing could have happened the way it did unless your husband, idiot that he is, abused you. Nothing could have happened the way it did unless you had been the victim of his relentless torture on your body and soul. And nothing could have happened unless I loved you the way I do. So you see, you are merely one-third of the equation. And you should be feeling only one-third of the associated guilt.

"Annice, what happened between us happened because we love each other, and how can love be a bad thing? You didn't seduce me just for the fun of it. It took you twenty years just to get to the boiling point. And what about God? Do you really think God intended for you to be so unhappy? Do you really think God intended for you to suffer what I consider to be the worst of all fates—to be unloved. You, the beautiful woman that you are, were cheated out of that by the one person in the world who was supposed to love you. It is not you who has sinned but it is you who has been sinned against. God is a forgiving God. If you have committed adultery, God has forgiven you. If you leave your husband, God will forgive you. If you choose to be with me out of love, God will bless you, bless us.

"Annice if you look beyond the immediate conflict and toward what will be the final resolution of this, you will be able to sustain yourself. You will not be alone. I will be there for you."

"But I've sinned," Annice said abjectly.

The doctor looked at her admiringly. With his hand he tilted her downcast face up.

"So have I. So has your husband. So has everybody the whole world over. And let he who is without sin cast the first stone, remember? We are all sinners, or did God make you a perfect person?

"But how do I get over it?"

"You don't. God made us so that we can be forgiven our sins but that we may not forget them. If we forgot them, how could we then remember not to commit them again? Our memories are sacred for that purpose."

The doctor began to quietly pace the floor around him. Annice knew he was delving seriously into the philosophical esoterics of the subject matter. She loved it whenever he did this, even to the point of smiling in the midst of so much tragedy.

"It is the task of every human being to carry their sins with them through life. They become part of us and make us better than we were before."

There was a brief abeyance before the doctor began his discourse again.

"You know, there are varying degrees of sin. They range from white to black and are colored with shades of everything in between. Some sins are almost white and pure as snow; simple lies, for instance, which are told to protect somebody's reputation, perhaps. There are sins that are light-gray in color, like perhaps stealing a car and hurting nobody in the process. And last, there are sins that are black as coal, like murder. And even within their own categories, each sin is given its own special consideration due its own circumstance.

"Take George Washington, for instance. He is the father of our country, a Revolutionary War hero, and yet he is also a killer! He willingly killed other men during the French and Indian wars and during the Revolution. Did he not? But, as a nation of people, we look upon him as an exulted figure. He is revered despite his crimes. And why? Because the conditions and circumstances necessitated it, and because of the greater good that came as a result of it. A resolution, which results in a greater benefit, is considered worthwhile, even if it is arrived at with methods which are detrimental. Nobody ever thinks of George Washington as a fiend. He is, instead, a noble man, a virtuous man.

"Annice Colby, you are a virtuous woman. You have been brutalized by a man who was supposed to love you. You want only to love and be loved. If the only way to do that is to commit adultery and leave him, then I say society will not hold you in contempt. To love and be loved is the eternal solution for us all."

"But I am not a president," Annice interjected. "Only people of prestige and privilege are afforded the benefit of the doubt."

"I disagree," the doctor stated strongly. "The true worth of a person is not measured by his wealth or status in life. We, as individuals, are the most responsible for applying our own worth. The essence of privilege and prestige are determined by how we conduct ourselves in our lives. We hold ourselves up to it each day of our life. It is more in our character, how we act, that identifies who we are as a person. Are we honest, hard-working, forgiving, loving, forthright, or are we dishonest, indolent, and hateful? Believe me, if George Washington had been any of these bad things he would never have overcome the sins he committed going to war. He would have never been president. And we wouldn't be speaking about him now.

"Annice, don't determine yourself by the sin you committed. You are more than that. It took you twenty years before you finally decided that you had enough, before you finally did something to bring about a resolution for the pain you were feeling. You really didn't have an affair. Affairs are when people who are attracted to each other physically give in to the temptation of the pleasure they hope to derive from being with each other sexually. You didn't do that. You weren't looking for sexual pleasure. You were looking for love. The feelings we had for each other were contained for all the years while you worked with me in this office and they were only brought out once you were in tremendous pain. And why? Why were we able to keep our desires in check for such a prolonged period? Why? Because of the moral good in each of us. Each of us, despite our weaknesses, had the desire to do what is right. But now your soul is at stake, and because your soul is of the highest priority, we can forsake the constraints of our morality. We are compelled by the greater good, and the greater good is for you to be free, free to be able to love, free to be able to be loved."

The doctor was momentarily out of breath. The soliloquy was over. Annice, too, wanted to break from the inundations of thought the doctor had evoked in her.

"Hold me," were the next words out of Annice's mouth.

In response the doctor scooped her into his arms and held her protectively and lovingly against him. They kissed. While the kissing ensued, the doctor happened to notice the wall clock in the room.

"It's time to leave," he announced.

The couple exchanged several flourishes of kisses before they reluctantly broke off their embrace. Annice compliantly began readying herself as she started putting her desk in order and collected her personal belongings. The doctor stood quietly nearby and watched her.

"You know," he finally spoke out. "There are places you can go, shelters, if you are afraid to go home. I could even give you a phone number or an address if you like."

Annice began to dawdle a bit and the doctor realized she was contemplating his offer.

"No, Christopher, I can't just leave him like that, without a word. Even though I do intend to leave him, I intend to do it with a certain amount of consideration, for myself and him. I've heard what can happen when a woman goes into one of those shelters. It involves making out an official complaint. Then the police have to get involved, and that ends any possibility anyone has for leaving someone in a peaceful way. Brute that Leslie is, I don't want to make things worse; and the worse is usually left for the one doing the leaving, in this case me."

"I think it would be best if you left now," the doctor said in protest.

"I know you think that," Annice returned. "Look, I've got to go now. I promise you it will be soon."

And with that, Annice rushed out the door. Just after she departed, the doctor realized that he had neglected to make any provision to see her over the weekend. Realizing that she was probably still somewhere out front, either in her car waiting for traffic to clear or possibly in her car doing something prior to leaving, he was just about to dash out after her when suddenly the phone rang. He was indecisive for a moment then realized that the indecision had probably cost him the chance of having caught up with Annice. He relented from taking up the chase and answered the phone instead.

"Hello, this is Dr. Haefner. Who's calling?"

The only reply the doctor received was a crackling sound coming from the other end of the line. It sounded as if it was a cell phone with a very bad connection. Something was interfering with the signal.

"Hello, this is Dr. Haefner. Can you hear me?"

Again there was no formal response. The doctor answered for a third time.

"Hello? Hello?"

Then, suddenly the doctor was struck by an idea. It's him! It's him! Quickly he activated the new listening device, placed in the top corner of his desk. He placed the phone's receiver directly in front of it. Then he spoke into the receiver one more time so the caller might resume his effort. Standing completely still and bending with his ear down to the receiver, the doctor waited. He could still plainly hear the same garbled communication coming through.

It was all too reminiscent to him. The scenario being played out was almost identical to the one which occurred a decade ago. Then, on the night of James's death, James had tried desperately to make contact with his old friend. He recalled it all vividly—the incessantly ringing phone, the garbled communication, the jiggling doorknob. This was a different instance, but the same, nonetheless. After several minutes, the message ended. The communication became dead silent. The doctor hung up the phone then rewound the tape. He turned up the volume and played back the message very slowly. He put his ear right up to the machine and listened, to every sensation of sound being played.

Most of the message remained incoherent but a few words began to crystallize out of the static. The words were cryptic but could be deciphered if careful attention were paid to them. The words which were discernable were: to . . . to . . . ole . . . to . . . ole . . . for . . . for . . . you. There were other words being said but it was only at this one spot on the tape that the words were clear enough to be known. Just to be sure he hadn't missed anything, the doctor played the tape through a second time. When it was over, he turned off the machine. He leaned back into his chair and wondered over the words and their meaning.

"If it was James, what was he trying to tell me?"

He pieced together the words in his mind. The word "ole" obviously meant "old." But what ramification did the word old imply? Too old for what? Too old for whom? Then it struck him. "He's implying that I'm either too old to be fooling around with two women, or he's meaning that I'm too old for Linda, or he means that Annice is too old for me since it appears that I have a chance for Linda. Wow!"

The doctor didn't know which of the three meanings were correct but it appeared that one of them was. Knowing James, the doctor ascertained that the correct one was that Annice was too old for him. He ejected the tape and tossed it into one of his desk drawers.

"Oh well, what difference did it make anyway?" he thought. "I'm not going to let any of James's opinions determine anything I do. My mind is made up. Hell, it was made up twenty years ago."

It had been a tedious day and the doctor was tired of thinking about all of the pertinent issues of the day. All he wanted now was a satisfying hot meal and a good night's sleep.

"Off to Herkimer's."

When he arrived at his favorite restaurant it was after 6:00. He was concerned that his later-than-usual arrival would mean that he might not get right in. Sometimes the restaurant gets quite full between six and eight o'clock. Sometimes there's even a long line of patrons standing outside waiting to get in. If that were the case today, the doctor already made up his mind that he would skip out on the place and just eat at home.

The doctor grimaced as he drove along, city block after city block, all the way until he reached the outskirts of town. He was greatly relieved, however, when he pulled to within eyesight of the establishment and found it to be only slightly more occupied by cars than usual.

"Not so bad tonight," he commented to the hostess once he was inside.

"Give it fifteen minutes," she replied readily.

"Then I'm glad I got here when I did," he countered.

"Table for one," she shot back.

"Yes."

"Then follow me."

She escorted him back, back to a corner of the restaurant where she knew he often went. There, the doctor waited several minutes before a waitress, flustered and harried, came to take his order.

"Are you ready to order, sir?" she asked in an exasperated voice.

"Yes. I'll have two hot roast beef sandwiches, a side order of fries, and a large chocolate milk, 2 %."

"Will that be all?"

"For now, yes."

During the fifteen minutes the doctor waited for his food he noticed how the ranks of the restaurant patrons were swelling. By the time it arrived the increase had all but filled the place.

Never had two hot roast beef sandwiches tasted so delicious, and never had a plate of golden fries looked so good or tasted so ideal.

Within ten minutes the meal had been devoured, and when the waitress returned to ask him if everything was to his satisfaction, he replied fervently, "It was a remarkable meal."

She gave him a pleased look and began clearing the dirty dishes off of the table. The way she worked around him lured the doctor into taking interest in her. Several times she brushed up against him, his arms and shoulders. At one instant her left breast was only inches away from his face. He could smell her perfume, some kind of lemon scent which he immediately took a liking to. And before it was over he swore he could feel her body heat luring him to her. The moment she stepped away he made a comment about her beauty, which she heard. She smiled but continued with her work. While she was attending the next table over, another whispered voice met her ear, another loving compliment. This, she attributed to the doctor as well, though he had nothing to do with. When he finally got up to leave, she purposely met him on his way to the counter.

"Thank you," she said in a deliberate voice, hoping the doctor would take the hint and ask her out. But much to her chagrin the doctor had no idea why she furthered her chances with him. He did not know that his old friend James had been the one to entice her.

"Thank you," the doctor replied, not knowing what more to say to the eager young lady.

Feeling somewhat rejected, she walked briskly away. The doctor made ready to pay his bill, and as an afterthought, allocated a sizeable amount of gratuity for the waitress. Before departing, he scooped up a handful of jelly mints for the car ride home. As he was exiting the entrance, he heard his name being called out. He turned toward a pack of people nearest him, observed them, but discerned nobody he was familiar with. Again his name was called and again he turned, this time to an unfamiliar couple heading in from the parking lot area where he had parked but farther out. He stopped. Upon their approach he finally did recognize the woman who had recognized him. It was James's older sister, Deb.

"Do you come here often," Deb quizzed the bewildered physician.

Not wanting to deliberately lie but also not wanting to divulge to her the frequency with which he actually patronized Herkimer's, the doctor deflected the answer by responding with his own observation.

"I can't believe you were able to recognize me. I don't believe I have seen you for more than a decade."

"Has it really been that long?"

"In terms of something like this it has."

"This is just so queer. You just called me up the other day too."

Deb started to go on and on, bringing up any old event from the past to discuss. She never introduced her male companion which the doctor thought extremely rude. She just kept reminiscing about the past, which the doctor found very annoying after about five minutes. His only out, he figured, was to keep quiet and hope she would soon exhaust herself. If that didn't work he would have to comment that they had better get inside before all the tables were taken. Just as he was about to mention that, Deb's companion motioned her to hurry up because he was hungry.

"Stop prattling. I came here to eat not start a talk-o-rama."

"Say, Chris, it was nice seeing you. Hope you make out with that project you're working on. And, oh, by the way, I have a keepsake here with me. Remember, you asked me on the phone if I had anything you could have to remember Jim by."

Deb reached into her handbag and pulled out a picture of her brother. She handed it to the doctor.

"Thank you," he said politely.

Once their little association was over, the doctor walked to his car and got inside. He sighed, relieved that his unexpected visit with Jim's sister had ended. He had never intended to pick up the keepsake. He took the photograph out of his shirt pocket and looked intently at it. It was a picture of James when he was maybe seven or eight, just at the time when they first met. It was intriguing. It was even more intriguing that Deb, of all possible people, had just happened to be at his favorite restaurant that particular night. He had never seen her there before. Hell, he had never even seen her in the city in all the years since James's death.

Then, suddenly, the doctor was struck by another unusual thought. Deb, he recalled, had mentioned that he had mentioned something about him doing a project—the project of course being the one he spoke of about James. But the doctor knew, distinctly, that he had not mentioned that to Deb that day he called her. He was sure about that. So how did she know about it? How?

Contact

There was only one solution: James. Somehow he had inculcated on his sister's mind the story of how the doctor was going to do a study of James's past for the benefit of future patients of psychiatry.

The doctor's late dinner and Deb's detaining conversation had made it so that when the doctor screeched out of Herkimer's parking lot and onto the New Danville Pike south, dusk had pervaded the surrounding countryside. As a standard of precaution, the doctor activated his car's headlights and proceeded at a cautionary rate down the highway. Up ahead, a mile or so distant, was the notorious Dead Man's Curve, one of the places where James had first visited him. Now, with the keepsake picture tucked away in his pocket, the doctor felt even more vulnerable to the possibility of James intervening upon him. Eager to get beyond that point of previous contact, the doctor accelerated his car's level of speed to slightly over the posted speed limit. He took the turn well and was just curving onto the straight road when suddenly he noticed a person located on the side of the road just a hundred feet ahead. Due to the darkening day, the figure remained obscure, but upon passing the individual the doctor noticed that he, whoever he was, had his right arm and thumb extended out from his body in the mode of a hitchhiker. Feeling relieved that he had successfully passed the point where James would have appeared if he had so intended, the doctor pulled his car over at a point just past the sojourner. His first instinct was that by aiding the needy traveler he would thwart any attempt James might make to visit him during his lonely drive home.

When his vehicle came to a stop, he unlocked the back door and waited for the hitchhiker to approach the car. During the moments that followed the doctor's mind grew increasingly suspicious. He turned around to see if he could see the person he had stopped for, and saw only an empty roadside. Disturbed, the doctor quickly relocked the back door and started to speed away. He screeched the tires as he did, kicking up dust and stones, which made his tires slide sideways and hampered his fast getaway. Once his car straightened out, he burst forward on the highway, desiring to get out of the situation as quickly as possible. Was someone playing a trick on him? he wondered. Was it James?

There was an enduring silence in the little stretch of time and highway since the doctor initiated his escape from the unusual incident. He was desperately attempting to ease his reaction that James had indeed been the lone highway hitchhiker he had just encountered, when suddenly, from behind him, he heard a voice call out.

"Hey, take it easy when you drive. You don't want to get us both killed do you?"

The doctor turned to the back of the car with a furious look on his face.

"If looks could kill," James stated with a snicker.

Now that the initial shock of being back with him was over, the doctor was ready for him. "How could I kill you either way, old friend, when you're already dead?" he stated sarcastically.

"What a terrible thing to say," James blurted out. "Is that all you can think to say to me after all these years. And anyway, your take on death is pretty much wrong. You say I'm dead, and in accordance to living that may be true, but in the broader sense of being in an existence, I'm all here—at least the part of me that matters."

The doctor found it too distracting to drive and hold a discussion with the ghost of a deceased friend, so he tried to think of some place where he could pull over and carry on an intense interactive discourse without being interrupted by anything else.

Though rather impressed with James's insightful remark, the doctor kept his thoughts in remission until he had decided upon a place for their conversation. Not far ahead was the Pine View Dairy, a modern roadside convenience store and dairy run by a family of farmers. When the store's entranceway came into view, the doctor turned into it and brought the car to a complete stop in a far corner of the parking lot.

"This is where I stop and you begin," the doctor said soundly.

"Begin what?" James asked.

"Begin telling me just what the hell this is all about."

"*This* meaning what specifically?" James asked innocently.

"*This* meaning—what are you doing back in the world? *This* meaning how you did it and why you did it. *This* meaning explaining it all."

"Hey! Hold your horses there, professor! One thing at a time, after all I'm only . . . human."

"You're not anything any more," the doctor purported.

"If you keep up with the snide remarks, I won't tell you anything. I'll just disappear and you can forget you ever saw me. Then what kind of explanation will you get about me. I'm one of the unsolved mysteries of the universe."

"OK, James. I'm listening."

"OK. To start, I came back because I discovered I could. I can't explain it any more than that. I discovered I could do it, so I did. Actually I believe I never really left—my spirit that is. I remember everything about my previous life. I remember it better now than when I was alive. I can place myself at any point of my life, any time, any place, any age. I can be there just as if I am there. It's almost as if another dimension has been revealed to me now. But the past is like being in a fog. It's all misty and vague in the sense that I can't interact with it. I suppose that's because events from the past can't be changed. Unlike the present."

"That's fascinating," the doctor proclaimed.

"Here, now, with you I can still interact. It took me a long time to be able to do so, ten years to be exact, but I accomplished it nonetheless. And the ten years it took had no meaning to me while attempting it. To me the time went by as though it were a day. For me the problem was you."

"How so?" the doctor interjected.

"You, you're only mortal. You have only a finite time to be alive and wandering the earth. If it had been harder for me to get here, it may have been too late. Ten years passed as a day. If it had taken, say fifty years, you probably would have been dead and gone. Then you would have been put to the test of seeing if you could have worked your way back. Because, back I believe is the only way spirits can get together."

"You mean you haven't detected any other spirit life in your other realm of existence?"

"It's weird, isn't it? In all the time since I left your world, I have not encountered one other like me, no one."

"Maybe that's because nobody likes you," the doctor remarked sarcastically.

"Aren't you the jokester," James replied.

"Sorry," the doctor conceded.

"Anyway," James concluded. "That's all I can tell you about how I came to be. To be or not to be, that is the question."

"Inconclusive," the doctor smirked. "So, anyhow, now that we've touched on the 'how' let's talk about the 'why.' Why have you come back to me?"

"That's the easiest question yet. I've watched a little bit of your life now. It's sort of like a soap opera. Your life is full of scenes which seem to go on and on and on, but never reach any conclusion. Now, this is your private life I'm referring to. You accomplish a lot in your practice, there you're a stud. But in your private affairs you're a dud."

"Is that so?" the doctor said challengingly.

"Yes, that's so!" James declared. "Look at you—you're what?—forty now? What do you got to show for it? You have never been married. You have no children. And you're thirty-nine-year-old married secretary has now recently become your lover. You're pathetic!"

"Who are you to judge me!"

"Who do I have to be!"

"Look, why does any of this matter? Why is my personal life of such great concern to you?"

"Because I came back to look out for you, be a big brother to you. Stop you from ruining your life. You may be this high and mighty head guy but it seems the only person you can't take care of is yourself."

The doctor wanted to change the subject.

"Why did you go see your brother Dave in prison?"

"Dave is a loser. I wanted him to see me so that he knew that I knew how much of a loser he was. Dave is a fool."

"Has there been anyone else? Have you materialized before any of your other old acquaintances?"

"No. The only other person I've interacted with was that delicious blonde you hired as a temporary."

"Yes, you somehow got her high. Tell me how you managed that—that's a real curiosity."

"No effort, really. I could tell she was a smoker so I just got hold of some of my old secret stash."

"Where?"

"At my old house, you know, Pine Street. I had pot hidden all over that place—under floorboards, in the ceiling behind some of the ceiling panels, in the old coal bin under the front porch, in the cellar. Hell, I even had some hid in my parents' closet—in their bedroom!"

"And you mean to tell me after all these years it was still there?"

"Yes!"

"So you got her all doped up and sent her to me."

"Hell, yes! And I did you a hell of a favor too. She was one wild and horny chick when I left her."

Through the duration of their conversation, the doctor was becoming increasingly sentimental. How could he not be? How often does any person have the chance to meet with the resurrected spirit of a close old friend? He felt sorry for James much in the same way he had always felt sorry for him. He wanted to know about how he died. He wanted to know if his speculations had been true.

"James, how did all of this come about? What happened to you down in New Orleans?"

James paused. It was apparent that he did not have a ready answer. Twice he began to speak but bit back his words. He looked over at the doctor with an angry glare.

"Why do you want to know?"

"Why wouldn't I want to know?"

"It all happened so fast. We . . . we were all partying: Julie, me, her sister, her sister's boyfriend, and there might have been some others. My memory of that night is unclear. It was supposed to be a gala for our engagement, supposed to be. I remember it was late. Everybody was stoned. I remember walking into the kitchen for a beer, I think. Anyway I remember being in the kitchen and I saw Julie's sister there leaning over the sink. I think she was puking. Anyway, I remember checking her out. I was so stoned. I went up behind her and started to laugh. Then I checked out her ass. She had one fine behind on her. I went right up to it and began grinding on her. And she really didn't care. I felt her. She was grinding me back the same way I was grinding her. She never told me to stop. As far as I was concerned we were in a groove. Then I started feeling her up. I put my arms around her and grabbed her titties. And I didn't stop there. I slid my hand around her waist and unhooked the button of her blue jeans. Then I reached my hand down over her panties and began feeling her. I was going to drop her right then and there and have her except for what happened."

"What happened?"

"It happened so fast I had no time to recognize anything about it. Someone put his hands around my neck and jerked me back. I had no time to think. His hands stiffened around me like a vise. He had me so fast I couldn't even yell. I jostled him around the best I could, but before I could even make a dent against him, it was over. I was dead. I was choked to death on the night of my engagement party by someone who was supposed to be a friend of my fiancée. Everyone who was there that night knew it too, including Julie. It was a conspiracy!"

"I knew it! I knew it too!"

"What do you mean you knew it?"

"I always knew, intuitively, that somebody had purposely killed you."

"How could you have known?"

"Just the way things didn't fit together. It didn't make sense, any of it."

"Explain."

"The whole thing. The account of the way you died—supposedly, that is. Don't you know? You were killed in a fatal car crash. You and your fiancée were driving along some remote country road when the car unexpectedly careened over the side of a steep embankment. The car rolled over a few times on the way down and you were killed—strangled to death by your seat belt. Your fiancée escaped without injury."

"That witch! That total black-hearted witch!"

James's face was charged with anger. He made motions as though he were pounding his fists together. The doctor curiously noted that the angrier James became, the more alive he seemed. His very face, the contour of his body, the entire definition and detail of his movements, seemed to become more precise. It was as though the doctor was looking through a telescope at some far away focal point and was now ranging in the clarity of the view. James seemed more alive the more reason he had for wanting to be alive. And right now, indeed, the doctor knew James wanted to be back, body and spirit, so he could seek revenge upon his former lover and friends. For James's sake, the doctor opted to change the conversation.

"Now that you're back, is it easier to come back each time?"

"It's like I told you already. I never felt the difficulty in it. The ten years that passed after I died, to me, were like a day. When I did make it, I realized it, but that's all. There was nothing more, nothing less about it. Right now I appear wherever and whenever I want, at least I think I can. The existence I have whenever I'm not here is unbounded by time. My perception of my existence doesn't change, only the context. Like, I mean, the background. I don't feel myself as being apart from the world except in the sense of being able to interact with it."

What James was saying sounded confusing. Rather than indulge him further on the clarification of his ability to access the world again, the doctor asked him another question about something else he was curious about.

"That night . . . that night you died, did you try to reach me? Did you attempt to make contact with me? That night, I was upstairs in bed when suddenly I heard the phone ringing. I raced . . ."

James laughed.

"I do remember. We were best friends, you and I, and my soul cried out for the security of that. I tried . . . I tried to make you aware of me, of what happened to me. You were the only one, the only one who would help me, and I knew it."

"I'm sorry, Jim. I didn't know it that night, but I knew it the day after. My father told me what had happened to you the next day up at Buchanan Park. Then I knew. I knew it was you. I'm sorry you died."

"Don't be sorry. Both of us knew I was going to die before I was thirty."

James's humor lessened the doctor's sorrow over finding out the truth about the way he had been killed. It had all come back to him—the pain, the guilt, the horror. The doctor's mind was reeling.

"Look, James, I'm actually enthralled by the fact that you found your way back into the world and I'm wholly intrigued that your purpose for doing so was to lend yourself to guiding my life, but right now I'm tired. I'm tired physically, mentally, spiritually. I'm going to have to ask you to leave. I need to go home. I need a good night's sleep. I feel depleted."

"There you go with the big words again. It's OK, Dr. Haefner, I won't bother you any more tonight. Go home and get your sleep. Sleep, it's so funny to think about sleep, something that's so relative to mortals, something I have no further need of. I'm so enduring now."

"Look, James, why don't we get together again real soon? Why don't we do it at an arranged time and place? It would be better for me if we saw each other that way. You . . . you could even set up an appointment to come and see me at the office either before or after regular hours."

James wasn't certain whether his friend was being serious or not about actually scheduling time when they could get together. To him it was a folly. Ghosts don't like to regulate their comings and goings in accordance with the real world. They are visitors, and visitors like to come and go as they please, thank you. To appease his old friend, James replied that he would try to pick a more opportune time to come calling.

Their conversation over, the doctor said goodbye. James took the hint and began fading from view. The doctor watched intently as James's form dimmed then diminished from sight.

Today's the Day

That night the doctor had been provided with such an intense sleep that when he awoke the following morning it took him several conscious minutes of thought to recall the disruptive event of the night before. Upon his initial recollection, he determinedly purged the thought from his mind and plunged himself into the activities of a routine weekend morning. He moved expediently into the bathroom and stepped into a hot shower. Amid the steam and rushing water he soaped, and soaked himself body and soul.

After showering, he dressed then departed his home, momentarily, to retrieve his morning paper from the end of the long lane which led from the road to his house. The outside air temperature was brisk and the short walk invigorated him. Back inside he was ready for a tasty hot breakfast. It had to be substantial. Within minutes he was pertaining to a pan full of hot sizzling eggs, a sauce pan simmering with hot chocolate, and a toaster heating two slices of toast. Once the eggs and chocolate were done, he applied them to a plate and cup respectively, then retrieved his slices of toasted bread and went about applying an adequate amount of strawberry jelly to them. With everything ready, he seated himself at his favorite kitchen chair and simultaneously ate his food and read his paper. Once, he got up and brought back the salt and pepper shakers so he could sprinkle more of each on his eggs. At one point, he looked up at the kitchen clock and noted the time: 8:15. He searched his mind as to whether or not there was anything of relevance, according to the time, he needed to pertain to and decided there was not. Suddenly he phone rang.

Who could it be? He deliberately ignored the first couple of rings, preferring instead to complete the article he was reading about some mysterious fish kill in a local lake. When he completed the last sentence, he got up. The phone was on its fifth ring. Whoever was calling was being persistent. Then it struck him. What about James? Could it be him? Suddenly the solitude and serenity of the quiet morning was breaking. The doctor felt as though he were an ice skater in the middle of an ice pond, when suddenly he heard the reverberating sounds—pings of cracking ice.

He picked up the phone to stop the ringing but prior to putting it up to his ear he pondered what to say if it were James. How could it be that his life was now being splashed full of interactions with the spirit of a dead friend?

"Hello," he answered in a terse voice, expecting James to respond with a wisecrack of some kind.

"Oh, Christopher, it's so wonderful to hear your voice."

Immediately the doctor's demeanor softened. It was Annice.

"Oh, Annice, I'm so glad it's you."

Instantly the doctor was drawn into Annice's world, a far better world than James's. The doctor responded with immediate concern for her, her situation. "Is it safe for you to be talking to me?"

"Nothing's going to stop me from talking to you," she replied. "And besides, you-know-who isn't here."

"Working?"

"No. He's off on some weekend excursion with some of his buddies. They left early this morning. They're taking their motorcycles up to Tower City for the weekend to go trail-riding. They arranged it months ago. I forgot all about it until two days ago when the threats started coming in. Last night he took me forcefully and told me that that should keep me until he got back Sunday night. He told me that if anyone else touched me or even got close to me, he would know, and I would be in trouble the moment he discovered it. But of course that's all nonsense. And you know what?"

"What?"

"It really doesn't matter to me. He doesn't realize how little bit of time I'm going to be around in his dark little world. But I don't want to think about that right now. I want to think happier thoughts. I want to think about you and me. I want to be with you. Do you have any obligations this weekend?"

"Only to myself," the doctor responded wistfully.

"And to me," Annice replied with a smile in her voice.

"And to you," the doctor said reassuringly. "When would you like to get together?"

"I'll do whatever you like," Annice announced.

"Then how about we get together this afternoon? We could meet, let's say, 1:30, in the back parking lot at work. That's a safe place for us to be seen together without anyone being suspicious of anything."

Annice, calling from her bed, noticed her appearance in the closet mirror as she spoke. She was bothered by her drab look—pale face, her hair all tangled, and she could tell that her breath was anything but fresh. Urged by the need to fix herself up, she restrained herself from engaging in what could have become a lengthy conversation and made her excuses.

"OK then, Christopher. I'll see you later."

"Will do," the doctor replied compliantly.

The doctor, elated at his fortune, decided to further enhance his good mood by listening to some tunes on the radio. He sauntered into the living room and turned on the stereo. Playing, on the-hits-from-the-'70s station, was a very coincidental song: *Today's the Day*, a song he very much liked ever since it came out twenty-five years ago. It was one of the few songs he liked from his time that he could not remember the singer. He listened to the words, knew them all, but still could not associate the name of the artist. He continued to listen, all the way through, then fretted when the song concluded without the disc jockey ever mentioning who recorded it.

Making his way back into the kitchen, he proceeded to the table where he gathered up his dirty dishes and carried them to the sink for cleaning. Another song that he liked was playing on the radio, and the doctor started singing along in a low voice. Partway through the song, the doctor was startled by the sound of a third person's voice, a chuckle, coming from somewhere directly behind him. He turned and was angered to see James, posed, sitting upright in an empty chair. The two stared at each other. The doctor deliberately held back from making any comments due to his anger. If he made James mad, he would be hard-pressed to get rid of him before he went off with Annice for the day. Finally James proceeded to talk.

"You're just like those old songs you listen to all the time. You are so predictable when it comes to women. You won't change. You act like she's the only woman left in the universe."

"Who?"

"You know who, Annice. Chris, you're crazy. What do you see when you see her? Do you see?"

"Suppose you get to the point. You're not making any sense."

"You're the one not making any sense, pal. Annice is on her way out, her looks, her beauty. She's getting old. You're getting old. You have an unbelievable opportunity right now with Linda. Linda is drop-dead gorgeous and you absolutely know it! You idiot! And you even had her that day I sent her to you. You had a woman who could be a model for God's sake. Why wouldn't you want her? Tell me why?"

"You forget one thing, my friend. You asserted that I had sex with Linda but you forget I also had sex with Annice. And believe me, there is no way to compare the two. Sex with Linda was lustful. Sex with Annice was love. The difference between the two is extremely one-sided, Annice's side."

"Yes, yes. So you finally tapped Annice. Congratulations! It only took you half of your life to do it. But see, that's precisely my point, Pip. Now that you've had her, move on to something else, something more lasting. Think about it. The best of Annice's years are gone. At the most, she has—what?—five, ten years left in her? Trust me, you'll get tired of her real fast once she loses her figure, and that's beginning to happen right now. Then take Linda. She's almost fifteen years younger than Annice. Just think of all those great years you have to enjoy being with her yet. You can't just throw that away, you can't. Take advantage of her now. Fifteen extra years of a hot, hot woman!"

"It's my choice to make, James, and I'll thank you kindly to allow me to make it without your interference."

"Whatever."

"Now that that's settled, let's talk about you. There are lots I'm curious about. Do you retain memory now that you're dead? I mean your entire existence is contained on an ethereal plane. How could you possibly collect memory now? Memory is a by-product of living and it is only produced by living life's experiences and tucking them away while there's a vessel to maintain them."

"Listen to this crap. Aren't you the dedicated doctor, always talking shop? The doctor is always in, isn't he?"

"Of course," the doctor replied. "I'm always focused on who I am, on what I am doing, on helping people, on helping you."

James felt the taunting lash of the doctor's words. In life the doctor had seldom, if ever, needed any help from James. And James knew it. Now, though, James was purporting that his main reason for coming back, into the doctor's life, was to help him, to be like a big brother to him, to help him choose the woman he would finally spend the rest of his life with. Without this purpose, James felt unnecessary, without any plausible reason for being around.

The doctor felt taunted by James's insensitive remarks about Annice's age. For everything that Annice had been through and everything she was still experiencing, the doctor wanted James to be made accountable for the things he had said. How terribly like him, he thought. Besieged by rage, the doctor lunged toward James, who was still sitting nonchalantly in the chair. His hands, held out ahead of him, were aimed directly at James's throat. He wanted to seize him, just as his assailant had done the night he died.

James saw it coming. He never stirred. Instead he waited, waited for his aggressor to come at him and flounder. Just as James expected, the doctor's lunge was met by the resistance of thin air. Just as the doctor's hands were about to clutch James's throat, they fell right through him. He hit the chair and was flung to the floor with it. James, meanwhile, simply vanished then reappeared in another chair. The doctor stumbled once getting up and looked over at his nemesis who had situated himself and was laughing it up.

James then addressed him. "You can't catch me I'm the Gingerbread Man."

"That makes us even then," the doctor reminded him didactically.

As he struggled to get up off the floor, the doctor placed his right hand on his left elbow which was hurt in the fall. He rubbed it more until he realized that James was displaying a cynical grin. Immediately he stopped. The doctor resumed his place at the table, hoping to figure out some way to get Jim to leave. James initiated the conversation again.

"Pip, you forget everything. All the way back when we were first interested in girls, we came up with a code."

"What code?"

"The Four-F Code: Find them, Feel them, Fool them, Forget them. Remember?"

"The way I remember it, it applied more to you than to me. Remember, I remained a legitimate virgin until I was seventeen."

"Della?"

"Yes, Della," the doctor freely admitted. "But I didn't find, feel, fool, and forget her. We stayed together for almost one year."

"Yeah, and I know why too. You were kissy-whipped. Once you started getting that sweet stuff you couldn't let go. She had you wrapped around her middle finger."

"No, you're wrong about that. We had a very egalitarian relationship as I remember it. We treated each other with respect. As I recall, our breakup was instigated by Della's father. After a time, everyone knew we were becoming very serious, including him. For some reason he didn't want us to be together once he realized it might be for keeps. He wanted Della to be with someone older. I think because he wanted her out of the house as soon as possible. He thought I was too immature to hold a steady job and marry her, so he introduced her to some guy he worked with. He was probably thirty—thirteen years older than Della. He had a good job, an apartment, and a car. Della, of course, resisted her father's interference but in the end her hormones got the best of her. She started letting the guy whack her and soon after that it was over. So you see your theory about the four Fs and me just isn't true. I may have joked about it with you but it didn't mean anything more than that to me. Della was my first and it was long lasting."

"He wasn't the only other person Della was whacking, as you put it," James remarked in a snide voice.

"If you're referring to you, you're a liar!" the doctor snapped back.

"How do you know?"

"I know."

There was a moment of silence between them as the doctor sought to quell his temper.

"Anyhow, today it's different. We're all adults. There are no upset fathers to contend with."

"No, only irate husbands," James shot back.

"And, you forgot, irritable old friends."

"Ha! Look Pip, You were always a sensible guy. Why don't you look at this in a sensible light? I know Annice is pretty. I wouldn't mind having a whack at her. But doesn't common sense dictate to you that that happiness you would have with her wouldn't last. I mean come on. She's got maybe ten years tops before she's old and gray. Is that where you want to be ten years from now, banging an old lady, especially when you could be sleeping with an attractive woman who will always be—what?—thirteen, fourteen, years younger than you?"

"Sex isn't all there is to a relationship, James."

"I think I know what it is. You're infatuated with the fact that you finally achieved one of your dream girls. You wanted in Annice's pants ever since we were teens. But I warn you, that will wear off long before you want it to. Damn it, Pip! She's too old for you! God almighty! Have some fun! Get it on with some younger woman. And while you're at it, have Annice too. It's like you used to tell me all the time, you only have one life to live, don't blow it."

"James, I'm so perplexed about you. You think this to be so, so important that you came back from the dead just to advise me on who to select for a life partner."

"Why shouldn't I? After all, we were best friends. What are best friends for? Why don't you start listening to me for a change instead of being caught up in the wonder of why I'm here?"

"James, I've heard everything you had to say but I'm still not convinced. It's my choice who I'm going to marry, not yours."

"I'm not choosing for you. I'm trying to persuade you who not to choose before it's too late. Think about it. Think about what you'll be giving up. You don't even know Linda well enough to say you could not fall in love with her. And I don't even have to mention her physical attributes. What are you going to get from Annice that you couldn't get from Linda?"

"Annice."

"What a goof you are! No wonder you became a psychiatrist—to keep yourself from becoming any crazier!"

"Actually," the doctor said in a high tone while standing up to stretch his legs, "I became a doctor of the mind because of you. And as far as I can determine, you came back to help yourself. I believe that the sins of your lifetime were so burdensome that you needed to come back to make atonement for at least some of them. So, what we really need to be discussing is how you can make up for some of the evil things you have done. Maybe a good way for you to begin would be for you to go down to Lancaster County Prison and help Dave out a little bit, maybe by telling him how sorry you are for all the times you punched him or got him in trouble with your aunt and uncle. Then, maybe you could . . ."

"Hold it! Hold it right there or I'm going to get royally pissed off! You know, you're a complete idiot! After all, I did come here and try to help you. And isn't that just like you, you superior-minded, egotistical idiot!"

"Say no more, Jimmy! Speak any more expletives and I'll hold no more conversations with you. I'll ignore you as if you weren't even here."

James looked up. His ghost began to lose its adjustment. It was almost as if he were trembling and it didn't seem as if he was in control of himself. The doctor looked on as the form sitting in the stationary position at the table began to vanish from sight. Just before he disappeared completely, he seemed to strengthen his hold. With his last ability he uttered a hopeless, "Forget you."

The doctor had won this round and the victory served to invigorate him. Now that he had bested James, he believed he would be free from any further interference from him at least for the day. And that meant that he and Annice would be free to be on their own. James had not made any attempt to visit Annice or the doctor while Annice was present. That could change but not likely today.

Having time to spare, the doctor proceeded to take a momentous walk through the woods surrounding his house. He wanted to ponder what he had said to James regarding his spur-of-the-moment theory that James had come back to atone for his sins. In truth, the doctor had no idea why he said it but in that moment of escalating emotion it sounded right. As he walked, the doctor openly debated the possibility of it.

"If James came back to help me, as he claims, how could that be if like he said he had no control of the time it took him to come back? He could have just as easily come back ten years from now as today. Why didn't he come back before this and lure some interesting young lady toward me? The doctor meandered through the thickly wooded river hills, speculating about the real meaning of James's intercession. There was just no way to know it.

When he returned, it was time to leave. He jumped into his car and started off toward town. Preferring not to take any unnecessary chances of running into Jim, the doctor purposely avoided his usual route, and at the junction where the New Danville Pike met Millersville Road, he detoured toward the small college town instead of heading down past Dead Man's Curve. He followed the Millersville road until he reached the Millersville Pike which joined Lancaster in two different directions. There he hopped on the Pike and bounded his way through the old suburbs of Quaker Hills and Bausman until he reached the city limits.

Saturday traffic in the city was lighter than he expected and he arrived at the rendezvous point quicker than he expected. He was early. Rather than remain conspicuous by sitting idly in the parking lot behind his office building, he preferred instead to go inside where he could wait for Annice privately. Annice, when she arrived, would see his car and know immediately where he was.

Once inside, the doctor made a stop in the waiting-room area where he scooped up a handful of jelly mints to munch on while he waited for Annice. He was in so jovial a mood that he began popping them into the air, one at a time, and attempting to catch them in his mouth. After his handful had been successfully devoured, a few first dropping on the floor, he decided to enter his private office and check up on the surveillance tapes which had been activated last night and programmed to run until early morning.

"Anything I can see with my eyes or listen to with my ears, I should be able to capture on tape. I want proof that this whole experience isn't just some figment of my overworked mind, although sometimes I wish it were." When he took out the tapes, he inserted two new ones into the recorders before reviewing the expended ones. He programmed the times for night activation, ten o'clock, then began playing the video through the sensing device to search for any anomalies. The sensor recorded several, which the doctor went through slowly. He became so engrossed at his task that he never noticed the noise made when Annice's Escort pulled up in the parking space beside his. She even entered the building and turned up in the outer office without his knowledge.

Annice flung her handbag onto her desk and sauntered toward the doctor's private door. At the entrance, she regarded him for a moment as he sat entranced in his bulky black chair, staring intently into some video monitor. Even as she stood there, he was oblivious to her presence.

"You look like a detective who's determined to crack a case," she interrupted.

The doctor looked up and was overjoyed at seeing her. Though he had found nothing in the tapes he was reviewing, he wished that James was here with him now seeing him with her, knowing that there was nothing he could do about it.

"I'm sorry, Annice. These are the tapes I told you about. I have come to a decision to start taping some of my more perplexing patients during their sessions. In a sense it's like adding another dimension to my work. It's one thing to actively participate in an interview with someone, and it's entirely another to be able to watch the process again as a third person. It allows me to add another perspective to the process."

"Are you going to do it with their consent?"

The doctor had never regarded this aspect of the situation since it was actually about picking up James's ghost. For an awkward moment he was speechless.

"Consent, of course," he finally added.

To change the subject, he commented on her good looks. Flattery was always one way to provoke change in any conversation.

"Just look at you," the doctor commented openly.

Annice was wearing a light-purple dress which clung to her curves as though it had been tailor-made just for her. It was a perfect match to her alluring brown eyes and shiny brown hair. The doctor stood up to her.

"You are the beauty, and I, the beast," he said with verve.

"I must be careful then, sir, for Beauty fell in love with the Beast."

"And no less is my heart for you."

The couple hugged, tentatively, then held on in a tight squeeze. Then they kissed. They kissed to the point of having to caution each other that they were not in the ideal place for things to escalate further. Despite their mutual desires to release their pent-up feelings, common sense prevailed and they began discussing what to do with their day.

"What did you want to do?" the doctor asked.

"I didn't have any plans except for being with you," Annice explained.

"Good then," the doctor responded. "We will be spontaneous."

"Spontaneous it is then," Annice concurred. "So, what shall we do?"

"That's a contradiction in terms," the doctor concluded, "for you can not plan spontaneity."

They both laughed.

"Seriously though, do you have anything you wanted to do?"

"Actually I do," the doctor answered succinctly. "How would you like to go on a little boat ride?"

"That sounds splendid," Annice declared.

"I have a friend who has a small powerboat. He keeps it down at the Pequea Marina. I'm sure if I called, and he wasn't planning on using it today, he wouldn't mind if we borrowed it for the afternoon."

"What kind of boat is it?"

"It's a Chris-Craft."

"A Chris-Craft? You're just being facetious."

"No, I'm serious. That's the name of the manufacturer of the boat. If I were the owner I would have to say that it belongs to me as Chris's Chris-Craft."

In the excitement of the moment, the doctor placed a call to his friend John Cool who was the older brother of his pal Dave. Just as he predicted, he got John's approval to use the boat for an afternoon excursion. After thanking John and saying his goodbye, the doctor suggested that they think about what provisions they wanted to take on the trip. Neither of them had eaten lunch yet and Annice admitted that she had been so nervous about their being together that she had had only the sparsest of breakfasts: coffee and toast.

"There's a country store down at the marina. We can purchase ready-made subs there and drinks. They also have snacks—potato chips, cupcakes, M&Ms, anything you like."

"Sounds like everything I want," Annice responded with a broadening smile.

Agreed, they made their way out of the office and into the back lot where the doctor insisted that, for their afternoon excursion, they would use his Buick.

"If I have to do the driving, I insist on using my car. It has immeasurably more leg room and the seats are cushier."

"I'm fine with that," Annice stated compliantly.

The doctor walked Annice to the passenger's side of his car then unlocked and opened the door for her, allowing her to enter. Annice blushed at his act of politeness.

"Except for you, I haven't had any man open a car door for me for years," she explained approvingly.

"It's simple courtesy," the doctor returned blandly.

"Thank you."

"It's something you deserve," the doctor added firmly.

The doctor proceeded to his side, got in, and buckled up. Realizing that Annice had not, he leaned over, grabbed her belt, adjusted it, and then clipped her in too.

"Thank you, Christopher."

Before the doctor could start the engine, Annice reached over to him and remarked, "You treat me so special."

"The way I see it, I'm over twenty years behind on treating you right," he replied.

The ride down to Pequea was a pleasant one. The doctor asked Annice if he could drive with the front windows down so they could feel the warm wind dance across their faces. Annice clipped her hair at the onset of the journey so it wouldn't become all twisted and tangled. The southern sylvan settings that surrounded them as they sojourned through the Susquehanna River hills would someday complement their lives on an everyday basis if they became a permanent couple.

When they arrived at the boat launch, they noticed an attendant already readying John's boat.

"All I have to do is gas her up," he replied once they introduced themselves.

"Splendid, we have to go to the store first anyhow," the doctor quipped.

"She'll be ready when you return," the burly middle-aged man assured him.

As they made their way toward the little store, the doctor noticed a spectacular boat sitting way up on the launch. It caught the doctor's attention immediately as he passed by.

"Look!" he shouted. "A Trojan!"

"What?"

"That's a Trojan boat. That was the company my father worked for all his life. They have been right here in Lancaster County since the '50s. When my father got out of the Air Force, he got his very first job at Trojan. They had just opened. He started off as a data-entry clerk then became a computer programmer. My father was working with computers since the early '60s, long before they became the phenomenon they are today."

"Are they still making Trojans today?"

"Not here. The company's history was a bit shaky through the '80s. Trojan was sold twice during that time; first to Whittaker, then to Bertram. Bertram eventually pulled the plug on the local operation. They moved all of the tooling out of Lancaster. In other places they still make Trojans but not like the Trojans that were originally made here. It was a bitter end for my father. The company declared bankruptcy. The employees filed a lawsuit to recover lost severance, back pay, vacation pay, and lost medical reimbursement. The company, locally, closed its doors in the early '90s, I think."

"What happened as a result of the legalities?"

"Most of the former employees received half or more of the monies they were owed. My father received everything he was owed. Most of that was in accrued vacation time."

"Wow!"

"Wow, yes, but it wasn't the victory my father wanted. He wanted the company to continue up to and beyond his retirement. When Trojan closed down, my father was only fifty-seven. He still had ten years or more to work before retiring. He hated what happened to his life."

"What did he do?"

"He went to work for Burnham Corporation doing their payroll. Oh, I forgot to tell you, my father, besides his data-processing job, also was the treasurer of the company's credit union for twenty-five of the thirty-five years he worked for Trojan. That's what made him qualified to work for Burnham in the capacity he did. He spent ten years there and now he's retired from both companies."

Once they reached the store, they went inside where they both went their separate ways to peruse what they potentially wanted to purchase. When they got to the counter, the store clerk counted up their selections together as the doctor indicated.

"That will be $10.50," the old woman stated.

"Here's twelve dollars," the doctor offered. "Keep the change."

Annice gave him a startled look. Outside she commented, "That's no way to beat inflation."

"She's a very nice old woman. She's poor. Every time I come here I purchase something from her."

"You mean you over-purchase something from her," Annice said tactfully.

"Once I paid two dollars for a fifty-cent cupcake."

Christopher was a kind and generous person and the sentiment for that was strongly felt by Annice. Her love for him grew stronger that day. It grew whenever he opened the car door for her. It deepened when he overpaid the old woman. It strengthened as they powered out across the calm Susquehanna and he made sure she was not being adversely affected by the boat's motion.

They visited several small islands located roughly in the center of the river. There they went in search of arrowheads of quartz, which were left by hundreds of years of Susquehanna Indian occupation. Much to their delight, they both found several specimens; some, complete. On their lucky island, they laid down a picnic blanket and feasted on their wares—subs, potato chips, cupcakes, and soda, a Pepsi for Annice and a Coke for the doctor. When the doctor took his last bite of the roast beef sub, he took Annice by the hand and walked her to a secluded spot. There he laid down the blanket and enticed her to join him for a quiet rest. Afterward, they resumed splashing about some of the lower islands before returning to the launch.

To each, The other

"I had a wonderful afternoon," Annice announced candidly as she helped her partner make sure that John's boat was properly cleaned and stowed before sending it back up to the dock. Once they had completed their scrutiny, they jumped overboard onto the concrete landing at the launch. The boat, which had spirited them away to their splendid afternoon, now sat empty, complacently, in the placid inlet of water that defined the entrance to the enclosure. Annice, having had one of the best afternoons in her life, seized the doctor by the arm and pulled him close to her. She then began administering a flurry of little kisses on his cheeks and lips. The doctor indulged her until he noticed the same attendant coming in their direction to accommodate their concern with the boat. He gently pushed her arms away from his face so she could see him.

Once the boat was dry-docked, the couple stood near the entrance of the marina and discussed their next move.

"I don't mind being spontaneous, Annice, but next on my agenda will be a discussion about dinner. I'm getting hungry."

"What did you have in mind?"

"Nothing in particular, but how about we go back to my place and cook up something special? I'd rather spend our time alone instead of going out someplace, if that's all right with you?"

"What do you have at home?"

"To start with, how about a Delmonico steak, well done, and cooked onion potatoes, and let's see, carrots simmered in steak gravy. Yes, that will do it."

"Sounds scrumptious. And what will we have for dessert?" Annice said teasingly.

The doctor picked up on the enticing way in which she spoke and pulled her to him. He squeezed her in a tender, loving hold, wanting to feel every part of her body against him. He slid his arms down the sides of her body, over her waist and behind. He whispered to her, "For dessert, I'll have you."

Their bodies quivered as they stood there, locked together as one. Neither one needed to say more. They departed, holding hands like lovers. Once they were in the car, the doctor opted to take Annice on a short sightseeing tour of the higher roads, directly above the launch area. The river road, which started at the marina, shot up into the hugging hills to a point about three hundred feet above the Susquehanna. Along the way up were old cottages leveled into the hill, built mostly back in the '40s by well-to-do businessmen who liked having a place to get away from it all. The cottages were equipped with electrical power and water but most did not have heat, since they were seldom used during the winter. The doctor's grandfather's brother used to own one; which one, the doctor didn't know.

When they reached the summit, the doctor pulled his car over in a small clearing so they could get out and look out over the river. The vista was breathtaking. The river, a mile wide, was steely blue in color and rimmed on both sides by vast stretches of green woodlands. The islands which they had just returned from complemented the aspect of color perfectly, like a brush stroke on a painting, several last details of green—tiny, but essential to the picture to make it a marvel.

The couple took a pleasant drive through the outlying hills before turning toward home. When they reached the doctor's reclusive Pinnacle Road home, a mere five miles from the marina, Annice made a comment relative to the last time she had visited.

"I see there are no yellow ribbons today," she said smiling.

"No need," the doctor remarked as they turned into the crunchy stone lane. "We're beyond that stage of the song."

"I see," Annice said with a hint of amusement.

When they got out, outside the garage, Annice speculated about how lonely it must feel, at times, living here, all alone in the woods.

"I'm alone but not lonely," the doctor countered. "This place is sedate. It's exactly what I need. Every day I deal with scores of people and their problems as if I didn't have enough of my own. This place enables me to continue doing what I do. Without it I . . . I just don't know."

They started inside.

"Besides, I get company. Sometimes some of my old friends stop by. And right now my brother Mark is around. You met him."

They passed through the threshold of the front door.

"And today, today I have you."

He turned to her. "Today is a precious day in my life because of you."

He reached out for her and she responded by embracing him. Their lips touched, tentatively, then passionately. After endless moments, mouth to mouth, they finally released each other. It was time to make a decision about how far this exchange would go. Their bodies expressed an urgency to join together now, while hot and ready.

"What shall it be? Before or after?"

"Before or after what?"

"Shall we partake of dessert now, before we've eaten, or just have a cool down and allow our other needs to be met first?"

Then, as if fate was crying out to be heard, the doctor's stomach let out a discerning rumble.

"The decision has been rendered," Annice announced jokingly.

"I may be hungry for the food, but I'm starving for the dessert," the doctor returned decisively.

It was a well-deserved meal and the doctor and Annice went to work to prepare it as if it were the most important meal in their lives. As a domestic pair, they discovered they were very compatible working together, something they both understood was very important should they soon enter into a serious relationship. The doctor commented on the subject while Annice was dicing carrots and he was peeling potatoes.

"I learned how to cook when I was only eight years old. I began by making hot chocolate every morning before school. Soon after, both my mother and my grandmothers taught me things that they knew. My mother taught me most of the basics—how to make your average dinners, spaghetti, roasts, homemade soups, French toast, filling. My grandmothers taught me all the specialties—how to make pies, cakes, homemade icing, cookies, scalloped potatoes, things like that. It was the combination of that learning process plus the story of the Little Red Hen that enabled me to become such a successful, self-sufficient cook."

"The Little Red Hen?" Annice asked quizzically.

"Yes. Don't you remember the story of the Little Red Hen? That was one of my favorite stories when I was a child. It was the story about the hen who went to all the trouble to bake bread, I think. All of the other barnyard animals noticed what she was doing, and of course, wanted to be able to participate in the spoils of her efforts. She told them each that they could but first they had to help her. She assigned each of them a task helping her in the stages of the making and baking of the bread, but each of them failed to show up to do it. Then, when it was all over and the bread was made, each of them finally showed up to eat it. But the wise hen disallowed them to have any, for they had not done the work which would have entitled them to a share of it. The lesson then being that only hard work brings with it all of the finer things in life. It's a lesson I've never forgotten."

Annice was amused.

"So a Little Red Hen did teach you," she responded jovially.

Once the potatoes and carrots were boiling, the doctor brought out a partially thawed steak from the refrigerator. He removed the packaging and placed it into a buttered frying pan to cook. Forty-five minutes later, the couple sat down to the satisfying result of their elaborate undertaking. Along with their food, the doctor poured them each a tall glassful of chilled water.

"I'm sorry," he said while pouring. "I forgot to get sodas out from the case in the garage."

"That's all right," Annice answered back. "Water is healthier anyway."

Before they ate, the doctor proposed a toast to their inadvertent choice of drink.

"To a healthier you," he toasted.

"To a healthier us," Annice replied.

Their meal stretched out for an hour as the couple discussed their day. Their conversations covered the island-hopping and their discoveries of Indian arrowheads. It also broached on the subject of Trojan, the prominent yacht builder again.

"You know, my father wanted me to work there once."

"Oh really?"

"Yes, but I'm not really a computer-oriented person and that's what my father did. Don't get me wrong. I like computers but I just didn't want to spend my entire life around them. They certainly do have their purpose in this age of information we live in, but outside of that, I personally don't have much to do with them. I don't have a personal computer here at home. I like to do my personal computations with a pencil and paper. It's an important skill to be able to budget your money in your head. I think that with the overuse of computers and calculators people begin to lose that skill. I would rather depend on myself to do it."

"But we have two computers at work."

"Yes, but there we really do have a need for them. I don't disagree that computers are very useful in the workplace. They are the best thing that's ever happened to compiling and retrieving data. And the more information you have to have, the more essential is their purpose. At home most people have tended to use computers for things other than processing information. There are exceptions, of course, but the majority of people who have computers in their homes use them to hook up to the Internet. And the extent of the Internet is buying and selling. Caveat emptor. The Internet is not a reliable place to purchase anything. Sometimes what you see is not necessarily what you get. A picture may be worth a thousand words but a computer image is not. In this dog-eat-dog world, people are out to get you. Fraud underlies thousands of Internet purchases every day. Take my advice and stay clear of it."

Before Annice could say anything further, the doctor, already on a tangent, began his often-added warning about Internet exposure on a personal basis.

"Every time you go online, you expose yourself to a potential of potent would-be identity takers. Give away your name, address, and social security number, and your whole world is theirs for the taking. I've even heard stories of convicted felons doing this while they're doing time!"

"It's true. You do have to be especially careful these days about safeguarding your identity."

The doctor was busy scooping up a forkful of carrots into his gaping mouth. After swallowing more water, he continued his oral essay on the pros and cons of the Computer Age.

"And there's one more thing. It's an extension of what I said earlier about maintaining and developing your computational skills. Brains need exercise. Besides the blood and oxygen they need to be able to function, so too do they need to be used to stay useful. All of us do, no matter how smart we are, no matter how dumb we are—we all need to use our brains continuously."

The doctor pointed to his head with his index finger. Then he tapped on it several times to get his point across.

"This, this is the only computer I'll ever need. It does all of my thinking for me and all it asks is food, air, water, and exercise. And I like to use it too for all it's worth. I like to read with it. I like to make grocery lists with it. I like to calculate my year-end taxes with it—not that I like the outcome. I like to learn with it. Annice, you're a smart woman. What do you think?"

"I agree with everything you said except I think you're too ready to dismiss the advantages computers have on adolescents in particular. You and I, because of our—how shall I say it?—our maturity, can not fully depict the advantages or the disadvantages of the computer on today's youth. Our point of view comes from a time when we did not have the value of the computer world. We weren't even introduced to pocket calculators until the ninth grade. There was no Internet, and personal computers in school were rare. I suspect our perceptions of their usefulness might be different if they had been part of our own experience. That's usually how it is. Attitudes differ according to experience. If we had the use of computers back then, we would probably feel more accepting of them now."

"So what you're saying is that my attitude may just be an admonishment of the younger generation based on the fact that, because I did not have their computer privilege and did not need it to be what I am today, I, therefore, am anxious to dismiss it entirely as unnecessary. That's a fascinating concept, one that I've never considered before. Annice, I'm proud of you. You're giving my brain exercise this evening."

"I have a better example for you," Annice continued. "Music."

"Music?"

"Music. Look, you're forty years old and this is the year 2000. Think. When was the last time you heard a contemporary song on the radio and liked it?"

The doctor pondered the question. He thought and thought and thought about it before finally coming up with a truthful answer.

"In all honesty I would have to say 1994—was it? That song by the Cranberries, "Dreams." And I really did like it."

"I liked it too," Annice replied. "And what about before that?"

"Before that . . . let's see . . . before that I would have to say . . . Madonna."

"Madonna! Boy, that really dates you. So let's see, that's one song out of a possible thousand, one song from the past decade's worth of culture. I think that by your own admission I have proven my point. So you see, Dr. Haefner, there is a relevance to actually being part of something."

"Annice, you're absolutely right. I can't believe I never thought of that before. I never connected myself to that postulation in its own purpose."

Annice had tendered a richly layered fertilizer atop the plop that was the doctor's brain. It had so invigorated him that he began to postulate theory aloud.

"Why does this happen? It happens to all of us. We lose interest in the things that were once important to us—our music, our friends, our culture. We take with us only those things that were a part of us during a particular time in our youthful lives. Is it because we are so easily swayed by ideals at that time in our lives? Then, when the real world hits us, we realize how necessary it is to abandon our ideals and render ourselves as combatants in a harsh reality—the work-a-day world, filled with responsibilities, jobs, spouses, bills, and children. But the question remains, what interstitial dynamic in each of us, that is so active and so intact while we are young, abandons us when we lose our innocence about the world? What is it? And why, why would it leave us—leave us just when we need it most?"

"But we do carry some of our interests with us as we grow older," Annice suggested. "We have our hobbies and activities."

"I'm not suggesting that we lose our interest in everything. I'm suggesting, rather, that we tend to lose the profoundness of our interest in the things we like or love, mostly. We tend to lose our ability to dream. Take for instance this analogy, most little boys dream of becoming space travelers, but instead of pursuing it, they instead abandon the idea based on the uncertainty of its ever happening. Take little girls for example. Most of them dream of becoming nurses or teachers."

"Or CEOs," Annice interrupted.

The doctor gave her a stare.

"That's an entirely different discussion," he stated with a grin.

Their conversation peaked with this lively discussion about the intriguing way most people lose their initiatives to live out their dreams. As a couple, these conversations brought them closer. Through the outpouring of their innermost thoughts and feelings, they had had a chance to grow intimately. Now, in addition to their intense physical attraction for each other, they had an intense desire to learn more about each other emotionally. What they discovered is that they were a lot alike, yet on the issues they differed on, they found that they could always come to terms with each other's opinions. More and more they found this out.

Another certainty came to each of them too; that was that the estimation they had of each other about who they were was true. Prior to their recent intimacy, emotionally and intellectually, they had held each other up to a certain standard of who this person really was personally. The doctor had favored that Annice was, of course, a very knowledgeable and easy-to-get-along-with person. He was right. But what he was surprised to find out about her was that she was intellectually as smart as he, in most interests. She could discuss with him world history, literature, old world and new, religion, and a multitude of other subjects. She could discuss them into the depths of their esoterics. She was a major contributor in their discussions whenever the doctor wasn't on a tangent about something.

Annice too, had good things to discover about the doctor. Not only was he the dedicated professional she purported him to be, he was also a very stimulating person to be around. He pursued knowledge like it was a bowl of Cocoa Puffs. He devoured knowledge about all things great and small. Everything they did, everywhere they went, his knowledge and interest went with them. On the little Susquehanna Islands, he described the Indians who once lived there, their culture, their ultimate demise. He described the geology of the Susquehanna Valley and the influence of time and human intervention upon it. He cared deeply about everything. He took nothing for granted.

There was one sad thought though. The doctor realized just how much Annice had been held back. How could a woman as bright as a shining star be relegated to being only a professional's assistant? Because of her marriage, because of the dynamics of her marriage, she had been subjugated into being a menial person—a person contributing pennies on the dollar of what she was worth. He's repressed her, mind, body and soul.

Their philosophical discussions lasted through dinner and dishes; and later, a mixed drink. About 9:30, the doctor noticed the time. It was getting late. Supposing Leslie happened to call for her. She wouldn't be there and there would be hell to pay. He hated to, but he purposely interrupted their engrossing conversation on the long-term impact upon society of the first generation to grow up in the prevalence of divorce. All evening long he had wanted to make love to her but how could he go from "Let's hope that the world learns from that mistake" to "Let's go back and get naked"? It would be too upsetting. She would consider him a phony.

Even if he had to let her go, the doctor knew, more importantly, that their relationship had strengthened through the course of the day. It was for the greater good that they would not end their day with a night of physical passion. This philosophy would carry him as he escorted her back into town then back home where he would slip quietly into bed, alone. It was important too that he be the one who suggested it was getting late and maybe she should go. It would look better on his character and she would, no doubt, appreciate it. So, though his heart was palpitating heavily and his insides were aching to join with the female part of her, the doctor conceded the situation. He stood up and stretched his arms to his sides. But before he could say anything, Annice too got up.

"Getting tired?" she asked.

"Somewhat," he replied.

"I have to go pee," Annice said simply.

The doctor reminded her where the bathroom was located, and in the intervening time he despondently located his car keys for when she returned, knowing fully well she would then ask to be returned to town. Thinking ahead, he also retrieved from the hall closet, two warm jackets. When Annice returned from the bathroom, she was startled to find the doctor standing by the front door dressed in a dark-brown jacket emblazed with a scene of a white-tailed deer on the back. Held in his hands was another jacket of similar make and style. He was holding it out to her.

"What's this?" she asked.

"This one's for you. It was a Christmas present from the past year. I've never worn it before."

"That's not what I mean. What are we going to do? Take a walk?"

"No. It's cold out. I thought you were going to ask me to drive you home now."

"What are you trying to do? Get rid of me?"

Though the sarcasm in her voice was glinted with a smile, the very thought of the doctor wanting to get rid of his beloved was appalling to him.

"I . . . I would never . . . I could never ask you to . . . ever ask you to leave this house. I just thought . . ."

"You thought wrong."

Immediately, the doctor came to the bothering sense of the situation and he remarked to her his concerns.

"Annice, I would like you to stay here tonight. It would be like a dream come true but I am deeply concerned for your safety. What if your husband calls for you tonight? You yourself said that he intends not to trust you. Don't you think he will call to check up on you, especially while he's so far away?"

"I appreciate your concern for me, Christopher, but I am not afraid to do this. This is what I want to do. If he does call or says that he did, I will just tell him that I fell asleep early. There is no way for him to know where I am."

The doctor looked at her with disbelieving eyes.

"And besides," Annice added. "I know him and what he does when he's away with his buddies. He's been out all day riding the trails, and right now he's probably drunk as a skunk with no phone around for miles. The place where they stay is a run-down old shack in the woods. It doesn't even have running water. They piss on the floor when they're too drunk to walk outside, and they don't care. Do you think I'm going to force myself to sit by the phone in hopes that the man who regularly abuses me decides to call to check up on me? Really."

With that said and no rebuttal from the doctor, Annice moved toward him slowly, helped him remove his jacket and the one for her, and placed them back in the closet.

"Come with me," she said in a provocative tone.

The doctor, in a panic, rushed over to lock the front door, then followed behind Annice as she made her way back toward the bedroom. Once there, Annice stripped to her purple bra and panties, the pair which she knew had so excited him before. The doctor moved nervously while removing his clothes, then faced her naked. Their pleasure was intense, more so than before, and they exhausted themselves on one another, having intercourse three successive times until they each slumped side by side on the bed.

Early the next day, the doctor awoke, taunted into consciousness by the relevance of knowing that his bed was being shared by his lover. He slipped out of bed quietly, trying not to disturb his Beauty. He dressed himself with a bathrobe and moccasins, took a long look at her lying peacefully on the bed, then left the room. Taking his keys with him, he unlocked the front door and made his routine walk down to the entrance of his lane to retrieve the Sunday paper. Back in the house, he plopped into his La-Z-Boy and began sorting through the paper for anything interesting to read. Within a few pages of reading, he began to feel hungry. It was 7:30, an appropriate time to prepare breakfast and wake his sleeping beauty. He went into the kitchen and prepared a double batch of French toast and enough hot cocoa for two. Then, while it was still hot in the pot, he walked back into his room and kissed Annice awake with a tender kiss atop her forehead. Her eyes popped open and she proffered him a kiss on the lips.

"Good morning," he said affectionately.

"Good morning," she returned in a soft, tired voice.

"If you hurry, I've made us a scrumptious breakfast of French toast and cocoa."

Annice propped herself up on the bed.

"I have nothing to slip into and I don't want to dress until I've showered."

"Come as you are," the doctor said in a jocular voice.

"Christopher, I am not eating breakfast in the nude."

"I was just being facetious," the doctor assured her. "Here."

He went into his walk-in closet and retrieved another bathrobe, one just like the one he was wearing, and handed it to her. She got up, took it, and wrapped it around her, drawing the cinch tightly around her belly.

The breakfast setting was relatively quiet compared to the loquacious meal they had shared the evening before. Evident in both their minds was the surreal ticking of the clock that marked their time together. Their conversations, which, previous to today, had been interspersed with playful remarks, were now more serious and terse. Tensions grew as time ticked away. Both felt forced by it. Both were reluctant to admit it. The doctor saw how it was ruining their precious time together and he finally overcame his reluctance to bring it up.

"Look! Let's not pretend like everything is OK."

Annice immediately put down her cocoa mug in front of her and gave Chris her full attention.

"We both know what is going to happen today. We can't avoid the unavoidable. Annice, the choice is yours. It's entirely up to you, stay or go."

Annice, upset and nervous, sat staring down at her cocoa cup, until she finally blurted out, "What are you saying?"

There was a momentary pause before the doctor spit out the hurtful words neither of them wanted to hear.

"You know what I'm talking about. A few hours from now we'll kiss and say goodbye. Then, later, even if by force, you will be with that jerk you call a husband. Just how the hell do you think that makes me feel?"

Annice felt awful. It was true. With or without her consent, Leslie would force himself on her. She was replete with sadness. At that moment, she felt entirely to blame for the horribleness that had overtaken her life. She began to cry. But the doctor felt determined and would not be swayed by her tears. If Annice was to ever be free, then she, and she alone, had to free herself.

"Look! You and I have been discussing this for weeks and you have yet to make any decision about granting yourself your freedom. Let freedom ring! Get rid of the jerk!"

In tears, Annice replied, "I . . . I know what you're saying is true, Christopher, but it's a harder thing than you think to just up and leave someone, especially someone whom you've been married to for as long as I have. It takes planning, planning and timing. And how do you think I feel about the whole situation especially about how it hurts you? I cry every night about it. I love you, Chris. I love you."

The doctor went to her. He reached down and touched the hair on her head. He glided his hands down the flow of her hair onto her shoulders. Next he tilted her sobbing face toward him.

"You belong to me, Annice, and I belong to you. I loved you ever since the first time I laid my eyes on you. I have loved you since before your husband ever met you. To have you leave me now, now that we have lived and loved together, would bring me more pain than I could ever imagine."

The doctor began to shed tears and his face told of the despair that dwelt in his heart. Annice turned toward him directly. Despite her willingness to desert her husband, she knew that she had to be sensible about it. With tears in her words, she told the doctor just so.

"My darling, I promise you with all my heart that I will be yours, and soon. But if I leave him now, without word, without warning, there will be trouble. He would retaliate against me, against you, and the thought of having him hurt either of us is too much for me to bear. It will be much easier on all three of us if I use the proper amount of discretion when I put all of this into action. Wait, darling, wait, just a little bit. Wait for me and it will all be worthwhile. And I promise you this. I will do everything in my power not to let him have me again, no matter what."

Lost Souls

It was just before noon when the doctor dropped off Annice at the back of his office building. He walked her to her car and opened the door for her with her key. Being reminded of his splendid kindness, she fell into his arms, throwing caution to the wind, and kissed him long and hard on the lips. Then the couple hugged, neither one wanting to let go. There were no words spoken between them, there were no words necessary.

Once Annice had pulled away, the doctor sat idly in his car and reflected on the time they had spent together—the boat ride, the dinner, making love, and discussing the eventuality of them being together. The thought of going home to spend an entire afternoon alone bothered him immensely. He noticed the time, 12:15.

"What to do?"

He thought whether he was hungry, but he was not. The enormous breakfast he and Annice had enjoyed sufficed to carry him beyond his normal midday meal. Since he was already in the city, he wondered if there was anything he could do while he was here. Then a thought struck him and he said it out loud.

"What about Dave Boller?"

He remembered the promise he had made to Dave the last time he saw him that he would come to visit him whenever he could make the time. And if ever he did have the time, it was now. Since his last visit, he had reneged on that promise and he felt a little bit bad about that. It inundated him, the idea of keeping one's promises. Think about the promises Annice had just made to him. Would he expect her to keep them? And if she wouldn't or didn't try, how awful would that be?

The doctor liked Dave but there could be no rekindling of their childhood days. They were worlds apart now intellectually, philosophically, financially, socially. And actually, while they were in each other's company, the doctor felt uncomfortable and out of place. Dave, despite his good nature, was a delinquent. He was a lost soul and one the doctor did not feel obligated to console. The doctor owed him nothing. But in the end, this is what freed the doctor into obligating himself to see Dave. It's different when you're not obligated. Having a free will is a powerful initiative. Thus, the doctor found it in his heart to want to spend time with an old lost soul.

"I will see Dave Boller of my own free will, not because I feel obligated, not because I feel guilty for having told him I would again and as yet have not, and not because James might have had an interaction with him again."

Free of the turmoil that had pervaded his spirit, the doctor drove to the Lancaster County Prison, which was located on the eastern end of the city, about two miles from his office. When he pulled up in the parking area, he began to feel apprehensive again about being there. Prisons were not a suitable place for an esteemed professional psychiatrist to be. It was a degrading experience all the way around, from the highly inquisitive entry procedure to the final exit.

Preferring to see Dave in a solitary setting, the doctor, as he had done before, requested that he meet him in his cell. He stressed to the guard that he was Dave's personal physician and that he had been allowed this privilege once before due to the confidentiality of their relationship. The attending guard placed a call to somewhere in the facility, meanwhile he shoved a form in front of the doctor for him to fill out.

The form was a statement the doctor had to sign, stating that he acknowledges that it would be considered a felony if he were to dispense any medications to any patient or person detained within the prison without the consent of prison officials. Failure to comply with this request would result in legal action. The doctor read and signed the form, and made no remark about the insulting document.

Within minutes, another guard appeared at the entry desk. She had been assigned to escort the physician to see Dave. The doctor couldn't help but notice her. She was an attractive dark-haired young woman who, even in her unbecoming uniform of blue and gray, looked alluring.

During their walk, she spoke pleasantly and once even brushed her hand into his. This time they followed the white-walled labyrinth in a different direction, other than the way to the cells. As they walked, the doctor popped his eyes in the guard's direction as if to say things were not right. His mind opened up on him. He wondered if James had something to do with this. Was all of this unnecessarily lavish attention his doing? Where was she taking him? To some distant far corner of the prison where she could provoke him with her feminine wiles? Finally, they reached their destination. They were standing in a wide-open area where three corridors emptied. Before them were two wide swinging doors with safety-glass windows eye-high in each of them.

"Your friend is at lunch now. Unless you prefer to wait for him out here in the hall, you may go in. Finding him may take some time. There are about five hundred prisoners in there right now."

"But I specifically requested to see him in private," the doctor contended.

"I'm sorry but there's nothing I can do about that."

"But I . . ."

"Lunch will last for another thirty minutes. I suggest you go in and find him."

The guard left without even offering her assistance.

"The least she could have done was go in with me and help me locate him," the doctor grumbled.

Up all three halls were series of row chairs which sat against the wall. Staring at the uncomfortable-looking plastic seats, the doctor contemplated his choices. He could wait and maybe somebody would come out and he could ask if they knew Dave and if they knew where inside he was, or he could go inside and walk amongst the prisoners in the hope of finding Dave without too much difficulty. Reluctantly, he entered. The room, full of prisoners, was noisy and confusing. The barrier provided by the massive wooden doors offered no hint of what was inside. After entering, he took a few steps then stood still and surveyed the population. He felt conspicuous. Looking out over the plethora of inmates, the doctor noted something that he had not previously considered. All of the prisoners looked identical, for the most part, in their County-issued jumpsuits. Finding Dave would be extremely difficult.

He had no choice but to begin parading up and down the rows of occupied tables. Nobody knew who he was. Nobody commented to him. But the rows and rows of eyes he passed followed his every move. After he had passed by a dozen or so tables he heard someone call out, a name? Whose? The doctor searched the eyes of those closest to him. Nobody identified themselves. He continued. Again, the voice of someone calling out persisted. This time it sounded clearer. The sound was emerging from somewhere close.

"Hey, Pip. Hey, Pip!"

The doctor whirled around. From the far corner, from a table he had already passed when he rounded out a row, came the very familiar sound of someone calling him by his old nickname. The doctor felt embarrassed, but all the same he sought out the caller from the population of strangers. Their eyes finally met and the doctor acknowledged Dave. The doctor approached, glad that they had connected before he had to immerse himself in the melee of disquieting men. When they met, Dave held out his hand invitingly. He spoke affably and told the doctor he was glad to see him but that he should have called first so that a more suitable time could have been arranged for their visit.

"Did something happen?"

"No, nothing worth speaking about. I came only because I said I would. And as you know, a promise is a promise."

"All right then," Dave remarked without thinking anything further into the unexpected visit. "Then, why don't you join in? There's plenty of food to go around. Today's jail-house special: Salisbury steak, with mashed potatoes, and corn. Oh, and along with that, applesauce with cinnamon!"

"Well," the doctor conceded. "It is past my lunch time and I haven't eaten yet. I suppose I could try. At least I can get a first-hand account of how my tax money is being spent when it comes to feeding our scrappers."

"OK," Dave responded jovially. "Wait here."

Dave left abruptly, insisting that he would personally attend to the matter of providing the doctor with a plateful of prison food.

"Besides," he said when he stood up, "it's not really a meal if one of us isn't eating."

From his vantage point at his corner seat, the doctor witnessed Dave, apparently persuading the clerk who was serving, that his claim of acquiring another plate of food for another person was legitimate. Successful, Dave returned with a duplicate portion of food and placed it down, directly in front of the doctor. Along with it he plopped down a wrapped cellophane packet of plastic utensils.

"This is your knife, fork, and spoon. Everything's plastic around here. I guess there are too many psychos."

"I would have never guessed," the doctor said facetiously.

He tore open the container of plastic eating utensils and immediately applied the knife and fork to cutting and placing into his mouth a piece of Salisbury steak. It was moderately hot and tasted delicious. The doctor was impressed. He ate each allotment in turn and was equally impressed. For the next several minutes, their conversations ceased as they each indulged themselves with their good fare. When they were done, Dave made a remark, stating that he was glad the doctor liked it.

"The food here is actually edible."

"It's more than that. It's actually very good."

Dave was curious, and now that the courtesy of extending his old friend a share in the midday meal had been accomplished, he wanted to speculate further as to why the doctor had bothered to see him, more than the reason of giving up his Sunday afternoon just so he could fulfill an old promise.

"Why did you come, Pip?"

"It's like I said, I came to see you."

"Oh, I believe you. But you also came to see if I had any further contact with the devil. Didn't you?"

"Actually, since you've asked, no. I've seen James a time or two since our last visit and he told me explicitly he wanted nothing more to do with you. And for you, you should take that the right way; which means, you won't have to be bothered by him menacing you."

"He told you that?"

"Yes."

"So now he's making direct contact with us. He can actually talk."

"Yes."

"So, what did he say?"

The doctor wasn't sure how much of the story he wanted Dave to know, but realizing that Dave was already involved, he decided to tell him a certain amount of what James had to say.

"So, Dave, since you've asked, have you had any contact with the devil?"

"As a matter of fact, I have," Dave reported. "Since the last time you visited me, he appeared once but it was pretty much the same as the previous times. He stood there, same as before, with his leg propped up behind him against the cell wall. He stood there, staring. Then, before finally leaving me in peace, he smirked. I know why he comes too. He comes just to torment me, to make fun of me in my situation. Hell, he should talk. He was arrested more times than Billy the Kid. You know it too. But he had all the luck. It's always that way; I mean, people like him, worthless losers, always finding some way out of trouble. Here I am, doing time for theft, and that guy was a full-time criminal. All he ever did was a few days in the Dade County Jail in Florida until they found out he was still a minor, then they had to let him go, free of all charges—dealing in dope, reckless driving, possession of a stolen vehicle, evading capture, and countless other charges—all dropped because of a technicality, all because they made a mistake and threw a juvenile in an adult prison. Unbelievable!"

The doctor listened to Dave's rendition of his recollection of James's criminal life. When done, he shared briefly some of his beliefs about why he believed James had returned. Before their conversation could really take off, an announcement came over the loudspeaker, stating that the meal period was over and all prisoners were encouraged to leave the dining area so it could be promptly cleaned.

Soon a long line formed, and one by one the prisoners passed through a checkpoint, exiting the dining hall. Dave and the doctor purposely loitered at their table until they assured themselves the last positions in line.

"This way, we won't get hassled when we explain who you are and that we are going straight back to the cellblock. The cellblock is located in the opposite direction of where everybody else is going. This way we have time to deal with them."

At the point of inspection Dave explained to the attending guard who the doctor was and that they had special permission to go to the place of their choice, Dave's cell, to discuss medical matters.

"OK, but remember, the visiting time is over in just thirty minutes."

Just at that moment another guard came into their presence. It was the same guard who had escorted the doctor to the cafeteria. She intervened on their behalf and informed the other guard that she knew of their situation and she would tend to them personally.

"Come with me," she spoke directly.

She led them through some of the inner corridors until they reached a back door leading into the cellblock area. When they arrived at the designated cell she, again, placed her hand on the doctor's back. The doctor felt her warmth pass through him and wondered whether James had anything to do with it. Dave's cell was unlocked and they simply entered it. The guard warned the doctor not to hesitate leaving the cell once the call for the end of visiting hours was announced.

"You don't want to end up getting stuck in here yourself," she said with a laugh.

Dave noticed the presence she gave Pip. And once she was gone from sight he noted, "She's got bedroom eyes for you, Pip."

"Not interested," the doctor said blandly. "The last thing I need right now is yet another woman flaunting her feminine wiles at me."

"Wow! You must be doing all right," Dave supposed.

"I have everything I need in a woman right now, thank you."

"But still, though, you have to admit, she would be a good one to have."

"She would be I'm sure. So why don't you throw some attention her way? You never know. Show her what a decent person you are. Maybe she would give you a chance. She's obviously looking for love."

"Yeah, looking for love in all the wrong places," Dave replied. "I'm nothing to her. I'm nothing but a loser. There's no way a woman like her would be interested in a man like me. I know it! You know it!"

The doctor was preparing a mental response to Dave's pathetic put-down, when suddenly, the sedate scene was interrupted by a loud, raucous laugh. It was James!

"How pathetic! A pity party!"

"James!" Dave called out.

"James!" the doctor shouted.

James was with them, and apparently, had been since they first entered the cell. He had heard everything that had transpired between them and had been provided with enough juicy information to now go on the attack.

"Both of you! Both of you are the sorriest excuses I ever came across when it comes to hustling a woman. What the hell is wrong anyway? You had the likes of me around to watch and learn from. You and you are both afraid of a hot honey. Maybe my best advice to you would be to become lovers; unless, of course, you're afraid of each other too."

Dave, for the first time, heard James's ghost. Hearing that voice again throttled him. He commented, and as he did, lunged toward the specter.

"Cuz, you're still the same crazy . . . !"

The moment Dave went after him, James knew he had him. The very instant Dave would have made contact with him, James decidedly disappeared. Dave toppled over. James immediately appeared again, this time in the spot Dave had previously occupied. When Dave got up, he turned to face his adversary again. The doctor warned Dave not to attack, but it was too late. This time James acted the aggressor. He held up his arms in defiance, and when Dave advanced on him, he swung one of his fists through the air as though he were going to slug him. Dave reacted to the feint by ducking, which caused him to go off balance and he crashed to the floor once more. This time, the doctor intervened on Dave's behalf and held on to him before he could advance on his half brother again in another futile attempt to thrash him.

"Don't stop him," James shouted. "I've been practicing for this ever since I returned."

"Why don't you go back to hell where you came from?" Dave suggested.

"Why don't you try picking on someone your own size, James?"

"You mean you?"

"I mean me!"

James relented. He knew fully that the only reason Dave fell was because he was tricked into thinking that he was like flesh and blood. The doctor taunted him further, even though he understood that any physical contact between them was impossible.

"Go ahead, James! I'm bigger and stronger than you. I can take care of you the same way I did when we fought years ago."

The doctor's futile challenge was made for Dave's sake so that he would be encouraged. The doctor wanted to prove to Dave that his nemesis was nothing to be afraid of either as a person or a ghost.

James flared up at the open challenge. His emotions swelled up inside of him. He wanted to strike like a panther in the jungle, taking his quarry unexpectedly, taking either of them down. He relented. He knew that Pip would not flinch the way Dave did, and therefore he could not make him fall. So, he did what he did when he used to get into predicaments where his opponent proved to be superior; he pretended to have gotten over the problem.

"Look, let's forget it, fellows. I was just carrying-on anyway."

So that things would cool off a bit, James deliberately looked away. Dave lurched his way over to his bunk and sat down. The doctor stood between them. He observed James, who had a strange depleted look about him, almost as though he had been in an actual fight. The doctor was the first one to speak.

"So then, James, why are you here? You told me before that you had no inclination to see your brother."

"Half brother," Dave interjected.

"You think I came here to be with that loser? Look at him! He's fat, freaky, and a fool!"

"Forget you!"

Turning to Dave, the doctor remarked, "Dave, you are officially discounted in the spirit world."

"Thank God!"

Turning to James, the doctor asked, "Then why are you here? What, that's worth anything, do you have to say to anybody?"

"There's that condescending attitude of yours shining through. As always. With you, there's no such thing as an interactive conversation, is there? Everything with you is so one-sided, your side. Anyone who ever talks with you has to constantly interrupt you just so they can get a word in edgewise. You are the worst, worthless, wordy word person ever."

"And you are an illiterate alliterator," the doctor stabbed back. "As for me, I am, what you could characterize a deliberate deliberator when it comes to dialogue. To clarify that, I would say that in any interesting conversation I usually prefer to provoke in-depth discussion rather than subsist on the surface of matters. And I don't do it just to hear myself think, rather I do it to satisfy both the matter and my mind, and hopefully, the mind of the person or persons I am engaged in conversation with. I enjoy delving into esoteric knowledge. And this, I do intentionally, to make me think, to make others think. And at the heart of all this is the quest to find truth. Truth is beauty; beauty, truth."

"I know where you're coming from," James purported. "Right now, you are acting like one of those ancient philosophers from the Golden Age of Greece. You're trying to sound profound like Socrates."

"I'm stunned, James. How could you, with your sixth-grade education, know anything about the Golden Age of Greece? Have you been studying ancient history in your spare time? In your afterlife?"

"Maybe I picked it up from you during one of your diarrhea-of-the-mouth sessions, or maybe I'm actually smarter than you think. Did you ever think of that? You know you and Socrates would have made a great couple. Together, the both of you could have searched the world over for beauty and truth, truth and beauty, and you could have done it in the way most intellectual Greeks did—as lovers."

To change the subject to the original intent, the doctor deliberately avoided any further comments about his Greek counterparts and referred instead to a continuance of the point he was making.

"There is an aspect of all this, too, you're not getting; that is, that despite my being a decisive speaker, I still remember what I have learned out of any conversation. Someone actually speaking to me may not realize it because of the way I defend my intellectual positions, but I can assure you, later, when I've had real time to think about all things that were said, I can usually conclude with a greater perspective, a greater insight, into what was being discussed. And that I owe to my oral partner. I can learn from anybody.

"Take for instance you, you and your insistence that I continue to waste my life away with all these tasty, tempting women you keep throwing into my life. In case you have forgotten, I did have relations with Linda, four times, if you are keeping score. I'm not entirely oblivious to what she has to offer as a woman, you know. And take for example today's security guard, the one you obviously influenced somehow to flirt with me. What were you doing, whispering thoughts to her about what a great guy I am? Or maybe you were doing something else unforeseen like titillating her sexual senses somehow. Do you really want to know what I think about her? I'll tell you. I think she is an attractive woman too and I wouldn't mind having her either, but see, therein lies the difference."

"What difference?"

"The difference between us."

"You're doing it right now, aren't you?"

"Doing what?"

"Doing what I said you always do. You're giving a speech. You're turning what could be simple-sentence answers into oral documents. You're complicating something that shouldn't be complicated."

"That's where you're wrong, James. But see, that was the essence of you. You lived your life too simplistically. Everything for you depended only on what was important to you at that particular moment and that's not the way life works."

"It worked for me. I lived an exhilarating life. I seized every day and got out of it everything I could, and I was extremely successful at it."

"But success does not necessarily bring about happiness."

"You should talk. Just look at you. You're forty years old and I don't see any wife or kids around you. What happened to you? In my thirty years I had three wives, three kids and thirty lovers, that's one lover for every year of my life. And that's my point about you. If you're not ever going to do what you call the right thing—that is, get married and have children—then why not try a little of my type of life style? At least you wouldn't be bored at night. It's silly and stupid to withhold from the delicacies of life simply because every little thing isn't exactly what you wanted it to be. You need to learn how to have fun."

"If I listened to you, I would be dead too."

James looked crossly at the doctor for reminding him of his death.

"You're right, I'm dead. I was murdered. I am what's left of a murdered man. You know, for all the contempt you hold against me for the things I did, at least I never killed anybody. I never hated anyone enough to kill them. That should count for something in my favor."

"That's not entirely true."

"That's not entirely true? I never killed anybody!"

"What about your dogs?"

"What! Snoopy! Taffy! They were dogs! Who would care?"

"They were living things which you played with like toys, and in doing so, destroyed them."

"Hey, I was just a kid then, you can't hold that against me. Besides, Snoopy wasn't killed. She ended up in a licensed-care facility. She went insane."

"Yes, you drove her there."

"And as for Taffy, she wasn't worth the space she took up."

"Still you killed her."

"Maybe so, but what's a dog's life?"

"And it wasn't just the blatant fact that you killed her either. It was the way you did it. It was methodical, malicious."

"Oh, and I'm sure you never killed anything, not even a fly."

"The life of a fly is not entrusted to me. The consequence of killing a living thing has more to do with what our responsibilities are toward that living thing. Snoopy and Taffy were in your care. It was your duty to take care of them, and instead of doing that, you turned on them. You were their demon."

The course of the conversation had gone too deep for James who always preferred to swim near the surface of ideas. He had a conscience. He needed to leave the conversation at once.

"You know, Pip, this is why we got along so well when we were growing up. We are exact opposites. We supply each other with so much controversy that it's exciting to be together. I live at one end of life's spectrum, and you live at the other."

"And never shall the two ends meet," the doctor affirmed with a latent cynicism in his voice.

"Don't say that. I was the perfect challenge to you. Our personalities, our thoughts, our philosophies struck each other like meteorites striking the earth and you loved it, lived for it. That's why I was, and still am, such a special interest to you. Hell, I'm probably the reason you became a psychologist."

"That's psychiatrist," the doctor corrected.

"Psychiatrist, psychologist, what's the difference," James stated.

"Actually . . ." the doctor began.

"Spare me," James insisted. "I haven't the time."

At that precise moment the approach of someone's footsteps could be heard in the corridor.

"Later, dude," James said in parting. He smiled at his former friend then frowned at Dave then faded away.

The security guard who had escorted both the doctor and Dave to the cell appeared.

"Time to leave," she said amicably.

The doctor turned to Dave and shook his hand.

"I'll see you soon, Dave."

"Back at you," Dave replied.

When the doctor and his escort started off, Dave gestured for him to take note of her like James had suggested. On that issue, Dave was more like James. The doctor acknowledged Dave's gesture, and in a distorted sense of acting out, he reached over and placed his hand on the small of the woman's back.

Once he was on his way, the doctor deliberately drove past Annice's house in the city. He hoped not to accomplish anything specific other than to possibly get a glimpse of her and feel closer to her. The stint in the prison had taken its toll on him emotionally. It made him feel too distant from her. He idled past her house but didn't see her. He thought about the promise she had made to him. Only me . . . Only me.

What would God Say?

Aside from the clouds, wind, and rain, Monday started off on a high note for the doctor as he received a very encouraging phone call just prior to his departure from his home. Annice had called him and whispered over the phone that she had been able to keep her promise. She reiterated her promise too, pledging that she would continue to strive to stave off her husband's sexual advances any way she could.

"I'm doing things now in preparation of leaving the relationship," she stated firmly before saying her goodbye. "I love you."

All throughout the day, the doctor was gripped at the heart by the realization that someday soon their love, their lives, would be fulfilled. He was in such a jovial mood that many of his patients made comment of it, and some, who enjoyed their time with him so much, were quite disturbed that their appointments were over.

Annice was kept busy at her desk making insurance inquires over the phone, filling out forms, and updating patient files. She did, however, manage to slip in an "I love you," on a small yellow Post-it note that she attached to a pile of documents she slipped into the doctor's office between patients. The event of the day, however, came just after the last patient departed. It was then that the doctor's dear old mentor, Dr. Horace Brain, burst through the entrance unannounced, unexpected, and highly excited. He was out of breath when he began explaining himself to the doctor's secretary, expressing to her his uncertainty as to whether or not he had been properly introduced.

"I'm sorry, my dear, but I'm an old fool and I can't for the life of me remember your name."

"My name is Annice. Annice Col . . ."

Annice stopped short of completing her name. It was distasteful for her to admit, even to herself, that she was the wife of such an awful man. In her mind she carried out the inevitable change that would come and she called it out inside her head, practiced it, again and again: Annice Haefner . . . Annice Haefner . . . Annice Haefner. Just the sound of it in her thoughts resounded vibrantly in her heart. She felt young and full of expectation as she had before her previous nuptials. The wonder in her heart had put her mind and body in a trance so that Dr. Brain knew that something was affecting her deeply. As a courtesy, he allowed a minute to pass before he made an interrupting sound in his throat. With no expectation for her to apologize, the doctor went right on explaining his unexpected presence.

"Be assured that I would never have come without notice unless the news I carried was of the utmost importance. I know that regularly Dr. Haefner sets aside this final hour of his day for himself, to reflect on the events of the day. Please tell him I'm here. Please ask if I can see him."

Annice had heard a lot about Dr. Brain in the recent weeks and she knew that the doctors had also visited each other. She compliantly communicated the arrival of Dr. Brain through the intercom to Dr. Haefner, who acknowledged the unintended visitor by shrieking, "Who?" into the intercom, then racing to greet him.

"What a pleasure it is to see you, Doctor. What an unexpected pleasure. Come in. Come into my office."

The two men had barely situated themselves when Dr. Brain, eager to spill his news, blurted out, "It's him! It's him! I can't believe it myself but it's him!"

"Slow down, Horace. Exactly what are you talking about? What do you mean it's him?"

Dr. Brain, sitting across from the doctor, leaned forward on his chair and steadied himself on the doctor's desk. He stared forward as though he expected the doctor to reach inside him and extract the hidden secret. Then, as if he were a second person in the room, playing a separate role, he leaped out of the chair unexpectedly and moved over to the wall behind him. He stood beside the obituary of the deceased James Cuzze and proclaimed, "It is him!"

The doctor, shocked, stood up from his swivel chair, and in disbelief, watched as Dr. Brain once again pointed to the faded picture inside the frame and proclaimed, "It is James!"

There was an enduring moment of silence before Dr. Brain, who had carried the exciting news with him for several hours now, burst forth in an unprecedented unburdening of the revelation he had made.

"I tell you. I tell you. It is James. The James represented here, in this picture of old. The very James who has aggrieved you all these years. I . . . I couldn't believe it myself when I put two and two together, but it's true! It's true!"

The doctor stood there, petrified, still waiting for the prestigious friend to clarify what appeared to be some sort of revelation. His mind was running wild. Had the doctor had an encounter with the ghost of his deceased friend? Had he?

"My boy, this I declare with no uncertainty. Your James . . . your James was mine!"

"What do you mean, Doctor?"

"James, James Cuzze, belonged to me. He was mine, my patient! Did you hear me? He was my patient first!"

Dr. Haefner was dumbfounded! What was Dr. Brain talking about? How on earth could James, who he knew almost all his life, have been any patient of Dr. Brain?

"Let me get this straight, Doctor, you say that James Cuzze, my James Cuzze, was a patient of yours? How? And when?"

Dr. Brain swayed from the wall, and without falling down, managed to get himself into one of the patient chairs across from the doctor's swivel chair. Dr. Haefner spoke.

"Look, Doctor, I knew James his whole life, mostly. He never, at least to my knowledge, ever submitted himself, either by his own volition or by force, to any sort of psychiatric care."

Dr. Brain nodded in acknowledgment of what his esteemed colleague was saying, but then added, "You said it yourself, Doctor, you only knew him most of your life but the very part you missed, just prior to your having met him, is the part where I participated in his life. Look, see what I have here."

The doctor, who was holding a file in his hand, thrust it forward across the desk. "It's all right there in black and white. See for yourself what I am saying."

Dr. Haefner carefully opened the file and began perusing its contents. The first page was a content page listing the patient, his name, address, and phone number, and beneath that was a short summary of a profile of the boy's troubles. The page read: James Cuzze, North Pine Street, Lancaster, Pa. 17603. Age 8, Juvenile. Legal Guardians: Mr. and Mrs. John Boller.

Underneath that information was a listing which noted the behavioral problems that the custodians were having. It read: Juvenile is exhibiting excessively in all behavioral aspects of his personality. This includes both fair-weather and foul-weather aspects. At times he is overly anxious, exhilarated, enthusiastic, and determined. At times he is overly obdurate, irritated, frustrated, belligerent, and angry. The parents have expressed their concern that as he ages these abnormal patterns will deepen. They fear James for what he might do to himself and for what he might do to them.

Though of the tender age of seven, James has been caught shoplifting from various corner groceries. He has been caught breaking into neighbors' homes, though without taking anything that didn't belong to him. Several times he has snuck out at night and stolen milk bottles from porches after deliveries had been made. There is one old man from the Pine Street neighborhood who claims that little James is always knocking off his hat whenever he is out for a walk. This James does by sneaking up behind him. Even in elementary school where discipline is the rule, James acts out abruptly toward his schoolmates and his teachers. This year, 1967, he has already been suspended three times, most recently for stealing his teacher's lunch bag from the cloakroom and arbitrarily tossing it out the schoolroom window. In short, James is a menace of a variety worse than the Dennis type!

Strangely, though, he exhibits a good potential for things academic. His grades range mostly from C to A, depending upon the subject. He also exhibits a talent for drawing. But despite his endeavors, despite his aptitude, he can't be controlled. nor can he control himself. The Bollers are at their wits' end and are requesting help in the format of mental health.

Subsequent papers noted the detailed summaries of several meetings with the Bollers and James. On the last page of the old file, the doctor read Dr. Brain's final analysis of James's family as he was noting them.

The page read: After our third group session, I am strongly recommending continued and more intensive therapy. The boy is a highly unusual case. At times he appears completely normal. At other times he is obnoxious and rude and shows not an ounce of respect toward authority of any type. Ongoing therapy may reveal that he is, as I suspect, suffering from the ongoing trauma of feeling unwanted. This case, however, is more acute than in any case I have ever encountered before.

Scribbled alongside the margins of the paper were words which revealed just how perplexed Dr. Brain was about James. Written were the words extreme, confusing, bewildered. Exclamation points peppered the page to note the emphasis he felt. And one phrase told all: unlike anyone I have ever seen!

The two doctors shared a collaborative look, a look of mystery. It was true. Dr. Horace Brain had dealings with James—before the time of his friendship with Dr. Haefner. There was a moment of silence between them as each reflected on the significance of the revelation. They had each shared in the catastrophe that was James and to each he had been and still was an enigma.

Finally Dr. Haefner spoke. "Do you remember what happened to his case?"

"Actually I do. I have record of it. My records indicate that my association with him was abrogated because of his defiance toward his parents in their wishes to have him continue his therapy. Several times I had to cancel sessions with him for his failure to show up. He would just disappear whenever it was time to come. There was nothing the Bollers could do about it. If they forced him, he threatened them. He tossed knives at them or threatened to kill them in their sleep. I have it all written down."

"This, this is all too incredible. You and I . . . that you and I had that same relative experience in life, that which was James!"

"So you see, my old friend, I preceded you in our wondrous endeavor to help him. And even way back then when I had my shot at him, I deemed him as a person probably beyond my abilities to control. Even then, I considered him as a disruptive person on a path of destruction. Whatever controlled him was unstoppable! Neither you nor I could have made a difference! So, what is this hold he has over you! Doctor, if you can honestly stand there and accuse yourself of rendering insufficient aid to that rascal of a boy, then I accuse you of holding yourself up too high, as being above the rest of our profession.

"If this is true then tell me and I will call you the most arrogant, conceited, contemptible person that ever walked God's earth. Tell me, Doctor, tell me, how it is that he possesses you so?"

Dr. Haefner pondered that thought a minute. Then he responded, "I know I am not entirely to blame for James. Especially now that I know I have you to share part of it," he laughed. "I am aggrieved by the loss of it all. Undeniably, I was the closest person to him, and undeniably, I had the best chance of all of helping him. You see, it wasn't just about figuring him out. That, I wasn't sure I would ever be able to accomplish. But actually helping him, maybe just enough, would have been all that was necessary for me to feel . . . to feel as though I had made a difference in his life. My problem was that I always felt inadequate to do so. All during the spawning of my professional life I waited, waited until I felt I possessed the necessary skills to deal with him. I kept putting it off, putting off any attempts to really make contact with him and somehow force him into my practice. Then, he died. And when he died, along with him died any chance I would ever have to respond to his suffering. Then, all I had left was regret. And regret is a sorrowful thing."

"All I have to say, Doctor, is that regardless of how you think about it, you can never be sure you would have ever been successful in helping him. Sure you could have applied time to him, but how beneficial would it have been? I ask you. Maybe the real reason you kept him at a distance and never really attempted to help him once you acquired your professional skills was that you knew him so perfectly. You knew him so well that you knew deep down the futility of what you expected. Doctor, I have to remind you that there is such a thing as an incurable patient. Don't be so certain about what you think you could have done for him. You're not God."

"No, I'm not," Dr. Haefner responded in a passive voice. "I am a licensed psychiatrist who has been in practice for about a decade. I've helped many, many people. Do you know, Dr. Brain, that in all my years of practice I've never had one of my former patients lose it altogether? No one that I ever treated has ever committed suicide. No one, regardless of their pain and suffering, has ever deemed their lives worthless. That's entirely because of me. It's because of my success that I feel so terrible about James. I could have helped him. I should have helped him."

"That's probably true. But remember, Doctor, he would have had to have been a willing candidate. Would he have been? In order for you apply your healing hands on him, he would have had to cooperate fully with your endeavor. Would he have?

"The time for really being able to help him passed you by, my boy. It was on my watch when that should have occurred. Even back then, there were legitimate therapies and medications available for him. And even though the medications were lacking, all he would have had to do would have been to continue in some ongoing treatment until some of the miracle drugs came along, like Prozac. Prozac would have been the prescribed medication for someone like him. Look at how it helped your mother. She was one of the first patients in the country on it and that was back in the early '80s. James, at the time, was still a minor. He would have received help if his parents helped him. The way I see it, it was their fault mostly. I treated him as a young psychologist and I don't feel as though I dropped the ball. I couldn't have forced them to seek treatment for him. Nobody could have, except possibly the courts, and they weren't involved. Stop blaming yourself for something that isn't your fault."

"What should I do?"

"What you should do is what I would do. Don't forget James. Use him. Use your experiences of him to help you with your work as a psychiatrist. Write down your experiences with him. Write down everything you can remember about him. Write down his faults and weaknesses. Write down his aptitudes and everything that was good about him. Write down what you thought was wrong with him. Write down what you think may have finally helped him. Write it all down. Then at least you will have established something tangible about him. I believe that if you establish something real out of the experience of knowing him, then you will feel as though you have accomplished something. There will be something there in place for whenever you need to occupy yourself with it. You won't feel that it's so necessary to convolute your mind with thoughts about him. You won't have to because there will be a place where it already is. And it will all be there in a perfect order. Who knows, you could turn it into an esoteric prize, an interpretation of immense interest. Hell, you could write a book about him."

"A book?" Dr. Haefner questioned the idea out loud. "It sounds plausible. I could call it *The Book of James*."

"You're title sounds biblical," Dr. Brain remarked.

"Oh, but that's the perfect implication," Dr. Haefner returned. "Nobody would be disappointed either. James was a classic. His life resonated in and out of what life's ideals are. He loved and hated people as no one else could. He was an angel and a demon to everyone he knew, and he knew too. Therefore, any religious connotation derived from the naming of the book is indeed applicable. I thank you, Doctor, for that."

The measuring of James's life in a religious aspect brought Dr. Haefner into a philosophical mind-set. He wanted to weigh out a certain amount of perspective about it while it was still fresh in his thoughts.

"The good of God dwells in each and every one of us. Likewise, the devil's evil does too. Determining how to quell the evil in us is our life's quest. In most of us we usually sway just a little in both directions and that's not too hard for our psyches to take. But for James and anyone like him, they have the pendulum swinging full swing. To them, decisions . . ."

Just at that moment the office door swayed open and Annice's face appeared. She hesitated until she was acknowledged.

"Annice, do come in," Dr. Haefner requested.

"I'm sorry for interrupting," she stated innocently. "I just wanted to let you know that it's time for me to leave."

Both doctors turned simultaneously toward their watches. It was already five o'clock.

"Well, I guess visiting hours are over," Dr. Brain said jovially.

"Why don't you stay? We'll go out for a bite to eat."

Before Dr. Brain could reply, Dr. Haefner excused himself from the room so he could speak to Annice.

"Annice, Annice," he spoke out as she was gathering her belongings. "Annice, we're going out to eat. Would you like to come?"

"I would, but I can't," she smiled and said.

Her smile was such that Dr. Haefner suspected she was being suggestive toward him. He ushered her out of his doorway and into the main office area.

"Excuse me, Doctor," he said as he exited the room.

With the door closed behind him he stood in front of Annice and reiterated his previous question to her.

"Would you like to come, with me?"

"Anytime, anyplace, anywhere," she said, resuming her enticing intent.

They kissed.

"Someday we will be together," the doctor said while she whisked her handbag up upon her shoulder.

"Together forever," Annice said in departing.

Back in his office, the doctor apologized for the extended
interlude he had spent with his office assistant. Their words, their
kisses had left him brimming with joy. The doctor's mind was
nowhere where it had been before and his esteemed colleague was
aware of it.

"Am I accurate in assuming that your altered mood can be
attributed to the time spent behind that door? Is she the one who
holds you . . . dispossessed from all others?"

Dr. Haefner felt confident in telling Dr. Brain everything about
him and Annice. He relinquished it all as they coursed through their
evening, first at Herkimer's where they enjoyed a splendid meal
together, then outside in the parking lot. It was a nice diversion for
Dr. Haefner, who found comfort in the way Dr. Brain evaluated
then validated their relationship. These were the first encouraging
words the doctor had heard regarding the sticky situation from an
outsider.

"You're both attracted to each other and respect each other. And
you are compatible as a couple. I wish you both the greatest success
in fostering your relationship."

Having his involvement with Annice as a diversion was relieving
to the doctor. Had he not had such engaging subject matter as a topic
for discussion, the doctor feared he might have opened up to the
doctor and promulgated, instead, the topic of James and his recent
involvements with him. He already knew what the result of that
would be. Dr. Horace Brain would not be subdued into believing
that a ghost, any ghost, exists. The only people he could completely
confide in were those whom James had already appeared to. And
now, now that it had been discovered that Dr. Brain had actually
had contact with James, James might, if he discovered who Dr. Brain
was due to his current association with Christopher, visit with him.
Then he would be a believer. Then they could discuss the miracle as
something that has happened rather than as one that may or may not
have happened.

The concept of it having been a miracle set off a spark in the
doctor's mind. He reflected upon it. He watched as his friend waved
goodbye from his vehicle and joined the traffic flow heading north

into Lancaster. It was late but the doctor could not leave just yet. His contemplations weighed him down and he did not want to be distracted from his thoughts.

The issue of whether or not it could be said that James's presence was a miracle inundated him with a burden of thoughts, thoughts that delved into the greatest depths of meaning, of solution, of purpose. Certainly the ability to transcend one's own death qualifies as a miracle. Then, if James, James Cuzze, nonetheless, has done this, surely the event can be viewed similarly. James is not God but God would have had to have had a hand in it. Then, if that's true, James's appearance could be nothing less than a miracle. It must have been God's purpose to send him. But, why?

The doctor stood in silence as he put together thoughts The power of his feelings for life, for love, helped inculcate in his mind one staunch belief, one final conclusion for this all.

"Annice!"

It was all for her and he knew that now. If miracles happen, they happen for a reason and the reason must be founded in love, for love is the essence of God. And Annice is the only source of love in his life.

Suddenly the doctor felt ashamed. Here he was purporting that a ghost had been sent by God to help him win love and he had just openly admitted that Annice was his only source of love. And what of God? What of the God who had performed this miracle? What of the God who had set forth into the world the only demon who could have secured his wrath, the wrath he could then apply toward determining once and for all that his love was meant for only one person. He became his conscience.

It came to him that since he and Annice had begun a physical relationship, he had, at times, actually prayed to God, prayed for God to grant them a favorable conclusion to their ardent belief that they were meant for each other. Prayer, though, was something that had, in most of his years since he left high school, eluded him. Prayer, he had always thought, was something too intangible to be useful in a person's life. It gave only the briefest relief to the person praying, and then if a prayer was not answered, usually led to increased anxiety in a person's already-troubled mind, since most people who pray are those experiencing some sort of despair in their lives. Prayer, then, can actually become a source of alienation from the Almighty.

Due to this perspective, the doctor had turned away from prayer as a source of expectation in his life—until now. His relationship with Annice was an adulterous one. Even though he strongly believed that it was based on pure love and its favorable result was for the greater good, he was still unsure of how God felt about it. His conscience was his guide, but he was still stepping into a quicksand of guilt about what he was doing.

Prayer was a reprieve. It allowed him to have a presence with God so he could plead his case. It alleviated his uncertainty in that at least God would recognize his sincerity in what he was doing. And if Annice was praying too, and he was sure she was, then God would be hearing from them both directly, and that has to be better than not hearing from them at all. Even if they were wrong it was the right thing to do. He was like a little boy again, believing, wanting to believe that God was there for him. He, all the time, would find himself preparing for the court of heaven. From the recesses of his mind came persuasions, arguments, contrivances, all pleas for their cause, pleas to God who sat in judgment of them.

In one of his arguments, the doctor pleaded that he knew now why love, in terms of a woman's heart, had always eluded him. It prevailed upon him that God must have been disallowing his closeness to anyone since he had first met Annice because they would eventually be together. He knew too that as a younger man he admonished God for not having brought to him that special someone once Annice had been taken.

And to God he proclaimed, "Having been weakened in the heart the way I was when she was gone, having nothing left of love to live on, having no hope, I did sinfully abandon you as my Creator. But this was not a sin of contempt, but rather, a sin of despair, of weakness you yourself made possible in each of us, your children. For this I am sorry.

"But something we have all learned in our lives is that good things happen to those who wait. And in relation to that premise, I have now reasoned and believe that this is what you have intended—that the love that is to come from this is worth my wait and has the power to diminish the transgression of how our union was formed.

"And last, I ask you to forgive us for how this came about. I do not suppose you have condoned our actions but rather understand them. It is because of the second-greatest gift you have given us that I beseech you to accept what we have done. Love is your greatest gift but our ability to act freely upon it is the reason we have done so. This, free will you have given us allows us to do so. You love us enough that you do not force from us a reciprocal love. Instead, you allow us to love or not to love you in return. It is from this accord that we have chosen."

And God would answer . . .

Escape

During the next several days, Annice, serious about her intent to leave Leslie, began in earnest to make some of the essential arrangements to bring the plan to fruition. With the exception of Christopher, nobody knew of her pending flight. She had managed to locate and had already visited a single-bedroom apartment very close to her work. She had already set aside enough money for several months of rent, a security deposit, food, and bills. She needed now only place another call to the prospective landlord, tell him she wanted the apartment and arrange a time and place for her to sign the lease.

Most of her personal belongings; jewelry, shoes, clothing, and keepsakes, she had already packed into small boxes and stored in various, obscure places. They were all around the house, in closets, corners, shelf space, anywhere convenient, so they could be gathered up in a hurry if needed. Important papers like her birth certificate, marriage certificate, checkbook, and savings passbook, she kept with her at all times, tucked safely away inside her handbag. She knew that on the very next provocation, any sexual or physical assault, she would flee, regardless of whether or not she had secured a place to stay.

For six days following her promise to Chris, she had been successful at keeping her husband off of her, pretending to be sick with headaches and nausea. He even openly suggested that she might finally be pregnant after twenty years of marriage and even flaunted the idea around to some of his co-workers and Annice's sister Amy. But Annice knew that time was running out. Inevitably, whether sick or sick due to pregnancy, Leslie would not tolerate not having relations with her. Her body was for his hobbies, a punching bag and a sex toy. By the sixth day, she noticed how increasingly irritable he was becoming. Soon he would be at a boiling point and would probably explode on her both with violence and violent sex.

On the seventh day, Leslie, overcome with suspicion that his wife was being unfaithful, devised a means to trap her. He went to his postal job as usual that day but while there began complaining of sickness, and as expected, he was sent home. He purposely went for a short drive to kill time, then drove home. He parked his car two blocks from his house on a block where nobody knew him, then began walking toward his house through a series of back alleys which led to the edge of his own backyard. When he reached the yard, he hopped the metal gate and stood in the shadows of the old trees which defined the property line. There he waited. There he watched. After a sustained viewing from the back of the house, he decided to go around front. It was dark and he knew nobody would bother him if they saw him. Out front, he sneaked up on the porch and peered in the two front windows. He had been away for over five hours, which amounted to an ample period of time in which Annice could have arranged for a lover to come to her. From the porch, he tried to ascertain the situation inside the house. There were lights on both upstairs and downstairs. The television set was off and he heard no music being played anywhere. He noticed nothing out of place, no unusual jackets or clothes strewn anywhere. He heard no voices and saw no figures of anyone, not even his wife.

Leslie felt annoyed. His adrenaline was flowing. He almost wanted someone to be there so there could be an altercation. He was pumped up and ready for a fight. He desperately wanted to catch his wife lying with another man. Then he would be able to justify the beating he had planned for her. It was exciting for him to think about it. He played out the scenario in his mind: Slipping into the house, he would hear them upstairs, laughing, giggling, playing around. He

would creep up the steps, slowly, quietly and wait at the top, wait
and listen for a while, listen to their playfulness, hear when they
begin their foreplay, hear his wife enjoying the pleasures of another
man, hear his wife's lover as he relinquishes himself over her. Then,
then, the confrontation would begin. He would break open the door
while they were both naked and vulnerable. He would strike at them
as they lay limp upon one another. Using the lamp he would bash
out their brains, possibly commit murder, a murder that under the
circumstances could be considered justifiable.

Leslie had tasted blood. He wanted reality to mirror the image
he had just sustained. Blood-thirsty and exacting, he placed his
hand upon the doorknob and turned it. It opened. He stepped
cautiously and quietly inside and closed the door behind him. He
stood motionless on the living room rug listening for movement or
sound of any kind. He thought about how happy things would be
if this scenario played out in real life like it did in his fantasy of it.
If he caught his wife cheating, he would have the right to beat her.
And he would make it a severe beating. He would leave an indelible
mark on her, a permanent mark, one that she would never forget
and one that he could always use against her. From the beating she
would get, she would forever be like a little lamb—a little lamb
always wondering when the big bad wolf would swoop down upon
her and devour her. She would never again be insistent toward him.
She would never again even attempt to resist his sexual advances,
perverted or not. She would be like a mistress, a servant, a slave. Life
would be wonderful.

Finally, he crept across the carpet then stood at the bottom of
the stairs. He listened. He heard the faint sound of running water
coming from the bathroom. He went up the steps to investigate. At
the top of the steps he listened further to the sounds coming from
the bathroom. The light was on and someone was splashing in the
tub. He lurked outside the bathroom door listening, trying to discern
whether his wife was alone or with someone. Several minutes passed
in which he heard only Annice splashing lightly in the water and
humming. Once he heard the shower curtain move and was sure, he
decided to make his move. He made a movement with his shoulder as

though he were going to burst unexpectedly into the room and startle whoever was there but the door resisted. It was locked. Infuriated, Leslie began pounding on the door with his fists, demanding that it be opened at once. Annice let out a cry.

"Who . . . who's there?" she cried.

"Who . . . who the hell do you think?" Leslie cried back, mimicking her meek voice in return.

"Leslie! What in God's name are you doing home now?"

"God's got nothing to do with it," he replied. "Just open the door before I break it open with my foot!"

"All right, all right," Annice cried back. "Why can't you wait until I'm done with my bath?"

Annice complied. She stood up in the tub and reached up for a towel she had hanging over the top of the shower curtain. Wrapping it around her she stepped out of the water and reached cautiously for the door. With a great deal of trepidation she unlocked it. The sound of the door's release was life-threatening. Instantly Leslie was inside and before Annice could return to her bath he had her.

"Let me go," she cried. "I'm cold standing here. I want to finish my bath. You're the one who interrupted me."

"I'll do worse than that," Leslie promised.

"Let me go!"

"No!"

Leslie stood there holding onto Annice's shoulders while she dripped water from her body onto the floor. It occurred to him that everything was in order in his home. Annice was alone. It also occurred to him that he was there for nothing. He grew incensed over the idea that he had to be there, that he had lost time at work for what turned out to be nothing at all. It was her fault. She was the cause of all this. If she had only been a more obedient wife, this never would have happened. He was stuck. He couldn't go back to work, which meant he could not go out to the corner bar after. There were too many snitches around and he couldn't risk being found out.

"This is your fault!" he shouted.

"My fault? I didn't decide for you to come home and sneak into the house for what reason I don't know."

"It's your fault and you're going to make it up to me!" Leslie demanded.

He squeezed Annice's hands until she let go of the towel that was wrapped around her. It fell to the floor and she was exposed before him, vulnerable and scared. He shoved her against the bathroom wall beside the tub and told her if she moved a muscle she would be punched in the head.

"Now that's a good girl," he said in a patronizing voice as he stripped out of his clothing.

Twice Leslie bent down to remove his shoes and each time he dawdled when his face was near her back. He kissed it each time. Despite not loving her, he did admit to himself she had a gorgeous body and he was very thankful it was his. He wanted something extra special from her, to make up for the fact that she was responsible for him having to leave work to check up on her. His wife was his to do with as he pleased. Pleasing her was no longer a consideration. He had, in accordance with a recent idea, opened up a new creativity in their increasingly one-sided sex life. And the lure of any once-forbidden act was now and forever with him. It enticed him to the point of no return. He forced her on the floor, face down, and attempted to take her. She would, forever be, his 'literal' piece of ass. For Annice it was a vulgar thing. The psychological pain she suffered was far greater than what would have been the physical pain if he had succeeded. It was for her, the point of no return. No longer could her physical body or emotional mind reconcile with his. 'Being as one' as couples strive to be, could never be.

Exhausted from attempting his deed Leslie departed. He went into the couple's bedroom and collapsed on the bed. Annice wept bitterly on the bathroom floor. She felt bitter. She had been violated, betrayed, and traumatized. There was no solace left for her, not in anything. Her husband had gone far beyond anything that could be considered a husband's right to have his wife. She thought about the conditions of their marriage, the promises they made to one another to love, honor, and obey. "Obey" had been a mistake.

Did a man, once he was a husband, have the inherent right to take his wife sexually whenever and wherever he wanted? In marriage, was his power supreme? Even if the means and manner seemed undignified? A man was supposed to be bounded by love and affection to the woman who would bring him happiness. But Leslie was no longer a man; rather, he was a beast, a beast with a black heart, who lusted only for himself and his own self-indulgences.

Annice knew that Leslie would never stop. Now that he wanted to use her in a way that he had not previously, he would never relent. As warriors do, they come back for more. It would be a unique pleasure for him, a private privilege, a sexual playground. Annice winced at the repulsive idea that from this day forward she would have to knowingly and willingly render herself to him this way whenever he wanted it. There would be no argument about it. The words of her mother rang in her head from the first time she had complained of being unhappy. "You have made your bed, now lie in it."

It was now or never. Annice had to act. She got up and toweled herself off. Too much had happened. Surely it would only be a matter of time until Leslie exploded on her again—and for no reason other than to amuse himself. The level to which he lacked respect for her, for himself, was astounding. Things could never be the same between them. This was it! This was all the excuse she needed to act! She would escape!

Leaving the bathroom light on and the door open, Annice was able to provide her bedroom with a soft illumination of light without having to turn on any bedroom light. Quietly she crept into the room. Her husband was asleep, lying quietly across the bed. This was her chance. Making as little sound as possible, she went from dresser drawer to closet and removed clothing, shoes, socks, and a few personal items. She carried them into the hall where she dressed. The remainder of the clothes, she bundled in her arms and carried down the stairs to the first floor. There she opened up the hall closet and retrieved a large bag, one she had prepared for such an occasion. She opened it and stuffed the remaining clothes into it. She then paused for a moment to consider what else she might take. There were other bags in the basement but she refused to get them, fearing the trap she would be in if he should awaken while she was down there and find her there. He would probably lock her in and leave her there, probably for days. A shoe box with more personal papers was in the pantry and she did retrieve it. Her car keys were in her possession. Ready, she glanced over at the kitchen clock, a cat-shaped clock with a tail that waggled back and forth to count the seconds. It had been a wedding gift from her sister. Tears were about to swell up in her but she swallowed them down. The clock struck the new hour. It was the start of a new day. It was the start of a new life.

Gleaming with self-assurance she walked out of the house that had been her home, the house which had seen the beginning and the end of her marriage.

Out on the street there wasn't a soul around: nobody to be witness to her defiant act of bravery, nobody to console or comfort her, nobody to wish her well, nobody to care. She escaped into the night, holding what was left of her former life in the few items that accompanied her. She reached the safety of her Escort and tossed her belongings inside. The departure from her former life had been hasty and not as prepared for as she would have liked. For a minute she sat idly in the driver's seat of her car and thought.

"What to do," she asked herself.

The strain of everything that had just happened to her had left her feeling depleted. Emotionally she was subdued and she struggled to find a strategy to follow to complete and make good her escape. A plethora of ideas flooded her mind. Should she go to her sister Amy's house and tell all? Should she dare to approach her elder parents and tell them the epic tales of her tragic abuse? Should she go to the office where she worked and just hold up there? There was no place to sleep but it was a place of safety. Annice felt overwhelmed. But a good thing happened from that burdensome feeling. She remembered Dr. Jeanne.

"I should still have her card somewhere I believe."

Annice clicked on the car's dome light and began rummaging around in her handbag for the card Dr. Jeanne gave her several weeks ago. Inside her bag she found a white envelope. It was the envelope where she was keeping the incriminating photos depicting Leslie's violent rage against her last month. Along with the photos she found the card. In addition to finding the card, she opened up her wallet and counted out her cash. There was $157. Besides the ready cash, she reminded herself that in her private checking account she had a balance of $750. In all it was enough, enough to help her start her new life. She regretted that she had not prepared longer. Just then Annice was startled by a set of headlights coming up the street. On impulse she locked the doors. She had to leave, for here she was a sitting duck and the hunter, though asleep, was not far away.

Annice looked precariously at the forlorn-looking house. There were no indications that any life stirred in it. She looked away. After starting her car she drove quietly away, knowing in her heart she would never return.

She drove several blocks down on College Avenue past the quiet homes of her neighbors. At Columbia Avenue she turned right, a main thoroughfare leading west out of the city. Two blocks down she stopped at a convenience store. She pulled into the parking lot and parked her car directly in front of the public pay phone. She got out. Unsure of the price, she deposited two quarters into the coin slot.

Hearing a sympathetic voice, Annice broke down. She related her situation to Dr. Detweiler entirely, replete with stories of her husband's abuses both present and past.

"I'm stranded," she pleaded. "Please help me."

"Are you OK to drive?" Dr. Jeanne inquired.

"Yes. I think so."

"Then come to my place. You can stay here with me until we sort things out. I live at 21 Roll Ridge Drive. Do you know how to get here?"

"Yes, that's over in the Manor Ridge Development. Right?"

"Yes, that's right."

Ten minutes later, Annice was sitting comfortably in Jeanne's quaint living room, drinking iced tea and talking. After several minutes of conversation, Jeanne suggested that they call Chris.

"But . . . but . . . it's so late," Annice protested.

"Nonsense, I'll bet you Chris will be glad we called. I know for a fact how he feels about you. He will very definitely want to be involved in this situation."

Annice sat quietly on the couch and listened as Jeanne placed the call. Next thing she knew Jeanne was right in the middle of telling him everything about her present state of affairs. Jeanne elaborated on the things she told him except for the ordeal she had just experienced. Though Jeanne's reactions seemed ordinary and quiet, Annice still felt a little embarrassed and worried about whether Christopher might be upset for having been called so late. Jeanne noticed Annice's anxious face and signaled for her to come over next to her. When she did, Jeanne attempted to calm her fears by putting her arm around Annice's shoulder. Jeanne then began holding the phone out a short distance from her ear so Annice could hear Chris's voice. Annice heard. His words were calm and he appeared to be completely undisturbed at being called at such an inappropriate hour. Finally, Chris asked to speak to Annice.

"So it finally happened. Are you all right? Anyway, I'm glad you left him. Now there will be a real chance for us."

"I'm . . . I'm so sorry for calling you so unexpectedly."

"Don't be. I'm glad it was me you called. Jeanne assured me that you will be able to stay with her for a while. You will be safe there too. Sometime tomorrow, we will begin planning what we should do for you. But whatever you do, do not, I repeat, do not show up for work tomorrow. That's the one place your husband will probably come to apprehend you."

"But what about you?"

"Don't worry about me, I'll manage. The most important thing is that you remain safe. Your job will be waiting for you once this is over."

"But what if he comes there and starts something with you?"

"I expect him to come but I don't care. I'm not required to tell him anything. If he hassles me, I'll order him to leave; and if he refuses, I'll call the police. It's as simple as that."

"Be careful, Christopher. I want you to be safe too."

Annice felt safe and sure in the midst of her two friends. She had hope now to carry her. Every moment of her life now was filled with the realization that now her life would be new. Though all of twenty years had passed it wasn't too late.

Jeanne had one spare room in the upstairs of her little home. She used it sparingly, usually for guests who visited her during holidays. It was always clean and ready. It came complete with a single bed, television, chairs, curtains, and a phone. Annice complimented her on how accommodating it was, telling her again and again how lucky she felt knowing she had someone like Jeanne in her life. Jeanne returned Annice's compliment, telling her she was pleased to do it and it made her feel good that someone trusted her for help.

Enlightenment

The following morning, bright and early, the doctor showed up, unexpectedly, at the Detweiler home. He had told Jeanne the previous night he might come before going to work. Jeanne had not related this information to Annice because in Annice's delicate condition she did not want her to be expecting him in case he did not show up. Jeanne cordially invited him in.

"Would you like anything to eat, Chris?"

"No, no thanks. I've already eaten. And besides I'm all out of sorts. I couldn't sleep much last night with all this going on."

"You love her, don't you?"

"Yes, yes, I do. Is it that obvious?"

"I am a woman, you know. And a woman can tell when a man is in love even if it is with someone else."

The doctor smiled.

"Is she up?"

"No. Last time I checked she's still sleeping like a baby. Why don't you leave her a note telling her you stopped by? She will appreciate that. It will be reassuring if she knows you cared enough to come over on your way to the office. Come, sit with me while I finish eating. We can talk things over for a bit."

The two doctors proceeded into the kitchen where they sat down opposite each other at the dinette set.

"I'm sorry I interrupted your meal," Dr. Haefner issued once he saw Jeanne's partially portioned plate of food.

"Don't be sorry. I'm glad to be involved in this. Annice is a wonderful person and I want to help her."

Taking a bite of her scrambled-eggs-on-toast sandwich, Jeanne inquired, "So, what's next for her?"

"Well, the biggest step has now been taken. She's already started looking at apartments. Once she has arranged that, I'll assist her in arranging the abrogation of her marriage. The rest is entirely up to him. He can avoid trouble and just allow her to go peacefully, or he can make trouble and then make it extremely difficult for him. With the help of a restraining order, we can keep him away while things are taken care of. As for her apartment, he will never know where she is."

"What about letting her stay with you?" Dr. Jeanne asked bluntly.

"With me?" the doctor asked in an unbelieving voice.

"Yes, with you," Jeanne returned in an upbeat voice which told him that it was time to cast off his attitude of protective friend and live up to the role of portended lover.

"If you love her, why don't you offer her a place to stay— yours?"

The doctor was a bit taken aback by Jeanne's bold proposition but he was ready with an answer, an answer he himself had already thought about when he had asked himself the same question.

"I would if I could, Jeanne. Believe me, I would. But I'm not an ordinary Joe. I am a professional man, a doctor, a psychiatrist. If I were to ever do such a thing I would be criticized severely by my fellow professionals and the general public. I could just see the headlines now: Esteemed Lancaster psychiatrist accused of having an illicit affair with a married woman. And it would probably be instigated by her estranged husband despite everything he's guilty of doing. It may sound a bit selfish at a time like this, but I actually have a reputation to think about. I am a responsible member of this community. It would be very irresponsible of me if I were to be selfish enough to indulge my passions in that way. I love Annice, but having her move in with me just seems so rash."

"It's spontaneous and sometimes that's the best way with love."

"It could also be foolish and stupid."

"You're not a fool, Chris, and if you did this, you could make it one of the smartest things you ever did. You would be with the woman you love. You could live with her, love her, protect her. For her it would be the safest place to be."

"I . . . I don't know," the doctor protested. "If we used the transitional approach it would be more appropriate. Besides, she has already looked at an apartment. And we haven't even asked her yet."

"The apartment is no excuse. She hasn't signed anything yet. She told me. As for asking her, there's no doubt she would sign on with you in a heartbeat, and heartbeats are what this is all about, isn't it?"

"She already has my heart."

"Then prove it to her. Show her how much you love her by being willing to take a little criticism from the rest of the community. Remember, let the person who is without sin cast the first stone. Did you also ever consider that she would be more at risk by her soon-to-be ex-husband if she were to go it alone? He could stalk her. And by doing so he could eventually find out where she moved to. Then if he did, where would you be when she needed you?"

"I . . . I just don't know, Jeanne. I have to think more about it but not right this moment. This is all too much on my mind right now. Look, if she ever gets into any trouble with him, I'll be there for her. Look, look at the time. I must be going now. Quick, get me a pen and paper. I'll write her a little note."

Jeanne got up and retrieved a piece of paper and a pen from one of the kitchen drawers and handed them to the doctor. He wrote Annice a brief message telling her not to worry and reiterating his stipulation to her not to come to work today. He handed back the note and excused himself to leave.

"Also, tell Annice that I'll stop over after work today to see how she's doing."

They proceeded to the front door together.

"Again, thank you," the doctor said with relief as he was about to exit the home.

"If you like, we could all have dinner together tonight," Jeanne suggested.

"If you like," the doctor returned, then left.

The doctor drove across town and arrived at his office ahead of his scheduled start time. Already waiting for him was Mr. Franklin, his first patient. They walked into the building together.

"I know I'm here early, Doctor, but I try to avert my forgetfulness by going places early. That way I'm seldom late and Bee doesn't raise a fuss with me."

Mr. Franklin suffered from the early stages of dementia which the doctor was no expert on. But because it was a mental incapacity, the doctor received patients like this, though usually just to ascertain their disability then refer them to other doctors, specialists who deal with the deteriorating effects of old age. So far though, Mr. Franklin had been hard to get rid of. He and Mr. Franklin were fond of each other and their time spent together went more like two old friends jawing at each other than a doctor dealing with a patient's dysfunction. The doctor cared for Mr. Franklin by giving him advice and profiling his deteriorating condition. Mr. Franklin was, though, a psychological specimen. If he remained with the doctor long enough, the doctor could see, exactly, how a person's personality changes due to the adverse effects of dementia. After seeing Mr. Franklin, the doctor was busy with two successive patients who both arrived at the same time for service. Then, and before the two additional arrivals came, he placed a call to a staffing office for help. To avoid the possibility of getting Linda back and all the complications that would go with it, he contacted a different agency. While he was with them in conversation explaining the requirements of the job, he had no idea that sitting across from him in the seemingly empty patient's chair was his old nemesis, James.

James, unseen, sat patiently, attentively, while the doctor concluded his call. Then, as expected, the doctor left the office to meet and greet his next patient. Immediately, James got up, and without a care or hesitation, he slammed the door to the office shut and locked it. The doctor whirled around toward his office door and went up to it. He tried to open it but it was locked. Next he went out to his patient and apologized that there would be a short delay in their treatment as he would have to find some tool and pry the door open.

Meanwhile, inside the office, James materialized. He seated himself in the doctor's chair and picked up the phone. He did not finger any of the digits but a call went through to Linda's apartment. She had been lying in bed sleeping when she heard the phone ring. With her eyes still closed she reached out beside the bed and picked up the phone. When she picked up, a voice spoke to her.

"Is this Linda?"

"Yes, it's me. Who's this?"

"This is Mr. Stief calling from the agency. If you are available today we would like you to go over to Dr. Haefner's. He needs help. His secretary is indisposed. Would you like to do it?"

"I . . . I don't know. I just got up and I'm nowhere near presentable looking. Maybe tomorrow, though."

"No! That won't do! He needs you today!" James demanded. "If you won't go today, you won't go tomorrow or any day for that matter. Now what do you say!"

"Hey, you don't have to be so tense about it," Linda declared.

"OK," James remarked. "But the order stands. It's now or never."

"All right, I'll go," Linda relented.

Linda didn't know quite what to think. Ever since she and the doctor had been intimate that last time he had only called her once, and even then she felt he had called her more out of obligation than desire. Reluctantly, she hopped into the shower, showered and shampooed, then dried off. Once she was admirably clean, her hair shining, she went into her closet to select something appealing to wear. This, she knew, could be her last chance to snag the doctor. And she reasoned, it should be easier, after all he knew he would be getting. To lure the doctor's sensibilities, she picked out a coquettish little black skirt and a white blouse to be her enticing attire. The blouse was practically see-through and she purposefully did not wear a bra under it. That, she knew, would be enough.

Linda arrived at the doctor's building less than an hour later, unannounced and unexpected. Before entering the building, she paused at the main doors and checked her facial appearance in a small compact mirror. When she entered, she did so with a confident stride, realizing she had been asked for and received. Inside the main office she was completely baffled by what she was confronted by. In the office, in the familiar chair she was supposed to be occupying was another woman!

Linda felt indignant. The woman in the chair was not there by any inadvertent circumstance. She was cheerfully acting the part of office assistant. She was already busy with a patient and Linda had to wait her turn in line.

"May I help you?" the auburn-haired lady asked.

"You may," Linda returned indignantly. "For starters how about getting the hell out of my chair!"

Startled by the remark, the woman automatically called for the doctor over the intercom.

"Doctor, there is a woman here to see you. She's claiming that you hired her to be your secretary."

The doctor, who was between sessions, came quickly out of his office to find out what was going on. Upon his approach toward the desk, Linda intercepted him from behind.

"Linda," he said in a subdued voice. "What are you doing here?"

"What am I doing here?" she stated in an exasperated voice. "You mean, what is she doing here," she stated, pointing to the forlorn-looking woman behind the front desk.

"What are you talking about?" he inquired in a perplexed tone.

"What do you mean what am I talking about? I was the one called by the agency this morning asking if I could be your replacement. And then I get here and here she is."

The doctor was aghast. He was the one who placed the call to the agency and he specifically did not call the agency who had previously hired Linda. How could it be that both women showed up? The doctor had to think up something quick to appease Linda, at least until he could explain the mishap to her in a friendlier atmosphere. In the present circumstance, he was already falling behind on the day and could in no way spare any time on unraveling this mystery.

"Look," he said to Linda with a serious intonation. "I don't know how this happened. I am not responsible for it. However, as you can see, I already have a replacement for the day. She was here first and quite frankly I don't have the time to get to the bottom of this right now. I have a practice here with people depending on me. That, not you, is my priority, first and foremost. As for you, as for us, we will just have to find an appropriate time to talk about this. I am sorry for the inconvenience this caused you. I really am."

Linda was becoming irritated by the doctor's nonchalant attitude toward her, as if her coming down meant nothing to him; this, after everything they had been through, through all of their love-making. She felt like a corporate stockholder who had just found out her stock's price had plummeted to zero.

"Look at me," she argued. "Look at me and tell me you don't want me."

The doctor looked at her but so did the strange woman behind the desk and so did the other patients and supporters assembled in the waiting room. To everybody present Linda's meaning was clear. She was availing herself, selfishly, to the doctor, who could only feign being ignorant of her folly.

"Linda, I'm sorry," he said with finality, then broke away from her capturing stare.

"Oh, how could you!" she declared then flung her pocketbook toward him. It missed. Humiliated, she catapulted toward the door, flung it open with a bang, then disappeared out into the hall. The doctor's first instinct was to follow her but he didn't. He couldn't. He turned toward his disbelieving audience and made a quick apology.

The altercation was over. Linda had been hurt but the doctor knew he was not responsible for it. He retreated into his office to think, telling his temporary not to allow anybody inside until he said so.

Reeling from the unexpected event, madder now than before, he picked up the phone and began dialing the staffing agency to give them a sound reprimand for screwing things up. From facing the window behind his desk he turned, still listening to rings, when suddenly he beheld James!

He was grinning broadly, and sitting prominently in one of his patient chairs. There was an aura about him, something indefinable, almost as though he were alive.

Immediately the doctor reacted to the specter's presence. He slammed down the receiver and bolted to the doorknob to lock it. Next he returned to his desk, sat down, and secretly activated the camera and audiotape from a controller beside his desk. James, seeing all and sensing what he could not, just laughed aloud.

"Don't you know, good sir, that vampires can't produce images? How then do you expect to see mine?"

"I did not know you were a vampire as well as a decadent demon desperate to dwell again in the land of the living."

"Bravo," James laughed clapping his hands.

"Good, indeed," the doctor replied sarcastically. "Now, what the hell are you doing here? I have a practice to run."

"Hey, you're the one who said that I should drop down here for a little tête-à-tête."

"Yes," the doctor said stiff-lipped, "but that was supposed to be by appointment only."

"Oh, stop being such a sour grape. You're just mad because Linda, your lover, ran out on you."

The doctor stopped cold.

"So it was you, you demon. What the hell is it that irks you so much for you to be constantly interfering in my personal life? A decent friend, alive or dead, would not meddle into the private affairs of a person they liked and appreciated. Why are you doing this?"

"Why, why, why. Why is that all that matters to you? If you were a decent friend, you would at least listen to what I have to say. You know yourself that as things go I was always much more successful when it came to women than you were, are, or ever will be. You should take your own advice and listen to the expert; in this case, me."

"James, I've told you all this before and there's really nothing more to say. I love Annice. I do not love Linda. There. Enough said."

"Nothing said," James declared. "I think you're just afraid of her."

"Afraid of Linda, nonsense."

"Afraid of her and women like her. Women who could really rock your world."

"I prefer a more stable world for myself, James. I always have. And you must admit it did me just fine, for I've lived a good life so far, a far better one than you did."

"All this talk about love, what is love anyway? Most people are in love with being in love but they're not really ever in love. When they do think they are, it's usually at the beginning of a relationship and that love that they feel is usually a hormonal love. Their love is nothing more than sexual desire and that wears off. And it will wear off for you and Annice too, mark my words."

"If that's true, as you say, then what difference would it make if I choose either woman? If my love, as I say, is really nothing more than sexual desire, then eventually it would wear off on Linda too. Wouldn't it?"

"Of course," James put in eagerly. "But there's a difference."

"What's that?"

"Annice is an older woman. You know it. I know it. She knows it. So with Linda, who's much younger than Annice, you would have more of the good thing longer, much, much longer. When you are 55, you could still be enjoying a woman of 40. Annice is 40 now. Fifteen years from now you would still have what you're so hot for now."

James talked on and on about the differences between the doctor's two prime choices in women, and the doctor waited patiently to refute him. At one point, he used the intercom to send out a message to his next patient that he would be taking them in just a couple minutes more. His new assistant then informed him that he was already fifteen minutes late and the patient had already left the office, mad.

"Now look what you've done, funny man. One of my patients has left me. That has never happened before. In all my years of private practice I have never let a patient down."

"Oh, yes you have," James interjected. "What about me? I remember how it was between us all those years we spent growing up together. You were always doctoring me about my behavior, about who I was, about why I did things. You were always trying to figure me out. Don't think I was a dummy about it. Really, though, I tried to humor you. I could see how you tasted for it, for answers, answers to try to help me, answers to try to help you. You never did, did you?"

"Did what?"

"Figure me out."

"Oh, I did, I believe, but I really didn't have to. I believe now that you knew all along what made you tick but you thrived on it, on being you. You knew that if I or anyone ever helped you put back together your broken pieces, the James you knew would cease to exist, and without his existence you would be relegated to a mundane life, a life like mine. And that, more than anything, scared the hell out of you. You knew exactly who you were as a person, as a person in relation to everybody else—your real parents, your aunt Betty and uncle John, your half brother, Dave Boller, your real brother and sisters, your party friends, and me. You knew everything. You knew you had to keep it because *it* kept you alive."

Dirty Words

The doctor's conversation with James had redeemed him. After a lifetime of thinking about him, of thinking about how he could have helped him, he knew now he could not have. It would have been impossible. James had to be who he was and little or nothing could have been done for him despite the greatest efforts. Even death did not escape this truth. James was still James, in life, in death. Eternity would not change him. So, the doctor was free, forever free from the dragging effect his friend had bestowed upon him.

Besides the exhilaration, the doctor felt something else of old. Every encounter the doctor had ever had with James had left him feeling a bit inspired. James, after all, was the epitome of a person who lived life to the fullest. In everything he did he exemplified this. And at times, the doctor had to admit, he had felt envious of how his friend was able to take in the pleasures of life. So now, as a final tribute to him, to what he was able to accomplish, the doctor decided to throw all caution to the wind.

As he began wrapping up his workday, he went through the formula in his mind. Against his better judgment, he had decided to take Jeanne up on her challenge. She was right. So was James but not in the way James had intended. Jeanne wanted him to take Annice right in despite any detrimental consequences. James didn't want him to take Annice at all, and yet taking her was exactly the kind of thing he would do. The way he dealt with life was that if he wanted something, he would take it. This time, for the first time in his life, he would act upon his impulses, his desires, his selfishness. He would take what he wanted, just like James had done.

Annice was out there ready to start life anew. Now that she had left her husband, she would never go back. It scared the doctor to think of this precious woman struggling on her own, alone and uncertain. He could not bear to think of her falling on hard times, paying rent, bills, and car repairs without anyone to help her. It was all too much. Annice, dealing with landlords and bill collectors, while all the time having her ex-husband snooping around, stalking her, just waiting for an opportunity to strike at her. He couldn't allow it, not since the day he first made love to her, not since the day they became one.

It was a simple plan. He would just go to Annice and tell her. When he left his office, he literally chased his temporary out, telling her he was in a desperate hurry to do something. The last thing he did before exiting the office entirely was to scoop up a handful of the jelly mints he liked so much to have something to munch on during his commute through the city on the way to Dr. Detweiler's. Assured that his new-found determination would work magic on his anticipations, he commented aloud as he started toward the door, "Thanks, old buddy. Thanks, James."

The moment he was about to turn into the hall, he heard a scuffling sound coming from the main entrance. He quickly locked the door to his office and turned to see who and what it was. In stumbled a man who the doctor vaguely recognized. It was Mr. Colby. Mr. Colby was less sure of who the doctor was, and in a stuttering voice, began introducing himself to the doctor.

"My . . . my . . . my name is Colby, Leslie. I'm . . . I'm looking for my . . . my wife. Is she . . . Is she . . . here?"

The doctor gave Mr. Colby a cold stare. He was obviously intoxicated and in no condition to even be out and about. In addition to his inebriated state, the doctor could see that Mr. Colby was also seething with anger. His face was crimson and blood vessels in his forehead were nearly popping. Every word he spoke came with a burst of pungent alcohol, enough to make anyone he came in contact with tipsy too. To deal with him, the doctor decided to address him in degrees of dismissal depending on Leslie's insistence.

"If you are looking for Annice, she is not here. She was absent from work today. Do you know what happened to her?"

"Hey, no you don't! What are you, asking me questions about the whereabouts of my wife? I came here to ask you so don't get smart with me."

"Mr. Colby, you are obviously drunk and should not even be here. Why would you persist in finding Annice in your condition? Do you have some special little treat for her—a thrashing perhaps?"

The doctor could not believe the words he had just spoke—words he had wanted to say to this man for weeks and weeks. He was being dominated by a character new to him, a character which could withstand the usual barrage of logic and reason he often battled with whenever he had to decide between passion and reason. Passion had won. Leslie was defiant. He raised his fists in retaliation, sending the message clearly that if the doctor insulted him further there would no doubt be hell to pay.

"Is this how you deal with all of your problems, Mr. Colby? If Annice were here right now, in my place, what would you do to her? What would you do?"

Leslie swung his fist and missed. He stumbled to the floor in a miserable mess. The doctor refused to aid him and instead put aside his briefcase in case Leslie got up to continue his assault. After standing in an attack position for a minute or more, the doctor invariably decided to take a different course of action against his assailant.

"Mr. Colby, I'll tell you what I'm going to do, I'm going to go back into my office and call the police. You have a heavy measure of charges piled against you—trespassing, assault, public drunkenness, to name three. Stay here."

The doctor let his guard down, certain that his opponent, lumped on the floor like a heap of mashed potatoes, couldn't possibly attack. He was wrong. The moment the doctor's back was turned, Leslie, lying in a feigned position on the tiled floor, sprung up after him like a jerk-in-the-box. He grabbed hold of the doctor's neck with both hands and jerked his head into the wall. The doctor stumbled but held his balance and did not fall down. Leslie was ready the second he resumed his stance, with an immediate left, right, left. The doctor, unready, took all three hits to the head. Two of the unexpected hooks landed squarely on his cheeks, the other on his nose, which began bleeding profusely. On his first attack, the doctor employed trickery. He stood in front of his attacker, stooped over as if he were seriously injured. He pretended to be administering to his nosebleed just so he could take Leslie by surprise. Just at the right moment, the doctor attacked. Like a storm that came out of nowhere, he threw three swift punches to Leslie's abdomen. Leslie fell back and hit the floor again, this time on his head. Once he hit the floor, he moaned and writhed, holding onto his head as if he were keeping it attached to his body. Uncertain that this too was a ruse, the doctor jumped down on top of him and held him by the back of the throat. The doctor's whole body, whole being, was throbbing with glee. He was experiencing a feeling he had felt only once before, when he had first taken James in a fight. He had a flashback of that troubled time in front of the porch. He held James by the front of the throat, up in the air, up against the porch rails. He had said, without words, that if ever, ever there were a conflict between them and James decided to use force, his force would be vanquished forever! Now it was Leslie's turn.

"Know this, Mr. Colby. I do know where your wife is. I do know. She has left you, left you for good, left your stinking sorry ass forever. I know all about the way you abuse her. I know everything. Those days are gone, as are you! Annice loves me and I love her and there's nothing you can do about it! If you try, if you try anything, anything at all against her, I will kill you. Do you get that? Annice has pictures of what you've done to her. She's confided in me and another physician already about your abuses. And that other person will remain anonymous, so if you come after me, there will still be another and another and another because you will now become infamous in the medical profession. We are standing ready to post your picture and the pictures of your abuses all over the Internet, all over the country, all over the world for that matter. So you see, it ends right here. Try anything, just one misplaced phone call, just one time where you're in the wrong place at the wrong time and it all begins—the police, the courts, the attorneys, the public scrutiny. You will see. It will be the end of your life as you know it. My advice to you is to get up and go and never come back. And leave Annice alone if you know what's good for you. Now, what's it going to be?"

Mr. Colby leaned upright on his elbows. He stared at the doctor with eyes of ice. The doctor stared back with eyes of fire. The two did not meet. Not a word was said, not a word.

Leslie staggered out, listless, defeated. The doctor followed. Once Leslie had sufficiently removed himself from the building and surrounding neighborhood, the doctor walked briskly to his car in the back parking lot. After getting in, he drove around to the front of the building and again surveyed the area for any sign of Mr. Colby. Assured that he was nowhere in the vicinity, the doctor proceeded to the Detweiler home. He parked several houses away and walked. When he reached a neighbor's home adjacent to Jeanne's, he turned onto their walkway and into their backyard. This, just in case. He next ventured over to Jeanne's back door and tapped lightly on it. Moments passed as the doctor moved nervously with his hands and feet anticipating the worst—that Annice might not be home, or worse yet, Leslie had successfully followed him and may still be drunk enough to fight. For enduring moments nothing happened. Finally the doctor knocked louder. Then came a response. Annice called out from inside the kitchen.

"Who's there?"

"Annice, let me in."

"Who is me?"

"It's me, Christopher. Please let me in. It's urgent!"

Annice opened the door and met the doctor's stern face with a frown.

"What's all this about? You look like you've seen a ghost. What's wrong?"

"What's wrong is right," the doctor responded as he entered the back door and, once inside, closed and locked it as quickly as he could.

He stepped over to her and looked her in the eyes. He placed his hands on her shoulders so she could feel the certainty and strength of what he was about to say.

"Annice, I love you," he began, "and if you love me too I have an offer for you, an offer that I insist you take from me right now. I had an inadvertent altercation with your husband today, just an hour ago. He came to my practice looking for you, presumably to hurt you. He was drunk as a skunk and looking for trouble. I had it out with him. I told him I love you and that you had left him for good just as you told me. We fought. I won. When it was over, he left knowing that there was nothing more he could do. He knows that if he ever comes after you, we will get the law on him for all the things he's done to you. Believe me when I tell you that he never will. So, now you are free in a sense but I don't want you to be free, except to me. What I mean is . . . Will you come with me? Will you come to live with me?"

Annice was dumbfounded. How could she ever have guessed that in the course of one day all of these things could have happened? She looked at him with resplendent eyes. He was her hero. She had been rescued by a love that had refused to die despite twenty years of life in between.

"Of course I'll come," she replied. "I could think of nothing better to do with my life than be with you. I love you, Christopher, and I know it's true. What I feel for you now is even better than what I felt for you when we were young." Annice paused. "Of course, there is one stipulation that goes along with my acceptance of your request."

"Of course, anything," the doctor returned, with a confused stare.

"The only condition I have is . . . that you will make me your wife."

"I wouldn't have it any other way," the doctor said adamantly.

The lovers kissed. They kissed as though the moment was eternal and time stood still for them. Their kisses spoke words their tongues could not—communication of the heart.

After packing up Annice's belongings, the couple took off. For Jeanne, they left a note, telling her, succinctly, they decided to be together. Their love was now stronger than their fear, and when they departed from the Detweiler home they did so with no apprehension about who might see them. They left holding hands, boldly, so that anybody looking would know they were lovers.

The doctor's mind was in a whirlwind as he drove along the familiar country roads toward his—their home on Pinnacle road. He was alive and young again, at least in his heart. He felt inside him the exact strength of feelings he had felt in his heart before when he first loved her. It was almost as if there had been no time between. The joy of love is a power like no other.

At home they unpacked and made love. They ate dinner then made love. They showered for the night then made love. Then they made love. It was life as neither expected it could be.

Days went by. Chris and Annice lived together and worked together as happily as could be. It was days before the doctor realized that he had not concerned himself with anything that had to do with the subject of James. But in accordance with that, he knew that he had finally rendered the final verdict about what their relationship was. James was James and that was all he could be. The end. Annice filled up his life now. Soon they were to be husband and wife. The doctor's preoccupation with the makings of their wedding kept him at an even farther distance from the subjective concern about James. He had not appeared since the last time he saw him. To the doctor's knowledge, he had not been seen by anyone—at least nobody had called him to correlate that information to him, not even Dave Boller. Apparently James was gone, gone as instantly as he had come. The relevance of him having come at all seemed to fizzle too. Except for Dave Boller's knowing about him, he was a secret; and a secret he had to remain. After all, what would be the point of making his transcendence anything of an issue now? There was no real proof that it really happened, and who would believe Dave?

As it happened, one Saturday, the doctor rode into the city with Annice as his escort. He had inadvertently forgotten his briefcase the night before and he desperately needed some papers that were in it. The couple arrived at the James Street office in the late morning and

Annice parked the Buick in the back parking lot. She decided to wait in the car while the doctor ran inside and retrieved his briefcase.

Inside, the doctor was happy to see that the case was just where he thought it might be, beside the inner door to his office, a place where he usually put it when he locked the door. He was about to pick up the case when something strange caught his eye. The expensive detection equipment that he had used to attempt to capture the entity of his deceased friend on was on. Immediately, he dropped the case and raced over to the equipment and stopped it from playing. Understandably curious, he rewound several minutes of the tapes then turned them on. The doctor was astounded by what he saw and heard.

"So, you finally did something about her. You were finally man enough to take her. The agony is that you wasted twenty years in the doing. If I were you I would have done what you did a long time ago. See, you always were so far behind me when it came to women. But you know, Pip, you couldn't have done it without me. You know, it was always you for me and me for you and that's the way it always worked best. So, now that you have her, I guess my work is done, unless of course you want me to be best man at your wedding."

The image of James was clear and precise during the initial part of the tape but then the image faded. And the peculiar thing too was that it was almost as if James knew too that he was holding on less and less to the reality of the living realm. His appearance seemed disturbed.

James looked ahead, desparingly, at his long-time friend.

"Don't hate me, man. Despite everything we went through, I never hated you. In fact, though I could never say it before, I really did love you, as . . . as . . . a friend, that is. What we experienced together is the stuff of life. You can't live your life in a pristine world, my friend, because the world is a dirty place, and you know, it doesn't really hurt to get a little dirty from time to time."

The screen went blank. The image was gone. James was no more. The doctor fell into a trance and did not notice it when footsteps came treading across the carpeted floor.

A voice spoke. "Chris, what are you doing? I've been waiting for you for fifteen minutes already."

The doctor, startled, turned around and met Annice's vibrant face, smiling at him in a way which told him she was on top of the world, a world they had finally made for each other, a world founded in happiness, a world founded in love. He paused then spoke.

"I . . . I'm sorry, darling. I was just reviewing something on tape that I needed to see. It . . . it was a message from an old friend of mine, some advice he gave me. I'm going to keep it and listen to it from time to time. For a long time I had forgotten that everybody's life is a differing example of how life can be put together. It is important to realize this—that we can take certain aspects of each other's lives, things that work well, and implement them into our own lives, tempered, of course, according to our standards. We can use them and thus be more useful, to ourselves and to others."

"Christopher, that's a little deep for a Saturday morning. How about we leave now and find something fun to do? How about if we go ahead and call John and ask him if we can use his boat and go out island hopping on the Susquehanna this afternoon?"

"Are you sure you want to? It rained a little last night. We might get dirty."

"Then what are we waiting for? Let's go."
The End?